"AN ACTION-FILLE[D] ... BEST!"—*Sou[...]*

Sergeant Bill Clark

of the Dallas Auto Pound discovered a woman's body in the trunk of an impounded car . . .

Vice cop Randi Stoner

was working undercover in a strip club to investigate a dancer's murder . . .

One remorseless killer

linked the two cases together—and sought revenge against both cops, at any price . . .

TARGET BLUE

is an electrifying novel by Terry Marlow, a pseudonym for a sergeant of detectives and a former SWAT captain with the Dallas Police Department.

"A GRITTY DETECTIVE NOVEL WHICH PROVIDES INSIGHTS INTO BOTH THE PHYSICAL AND PSYCHOLOGICAL DANGERS OF POLICE WORK."
—*Wichita Falls Times*

"DOWN-AND-DIRTY . . . CINEMATIC . . . FASCINATING."

—*DeLand Sun News* (FL.)

TARGET BLUE

A NOVEL

TERRY MARLOW

JOVE BOOKS, NEW YORK

This is a work of fiction.
The characters and events described in this book are imaginary,
and any resemblance to actual persons, living or dead,
is purely coincidental.

This Jove Book contains the complete
text of the original hardcover edition.
It has been completely reset in a typeface
designed for easy reading and was printed
from new film.

TARGET BLUE

A Jove Book / published by arrangement with
G. P. Putnam's Sons

PRINTING HISTORY
G. P. Putnam's Sons edition published September 1991
Jove edition / April 1993

ISBN: 0-515-11056-6

Jove Books are published by The Berkley Publishing Group,
200 Madison Avenue, New York, New York 10016.
The name "JOVE" and the "J" logo
are trademarks belonging to Jove Publications, Inc.

PRINTED IN THE UNITED STATES OF AMERICA

10 9 8 7 6 5 4 3 2 1

To the men and women of the Dallas Police Department and to police officers and their loved ones everywhere who bear the scars in body and soul of wounds suffered in the line of duty.

TARGET BLUE

BOOK ONE

A DAY IN THE LIFE

CHAPTER 1

Friday, Dawn

On a residential street a few blocks off Singleton Boulevard in West Dallas three young men sat waiting in a white Monte Carlo with blackout windows.

"It's nearly sunup, man," one of them bitched.

"So?" the driver answered, watchful.

"So I'm freezin' my butt off out here for nothin'. They ain't comin'."

"They're coming," the driver assured him.

"At least fire this mother up and let's get a little heat goin'."

"Yeah, Frank, that'd be a very intelligent thing to do. Wouldn't it?" The driver turned to look at the man beside him. "Turn on the car, sit here with the exhaust puffing smoke and the motor running. That wouldn't be suspicious, would it?"

"Aw, man . . ."

"Just like you think it would be smart to sit here and smoke a pack of cigarettes, right? Nah, that wouldn't tip anybody off, lighting matches and sucking on cigs out here in the dark. I swear, Frank, you're so smart I don't understand for the life of me why you ain't in charge of this whole operation."

"Lighten up, Willy, Jesus . . ."

"How do you feel about that, Johnny?" the driver asked the one in the backseat. "Don't you think Frank should be running things, since he is so smart?"

Johnny smiled at that but had nothing to say. He seldom did.

3

The three of them were cousins, sons of Mexican immigrants, but for reasons of their own they called each other by Americanized names rather than the ones their parents had given them.

"There, you see, Frank, Johnny thinks you are smart, too."

"Smart enough to know this is bullshit," Frank muttered.

"You're right, Frank. They ain't going to show and this is all for nothing. Only tell me, niño, what is this here?"

Frank looked where Willy pointed and saw a van stopping at an apartment complex directly in front of the waiting Monte Carlo.

"Get ready," Willy said. Frank and Johnny reached beneath the seats and pulled out Ingram MAC-10's, blunt and ugly little submachine guns not much bigger than pistols. To the snout of each of these was attached a silencer, a six-inch tube.

They watched the driver of the van open his door and step out, looking up and down his street and then in their direction, apparently right at them. Instinctively, the three in the Monte Carlo ducked low, but the van driver gave no sign that he had seen them. When he walked around the front of the van and disappeared behind it, Willy cranked the Monte Carlo.

The driver of the van, a black man who had spent most of his life in the tropics, was miserable from the cold and hurried to open the sliding door on the right side of the van and unload his two passengers. He was bundled up in an army-surplus parka with a fur-lined hood which he had snugged down tight around his head before leaving the warmth of his van. He probably did not hear the Monte Carlo's engine rumble to life, even though sounds carried surprisingly well in the cold early-morning air. He almost certainly heard the squealing of tires as Willy whipped the Monte Carlo around sideways and slid to a stop parallel with the van. But by then it was too late. By then Frank and Johnny were already out of the car, even before it stopped. They were already dashing to their places, one at either end of the van, so they would not have to worry about shooting each other.

The van driver saw Frank first, as he passed in front of the windshield of the van, and was fumbling, trying to get his pistol out of his coat pocket, when Johnny started shooting from behind him.

Of Johnny's first long burst of a dozen rounds, four hit the van driver, one in his leg, one in his left buttock, and two in his back. One of these blew out a lung and the other severed his spinal cord. The van driver wobbled and jerked, then pitched over on his face on the hard, cold ground.

One of the two passengers inside the van tried to run and Johnny shot him. Frank went after the other one, who stupidly tried to hide. Frank found him trying to stuff himself into a ball beneath the seat. The frightened man screamed something, but he was talking too fast for Frank to make it out. Frank poked his gun up under the seat until he felt it touch the man and then he opened up, cranking a full magazine, thirty rounds, into the jabbering man. He worked the gun back and forth to make sure he hit the man everywhere, and then he reloaded, slapping a fresh clip home as he surveyed the scene. All three men from the van were dead or dying, and less than sixty seconds had ticked off since they had bailed out of the Monte Carlo. Not bad.

"Hey, Johnny," he stage-whispered. "Look at the shit these guys were hauling." Frank had opened a suitcase and held up a handful of crack vials to show his partner.

"Leave it," Johnny said.

"Aw, man . . ."

Johnny did not say anything more. He loaded a fresh clip, scooped up the empty Frank had let fall to the ground, and walked from the driver to the passenger who had tried to run, pausing just long enough to pump a bullet into each of their heads. Then he jogged around the rear of the van to the Monte Carlo and got in.

Frank dallied, because he knew how much money a whole suitcaseful of crack was worth, and it made no sense to him to leave it behind. If Willy did not want it, that was fine for him. Frank would move it on his own and keep the proceeds. But there would be trouble. He heard Willy gun the engine, meaning he was ready to go and that he would leave Frank if he did not get a move on.

"It don't make no sense," Frank muttered, finally deciding

he would follow orders and leave the dope. He threw his handful of ampules into the van in disgust and turned to go.

Frank saw the old woman at the same time she saw him. Like the dead van driver, the old woman was dressed for the weather. She wore a heavy coat that was a hand-me-down from the white woman she did housework for, buttoned up to her chin and its collar turned up, and a wool scarf tied in a bow at her throat. Also like the van driver, she was black. It was a black neighborhood, and she knew at once that this Mexican boy meant trouble. Her left hand was jammed deep into her coat pocket. Her right hand, snug and warm in her new blue mitten, held the strap of her big purse. She did not recognize the thing in his hand as a gun because it did not look like the guns she knew, the cheap handguns she had seen all her life. She thought it was a club, some kind of pipe. It was not being robbed she minded; she had decided long ago to give up her purse to anyone who wanted it that badly. It was the way these young men sometimes were so rough about it, knocking old women down, beating them and all. The old woman did not want that, so she planted her feet as solidly as she could and held out her purse to Frank.

She did not see the man on the ground beside the van. Or if she did, she did not know it was a man. Her eyes were bad at any distance, and even Frank's face, which was within five or six feet of hers, was none too clear.

"Here," she said, holding out her purse to Frank. "Take it if that's what you want. Ain't no use in any rough stuff."

The only thing she saw really clearly in the whole business was when Frank raised his gun and held it at arm's length. It was pointed at her head, and the black eye of the muzzle was close enough so that it came crystal clear to her. At first, she did not realize what it was, and when she did understand finally she opened her mouth to scream. And Frank shot her. Before her scream could rise from her throat and out her mouth, he put a bullet there. Her lips slapped shut with the impact of the slug at the back of her throat, and Frank noticed before she crumpled to the ground that there was no sign of a wound on her face. It was as if she had swallowed the bullet. Then he leaned over the little heap she made on the ground and shot her once more, the muzzle of the gun pressed to her left ear, to make sure.

Then Frank ran to the white Monte Carlo, laughing as he went because the old woman had swallowed his bullet, and the three men drove away.

Sergeant Marino of CAPers was at the West Dallas scene, drinking coffee from a 7-Eleven plastic cup and chain-smoking Vantage Ultra Lights. He was standing inside the corral of yellow tape with black lettering that spelled out POLICE LINE— DO NOT CROSS. It was a busy place. A couple of uniformed Patrol officers stood with their jacket collars turned up against the cold. The freezing rain had stopped and now there was a little snow in the air, tiny flakes flitting here and there like ashes from a fire, snow that would not stick on the ground but stung their cheeks.

They were about done. Officers from the Physical Evidence Section had fired off a thousand camera flashes, the technicians had marked with chalk or spray paint every spot where they had found a spent shell casing or anything else they thought might have anything to do with the four murders. Technically, four victims made it a mass murder, but it all went down as four strokes on the Uniform Crime Report at the end of the month. The van had been dusted for prints, swept, and vacuumed. Technicians from PES marked the locations of the scattered vials of crack. Everything in the van that could be removed without using tools had been taken, each item individually marked and bagged.

The bodies, each placed inside heavy dark green plastic bags with paper bags on their hands, just in case, were being loaded into ambulances for the ride to the Dallas Forensics Lab at Parkland Memorial Hospital, where autopsies would be done. The man who would do some or all of them, an assistant medical examiner everybody called Doc, had finished his work at the scene and lit a cigarette, then pulled his gloves back on. He was a short, fat man and wore what might have been a homburg. It was battered and glistened with rain and snow on the crown and brim. The little man wore a cashmere-looking overcoat with a plaid scarf tucked around his throat. Marino noted the old stains on the sleeves of the coat and thought that

Doc looked like a once-prosperous man who had fallen on hard times. Or maybe he just dressed down for murders.

"Any surprises, Doc?" Marino asked.

"Pretty standard for this sort of thing. Automatic weapons, overkill. Gangs, I imagine."

"You know it," Marino grunted.

"The old woman?" Doc wondered aloud.

"Bad luck. Tried to catch a bus at a piss-poor time."

"Yeah. There was a hell of a lot of crack left in the van. Did you see?"

"Enough to run a crack house for a day or two. That's what these three were doing, resupplying a crack house."

"Do we know where?" Doc asked.

"We will before long. My troops are going door to door."

"Why didn't the shooters take the crack? It's worth thousands retail. Why leave it for the cops to impound?"

"They were sending a message. This is their turf and they don't want any poaching. If the dope was taken, it could have been anybody, rip-off artists. This way, there's no question what it means."

"So you know who did this."

"More or less."

"Case closed, huh?"

"Sure, Doc. All I have to do is prove it," Marino grinned tightly, thinking that his only witness was the old woman with blue mittens in the body bag.

Sergeant "Wild Bill" Clark came late to his boss's retirement party in the Auto Theft offices downtown. It was about what he had expected: Work had ground to a halt in the Auto Theft Unit, his crew was there, scratching their butts and cutting up, and all the clerks and secretaries were standing around smiling, holding Dixie cup punch drinks and slabs of white cake on paper plates. And there in the middle of it stood Eugene Felty, testing the rod and reel they had given him and trying to look as if he were having a good time.

There were others there, too, some of the regular Auto Theft investigators and some friends of Felty's from other outfits. A couple of them looked old enough to have been in Felty's class at the academy. Clark knew most of them, but there was a new face here and there in the crowd.

"Well if it ain't Wild Bill," Felty announced when he saw Clark come in. "Better late than never, I guess."

"Why, you old fart, I thought you'd be gone by now," Clark answered.

"Not without making sure you showed up for work at least once this week."

"Boss," Clark protested, "I work every day, you know that."

"Only if I believe what I read on the time cards." Felty grinned and waved Clark toward him. "Come here, you bum. I got somebody for you to meet." Felty put his left hand on Clark's shoulder as he came near and extended his right hand toward a young-looking guy who was standing off to one side, apart from the others. "Lieutenant Bonny, this is Sergeant Clark, Wild Bill. I told you about him."

"Sergeant Clark, how do you do," the young guy said, not really smiling.

"Hi," Clark answered, not caring for the mechanical handshake he got from his new boss.

"We call Bill and his crew the Junkyard Dogs. On the books it's the Salvage Unit. They know more about cars than you'll ever need to learn to run this unit. They look like hell, but if you give 'em their head they'll do good work for you."

"I'm sure," the new lieutenant said, but he did not sound as though he meant it.

"Bill, do the honors," Felty said. "Introduce your gang to the lieutenant here."

"Uh, okay." Clark nodded, then pointed out each of his men as he named them. "This is Boots Hamaker, next there is Smoky Tunnell. He's got that wrist taped because he still hasn't figured out he's too old to rodeo. The big guy there with the double helping of cake is Nacho Hernandez. He'd still be a pro wrestler if he hadn't got too fat to find trunks that fit . . ."

"Macho?" Lieutenant Bonny interrupted to ask.

"No, sir. Nacho."

"I see."

"And those two down at the end of the table, they're our

wheel men if we ever need a getaway car. The long-haired one is Wheels Winager, the other there is Crash Kopeck.''

"Good morning, Chief," Felty interrupted, moving toward the door to offer his hand to Chief Orville Knecht who arrived otherwise unnoticed, with a couple of deputy chiefs in his wake.

Knecht was running behind schedule and was not in a good mood. He had just promoted three new sergeants but they all had been white, no help with the Affirmative Action thing. They had no witnesses on the West Dallas mass murders and no real leads but plenty of conjecture. At his two-o'clock meeting with the assistant city manager he would be doing a lot of explaining and he thought, as he shook Lieutenant Felty's hand, that he would not mind trading places with the grinning and apparently carefree son of a bitch.

"Gene"—Knecht smiled over their handshake—"sorry I'm late, but you know I wouldn't miss this for anything." Knecht turned to a deputy, who handed him Felty's retirement certificate.

The chief looked over the roomful of investigators, nodded and smiled at each of them, spoke to the ones he recognized. A couple of them had been near Knecht in the academy and he resented them. They looked younger than he felt. And why shouldn't they? They put in their eight hours and go home, or to the DPA Club or wherever. He could not remember his last eight-hour day, or a day off when the phone did not ring, for that matter. They were playing games, these guys, cops-and-robbers. Look at them, smoking and joking, not a care in the world. All they had to worry about was keeping their paperwork caught up. When was the last time an investigator got fired because the crime rate was up? You didn't see these guys sweating bullets every month when the Uniform Crime Report came out.

". . . so nice to meet you in person," Mrs. Felty was saying.

Chief Knecht replied in kind and found something nice to say about her husband, the man of the hour. Then he made his "end of the road and a new beginning" speech, the Public Information Office photographer he had brought with him snapped a few photos, copies to Felty, and that was that.

The chief's little entourage made its way out the door, and

Sergeant Clark decided to make another pass at his new boss.

"Lieutenant Bonny," he said. "I'll be heading out with my gang in a minute. If you'd like, I'd be happy to take you out to the pound, walk you through our operation."

"That won't be necessary." Bonny half-smiled. "I want to go over the books with Lieutenant Felty while I have the chance. Don't let me keep you from getting some work done."

"You guys leaving already?" Felty asked.

"Hey, there's no truces in the war on crime, Loo, you know that," Clark answered.

"Huh?"

"And," Clark went on, drawing Felty aside and whispering in his ear, "on behalf of my troops and myself, I'd really like to thank you for finding us this little tight-ass to take your place."

"It won't kill you to hear the book quoted once in a while. You dogs keep getting results, he'll warm up to you."

"Maybe, but life was so simple with a burnout like you at the helm."

"I spoiled you. That's your problem."

"No doubt about it."

"Don't forget to swing by the club later, Bill."

"Wouldn't miss it."

Clark and his men excused themselves, Clark hoping his new lieutenant would be at the Dallas Police Association Club that evening for the real party. He hoped that Bonny would turn out to be a drinker, at least.

Randi Stoner hustled down the hall from the elevators toward the Crimes Against Persons Section, her high heels clip-clopping on the tile floor, the echoes caroming off the cavernous walls. She nearly took a spill descending the steps two at a time from the level of the old Police and Courts building to the floor of the old city hall.

A head popped out of the press room as she drew abreast of it. It was Bobby Thurmon, a police-beat reporter for one of the papers.

"Is that you making all that noise?" he asked as she passed. "I thought it was a cop on a goddamned horse!"

He was smiling a kind of a smart-assed smile, but she did not bother to answer. She did not want to be late. Screw you, buster, Stoner said to herself. She was wearing a T-shirt and a tight-fitting pair of faded jeans that wrinkled snugly at her ankles. That was why she had not taken off her fake-fur jacket even though the building was stifling hot after the cold outside. "Dress easy but not sleazy," the sergeant had said. She was not sure she had got it right.

Randi Stoner asked for Sergeant Grouton, and the clerk at the front desk in the Crimes Against Persons office pointed toward a closed door. Stoner knocked and slipped inside to find her sergeant and the two men assigned to work with her already sitting around the table in the little room. There was also a man she did not know, a grizzled little man with his shirtsleeves rolled up to show tattoos on both forearms.

"Excuse me." Stoner smiled. "I hope I'm not late?"

"Couple of minutes." Grouton nodded. "Which way did you come in?"

Stoner pointed over her left shoulder with her thumb.

"You came in the front door?" Grouton asked.

"Yes, sir."

"Don't ever do that," he said. He sounded tired but not angry. "This setup has back doors. They're for undercover cops to use so they don't get burned."

"Oh."

"There could be anybody up front there. That's why we moved our office out of Police and Courts. It's not good for undercover officers to be seen coming and going at City Hall, okay?"

"Yes, sir. Sorry."

The two vice cops she had been assigned to work with were exchanging looks and grins.

"What are you two ladies tittering about?" Sergeant Grouton demanded of them. "It's your job to tell her this stuff. How's she supposed to know if nobody tells her, huh? Okay?"

They shrugged and gave her an apologetic look apiece. Stoner settled into the only empty chair and wanted the briefing to go on; enough about her.

"This is Investigator Green. He'll be working on this with us."

"You haven't missed anything," the tattooed man assured her. "We were just catching up on another case."

"The big killing in West Dallas this morning," Sergeant Grouton told her. "You heard about it?"

Stoner nodded. There had been something on the car radio, but she had spent her morning shopping secondhand stores for the fake-fur jacket.

"So anyway, that's all we have on that," Sergeant Grouton said, closing that discussion.

"Here's some mug shots," Green said, dealing out the five-by-seven-inch glossies, front view of an ugly and dangerous-looking man with a broken nose that lay thick and flat between deep-set eyes. He had long, straggling hair in the photos, and his lips were stretched into an idiot grin as if he thought that might change his looks. White letters stuck into grooves in a black placard beneath the man's throat spelled out his ID number, a date from last summer, and the letters *DSO*. "He was in the county for aggravated assault, beat the hell out of one of his girls. He's been handled before for drugs, speed mostly. He's a biker-type, dirty as hell and runs with a mean crowd. No real gang affiliation, as far as we know."

"What happened on the aggravated assault?" Stoner asked.

"Dropped. Complainant got amnesia."

"Oh."

"We're looking for him on a killing. Girl's body turned up last week out in Pleasant Grove, in a creek bed. Here's the crime scene shots."

Green handed the black-and-white photos around the table. The victim was young and might have once been good-looking. She was lying on her back in weeds that looked waist high. The brown winter grass had been trampled down around her as if there had been a struggle. Her legs were spread apart, her knees bent, and her arms were pinned under her body. There were places on her stomach and both breasts that looked like sores of some kind. Her head lay over much too far toward her right shoulder. Her throat was gashed down to the spinal cord. Stoner could actually see the gray and white of the bones. There was something protruding from her vagina, something round and dark. The next photo she saw was a close-up.

"She was burned over the chest and stomach, probably with a cigar," Green told them. "That's a beer bottle with the neck broke off. M.E. says he did that before he killed her. She was also raped, vaginally, anally, orally. Semen from at least two men. Wc think thcy had her out there awhile before they finished her off."

"Who was she?" one of Stoner's partners asked. J.D., the younger of the two. He was about Stoner's age, but he had been in Vice a couple of years. The other one, Larry Potter, was the old head, on his second tour in Vice.

"She went by the stage name of 'Krystal.' Her and about half of the other titty dancers in town. Real name's Holly Jean Russell, nineteen years old barely, had a birthday a month before she died. She was from out in West Texas, somewhere around Borger, I think. Left home right after high school, headed for the big city to break into show business."

"Jesus," Larry sighed. He had kids older than this girl.

"Show business?" J.D. asked.

"Well, I guess shaking your tits in a bar looks like show business to a kid like that. She read something in a magazine about Dallas being the 'Third Coast,' thought she was going to get discovered and end up in the movies."

"This guy did it?" Larry asked, looking at the picture of the ugly man with the flat nose.

"That's what the snitch says. Claims to be a witness. He's damned sure qualified."

"Have you filed on him?"

"Yeah, sealed indictment. We're trying to keep it quiet. If he spooks, he'll haul ass for who knows where."

"Will the snitch hold up?" Larry asked.

"Probably not. We do have a little bit of physical evidence, though. Body chemicals match up, and believe it or not we got a partial print off the bottle. Of course he'll claim he tossed the empty and somebody else used it to frame him. He sells enough methamphetamines to buy a good lawyer who'll point out the chemistry might not be exclusive and all that shit, but if we can get him off the street with a high bond maybe we can shake out a witness or two. From what I hear, he don't make any secret of being an enforcer. He specializes in girls about this size here. Starts 'em out dancing, street whores when they get too much mileage on them. Y'all ready for the specs?''

"Shoot," J.D. said.

"His righteous name is Jefferson Lee MacAnnaly. D.O.B. of six, ten, fifty-seven, making him thirty-three years of age. Street name's 'Mack the Knife.' He's a big boy, six foot four and around two sixty. He's supposed to carry a boot knife at all times and never gets too far from a gun, although he don't usually carry one on him when he's in the clubs. For that, he uses one of his 'speed' whores, like a gun bearer. Let her take the felony rap if the cops bust 'em. Sells speed, has friends that cook speed, uses the shit himself, and makes everybody around him use it, too. When he's not showing off on his big Harley motorcycle, he drives a van. A 1976 Ford Econoline with a real fucked-up paint job, mostly orange, with a lot of primer. He tinkers with it, changes the looks, got plates on it that come back to somebody else. Last-known address is the one he gave the county, but he was lying about that. That's it.''

"Where's he from?" Larry asked.

"Oklahoma's all we know. He's only been handled that once in this part of the country, and people don't like to talk about him. I understand he travels quite a bit.''

"Okay," Sergeant Grouton said, his lips pursed like something in the room smelled bad. "What's the deal?"

"You put your female officer in one of the topless clubs undercover and she keeps her eyes and ears open. We know the ones he hangs out in and as long as he doesn't know we've filed on him it stands to reason he'll turn up, or else she might hear something.''

Stoner looked at her sergeant with a question in her eyes.

"Makes sense to me," Grouton said, returning her look evenly. "You can dance, can't you, Randi?"

"Well . . .''

"Didn't they tell you about that, Randi?" Larry cut in. "About the titty requirement for this job?"

"They said I had to have 'em. They didn't say I had to show 'em," she shot back.

"Oh," Sergeant Grouton said, nodding. "In that case, why don't we just see if we can get you a job waiting tables?"

"Yeah, I think that'd do," Green added. He was not sure they were kidding.

"Okay with me," Stoner said.

Wild Bill Clark was on the phone trying to line up a lunch date when his other line bleated for attention. It was one of the Public Service officers assigned to the pound yard, calling to report a strong odor from an impounded car.

"Nacho!" Clark yelled.

"What?"

"Run down in the yard and punch the trunk lock on this Lincoln, will you?"

"What's the deal?"

"PSO reports a strong odor."

"Aw, man . . ."

"Do your duty, my man. Serves you right. If I hadn't spied you at that candy machine in the hall I would never have thought of you."

"Didn't I get the last one, Sarge?"

"Could be. That would be the dead dog, or was that the week-old stringer of catfish?"

"The catfish. I can still smell them goddamned things, man."

"Stout heart. Do your duty."

Hernandez stomped out of the office mumbling.

"I already told 'em to have the PSO stand by to hold the punch for you. Don't bother to thank me—that's what I'm here for," Clark called after the big man as the door slammed.

He had paperwork on his desk, but the Junkyard Dogs were in what Clark liked to think of as a lull in the action and he could not bring himself to face the printed forms and all those numbers.

They had just wrapped up a combination sting/raid deal with the state boys that had closed down three junkyards and one of the bigger auto-theft rings uncovered in the Southwest in the past five or ten years. They all had put in extra hours, and he was letting his troops catch their breath before starting anything else.

He pushed the paperwork aside and punched line one again. The woman on the other end of the line sounded more than a little interesting. She was a teller at his bank whom he had known casually for a year or more, and he had finally decided to take the big step and ask her out. It was going well, and he did not realize that Hernandez had been gone long enough to drive down into the yard when he heard him calling on the radio.

"Twelve Thirty-two to Twelve Thirty."

Putting his teller on hold again, Clark opened his desk drawer and dug through the flotsam until he found his portable radio. "Go ahead, Thirty-two."

"You want to meet me down here?" Hernandez asked.

"What's the nature?" Clark returned, thinking of his phone call.

"We got a Signal Twenty-seven down here, man."

"Well, of course we do," Clark mumbled, careful that he was not transmitting over the radio. A Twenty-seven was a dead person. "My first prospect in over two months, and . . . Naturally, it's a goddamned Twenty-seven. Ten-Four, I'm en route." He made excuses to his teller and hung up the phone.

Clark hurried out of his office to his car parked outside and drove down the long lane that ran alongside row upon row of impounded vehicles of every description—lost, stolen, wrecked, and simply abandoned cars, trucks, and vans as far as the eye could see. Checking the lane numbers as he jolted past, he turned to his right and found his investigator and the PSO standing at the rear of a pale yellow Lincoln Town Car. Hernandez was standing, at least. The PSO, a kid who looked like he was just out of high school, was on his knees, vomiting.

When Clark got out of his car, Hernandez fixed him with a wounded look, as if he thought his sergeant had known about this all along. As cold as it was in the unsheltered lot, the smell from the open trunk was staggering. Clark cupped his hand over his nose and mouth and looked inside.

"Jesus H. Christ," he said when he saw what was there.

"My sentiments exactly," Hernandez said.

"Okay," Clark said. "Close the trunk. You stay here with it. Nobody touches this car for nothing, you got it?"

"I got it."

"I'll make the call."

"Easy for you to say, Sarge."

Back at the pound complex, Clark went to the nearest telephone and dialed the number for CAPers. When the clerk who answered told him everybody was in a meeting with the captain, he insisted she interrupt the meeting.

Marino walked into his office in Crimes Against Persons just as the clerk up front buzzed through to tell him there was a call on line two.

"Marino," he said.

"Marino, this is Clark at the auto pound, and we just found a body in a car trunk."

"Crap. What does it look like?" Marino grumbled.

Clark thought about that question for a moment, but only said, "Like it's been in there awhile. But I can tell she's a white female, blond, and cut up from one end to the other."

"This is not the day for . . . Okay, Clark. Have you called for Physical Evidence yet?"

"No. You were the first call I made."

"Right. Stand by. I'll get some people on the way."

As soon as he was off the phone, Clark went into the pound office to pull the ticket on the Lincoln. By the time CAPers showed, he wanted to know all he could about the Lincoln.

CHAPTER 2

Friday, 2:00 p.m.

Chief Knecht was ushered into Bobby Klevinger's office. Knecht never looked at City Hall without thinking it looked as if it were about to fall over. This was the "new" City Hall, designed by somebody famous, with a "lagoon" fountain and modern-art flagpoles out front. The thing was, the building was bigger at the top than at the bottom. It did not seem right to Knecht, as if someone had looked at the blueprint wrong and built the thing upside down.

"I appreciate your coming over, Chief."

Knecht smiled and nodded. Like I had a choice, he thought to himself. Klevinger was the assistant city manager–public safety, Knecht's boss.

"I expect you know why I wanted to visit with you," Klevinger said. "It's this union thing."

"I beg your pardon?"

"The move to organize the Police Department. I want your feel on it."

"Well . . ." Knecht was not sure what Klevinger wanted to hear, so he began tentatively. "There's been union talk for years, but . . ."

"It's a bit more than talk, isn't it? Didn't you see this?" Klevinger opened a manila folder he had brought with him from his desk and put photocopies of a local newspaper story on the table in front of him. Knecht had seen it, as a matter of fact, a

19

couple of days before. It was a longish piece, an update on the Dallas Police Association, the newer Patrolman's Union, and the Combined Law Enforcement Association of Texas, known as CLEAT.

"Yes," he said. "I read it."

"Well, what do you propose to do about it?"

This was not what Knecht had expected, and he changed his mind about a cup of coffee to stall for time. When he returned to his seat, he began, cautiously.

"I think the main thing is the troops aren't sure they have the support of management, and . . ."

"Which management?" Klevinger cut in. "Do you mean you and your chiefs or city management?"

"I don't think they make the distinction. The department's been through a rocky few years. We had to ask the officers to do without raises two years in a row, last year it went down to the wire on a pay cut with the revenue shortfall projections. You know better than I about that."

"Freezes and cuts have been citywide, nobody's singling out the police."

"Yes, sir, but they tend to think they should be singled out. Cops don't see themselves as being the same as sanitation workers and parks employees."

"I know . . ."

"And the pay issue aside, there has been a lot of criticism of the department by city council members. That's to be expected, taking the long view. Going to single-member districts, increasing minority participation, all good things mind you, it's to be expected that we have to take our turn in the barrel. But I think you and I can agree some of the rhetoric has been excessive . . ."

"Can we? I'm not so sure. When your department has these questionable shootings . . ."

"Two last year, one officer ultimately exonerated and the other fired and filed on. With twenty-four hundred officers working two hundred twenty days, Mr. Klevinger, we put in five hundred twenty-eight thousand workdays in a year. There were four hundred and eight assaults on officers last year, and we don't report scuffles. Our people were involved in more than three dozen exchanges of gunfire, and, yessir, we had two questionable shootings. Shit happens.''

"Let's don't . . .''

"Not to mention that my department has been under pressure for fifteen years to lower entry standards so we can hire more minorities . . .''

"Change your standards, not lower them.''

". . . and now it's our fault if our level of performance reflects those lower standards in any way . . .''

"Now . . .''

"Not taking into consideration, of course, that our population increased by two thousand a week throughout the Sun Belt boom days and our people are spread so thin . . .''

"Chief . . .''

"And we've not been authorized the positions we need to meet demands for service, nor the money to train, support, and equip the people we have. And another thing. We have the cleanest, most honest crime-reporting system in the country, and what is the payoff? We catch hell because our crime rate is up. Nobody seems to understand our stats are high because we report our crime, we don't hide it.''

"Chief, let's not have this conversation again. I want to talk about police unions.''

"We are talking about unions. Nothing I've said here is secret. The troops know all this as well as I do. That's why some of them are talking union. They don't think their interests are being looked after.''

"It's not an easy job, Chief. That's a given. But as to the union . . .''

"Give me the additional two hundred officers your bosses have promised over the next two years, decent pay raises, and the money we need for equipment. Keep your promises and there won't be a union here.''

"Are you questioning our intentions on the additional positions, Chief?''

"No, I'm questioning your delivery. Good intentions won't get the job done.''

"I'll bear that in mind.''

"Excuse the soapbox.''

"You sound like a union organizer yourself when you get going."

"Hardly. If you think there are problems with the Dallas Police Department now, if a union comes in, you'll cry like babies and long for the good old days."

"I can assure you, Chief, that neither I nor my bosses want to drive the police into the arms of the organizers. A key issue, though, is collective bargaining. The DPA as it exists presently can insist on that, but of course it would require a public referendum. They tried that in 1974 and the voters shot them down three to one."

"Yes, sir. And I think they would vote it down again today, but I'm not as sure as I was then. There've been a hell of a lot of police funerals since seventy-four."

"Yes. Times have changed, there's no question about that. So, bottom line, your view of this is that our best response is to throw money at it."

"Our best response is to keep our promises."

"Well, thank you, Chief, for stopping by."

"Yes, sir."

Paddy Maguire was going to be on television, and he was not happy about it. He had been a sergeant since nine-thirty that morning and now it was a quarter to three. Paddy had spent the day trying to make the transition from Vice to Community Services, and it had not been easy. There was a crowd of angry neighbors out in the parking lot in front of his storefront police community center, being orated to by a handful of self-appointed community leaders, and Channel 8 was on the scene with their Minicam. Just before he walked out the door to try to explain why the Dallas Police Department had decided to close the center, one of his PSO's caught him and handed him a phone message. He could not make out the man's handwriting.

"What is this?" he asked.

"I think that's what he said his name was," the PSO answered. "He was just kind of whispering. Bolo or something like that. He said you could get him at that number later this evening."

"Bolo," Maguire thought. "Lobo." It was from Lobo, one of his snitches. "Did he say what it was about?"

"Something about some badassed Mexican name of Frank, that's all."

"Okay, thanks."

Maguire slipped the note into his shirt pocket and checked to see if his hair was combed. He would try to remember to make the call, but right now he had bigger fish to fry than some badassed Mexican.

Randi Stoner drove her undercover rattletrap Honda past the front of the club, around the corner of the building, and parked. It took her a couple of minutes to get out of the car because it felt like stepping off the high board the first time, when the pool below looks like a place mat. She took a couple of deep breaths to steady her nerves, checked herself in the rearview mirror, and then she did it.

She pushed through the front door of the club, trying to look like she did it every day. Inside, she found herself in a small vestibule with another door opposite the first. On her left behind a ticket window sat a woman with a face like a bulldog and hair too black to be real. Randi waited while a couple of men paid at the window. There was a loud buzz, and the men pulled the second door open and disappeared inside. Through the closing door Randi saw colored lights and a cloud of smoke. The din of the music was deafening. Larry and J.D. had been right; a body mike would be useless with all that noise.

"Can I hep yew, hon?" the cashier asked, her eyebrows raised.

"I'd like to speak with the manager," Randi said, leaning near the hole in the glass to make herself heard.

"In reference to whut?"

"About a job."

"Are you a daincer, hon?"

"Waitress. I'm supposed to ask for Charlie."

"Go rat on in," the old woman said.

"Thank you." Randi smiled and pulled the door open.

The inside of the club was dark except for blue lights screaming down on three stages. A sound system boomed the theme song from the movie *Flashdance* through speakers the size of compact cars hammering at each other from every side. Randi stood inside the door, waiting for her eyes and ears to adjust, and watched the dancers working.

On the main stage, a blonde was dancing with her back to the room. Bent over at the waist, she was looking between her legs and shaking her butt at a gray-haired man perched on a stool almost within arm's reach of her. She was wearing black spike heels and a G-string, a sequined heart-shaped one. She leaned down over the old man on the barstool and shook her breasts in his face. She danced away out of reach when Pops tried to grab her, and the guy fell back on his stool, laughing like crazy.

There were two more dancers on smaller stages, at the other end of the room. One was black, slender, and lithe, in a silver G-string that sparkled in the spotlight. All three stages were lightly attended, probably two dozen men in all. It was early.

Randi saw only two waitresses, and was relieved to see that they were not topless. They were wearing costumes she would not have picked herself, miniskirts and smallish red vests that showed their middles and a lot of cleavage. But not topless, anyway, and that was something.

"Can I help you?"

It was a voice accustomed to being heard over the music, and even without the touch of his hand on her arm it would have been enough to startle her. She jumped, but his hand closed on her arm and she did not go far. When she turned to look at him, he was all smiles.

"Take it easy, baby," he said. He was skinny but tall, with black hair combed straight back, and he was wearing a baggy dark suit and a shirt that might have been the same color. He had a sleazy smile, or maybe she was not being fair. His eyes were busy, looking at her and back and forth, keeping an eye on things. He was not bashful about looking her over.

"My name's Randi. Randi Stevens. I called about a job?"

"Who? You called?"

"Yes, I called a little while ago. You said to come on over. You're Charlie, aren't you?"

"That's me. You dance?"

"No. It was about a waitress job."

"How come you don't dance?"

"Look . . ." Randi pulled her arm free of his grip. "Do you have an opening for a waitress or not?"

This was the first club she had tried, and there were a couple of others that would do just as well. Mack had more than one hangout, and if this guy was going to turn out to be some kind of . . . But what the hell, she thought, the others aren't going to be any different.

"Come with me," Charlie said.

Randi thought about leaving but did not. Instead, she followed Charlie, sidling after him between two tables full of customers. As she turned to pass between two chairs, one of the guys watching the main stage ran his hand up her leg. She jumped again and let out a squeal. The man laughed and leered at her, then the others chimed in when they caught on. She felt her face reddening as she pushed through. Try to get over that, she told herself, it only encourages the assholes. She made a note to come back someday when she had her badge and gun with her.

She wondered if this job interview was going to happen in a toilet and was relieved when Charlie went to his left past the men's room and unlocked a door that had a little novelty sign glued on it that said THRONE ROOM.

"Step into my orifice," he said, still grinning.

She sidled through the door past him and was not surprised to find that his "orifice" looked like it might have been a broom closet originally, with a window added that looked out on the club. When he closed the door behind her, she noticed that the music was surprisingly muffled. The office walls were heavily insulated, which they would have to be if he ever wanted to talk on his phone and be heard. Meaning that nothing that happened in here could be heard outside, Randi noted.

Charlie settled into his chair behind the desk, leaving Randi to stand.

"That's all right. I'll just stand, thank you," she said.

"Huh? Yeah, right." Charlie laughed. "Right. So, listen, how's come you don't wanna dance, anyway?"

"Look, Charlie, I don't know you and you don't know me, so it shouldn't hurt your feelings if I tell you that not only do

I 'don't wanna' dance, I don't really want to work here at all. I'm not particularly excited about being a waitress period, but it happens to be all I know how to do. And I hear a good waitress can make more here than at Denny's.''

"It's your tits, right?" Charlie nodded knowingly, his brow furrowed. "You're ashamed of your hooters. Am I right?"

"Not particularly. Look, I don't know if this is going to make sense to you, but I am somebody's momma, can you understand that? I have to work because I have to take care of my kid."

"Jesus, you're breakin' my fuckin' heart, girl. That's my point exactly, right there. Why run your ass off waiting on tables when you can make a hell of a lot more money dancing. You like getting your ass grabbed?"

"Not particularly."

"I didn't think so, the way you jumped outta your drawers when that clown groped you on the way in here. They do that with the waitresses, unless you really know how to handle yourself, which I don't think you do. When you're dancing on the stage, if one of them comes after you, we'll throw the son of a bitch out on his fuckin' ear. I don't see the distinction, myself, not when you compute into it the money differential."

"Fine. But I do, and that's what counts. Look, if you don't need a waitress . . ."

"I can always use good help. I just think you're wasting your . . . talent, that's all. It makes me wonder when a chip like you comes in here and she don't want to dance. You know what I mean? Maybe the older broads, okay, that makes sense. But you ain't that old, and you ain't fat, so . . . You know?"

"Look . . ."

"You ain't one of them sociologists, are you?"

"What?"

"From the university, you know, doing one of them research deals. I heard about them deals . . ."

"Don't be ridiculous."

"Or a reporter?"

"Okay, okay," Randi broke in on him. Cop had to be his next guess. "I'll make you a deal. Let me warm up to it. Let me start out waiting tables until I can get the feel of the place. Then I'll give it a shot. How about that?"

"You could do Amateur Night."

"I beg your pardon?"

"Amateur Night, every Wednesday. It's on the level, too, more or less. Well, okay, most of the girls that dance ain't really amateurs. They work other clubs, they dance in here and we act like they're squares off the street. Hey, the customers love it. Sometimes we even get real amateurs. Wait'll you see, you'll love it. It's a blast."

"Yeah, that's an idea. I'll see about doing Amateur Night." I'll call in sick on Wednesday, you prick, Randi thought. "So how about it, do I get the job or what?"

"What the hell. Yeah, yeah, I guess so. Here, I've got something you need to fill out."

Charlie opened a drawer of the filing cabinet and reached inside. He handed her something. She was expecting an application form, but he handed her a waitress costume.

"Fill this out, get it?" Charlie laughed. "I love it. Fill this out."

Randi smiled stonily. "When do I start?"

"You did already. Slip into that and go to work."

"Tonight?"

"No, I'll pencil you in for the fall season. Why the fuck not tonight?"

"It's my kid. I've gotta get a baby-sitter. I'll be here tomorrow night. What time?"

"Whatever time you like, dear. Whatta you think, I'm runnin' a business here or something? I thought you wanted a goddamned job."

"I do, I do, but I can't work tonight. My little girl's at home by herself. You know how it is."

"Yeah, and I know it ain't gonna be like that with me, baby. You work for me, you have your ass here, on time, every fuckin' day. You understand me?"

"Sure, you bet."

"You bet my ass. First time you call in with some bullshit about your sitter can't make it, the first time you leave me stranded high and dry, your ass is fired. You understand me?"

"Don't worry about it, Charlie. I'm dependable, you'll see."

"Okay, then. Tomorrow. Be here at three o'clock. You'll work till closing."

Bobby Thurmon followed Lenny Stuyvesant up the narrow stairs from the biting cold of the street toward the raucous jukebox music and the smell of stale beer on the second floor. Bobby had only been to the DPA Club once before and he had never been to a party there. It was a bar owned and operated by the Dallas Police Association, a haven where the cops could go and get shit-faced without getting into any trouble. Cops only, and their guests. He had not been invited, but he knew Lenny would not have any trouble finding a sponsor and hoped that would do for him as well.

At the landing, Lenny leaned on the banister to catch his breath. Lenny was up in his sixties, and nobody was sure how long he had been on the police beat. He had seen a couple of dozen young guys cycle through the pressroom, starting out covering the cops, then either quitting or moving on to bigger and better things. Lenny liked the cops. Bobby Thurmon thought he liked them too much. But the old man had outrageous sources and some great war stories. You could not beat him on anything worth covering. Christ, Bobby thought, he looks more like a detective than the real ones do.

Bobby looked past Lenny down a hall. To the left he heard the clicking of balls on a pool table, and somebody cursing his luck. To the right an open door led into the club proper, the beer joint with its jukebox, a little stage, and a dance floor. When Lenny was up to it, they went in, and somebody at the table nearest the door called Lenny a son of a bitch and offered to buy him a beer.

Lenny shook hands around the table and introduced each of the cops to Bobby, but the music was playing pretty loud and he was not as good with names as he should be. He smiled and returned each of the cops' waves or nods. They were mostly older guys, Bobby noticed, and he had seen most of them around the Police and Courts building. Veteran detectives, gatekeepers.

"I just wanted to stop by and say *adiós* to Old Man Felty," Lenny was explaining to one of the cops.

"Yeah," the cop answered, one eyebrow cocked. "Can you believe that shit? Is that legal, Lenny?"

"What?"

"For a man to retire that's never worked a day in his life. That's against the law, ain't it?"

"You're probably right," Lenny answered, laughing. "I guess the fix's in, huh?"

"Gotta be. Hell, he'll never know the difference, except he won't have to drive in every two weeks and pick up his check."

"I'll tell him you said that."

Bobby saw the party, maybe a dozen men sitting and standing around a long table on the other side of the dance floor. The men looked like cops, and the women with them looked like wives. But then Bobby was still new at the business.

Lenny Stuyvesant did not just cross the room to get to the party; he worked the room, and he reminded Bobby of a politician pressing the flesh. He really works at it, Bobby thought.

"What're you drinking?" Bobby asked Lenny.

"What?"

"I'm going to go to the bar and get something. What're you having?"

"Nah, come on. They've got beer at the table."

"Okay for you," Bobby answered, leaning close to make the old man hear him over the music. "You're invited. I'll meet you."

"Whatever."

Bobby bought a bourbon and 7-Up at the bar and made his way to the party table. Again Lenny introduced Bobby around, and Bobby nodded and smiled, not trying very hard to get all the names straight. He could not remember anything unless he wrote it down, and he had no intention of breaking out his reporter's notepad under the circumstances. He knew all this was off the record. Lenny had been emphatic about that.

These guys did not have real names, he noticed. They were Wild Bill and Smoky, and the big Mexican was Macho or Nacho or something like that. Wheels and Crash shook his hand, but he was not sure which was which. The jukebox was awfully loud and cigarette smoke hung over the table like smog or . . . He could not come up with a better simile and let it go.

The women were sitting down, most of them, and they had real names. The record on the jukebox finally ended, and when the next one started, two or three of the ladies hopped up and dragged their men onto the floor to dance. It was all country-and-western dreck, and this was a sappy slow one.

It was not hard to figure out which one was the guest of honor. Lieutenant Felty was leaning against a chair at the head of the table, where a woman Lenny introduced as his wife sat smiling up at the men. Bobby thought Felty looked old enough to retire. He was a tall man, but his shoulders were rounded, pushing his head out over his chest. His hair was gray and thin, but he looked happy. He eyed Bobby with a mischievous squint and said something derogatory about reporters in general. He was drunk, but handling it pretty well.

One of Felty's men came up and asked Mrs. Felty to dance. She jumped at the chance and they were off.

"That boy's a daincing sumbitch," Felty announced with a proud shake of his head, like somebody's father.

Bobby watched the couple slide across the floor in time with the music.

"Yeah, they dance nice," he offered.

"Well, that's dancing there," Felty said, "but wait till they play something lively and you'll see them *daince,* by God!"

"Oh," Bobby said, nodding as if knowingly. He was not from Texas.

By the time Sergeant Dan Spencer got his search warrant signed by a judge and drove back to the meeting place, the state chemist was there already, waiting with the rest of his people. Spencer was Texas Department of Public Safety Narcotics, a state police plainclothesman in charge of a team of undercover narcotics officers. It was dark as pitch, but the snow had finally stopped. Spencer pulled his car, a maroon Lincoln his team had seized from a trafficker, off the gravel country road and up the bumpy rutted drive past the old farmhouse that somebody used now only to store their hay out of the weather, and nosed around the corner of the house with his lights out. Behind the house he could make out the shapes of three cars, two of his guys' unmarked units and the local deputy's car that was supposed to be unmarked, too. It was a white Ford LTD with a spotlight mounted in front of the driver's door at the edge of the windshield. Spencer's guys were driving seized cars, too, a Trans Am and a Bronco II. There were his three men and the chemist, all sitting in the LTD with the motor running so they could stay warm with the heater. Burn the other guy's gas, Spencer thought to himself.

Spencer and the deputy got out of his Lincoln and squeezed into the Ford. Spencer introduced the deputy to the chemist and then in a few words brought him up to date.

"Deputy Mitchell here has a confidential informant, guy who works off and on hauling dope, says there's a lab in a barn on a farm not far from here. He knows the people, knows a lab when he sees one, says he was in there within the last twenty-four hours and they were cooking."

"Any problem getting a warrant?" the chemist asked.

"No. Deputy Mitchell signed the affidavit. The snitch put it down good, lots of detail, volume, the smell, how long it takes to cook a batch, real good setup. He's working off a possession case, been reliable in the past, everything."

"How did he say they're set up?" the chemist wanted to know.

Spencer gave the chemist the deputy's affidavit and his notebook with all the details, and they all kept quiet until the chemist was through looking it over. The chemist was there to make sure that the lab did not blow them up. Cooking methamphetamine is a dicey proposition, involving ether and precursor chemicals, all heated and under pressure. With real chemists, it would be risky. With the kind of whacked-out dopeheads who made their living running clandestine labs, it was like juggling nitroglycerine. The way they found labs sometimes was the damned things blew up, took the roof off a house and burned what was left like napalm. So they did not rush the chemist. They wanted him to know as much as he could about what they were getting into. Spencer rolled down his window and lit a cigarette. The chemical part of it was Doc's problem. Spencer was thinking about a hike through the woods and a pack of dogs.

• • •

"What do we have on her so far?" Dave White asked, leaning his chair back against the wall behind his desk.

The Internal Affairs Division office was empty except for White and his partner, Bob Marx. It was after hours on a cold and snowy Friday evening, and everybody else had long since gone home. White and Marx had a new assignment, and White was wondering why it could not have waited until Monday.

"Hangs out with characters, frequents bars and clubs known for trafficking."

"She's working Vice undercover, for Christ's sake. Where's she supposed to hang out?"

"There's a problem with the times. The captain had Inspections pull time cards, and she's doing too much of her hanging out on her own time."

"He had Inspections do it? So we don't trust the Vice supervisors either?"

"It's not that, I don't think. Just a precaution. Unless she's working off the books for some reason, like I said, she's doing a lot of this stuff on off-duty time."

"What about her partners?"

"They check out all right."

"Bob, what's our source on this?" White asked, betting he already knew. And he was right.

"What else? A snitch."

"Right."

"Don't turn up your nose, David. Where would cops be without confidential informants?"

"Yeah, yeah. What's this one's story?"

"There's two of them, as a matter of fact."

"And they put a story together between them, and . . ."

"No. Two different cases, two separate snitches. And their stories match up pretty good."

"That's it?" White was not crazy about his job, anyway. Working Internal Affairs was seldom a smart career move, and it had not been his idea.

"Well, there is this," Marx answered. He squinted one eye and gave his partner a little smile as he tugged some stuff out of a manila envelope.

"What is this?" White asked, dropping his chair forward and

leaning over his desk as Marx spread the contents of the envelope across the calendar blotter.

There were fifty or sixty small loose-leaf notebook pages, with names and addresses, phone numbers, pager numbers, a lot of scrawled notes. And photos, mostly Polaroids. Faces out of a biker movie. Men with long hair and beards, tattoos, posing with guns of all kinds. There was one snapshot of a dude with a bandanna shooting dope into his arm and grinning like a loon. White shuffled through the pages and came to pictures of women. Most of them looked like what they were, speed whores, scrawny and nasty with eyeballs like headlights, high on methamphetamine or cocaine or heaven only knew. A few of them were cleaned up pretty good. He wondered if any of them were before-and-after, and studied them closely. He decided a couple of them were: one kid who was actually cute in one photo and looked like one of the witches in *Macbeth* in another. He did not think very much time separated the two pictures. It was a hell of a life.

"What is this?" White asked again.

"They call it a 'schiz book,' took it off some doper in a raid."

"They're proud of this shit?"

"Hell, yes. See, it's full of nicknames, street names, phone numbers. There's a couple of poems, too." Bob Marx had worked dope before he came to IAD.

"I can't believe they'd keep all this stuff."

"They're speed freaks. They can't remember phone numbers, or names either. Without pictures, they'd forget what their friends looked like."

"And what does this have to do . . ."

"That one there," Marx answered, pointing to one of the photos. A white female, mid-twenties, thin, she was wearing faded jeans and a leather vest with buckskin fringe, and was holding the vest open to show her breasts for the camera. "Enough of the tits, Dave. Check the face."

Her eyes were the first thing White noticed: too big, crazy-looking. Her smile was big and crooked. She looked like she was high as a kite. "Okay . . ." White said, nodding.

"And this . . ." Marx put the most recent police department yearbook on the desk beside the other stuff.

White saw the one he meant before Marx tapped the yearbook photo with his index finger. The photo in the book was black-and-white—an open, smiling face with dark hair pulled back according to regulations. She was wearing a uniform.

"She was still in Patrol then," Marx said.

"It's her, I guess." White nodded, looking back and forth at the two pictures. It was not easy to be sure.

"It's her, all right."

"Hell of a deal," White said, pursing his lips and nodding some more.

"Yep."

"Maybe she got carried away playing the part. It could happen."

"Maybe. She's stoned there."

"Looks like it."

"It could happen, but if she was on the level, she would have reported it."

"Yeah, but . . ."

"*But* nothing. Tightroping is like pearl diving in a septic tank. There's about a million ways to screw up and whether you do or not, you can still come up smelling like shit. But she ain't playing straight, I know that."

"You don't think this was in the line of duty?" White asked.

"I don't think."

"So let's pull her in, see what she has to say for herself."

"We'll probably end up doing that, but there's more to it."

"Okay." White sighed and rubbed his eyes with his hand. They could just get her statement, wrap it up by midnight, and that still left him Saturday and Sunday. But no-o-o-o . . .

"The Vice Control Division has a problem. A leak."

"You want some coffee?"

"Nah. You listening?"

"I'm listening," White said over his shoulder on his way to the coffeepot. "A leak. Transfer the bitch. That's simple enough. Put her back in Patrol or ditch her in Records or something."

"We gotta solve the problem, not transfer it."

"So?"

"So we're gonna work a sting on her."

"Get outta here." White laughed.

"I'm serious."

"I'm not sure we're qualified. Are you?"

"It's gotta be us, so when the deal comes down, she's the only one with access to the information. Then if it leaks, we got her."

"Yeah . . . but where is this deal going to come from?"

"That's all being handled upstairs. Our job is going to be surveillance. You up for a little around-the-clock?"

"Don't tell me that."

"What?"

"I got plans. This couldn't wait till Monday?"

"Attaboy, partner. Love that attitude."

"When do we start?"

"Tonight." Marx grinned. "You need to make any calls, let somebody know your plans changed for the weekend?"

Dave White looked at his watch. "Nah," he said. "It's too late now."

"Then we might as well get going." Marx dumped the stuff off the desk back into the manila envelope, and both men put on their overcoats.

"What about the rest of the Vice guys, the officers working with her?" White asked.

"What about them?"

"Have they been told about this?"

"Think that through, Dave. 'Listen, Officer, don't tell a soul, but we think maybe your partner there, Officer Stefanie Nugent, just may be dirty as a toilet bowl in a crack house.' Word might get back to her, don't you think?"

"Yeah, but . . ."

"No *buts*. Anybody working with her just better be on their damned toes, that's all."

CHAPTER 3

Friday, 10:00 p.m.

Curtis was pissed and Ned knew better than to interrupt him, so Ned leaned against the wall and concentrated on punching bullets into the curved banana magazine with his gloved thumb. His AK-47 lay on the floor beside him, already fed with a thirty-round clip and another taped to the first upside down so he could reload in a hurry. There were a couple of more magazines beside his left leg, loaded and ready to go. Ned was a practical man, and these were evil times.

"Stupid greaser shithead motherfuckers! They don't know who they fucking with, man!"

Ned had never gotten used to Curtis's Jamaican accent. Ned was South Dallas born and bred, one of the handful of Americans ganged up with the Jamaicans who had taken over the South Dallas crack cocaine trade. He didn't give a shit about their "posses" or any of the rest of it, but he had to hand it to them when it came to distribution. They had solid dope connections and no shortage of homeboys from the island to sit on their butts in crack houses and peddle the shit for them. And they were some stone-cold fuckers, too. He had seen them do some seriously evil shit to people, and he knew not to mess with them.

At the sound of footsteps in the hallway outside, Curtis stopped raving in midsentence and Ned laid the magazine he was loading softly down on his leg and picked up the AK-47.

Visitors. Ned watched Curtis slip a pistol out from under his jacket and check it. One of them big-butted 9's, Ned could tell. These Jamaicans love them sonsabitches that shoot fifteen or sixteen times at a whack. Because they can't shoot worth a shit, he told himself. Make up for it with firepower.

Two voices came through the door, one after the other. Some of that Jamaican slang bullshit Ned could not make out. Curtis answered with some more of it and then eased the two-by-four out from under the doorknob and told them to come in. It was Stone and Reggie, Curtis's main henchmen.

The three Jamaicans put the board back against the door after Curtis stood looking down the hall back and forth, letting the cold air in until Ned thought about saying something to him. Making sure his boys weren't tailed. Then the three Jamaicans made a little circle in the floor and starting talking some shit. Ned could make out enough of it to do him. He knew what was up anyway. Willy and his Mexicans had whacked some of Curtis's people, and Curtis was down for the payback. Ned did not like it that the Jamaicans were firing up some of their own crack, because he knew they would be crazier than a herd of goddamned bats by the time anything got done. But that was their business. He just made sure he got all his magazines loaded.

Sergeant Spencer put his three men, the deputy, and the chemist in two cars for the run from their meeting place to the place where they would leave the cars and hike in to the lab.

"What do you think, Doc?"

"Sounds pretty standard," the chemist answered. "Of course 'standard' is a relative term with these crazy fuckers."

The two cars rumbled down the country road, past the main aluminum frame gate. From the main gate in daylight you could just make out the roof of the ranch house beyond the crest of the hill. Beyond that was a big barn and a windmill with a water tank. The lab was in the barn. He could not see them, of course, but he knew that running loose in the pasture between the main gate and the second gate there was a pack of dogs, three or four pit bulldogs to deter any intruders. Or to kill them, if they insisted. Spencer had other ideas.

Within a minute or two they crossed a bridge, and the deputy cut his headlights off and pulled over to the side of the road. Spencer did the same. They would go in here, into the woods.

Spencer made sure the man who would go in front, his point man, had the special gun, the pistol with the funny barrel, and he double-checked it to make sure it was ready to go.

The chemist stood back and watched the others make their last-minute checks and get ready, noting that the troops had removed the dome-light bulbs in both cars so no lights came on when a door was opened. He could not make out what Spencer had in his hands. It looked like a cane pole with some kind of gadget rigged up on one end. The chemist had a revolver tucked into his belt in case things went so wrong that he needed it, but he was not enthusiastic about it. That was the other men's department.

The doc worried about the contents of the bag he would take. He had a respirator in there, a disposable sterile suit with boots and gloves built in, among other things. As if the risk of being blown up weren't bad enough, he knew there might be subtler dangers. Depending on what this gang of clowns was trying to make, there could be toxic fumes to inhale or maybe some of the hotshot new analogues, in which case inhaling microscopic airborne particles or even skin contact could be instantly lethal, carcinogenic, or possibly just provide him a lifetime supply of psychotic episodes.

Spencer followed his point man by a couple of paces and stayed just to the left of him so he could see ahead also. Next came the deputy, another DPS man, then the chemist and Spencer's third man brought up the rear. His job was to stay up with the rest of the team while also keeping an eye out behind them. Due east through the woods for fifty yards and they should come out just about even with the west end of the ranch house. The barn would be to their left at about forty-five degrees. From the edge of the trees, they would have to cover another twenty yards of clear ground.

All of them had portable radios rigged with earpieces and hands-free microphones. In addition, the deputy had his department's radio, in a case on his belt, turned off. He had brought the ''round badges'' from the state in on this thing because he did not trust some of his fellow officers, and he was not taking any chances. Nobody else in his department knew about this. When the thing was all done, he'd call in and get word to the sheriff. Then he would see how things went from there. It had occurred to him that he could lose his job over it, but on the other hand it was not long before the next election and he had been giving some thought to getting into politics himself lately.

There was no warning at all. As careful as the cops tried to be, stepping gingerly over the snowy ground, frozen mud and twigs crackling underfoot anyway, as quiet as they all tried to be, none of them saw it or heard it coming. The first thing any of them heard was when the point man choked off a short scream.

Dunk stood waiting in a dark corner of a downtown parking lot and cursed when he saw the snow had come again. He looked up at the dervish skittering flakes and saw the lights of the tall buildings behind him, their steel-and-glass sides towering over him so high that they seemed to converge in the sky above him.

"Shit!" he said, turning up the collar of his brown leather jacket to warm his neck. Dunk was not his real name, but he did not care and did not know anyone who did. He was a lean and rangy young man and might have been a prospect at some basketball powerhouse if things had worked out differently. There was no place for him to go.

He had stashed the Firebird a block away in a place where it was not likely to be noticed, with the cool plate on the rear end. All he needed now was for the people to show, and then it was off to someplace warm for the old dunker—Irene's place. Yes, Lord! Come on, you pepper-eating motherfuckers, I got plans.

They cruised by once. On the second pass, the Monte Carlo stopped across the street long enough for somebody to slip out of the passenger door. Then it cut sharply into the lot and came toward him. Dunk brought his hands out of his pockets so the people in the car could see they were empty. He affected what he hoped was the appropriate degree of nonchalance, allowing for the snow and the biting cold, his head cocked to one side and one hand making half of a "safe" sign like a baseball umpire.

The Monte Carlo came toward him, then veered right and circled him. Are these cats hinky or what! Dunk thought, beginning to wish he had never made the connection. Finally, the car bobbed to a stop with the passenger's tinted window within arm's reach of him. He waited, smiling and trying not to dance from one foot to the other even though the cold wind made it seem the only thing to do, and wondered if he ought to think about using some of the money he would make off this deal to buy a gun. Dunk had never seen himself as a gun type of person, but goddamn, these Mexicans were some spooky sons of bitches.

Down came the window, and it could have been a lot better for Dunk. It was the dude they called Frank, with them hot-cold crazy goddamned eyes and that shit-eating grin all the time.

"My man!" the Mexican in the car sang out, not too loud, because sound carries downtown at night, especially when it is cold.

"What's happ'nin'?" Dunk answered.

Crazy Frank did not show his hands for any handshaking or high-fives or none of that shit, and Dunk wished that he had. He worried about what the crazy Mexican had in his hands. Maybe I need some kind of partner, Dunk thought, some badass outlaw to back me up in this kind of crap. He made a note to think that through later.

"Dunk!" the driver called out, just enough to be heard.

"Thank you, Jesus," Dunk muttered under his breath. He knew the driver, a dude named Willy. He was cool, he was sharp. Willy was a Mexican all right, but he was a businessman. Don't ever want him to sic that crazy motherfucker on me, Dunk thought, but I certainly am glad he got the leash in his hand.

"You got it?" Willy asked. All business.

"Did I say I would?" Dunk grinned, his hands palms up, one eye on the passenger.

"You got it?" Willy asked again. Same voice, same tone, just like the first time never fucking happened.

"Yeah, I got it."

"Where?"

Dunk told him.

"Keys?"

"Here you go." Dunk handed the keys through the passenger's window, a hell of a lot closer to the crazy one than he wanted to get, close enough to smell whiskey on his breath, some of that tequila shit probably. Willy reached across and took the keys. The crazy one still did not show his hands. Ordinarily, Dunk would see the money before he handed over keys or let on where the car was or anything like that, but this was not ordinarily. Looking at the crazy one without wanting to let on that he was studying him had led Dunk to lower his expectations for this deal. He would not have minded if they tore ass and left him standing there. He was thinking more about life and less about money the longer he studied the face in the car window.

"Good," Willy said. "You're a professional, man, and I respect that."

Dunk nodded. He took some pride in that, and coming from Willy it meant more than it might have. Dunk's thing was he could steal the hot GM cars and pass them on with keys, and the steering column intact. Kids steal these goddamned Trans Ams and Firebirds, it's easy. But they fuck up the steering columns and you can spot that shit a mile away. When a man buys a hot car from the dunker, it is cool. Key fits, the column looks right, and the plates won't get you in no trouble. That's the difference between a pro and an amateur. Of course, if the cops go snooping down around in there looking at VIN numbers, that's something else again, but you don't expect a street operator to cover that angle. That's shop work there.

"I want to make you a deal, Dunk," Willy said. Willy was talking across the front seat of the Monte Carlo, past the crazy one, through the window on the passenger side, and Dunk had no trouble making him out, but the thing was, it was like Willy was whispering, seriously. Just whispering, like he could send his goddamned voice wherever he wanted that son of a bitch to go without even trying.

"A deal, huh?" Dunk answered, still smiling, thinking, What is this, "Let's Make a Deal" or something?

"Yeah, a good deal. I told you fifteen hundred cash, right?"

"Right." You damned right, Dunk thought, and that's why I went for it, because that is three times more than anybody else would pay for a two-year-old Firebird, clean or not. So what's the deal?

"Which is an outrageous price, you and I both know that. Right?"

"It's a good price, Willy."

"It's outrageous."

"Okay, outrageous."

"Are you cold, man?" Willy asked.

"No, I'm fine." The last thing in the world Dunk wanted was to be invited into the Monte Carlo. He did not figure he would ever see sunlight again if it came to that.

"Suit yourself. So, here's the thing. I got the cash right here, see?" Willy held up a wad of bills that looked fine to Dunk, who nodded.

"So I can pay you the fifteen hundred for the ride, and I don't mind doing that. The thing is . . ."

Here it comes, Dunk thought.

"The thing is, I like you. You are a professional, like me. I respect that. So I want to do something better for you. I want to do something that will, you know, give you a shot."

At the word *shot,* Dunk could not help cutting his eyes full on the crazy one, and the crazy one could not help giggling. Sweet Jesus, Dunk thought. Sweet fucking Jesus.

"A shot, you know what I mean. An opportunity. I want to set you up in a business of your own, man. Here it is, your choice: fifteen hundred cash like I told you or, behind door number two, *ta da!*" Willy held up a trash bag in one hand and the cash in the other.

"What?" Dunk asked, because it got quiet and he felt like Willy expected something out of him.

"Crack, man. A money machine. Fifteen hundred cash or a grand and two hundred units of the American fucking dream, man. Good stuff, stout shit, I promise. You sell this shit for five bucks a pop, you're talking a grand smooth. That makes two thousand instead of fifteen hundred. And when this is gone, I'll make sure there's more because you're going to need more, you're going to have you a demand problem on your hands, Dunk. You're going to have people trying to whip your ass to give you their money. Well?''

''I don't know, man . . .''

''I'm talking about a grand for a five-hundred-dollar car and I throw in the crack at no cost to you and you make another fucking grand in a week, maybe less, and then you're in business, and you don't know? Help me understand, man.''

''I . . . You know, I just don't see myself standing around on the corner, you know, holding that shit. 'Hey, mister, want to buy some dope?' It ain't me. You see that, don't you? I like it clean, in and out, move the ride and go on. I don't think standing around with all that shit, moving a dime at a time . . .''

''I gotcha, man. I see your problem.''

''You do?''

''Certainly. It's a matter of perspective. This is not a one-man operation we're talking about here, home.''

''It ain't?''

''Is General Motors a one-man outfit? Does Lee Iacocca build the fucking cars with his own hands? You gotta expand your horizons, home.''

''You're saying . . .''

''Exactly. I'm saying you find some street fools to move the shit for you. They buy it from you, you understand. You cannot do this shit on consignment. They move it, they stand on the corner with the shit in their pockets and flag down unmarked squad cars and all that shit. You wholesale it, that's what I mean. Open up a whole new goddamned territory.''

''I see what you mean. Yeah, yeah, I see it now.''

''All right, Dunker. You think about it.''

Dunk would think about it, all night. He would also give some thought to the late Lonnie Johnson. The last he knew of Lonnie, the kid was bragging around about getting in with some fast-lane Mexican dudes. Next thing he was in the paper for getting shot by a cop. Dunk knew Lonnie to steal cars, not to be no badass. He would definitely give it some thought.

• • •

It was a Rottweiler, a black son of a bitch the size of a timber wolf, so goddamned devil black they could not see anything about him but his bugged-out eyes.

The point man had the beast on his left arm. The dog had come flying out of the night and the brush at him and latched his steel-trap jaws down hard, and now the man could not shake him off. He had fired the dart gun into the dog at point-blank range, the muffled blast of the gun's compressed-air propellant and the dull thud of the dart's impact almost simultaneous. But the dog held on, and Sergeant Spencer was amazed that his man did not cry out. He had to be spiking on fear and adrenaline, but he said nothing, only growling himself through clenched teeth like the dog.

Spencer raised the pole like a spear and jabbed out twice, and each time there was a harsh sizzle and a burst of bluish light out at the end of the pole where the gadget was mounted. Twice more Spencer lunged and then the point man toppled to his left and went to the ground, the weight of the dog dragging him down. The big dog lay inert and rigid upon the ground, as if he were dead.

"Are you all right?" Sergeant Spencer whispered to his man.

"Terrific," came the muttered reply.

"Did he get his teeth in you?"

"Nah, I don't think so. Can you pry his mouth open?"

"No way. Hang on." Spencer drew a knife from his belt and snapped its blade open with a flick of his wrist, holding his spear gadget in his left hand. He knelt beside his man and the dog on the ground and then turned toward the chemist.

"Take this for me, will you?" he asked.

The chemist took the pole from him and drew it back to see what the thing was on the end of it. It was a "stun gun," a rectangular plastic box the size of a walkie-talkie, battery powered, with two contact points sticking out like pointed ears. When it was switched on and pressed into contact with a body, it discharged an electrical shock between the two points. It was supposed to jolt a man hard enough to incapacitate him without any permanent damage. That was what Spencer had done to the dog, jolted him. Four or five times.

Spencer was on his knees beside his point man, feeling cautiously where the jaws were locked down. Once he had located the teeth, he used his knife to cut the material around the bite. When he had made a circle around the dog's head, the man pulled his arm free and struggled to his feet. Spencer rose with him and insisted on looking at his arm.

"I don't see any blood," he said.

"Nah," the point man answered. "All he got was the material."

The chemist saw that the man's jacket was a heavy, quilted nylon. That was all the dog had gotten into his maw. A tiny bit more, and he knew he would have been trying to stop the man from bleeding to death. He looked down at the dog, not wanting to risk using a flashlight to get a good look. The beast lay perfectly still, and the chemist reached down and put a hand on its throat.

"He's breathing."

"Cut his fucking throat," the point man suggested.

Sergeant Spencer stood over the dog with his knife in his hand, and looked like he was considering it.

"That's not necessary," the chemist assured them. "He's out, stiff as a board."

"What's the goddamned deal on that dart gun, Sarge?" the point man wanted to know, keeping his voice low but not disguising his pique. "I thought that shit was supposed to knock a dog out like a light."

"Not exactly. The vet said thirty seconds. Longer if he was active."

" 'Active'?" the point man shot back.

"Yeah, you know, jumping around."

"Waggin' his tail, shit like that," the point man's voice was a bit louder now. "Jumpin' up and down and wanting to play . . ."

"That's why I brought the stun gun for backup. We got 'im off you, didn't we?" Sergeant Spencer had his hand on the man's shoulder, and had moved in very close to him so he would not raise his voice any more. "Okay, we've screwed around long enough. You got the point, right?"

"Yeah, yeah. Only I take the spear."

"Suit yourself."

And they were off again, the point man now at least as concerned with another dog attack as he was with the quiet and careful placement of his feet so that he did not trip any flare or booby-trap trigger wires. They all knew that speed cooks were known to rig up shit like that to protect their labs. But in the point man's mind, the problem of dogs was more immediate.

The DPA Club had almost emptied except for the Felty party, and some of them had drifted out. Wild Bill Clark, Mr. and Mrs. Felty, and three of Clark's Junkyard Dogs remained at the table. All the women except Mrs. Felty had gone, and all the men who had women to go with. Reminiscences had run their course, and all that held these stragglers in place was Lieutenant Felty's reluctance to say good-bye for the last time. There had been all the usual bullshit about keeping in touch, but they all knew that when you left you were gone for good. Felty had been in the business a hell of a long time. He was ready to quit, but still, turning loose was not easy.

Lenny Stuyvesant rose shakily to his feet and said his good-byes with inebriated eloquence.

"Now, as for my young friend here," he said, rolling the palm of his hand like a maitre d' to show he meant Bobby Thurmon, boy reporter. "I'm not sure some arrangements shouldn't be made for his transportation."

"Huh?" Thurmon wondered aloud. He couldn't imagine why the old man would say that about him, because it had not yet occurred to the younger man that he was shit-faced. He long since had yielded on his principles about buying his own drinks and had for a couple of hours been sharing the endless pitchers of beer the nice waitress kept bringing to the table. Thurmon began an indignant and carefully worded rebuttal of the old man's insinuation that he might not be up to driving himself home, but when he opened his mouth he only made an odd sound that bore no relation to the speech he had in mind. The others at the table laughed good-naturedly.

"Closing time, gentlemen," sang the waitress with a tired but pleasant smile.

• • •

Sergeant Spencer and his men reached the edge of the woods without any more adventures. Two of the state agents took up positions covering the barn. They all rechecked their radio gear and weapons, then Spencer announced in a loud, clear voice that must have carried for miles: "Police. We have a search warrant!" No reason not to; the dopers had no way to dispose of a lab in anything less than half an hour, and Spencer knew that when dopers shot at cops on raids it was usually because they did not believe they were cops. Hijackers were a hazard of the trade, and speed cooks were a schizy breed at best.

No sound answered Spencer's announcement, and after repeating it quickly, he and one of his men, accompanied by the deputy, went inside. The man-sized door cut into the big double doors in the front of the barn was closed but not bolted. The dopers had not been expecting any visitors. The three slipped quickly and quietly through the door, immediately fanning out and moving in crouches to the first available cover. Spencer pressed himself against the cold crumpled fender of a pickup truck. The deputy dropped to one knee behind a wooden post to the right of the door. He would stay there, just inside the door, and cover the other men's backs. The open loft above the barn floor was his responsibility, too.

Spencer and his man leapfrogged the length of the barn, one moving forward while the other stood or crouched behind cover ready to shoot or shout a warning. Spencer was moving cautiously across an opening between a tractor and a flatbed trailer toward a dim and dangling light bulb hanging from the darkness overhead on a wire when he heard a man's voice.

"Who the fuck's out there?"

Spencer dived forward, tucked his head, and rolled up into a sitting position in the shadows where an overturned fifty-five-gallon drum blocked the light of the hanging bulb and froze. He heard the sound of a door opening on rusty hinges.

"I said . . ."

Light spilled into the barn through an open door on the left side near the rear of the place, past the silhouette of a scrawny man with long, wild-looking hair. Spencer aimed both his revolver and flashlight at the man's face and clicked on the light.

"Po-lice! Don't move!"

"Son of a bitch!" the man spat, disappearing into the light beyond the door. He yanked the door closed as he went, but it did not close all the way.

"Po-lice, goddamnit!" Spencer yelled after him, keeping the circle of his light centered on the doorway. "Step out here and show me your hands."

"Po-lice, my ass!" a second voice barked from the other side of the door. "You don't expect us to fall for that shit, do you?"

"Suit yourself. I'd just as soon put some tear gas in there and see if we can fire up that shit you're cooking."

"Hold on, man, hold on a second with that tear gas bullshit."

There was only so much they could be doing in there, Spencer knew—dumping a batch, maybe. Not enough to beat a lab rap. There was too much gear involved. And even these freaks knew not to get in too big a hurry trying to tear down a rig. If they were crazy enough, they might be thinking about setting up some kind of booby trap, though . . .

"Time's up, asshole. Let's see a show of hands."

"Okay, okay, we're comin' out, man."

The two agents posted outside could hear the voices from inside the barn, and from their respective positions at the front and rear of the barn, both of them on the near side of the building so they could keep each other in sight, they watched to make sure nobody slipped out. The one near the front was so intent on the barn that he did not pay enough attention to his secondary assignment, which was to keep an eye on the house up the hill, to make sure no trouble came from that direction. So he did not see the man roll out a window and duck-walk into the shadows of the shed at the rear of the house. He did not know anyone was about up there until he heard the big Harley cough and rumble to life.

When the agent turned toward the noise, he saw the bike as it charged out of the shed and the rider as he leaned hard to his left to make a tight turn around the corner of the house, heading for the long driveway and the road out front. But he leaned too far, and the ground was cold and hard, the muddy ruts the dopers' cars and motorcycles had cut into the backyard gritty and slick, and the motorcycle went down hard on its left side.

The figure of the man disappeared beneath his bike for an instant.

The agent thumbed on his light and aimed it at the fallen bike. Before his eyes had registered the bike, he saw an orange flash and an instant later heard the sound of the gunshot. A whisper of lead hurtled past him, high and a little left, and then there were two more shots. The agent tossed his light away from his body and dropped prone in one motion. Spencer's voice rattled tinnily in his radio earpiece: "What the hell's the deal out there?"

One bullet hit something near him and then whined endlessly as it caromed off into the night. He rocked his shotgun up in front of him and fired, unable to see even the barrel clearly, as he saw a flurry of motion around the motorcycle and heard a deep voice cursing. He heard the pellets hit something metallic and he worked the pump and fired again. The motorcycle's engine roared and the man astride it let loose with a bloodcurdling scream, and then the bike and the man were gone around the corner of the house. The agent wanted to dash up the hill toward the house, angle off to his right in hopes of getting a shot. But he did not. His primary job was here at the barn. He retrieved his light and switched it off, then lowered himself again into the shadows and called Spencer on his radio.

"What's going on out there?" Spencer repeated over the radio. One of his outside men had confirmed gunshots but couldn't tell any more than that. The other had not answered. Spencer was cranking a dozen possibilities and options through his mind when he heard his man's voice.

"I'm okay. No problem, carry on."

"What's up?" Spencer insisted.

"One subject fled the house on a motorcycle."

"You have shots fired?"

"Ten-Four. No damage. Not on this end, anyway."

The shooter on the Harley had not looked hurt as he rode away, but the agent could hope. Maybe they'd find him bled to death on the road somewhere.

Inside the barn, everybody's options expired.

"Time's up, assholes," Spencer served notice. "Come out nice or fucking die!"

"Yeah, yeah, right with you, man."

The door opened and the scrawny one came out with his hands up. Spencer directed him to lie down spread-eagle on the barn floor, and he did so without any hesitation. He had heard shooting, too.

"Let's go, in there," Spencer called to the other one, reminding himself that there might be more than one still inside the room.

"Come on out, Spike," said the one on the floor. "They're cops, for real."

The second one came out then and joined his partner on the floor. With Spencer and the deputy covering, the point man moved in to handcuff and then search the two. When they were secured, Spencer and the deputy moved closer to the door that led into the lab.

"Anything you need to tell me about your lab, men?" he asked.

"What's to tell?" the second one asked, the one who had not wanted to come out.

"Like would there be anybody else in there? Or maybe some booby traps, anything along those lines?"

"Get real, man," snorted the second man. "This ain't the fuckin' movies."

"Fine. Get up."

"What for?"

Spencer lifted the man to his feet and got a good grip on him, then pushed him ahead toward the door. They were within a yard of the door when the man stiffened and started to talk.

"You wanna be careful of the cooling tower hookup," he said.

"I do?"

"Yeah, it's a little tricky, see . . . and, uh . . ."

"Just hold the thought, asshole." Spencer called on his radio for the outside man covering the rear of the barn to send in the chemist. To the doper, he added, "You can explain all that to my friend."

Spencer left his point man and the deputy to keep an eye on the prisoners and took a minute to show the chemist inside the barn to the door of the lab before he went outside to check on his man about the shooting.

"Let me look you over," he told the agent when he joined him at his position. He wanted to be sure the man had not been shot without realizing it. It could happen, especially in this freezing cold. He could not find anything. Satisfied for the moment that he was all right, he told him to stick chilly until the chemist gave the all clear.

"Goddamned shame," he muttered under his breath. "There ain't enough cops you can trust in this county to do the job right."

Mack pushed the big Harley-Davidson as hard as he dared, roaring down the winding country road without lights. He fish-tailed around a long curve and damned near lost it, then screamed across a frozen muddy patch where somebody had crossed with a tractor, and finally eased off the throttle. He looked behind and saw nothing, nobody coming after him, so he pulled the big bike over on a low rise where he could see any car that came his way. He climbed off the bike and checked to make sure he wasn't wounded. So much for lying low in the quiet countryside. He was heading back to town. It was just as well. He had business to attend to.

Element One Fifty-two, Corporals Jackson and Terry, got the suspicious person call and Terry honked his horn to signal his partner to get off the pay phone. Jackson turned to look at him with a question on his face, and Terry flashed the number of the call: Signal Thirteen, suspicious persons. Jackson wrapped up his call and walked to the car, looking worried.

"What's up, partner?" Terry asked.

"That was my wife. It's the boy again."

"Now what?"

"He's slipped out of the house. She doesn't know where he is."

"We could call the beat element . . ."

"No, he'll be back. I'm just afraid of what he's getting mixed up in. Last time, he told us he slipped out to go see his girlfriend. That would be bad enough, but I think he's getting mixed up with a bad crowd. Drugs, maybe gangs.''

"How old is he?''

"He'll be seventeen in two months if he makes it, if I don't wring his neck first. What's the deal on the call?''

"Carefree Apartments. Supposed to be juveniles smoking crack in one of the apartments, second floor.''

"Great. You don't have kids, do you?''

"Not yet. We've only been married a year and a half. Jill wants kids, but, I don't know . . .''

"Don't have kids, take it from me. Not these days, not if you work nights.''

Jackson and Terry rolled into the parking lot of the abandoned apartments, the headlights of their marked patrol unit turned off. They "code 6'ed" on the car radio to announce their arrival. They eased out of their car and closed the doors silently. The two officers, one black and one white, stood looking up into the run-down building, listening.

"I don't hear anything,'' Terry said softly. He was the junior man, two years out of the academy. He was twenty-eight and a failed third baseman in the minor leagues. He cocked his head to catch any sounds from the apartments and tapped lightly on his right thigh with the shaft of his flashlight, absentmindedly mimicking a gesture he had picked up standing in on-deck circles in small-town baseball parks.

His partner, Bill Jackson, used the portable radio on his belt to ask the dispatcher if they had a complainant.

"Negative, One Fifty-two. They hung up. No additional.''

Jackson acknowledged this and made a face at his partner as if to say, "What did I expect?''

"I don't see nothin', I don't hear nothin', partner. What the hell, let's just clear,'' Terry offered. If the complainant did not care enough to give a name and number, he did not care enough to go stumbling through the place.

"We oughta take a stroll through first, don't you think? Or they'll just call back.''

They moved away from their car, across the narrow yard strewn with trash and up the stairs with concrete steps and wrought-iron banisters. The apartments had been vacant for a couple of months, and kids were bad about breaking in to party. Terry was in no mood to chase juveniles. It was too damned cold, and you could not see shit in a dump like this. The kids were quick as rats and knew their way around. It had not been a year since he took a spill in a place like this and had put in sixty days on light duty with a cast on his ankle.

At the top of the stairs, they separated, each of them moving to a wall as they advanced down the dark hallway, stopping to test each door and to listen for the sounds of movement inside.

"P-s-s-s-t!" Ned signaled to Curtis and his boys to shut the fuck up and they did, all three of them turning to look at him with their eyes big and their eyebrows raised. They were stoned for real, he could see that.

Curtis raised both hands palms up to ask what was up, and Ned pointed toward the window. None of them said anything, none of them even looked like he was breathing. The whole place was stone silent, except for outside somewhere they could all hear it now. Like shoes scuffing on the concrete outside, something dragging along the wall, coming their way.

Somebody in the foul-smelling apartment cursed under his breath, and then all Ned could hear was the muffled metal noises the guns made as the three of them grabbed their pieces and got ready.

There was one window in the wall that faced the hallway, and it was boarded up with strips of plywood held in place with two-by-fours. All the window glass in the building had been busted for the hell of it, and there were no lights working anywhere except for a streetlight out in front that made the hallway outside gray instead of black. Inside, there was just the candle. Ned remembered the candle and snapped his fingers to make Curtis look at him, then pointed to the damned candle. Curtis nodded, then reached behind him and pinched the candle out with two fingers.

Through cracks between the plywood sheets a shadow appeared, blocking the dim light. Ned tore his eyes away from the window for a second to look at the three men in the room with him. All of them were crouched low on the floor, all of them pointing their guns at the front, at the window or the door. Tight as a guitar string, he thought. Catgut.

"Motherfucking greasers," whispered Reggie. "Sneaky maddog Mexican motherfuckers . . ."

It had to be them, Ned thought, old cool Willy and that stone crazy fucker he ran with. And that other dude. What did they call him? Should have checked the back way out, he cursed himself.

The doorknob on the front door clicked softly as it turned. It was not locked; kids and derelicts had screwed up all the locks in the place. But the door would not open, because Curtis had stuck the two-by-four back under the knob when he let his boys in.

It all happened at once. Ned heard Reggie or Stone scream, a wild-assed wordless rattling goddamned thing. The room lit up like there were lightning bolts turned loose in there all of a sudden, and the stench of cordite filled the place so bad it burned his eyes and made tears come, and the stuttering clatter of first one and then two and then three guns all banging away beat against the walls like some crazy motherfucker laughing. He saw the door being chewed up with the slugs like there was a chain saw at work on it, until he could see through it, where chunks were eaten out of it and he could see the gray light from outside through the door. He fired, too, but he was careful with his, one short burst in the direction of the door, then switch and another short one, just one-two-three at the window, and the boards on the window danced and shot splinters in the air and he made holes in it, too, and then he shot through the window again, holding lower this time and pushing the muzzle of his AK down as he finished off the burst, so the last of it slapped into the wall beneath the window in case they had dropped down there for cover. He had half of his first clip left when the other three ran dry and scrambled to reload and the aftermath of all the shooting echoed in the little room and the last he heard of it was the rattle of their spent brass on the floor around them.

One of them screamed again, like he had got off over all the noise they had made, and when Ned saw they were reloaded he dropped the clip out of his piece and flipped it over so the one he had taped upside down to the first one faced up, and he rammed that one home. They were all ready now.

Pop! Pop!

After all their thunder and lightning, it did not sound like much, just two pissant dull pops from outside. Ned heard one of the rounds screech through the boards on the window and something nasty off to his left. He looked over there and it was Reggie, who had started to get up as soon as he had reloaded. Now he was dancing like a crazy man up on his toes, his knees together, with his elbows up and his head down, looking down at himself and he was saying something Ned could not make out, some of that Jamaican shit real fast, and Ned knew Reggie was shot.

Scraping noises from outside, and Ned heard somebody talking, talking numbers, something about fifteens and threes and shit, and there was a funny sound to the voice, like it crackled and echoed or something. Reggie was all over the goddamned room, and now he was screaming.

"Shot my man! Shot my man!"

Stone was screaming now, too, and Ned saw him spring up and run toward the window. Ned stayed where he was and he saw that Curtis did, too. Curtis did not move at all except to crane himself out of the way of Reggie when he came wailing and dancing by.

Ned watched Stone when he got to the window and he saw him jump to his left and there was another *pop!* from outside and then Stone stuck his Uzi around the edge of the window and cut loose with a long burst. And then Stone put half his face around the edge of the window and Ned saw him hold the Uzi up with both hands and he shot some more; he kept shooting until the gun was empty and brass was falling all around him like a hailstorm.

"Got that motherfucker!" Stone sang out when he was through, and he went to work reloading.

"How many of them?" Ned asked.

"Don't see but two, and they both through," Stone answered. "I done for dem bot."

"Two?" Ned asked, and he and Curtis exchanged looks. That did not make any sense.

"Check outside, Stone," Curtis ordered.

And Stone was so stupid he wanted to. He opened the door without bothering to move the two-by-four that had held it closed, and Ned realized that it had been shot into pieces.

"It ain't but just dese two motherfuckers!" Stone sang out from the hallway where Ned could see he was staring down at the two they had killed in front of the window.

"Look the other way, too," Curtis called out.

Stone looked back and forth, up and down, and grinned in at them. He held up his hands to show them there was nobody left out there to kill.

"Check it out," Curtis told him.

Ned still thought it was a trap but he figured the odds were better outside at that than in here with Curtis if he crossed him, so he got up and moved quickly but carefully to the door. He heard something behind him as he went and looked over his shoulder to see Reggie crumple to the kitchen floor. He was not screaming anymore.

Ned watched Stone as he steeled himself to step through the door, expecting to see the crazy man start taking hits any second. But he did not, and Ned inched around the doorpost, looking first to his right and then to his left. They had made a hell of a racket, he thought. But when he looked to his left and saw the two of them lying there, he knew it was much worse than that. "Jeezus motherfucking goddamn Christ!" he whined when he saw the two dead men. "Cops! Motherfuckin' goddamn cops!"

"What is it?" Curtis asked from inside.

"Come see for you goddamned self," Ned shot back. No use to be afraid of Curtis anymore, he knew. He knew he had worse trouble than Curtis now.

Ned could not take his eyes off them. The white one was all shot to hell, purplish blood and all kinds of juices and shit running all out of him. He was on his back on the concrete just beyond the window, but Ned could tell from all the shit outside the door that the white boy had got his in front of the door. A dark thick trail like slime behind a slug ran from the door to the dead white boy. The black one was just the other side of the white one, and Ned saw that the black one had hold of the fake

fur collar on the white one's jacket. He had ahold of his partner
with his left hand and his pistol was still in his right. The brother
was the one got Reggie, Ned knew. The white boy's gun was
still strapped down in his holster.

"Where did you think you was takin' him, man?" Ned asked
aloud. It was a long way down that hall to the stairs, and
damned little cover on the way. "And couldn't you see the poor
motherfucker was dead already?" Ned heard sirens coming
alive, not far off, and tires squealing. He looked down at the
black cop's radio. It was lying on the ground beside him, where
he must have dropped it to grab his partner. Only had two
hands, didn't you? The thing was full of cops' voices, yelling
like their blood was up.

"Let's go!" Ned screamed, trying to drown out the radio
voices and the banshee sirens and the sight of the dead cops.
"Out the back, let's go, goddamnit!" He started into the apartment, had to step back outside and grab Stone to make him
come. The dumb son of a bitch had been leaning down over the
black cop, reaching to take the revolver out of his hand. "Dumb
motherfucker!" Ned yelled at Stone. "Like you need that piece
a shit thirty-eight!"

"Trophy, man!" Stone grinned back at him.

"Evidence, man!" Ned answered. He thought it would feel
good to kill the Jamaican son of a bitch, but there was no time.
"Let's go!" Ned dragged Stone back inside the apartment, and
he could hear Curtis at the back door kicking down the boards
and clearing the way out.

"Hey, man . . ."

It was Reggie, on his hands and knees with his butt up in the
air, looking up from the pool of his blood that was spreading out
around him on the linoleum kitchen floor. He was bleeding like
crazy, and Ned had seen enough of that shit to know the cop's
slug had cut an artery. He was done for, because they damned
sure couldn't be taking him to no hospital and there was nothing
they could do for him themselves.

"I gotcha," Ned said to him as he tried to avoid stepping into
the blood and took Reggie's hand. He reached under the man's
arm and looked around to see if Stone was going to help him.
But from the opened back door Curtis with his Uzi up at eye

level pumped four rounds into Reggie's face and Ned let him go, shutting his eyes against the spray of gore and the scampering racket the dead man's shoes made on the slick, nasty floor.

Ned looked up at Curtis, who was looking down the barrel of the ugly little gun at him. Ned did not move or say anything, because he was afraid he would tip Curtis that he was thinking about swinging his own gun up, and then Curtis lowered his and motioned Ned and Stone to get a move on.

"No time for that shit," was all Curtis said.

The Auto Theft cops had decided that Wild Bill Clark would take Bobby Thurmon home with him. Clark was batching it, and the kid lived too far out of the way for anybody to be bothered with taking him to his own place. Clark was coming in early the next morning, and he could drop the kid off at Police and Courts.

"Not necessary," Thurmon assured them all. But since his head was on the table and his mouth was on his arm, they did not hear him.

Stuyvesant had gone, and Thurmon remembered that he had not asked the old man the question. He had meant to ask him why he had volunteered to show Thurmon the ropes. They were supposed to be competitors. But he had forgotten to bring it up, and now it was bothering him.

The waitress and the bartender were closing the place up and there were only Clark and the Feltys left, except for a pair of dour men at the table by the front door nursing coffees. They had been pointed out to Thurmon as Homicide detectives on call for any major cases that came up during the wee hours. Thurmon heard the pager and saw one of the two make his way to the phone. He was back in a minute and nodded to his partner. They stopped by on their way out to say good night.

"You're well out of it," the older one told Felty, shaking his hand.

"What's up?" the ex-lieutenant asked.

"Two officers down in the One Fifties."

"How bad?" Clark asked.

"D.O.A."

"Both of them?"

The older man nodded.

"You got names?" Felty asked.

"Jackson and Terry," the old one answered, looking at his little notebook to be sure he got them right. "Kids. What the hell, they're all kids to me."

Clark held up his hands to ask silently if there was anything they could do.

"It's covered," the old man said.

"What about suspects?" Felty asked.

"One dead at the scene. Maybe some more ran off."

The old man with the sad wrinkled face wished Felty and the missus luck and excused himself.

"Hell of a way to . . ." Felty began.

"What's up?" Thurmon asked, lifting himself off the table to find everyone looking solemn.

"Party's over," Clark said.

BOOK TWO

THE HUNT

CHAPTER 4

Saturday, 7:00 a.m.

Bobby Thurmon awoke on a sofa in a strange room. There was a sound he could not place, something gurgling ominously. He remembered the cop's retirement party, Lenny Stuyvesant accusing him of being too drunk to drive home. After that, some desultory conversation and the slap of cold night air upon leaving the DPA Club.

" 'Morning."

One of the cops from the party stepped into the room . . . Wild Bill something.

"Want some coffee?" Clark asked.

"Yeah, thanks."

The aroma of coffee assured him that the gurgling was only a coffee maker dripping into a pot. Thurmon elbowed himself into a sitting position. Early light sliced through venetian blinds on a big window in the wall opposite him.

"Sorry to put you out," he called to the cop, who had gone into the kitchen, where he was making noises with eggs and a skillet, rattling plates and cups.

"No trouble."

"I don't usually overdo it."

"Happens to the best of us. You can return the favor for me sometime."

"Well, I really appreciate it." Thurmon untangled his feet

63

from the quilt the cop must have draped over him the night before and stood up. He had felt worse.

"Mind if I freshen up?" he called out.

"Wish you would. Bathroom's around the corner there. Help yourself to a razor, stuff's in the medicine cabinet."

Bobby's hair was matted and standing up in back from sleeping on the couch pillows, and his eyes looked like bullet wounds in the mirror. When he had freshened up as well as he could, he went back into the living room and found a cup of coffee steaming on a coaster atop the Plexiglas table set in front of the couch. The television was on. It was a local anchorman reading a bulletin.

"What time is it?" Thurmon asked, trying to focus his eyes on the hands of his watch.

"Quarter to eight. I programmed the VCR to catch a movie last night and got this in the bargain."

"We interrupt regular programming for this news bulletin," said the TV newsman. "Two Dallas police officers reportedly were shot to death upon responding to a suspicious person call in a South Dallas neighborhood that has been described as a hotbed of drug abuse. This occurred just moments ago, and our mobile news team is en route now to Parkland Hospital for a report. Repeating, two Dallas police officers were reported slain by gunfire in a South Dallas apartment complex known for drug problems. Their names are being withheld at this time pending notification of their families. We return you now to our regular programming, and we will be back with you as soon as our mobile news team has more details. Police Chief Orville Knecht is at Parkland Hospital at this time, and we will bring you a report as soon as more information is available. Please stay tuned."

"Jesus," Thurmon muttered. "Where was I?"

"Drunk at the club."

"Terrific. Where's your phone?"

Clark pointed to it and went back into the kitchen. Thurmon dialed his editor, and his mind lumbered into action as he waited for an answer.

"Where are you?" the voice on the other end asked, not angry yet.

"I'm . . . with an officer who's . . . close to the investigation, working a background angle. What's the latest?"

"What kind of angle?"

"You know . . . human interest."

"Get it on paper. I want to see it this morning. Early."

"Naturally. Anything new on the shooting?"

"They've released the names of the officers. Bill Jackson, thirty years old, seven-year veteran. Chris Terry, twenty-eight, two years. Terry used to play minor-league baseball. First time they've had a black officer and a white one killed in the same incident, for what that's worth. One suspect dead at the scene."

"Okay," Thurmon answered. He had fished out his notepad and scribbled it all down. "See you shortly."

"With a story."

"Right."

"You got your ass in a crack?" Clark asked, as he brought two plates to the coffee table.

"Not really. I can work off the offense reports, get something in on it by noon. They had plenty of coverage last night with the deadliners. Did you know the officers?"

"Jackson broke in at Southeast on my old detail."

"Was he white or black?"

"Why?"

Bobby shrugged. He had lied to his editor about having an angle, but maybe Wild Bill could put him on to something. "Do you know any more about it now?"

"Some. More coffee?"

"Please."

"I've been up awhile. I made a couple of calls."

"Anything you can tell me?"

"Like what?"

"Anything. I need an angle."

Clark turned to look at him, studied him for a moment.

"I don't know anything about that," Clark said finally.

They ate breakfast, both of them thinking, neither talking. The movie Clark had taped was a western, John Wayne in the cavalry. Before it ended, there was another news bulletin, a bit from a reporter on remote at Parkland, a two-shot of the reporter and Chief Knecht. The chief looked sleepy, tired. You could tell both of them were cold. They were standing outside the emergency room entrance, with cops milling around and ambulances in the background. The reporter asked the chief about reports that the cops had been killed with assault rifles, and Knecht did not deny it. He said something about waiting for the medical examiner's report, preliminaries on the autopsies. Knecht made a little speech about the men and women who lay their lives on the line every day. He declined to speculate about anything else and said his heart went out to the fallen officers' families. Then he excused himself.

"What do you think of him?" Thurmon asked when the movie resumed.

"John Wayne?"

"Chief Knecht."

"He's a suit."

Thurmon took three aspirins midway through his bacon, eggs, and toast, and was feeling pretty healthy by the time the movie ended a few minutes later. The tape cut to a shot through slats or louvers of men working on a car in a garage of some kind.

"It's funnier like this," Clark offered, switching the tape to fast forward with the remote control.

The men flew around jerkily, not working on the car but stripping it. Off came the doors, the bumpers, fenders, hood, and trunk lid. Out came the seats, what must have been the stereo, and some more stuff from the passenger compartment. Off came the wheels. A long-armed winch of some kind was pushed into the frame, a chain was lowered into the guts of the car, and Thurmon watched the men winch the car's engine up and over, into the bed of a pickup. A tarp was thrown over the stuff, leaving nothing in place except the remains of some poor bastard's car. It reminded Bobby of a thing he had seen about piranhas, where you see a dead calf lowered on a rope into a river that boils alive for about thirty seconds and then what is left of the calf is pulled out and there is nothing there but a skeleton.

"What is this?" Thurmon asked.

"Surveillance tape."

"It didn't take them long . . ."

"Nah, that wasn't quick. Quick is when they find a car on the street somewhere and a crew falls on it out of a van. These guys you saw were taking it easy. That's why they rented the garage space, it was hot and they wanted a place where they wouldn't have to work so hard. We rented them the space, working a sting."

"What did they do with the stuff?"

"Sold it to a salvage yard over in Arlington. That's the funny part."

"What?"

"See, the owner, he turns in a claim on his insurance. The insurance company goes low bid on replacements, meaning they buy the stuff from a salvage yard. So what happens is the thief sells it to the salvage operator who sells it back to the car owner. Guy buys back his own shit. It's hilarious."

"Why doesn't somebody do something about the salvage yards?"

Clark rose and took his empty plate back to the kitchen. He stopped at a closet on his way back and pulled out a jacket. It was nylon, like sports teams wear, royal blue with white trim. Clark showed him the front of it, the words "Wild Bill" in silver-threaded script over the heart. Above the name was an emblem about the size of a Dallas police badge—a bull's-eye, in the center of which was a silver bulldog's head, cartoonish, with a twisted snarl showing sharp teeth, and a black collar studded with silver spikes, like something you would see painted on the fusilage of a World War II bomber. Clark showed him the back, the same design only much bigger. In black block letters around the blue ring of the bull's-eye was printed DALLAS POLICE SALVAGE UNIT—JUNKYARD DOGS.

"Sharp," Bobby said, nodding.

"That's what we do. Auto Salvage Unit."

"I see."

"It would help if insurance companies would buy factory parts only. Of course, it would also help if they'd keep thieves in jail when we catch them."

"They don't?"

"The fat man in that video . . ."

Thurmon looked back at the TV screen, which was blank now, the tape having run to its end.

"Yeah?"

"One of the biggest car thieves in town. He got three years, probation."

"Why?"

"What difference does it make? We did more time sweating in that cubbyhole on surveillance than he did in jail."

"He's back stealing cars again?"

"Been filed on twice since he's been on probation."

"So they'll revoke him and send him off."

"Nah. They tell me there's no room for him at the joint."

"The prison overcrowding, that's really a pain in the butt, isn't it?"

"Yeah. You know, they were going to put up army tents, Quonset huts, like that, to make more room, but the commies and cocksuckers said that wouldn't be humane. Where were those sonsabitches when I was in the army? I lived in a goddamned tent for two years!"

"Commies and cocksuckers?"

"Lawyers."

At mention of the word *lawyers,* Clark spat. Bobby wondered if he always did that.

"I take it you're not entirely satisfied with the support you're getting in the war," Bobby said. He still had his pad out from the phone call to his editor, but he had not written down anything Clark had said.

"War?"

"The war on crime. Like the mayor said."

"I only know three things about the war on crime."

"What?"

"One, it's a real war. People are dying. Two, we're losing. And, three, nobody gives a shit but victims and cops."

CHAPTER 5

Saturday, 8:30 a.m.

As he drove toward downtown, Clark was thinking about this kid Bobby Thurmon. Clark did not know him, and he might have said too much already. Lenny Stuyvesant vouched for him, and that was worth something. He thought about this and a couple of other things as he drove to work by way of the downtown downramp so he could drop the kid off. Saturday was Clark's day off, but that was only on paper. He and his troops worked when there was work to do and played when there was not any. Felty had understood, but he did not think the new lieutenant would.

Clark swung into one of the parking lots on Commerce Street in the same block as the Police and Courts building. He was not authorized to park there normally; it was reserved for deputy chiefs and up, and some of the cops who had the pud jobs in headquarters. But on Saturday morning, none of them were around to worry about it.

"Thanks for putting me up," Thurmon said with a handshake. "I owe you one."

"Forget it."

"Maybe there's a story in what you were saying about the war on crime."

"It ain't news that the system's off the rails. Also, don't quote me and don't ever put my picture in your paper."

"Why not?"

"Lots of reasons. I don't mind talking to you, but it's on . . . What do you call it?"

"Background."

"Whatever, I just don't want to see my name or my face in the goddamned paper."

"No problem."

Thurmon started to get out of the truck, and Clark motioned him to wait. He had a lot on his mind, and things to do. But it had occurred to him a time or two along the way that it could help to have a friend in the press.

"I don't know if anybody has this yet," Clark began. "Press, I mean. It's not a secret, but I don't think anybody's made a point of it . . ."

"What?"

"It looks like the way it went down was this: Jackson and Terry went on the call, anonymous complaint, they're walking down the upstairs hall checking doors and windows looking for kids doing crack, right?"

"Okay," Thurmon said. He took out his notepad and pen. "Do you mind?"

"Write anything you want except my name."

"Okay."

"And it looks like the shooters were in one of the apartments. They cut loose through the door, dropped Terry on the spot. Jackson in about ten seconds flat puts out the 'assist officer' on his hand unit, his portable radio, and he gets off three rounds with his side arm. He gets off three shots and also he grabs his partner and he's dragging him out of the line of fire when one of the shooters pops him."

"He was trying to save his partner?"

"That's how it looks. From the way the bodies were. Terry was on his back, Jackson behind him, or over him, whatever you want to call it, and he had Terry's jacket collar in his left hand, his weapon in his right."

"Jesus."

"Yeah."

"Which one did you say was the black officer?"

"I didn't. What difference does it make?"

"It's a logical question, isn't it? Anybody who reads the story will want to know."

"Jackson was black. I didn't know the Terry kid."

"What about family?"

"Jackson? I think so, back then. But I haven't kept up with him."

"Any kids, any military service?"

"Hey, call the Public Information Officer. I thought you wanted an angle."

"Right. I appreciate it."

"Forget about it." Clark waved him off, thinking he did not want the kid to forget about it at all. He was thinking he did not mind if the kid thought he owed Clark a couple of favors.

"I gotta run," Thurmon said, sliding out of the truck. "Keep in touch, Wild Bill."

"Uh, just Bill will do fine, scribe."

"Whatever you say."

"See you."

The kid ran off toward the back loading dock of the building, and Clark eased out into traffic. He had his radio on KRLD for news and weather. The news was rehash and bullshit, background stuff, nothing about suspects. They had found witnesses who said it had sounded like a war, and somebody confirmed they had found a lot of empty brass in the shooters' apartment, but shied away from the reporters' estimates of one thousand or two thousand rounds. When Clark had gotten hold of Marino in Persons, the police count had been something like a hundred and forty rounds. That was plenty, Clark thought. Nine millimeter and 7.62, most of it nines. A couple of Uzis or MAC's maybe, and one guy with an AK-47. If the dead man with the Rastafarian dreadlocks was not a Jamaican, that would be a scoop.

Chief Knecht was catching hell from all sides, which was neither here nor there to Clark. The DPA was at it already, about the cops being outgunned. They had been after Knecht for months to issue automatics. The spouse auxiliary got some airtime, too, said they were still mad about Knecht going back to one-officer units. Clark did not see where that fit in, since Terry and Jackson had been working a two-man car. After a rough stretch the year before when two officers working one-man were killed, they had gone to all two-officer units. Naturally, response time went to shit because that cut the number of units almost in half. The citizens raised hell, so Knecht went back to mostly one-officer cars, with two to a car in the hot spots. That pissed off the minority spokespersons because they said the cops were singling them out, putting two-officer units in minority neighborhoods. Knecht came back with maps and charts to show that cops were assigned according to the calls and crimes, but talking facts in a deal like that was like shooting blanks in a war.

It was almost nine when Clark pulled into the lot and parked his pickup next to Boots's and Smoky's cars, not surprised that they had gotten there ahead of him. He jogged in the cold morning breeze past the guard shack, around the corner of the office building, and ducked inside through the door that he was glad to find unlocked.

The Lincoln was there, and he saw when he walked in that there were dried patches of Super Glue all over it. The PES troops had done that looking for fingerprints. Physical Evidence Section technicians had gotten first crack at the car because of the murder, and now it was his turn to go to work on the vehicle itself. There was black powder, too, brushed on in likely places. The glue, which the technicians liked to call cyanoacrylate because it sounded more technical, had dried in grayish blotches here and there. Clark did not know if they had had any luck. He would make a call to see about that later.

Boots and Smoky were standing beside the wall phone at the rear of the work bay, which ran up half a floor beneath the offices in the building proper. The overhead doors were down and locked, but cold wind whistled in underneath them, and Clark was glad to see that his guys had the coffee on. Boots was pouring a cup for him as he walked up. Smoky was on the phone.

"Calling the little woman already?" Clark asked, mugging at his watch. "Or didn't he make it home last night at all?"

"You know how it is, Sarge." Boots shook his head.

"This is official police business, Sarge," Smoky protested.

"I'm checking to make sure PES is done with it before we get started."

"Good."

"I guess you heard about Jackson and Terry," Boots said.

"Yeah."

"This year's getting off to a worse start than last year," Smoky put in, apparently having been put on hold.

"It goes in threes, you know," Boots pronounced.

"Bullshit." Clark tried the coffee.

"You know it does, Sarge. Like airplane crashes."

"Okay, it goes in threes. Four last year and two last night. That's six—two sets of three. So that's it."

"Naw, I think it's three shootings. I don't think it's by body count."

"Give me a break."

"Yeah? Right, uh-huh. Okay, thanks. Bye."

Smoky hung up the phone and nodded at them.

"She's all ours," he said. "They said they didn't care if we want to leave her where she is and not bother dragging her around to our bay."

"Good."

They finished their coffee and commiserated with each other about how things were going to hell and it was getting tough out on the streets, and then it was time to go to work.

Clark found a tarp and some scrap rags to stuff underneath the overhead doors to keep out most of the wind, and Boots and Smoky got down to business with the Lincoln.

It was a pastel yellow Town Car, four door, a 1987 model. The Physical Evidence Section had left the trunk closed, and the Auto Theft cops did not open it. That could wait. They opened all four doors and the hood, and Boots started with the Vehicle Identification Number while Smoky checked for the "Nader sticker." Clark watched them and made a couple of phone calls.

As he waited for an answer, Clark looked over the clipboard his men had left on the workbench: a thin collection of computer printouts, copies of pound tickets, and offense reports that was the beginning of the file they would build on this car. He read over the registration checks. "Not Reported," by VIN and by license plate number. "Clear" on the computer check for stolen. Sergeant Marino was not in; they expected him anytime. Clark rang through to his own office upstairs. Hernandez answered.

"Nacho," Clark grinned. He had not told any of his guys to come in today. "What are you doing?"

"Eating breakfast. Where are you?"

"I'm downstairs in the PES bay. We're going over the Lincoln. While you're resting, jot down this VIN and license. Check to see if we might have had the car in the pound before."

"M-m-m-f." Hernandez acknowledged the numbers Clark read off, with his mouth full of some junk-food breakfast he had bought off the "roach coach" that stopped by the pound every morning.

"Give me a buzz down here if you get anything," Clark said.

"M-m-f."

"Sticker's been peeled," Smoky announced, crouched beside the open driver's door.

The "Nader sticker" was supposed to be on the trailing edge of the driver's door, and officially was called the Environmental Protection Agency Notice. It was supposed to include the complete Vehicle Identification Number and provide mileage and emissions estimates. It was printed on a plastic material with glued backing that should hold it in place for the life of the car. It was made so that it self-canceled if it was removed, so it could not be taken off one car and put on another. A missing sticker meant the car was almost certainly stolen, although their computer check had not shown any stolen report on this one. It was possible that the door had been damaged and either repaired or replaced, but Clark did not think so this time.

Boots found a VIN plate where it was supposed to be, on top of the dashboard in front of the steering wheel up near the windshield, where it could easily be read from outside the car. It looked good, with the right kind of rosette rivets. He copied down the whole number—seventeen characters in all, numbers and letters. They would tell him the factory where the car was made, its restraint systems and engine type, the year and body style, and the car's completion sequence—whether it was the first or last off the line or somewhere in the middle at a particular plant in a particular year. He could find out from the manufacturer where the car was sent from the factory, which dealer sold it new, and from there he could fill in the life history of this particular car. He liked to think that what he did with stolen cars was like a pathologist doing an autopsy on a murder victim.

"How's the number look?" Clark asked him, hanging up the phone. The secretary in Persons had promised she would have Sergeant Marino call him as soon as he got into the office.

"It matches," Boots answered, comparing the numbers he had jotted down in his notebook to the Lincoln entries in the National Auto Theft Bureau handbook on his lap. "Right body style, engine. Rosette rivets."

"Uh-huh."

"Smoky." Boots, sitting behind the wheel of the Lincoln, looked out at his partner, who was leaning over the left fender looking for an engine number.

"Yeah?"

"You got that super-duper homemade VIN-pulling instrument with you?"

Smoky pulled a knife out of the little pouch clipped to his belt and passed it through the open driver's door to Boots. It was a stainless-steel kitchen knife which he had hammered in a vise and bent over to form a hook at the end.

"That's par for the course," Smoky mumbled beneath the hood. "Make fun of my equipment, but you always want to use the son of a bitch."

"Trying to make you feel useful," Boots answered, reaching through the steering wheel with the knife and then cursing.

"Well, use it right," Smoky lectured without looking up. He knew Boots. "Get out of the damned car like you're supposed to."

"Deficiency in design," Boots grumbled, stepping out of the car to stand just in front of the open door where he could look down through the windshield at the VIN plate as he reached in with the knife and hooked one edge of the plate. He tugged on the plate, tentatively at first, then harder. It did not budge. He had expected the metal plate to pop free. He had thought the thieves probably had cut the rivets to get the VIN plate out of another car and glued it in place on this one, but no dice. He could tell by its resistance that the rivets were whole. "I'll be damned."

"What?" Clark asked.

"Looks good so far. Smoke, you found a number yet?"

From a contorted position with his head shoved down between the rear of the engine and the fire wall, Smoky inched his check mirror into place to read the number. With his other hand, he shined his Mini-Mag flashlight down onto the mirror. The surface of the engine was grimy, and he laid the light down to get a rag to wipe it.

"I think so. Get ready to write."

"Ready when you are," Boots answered, notebook in hand.

"Okay, I think I can get it. Let's see—One, Lincoln, Nolan, Nine—nah, screw it."

"What?"

"Son of a bitch's been restamped."

"You sure?" Clark asked.

Smoky did not bother to answer. He wiped the engine boss again and the misalignment of the stamped characters over the originals was clearer. It was a good job, all right, but he was sure.

"Can you make out the originals?" Boots asked.

"Nah, not from here. We'll have to pull it and grind 'em."

It would take a little time, Clark knew. They'd winch the engine out of the car and grind the numbers off, polish the boss down smooth, then hook up a battery charger, one clamp to the engine, the other to a six-inch wooden stick wrapped with copper wire laced through aquarium filter stock. Then they would dip the stick into a plastic cup of acid like an oversized Q-tip and use it to wipe over the clean boss in hopes of "raising" the original numbers. The theory behind it was that the act of stamping the numbers changed the density of the metal and made those areas react differently to the acid and electrical current, making a kind of ghostly tracing of the characters. Of course, the restamping had a similar effect, and sometimes you could not coax the original numbers up clearly enough to read them. Clark figured it worked one time in three, maybe a little more. And it had a lot to do with who was trying it. It was more art than science, and they all knew who was good at it and who was not.

"Before we get into that, see what you can get off the transmission. Maybe they overlooked it."

"Right." Smoky clambered out from under the hood and stretched. "Look out," he announced, to let Boots know he was firing up the lift.

"Take her away," Boots called out from the front seat, where he was in the process of removing the dashboard.

The big hydraulic lift rumbled up, and Smoky stopped it when the Lincoln was about head high off the shop floor. He locked it in place and stepped underneath the car with his flashlight and rag.

"Shi-i-t."

"What?" Clark asked.

"Take a look."

Clark joined him beneath the car and looked where Smoky pointed. This time it was obvious.

"Okay, they didn't forget about the transmission." Clark nodded. "Hey, Boots, how're you doing on the dash?"

"It's coming."

"Well—"

The workbench phone rang and Clark answered it. It was Marino returning his call.

"What's up?" the homicide sergeant asked, sounding a little tired. He was supposed to be off on Saturday, too.

"We're looking at this Lincoln, the one with the Twenty-seven in the trunk," Clark answered.

"Yeah." Marino did not sound as if it was at the top of his list. "So?"

"So it's gonna be stolen."

"No surprise."

"Yeah, a pretty damned good job, though. Professional," Clark added.

"Lot of that going around."

"Not exactly," Clark insisted. "This ain't shaping up like an everyday off-the-street deal. It's been through somebody's shop."

"Yeah?"

"Yeah." Clark waited, but Marino did not have anything else to say. "So, am I boring you or something?"

"What? Nah, man, I'm listening."

"What do you think?"

"About the car?"

"No, about the fucking Cowboys, Marino. What the hell are we talking about?"

"Look, Bill—"

"I read the papers, Marino. I know your boat's loaded, but—"

"Okay, you got my full attention," Marino promised. He did not sound apologetic, but Clark could hear him telling somebody in the background to wait a second. "What?"

"Who was the stiff? What do you have on her so far?"

"Titty dancer. My people are in her apartment now, looking. Maybe we'll get some names, phone numbers."

"Where did she work?"

"They move around. You know how they are. Greenville Avenue, mostly."

"Okay. Is that it?"

"So far."

"Let's keep in touch on it. All right?"

"You bet, Bill. Why not?"

"We've got the offense number. Have y'all done any supplements yet?" Clark asked.

"Probably. You want copies?"

"We can pull 'em up on the auto pound terminal."

"Right. That's it, then?"

"I guess so. I'll get back to you as soon as we have the car thing nailed down."

"Thanks. I appreciate it."

"Yeah, 'bye." Clark hung up and it was not the first time he had felt a little pissed-on by the big boys. That's what happens when you let a cop wear a suit to work. His IQ jumps twenty points and he's only got time for the big deals, which do not usually include stolen cars, unless there's a barnful of them.

Nacho Hernandez shoved the little door open at the windy end of the shop and stumbled in, bringing the cold in with him.

"I'm impressed," he announced.

"Good." Smoky smiled at him from beneath the Lincoln. "Now shut the goddamned door."

"Really," Hernandez went on, grinning. "I think they did a hell of a job."

"Who?" Clark asked. Hernandez had something, and he delighted in knowing anything that everybody else didn't. "What are you talking about?"

"Look at this." Hernandez brought Clark a Polaroid snapshot taped to a four-by-eight-inch sheet of heavy card stock. Clark took it from him. "You were right, Sarge." Hernandez beamed. "We had it before. As a matter of fact, we sold it."

"Yeah, I see." Clark said, studying the car in the photo. You could tell it was a big car, but it was burned so badly you would not necessarily have guessed it was a Lincoln. There was nothing left of it to suggest its original color—just a twisted hulk of charred body metal and bumpers. It had come in after it crashed and burned, according to the accompanying notes. The insurance company settled with the owner, and nobody wanted it back. After the time limit ran, the police department included the hulk in its weekly auction and tried to get enough for it to cover the towing and storage costs. Salvage yards bought wrecks like this for parts. Sometimes the only parts they were interested in were the ID number plates, which wound up on stolen cars of the same make and models. It happened often enough that Clark had started keeping a "burn file," with photos. The VIN numbers on the burned car were the ones on the Lincoln Clark and his men were working on. The license plates on the burned car would have been too screwed up to use, so the thieves probably filed for a salvage title on the wreck. That would explain why the registration was not yet in file.

"Boots!" Clark waved him over.

"Yeah?"

"Take a look at this."

"Aw, man," Boots moaned, looking at the Polaroid. "I hate it when that happens. There's no way this is the same car."

"No shit," Clark agreed. "So look again."

Boots had the dashboard out and expanded his search this time to the edges where the dash frame met the cabin walls.

"Here we go."

"They replaced the whole dash frame, didn't they?" Clark asked.

"Damned sure did."

"You don't see that every day," Smoky chimed in.

"Lower it, Smoky," Clark said.

"Coming down," Smoky warned his partner.

"Lower away."

When the Lincoln was back on the ground, Clark took the keys from Boots and went around to the trunk.

"Aw, Sarge," Smoky protested. "You don't have to—"

"Right." Clark grinned. "Hernandez, this trunk is your baby. You come open it."

"Not today, gringo. I did that shit already."

"I don't want to intrude on your find here," Clark insisted. "You sure you don't want to do the honors?"

"No hablo inglés." Hernandez turned on his heel.

"Sarge, we kinda oughta save that for last. Don't you think?" Smoky was serious about not wanting to deal with the odor from the trunk. The shop was sealed up against the wind and warm. It would not be anything to laugh at.

"We're just about down to last, Smoky," Clark said. "You and Hernandez see if you can come up with any packing slips out of the seats and quarter panels. Boots?"

"Yeah?"

"You pull the engine and get started grinding numbers."

"Aw, he ain't worth a shit at that, Sarge," Smoky protested. "He couldn't find a number in a phone book."

"Professional jealousy," Boots rejoined. "Textbook case."

"Get to it," Clark said, pocketing the keys for the time being. "But if we don't get anything off the block or transmission and if there ain't any packing slips, we're gonna be down to checking the trunk for stickers. Smoky, did you check for stickers on the underside of the hood?"

"Yeah, no luck."

"Then I don't guess there's any reason to think they might've left any on the trunk lid."

"Hell, let's give it a try," Boots offered, "before we start pulling the engine and everything."

"I guess so," Clark agreed.

Clark unlocked the trunk and eased it open, and the smell was as bad as he had expected. It was bad enough that he took the time to rig up a way of propping the small door in the overhead door open to let the air in. There were worse things than being cold.

"Nothing," Boots anounced.

"Any luck in there?" Clark asked the two men working on the seats and quarter panels.

"Nothing in the seats," Smoky reported. "We'll have the panels off in a little bit."

"Let's look at the gas tank," Boots suggested. He had crawled underneath the car to check something.

"Why?" Clark asked.

"Stress marks on the bolts. Somebody's been messing with them."

"I'll get the siphon hose."

Clark and Boots drained all the gas out of the tank while Hernandez and Smoky finished up their search of the car's interior without any luck. Then they raised the car again and unbolted the tank from the frame.

"Goddamn!" Smoky bellowed when the tank came away into his arms.

"What?"

"I thought y'all drained this son of a bitch."

"We did."

"Then there must be a body in here, too. It weighs a ton."

CHAPTER 6

Saturday, 2:00 p.m.

Clark pushed open the door and stepped outside when he heard the car pull up. He saw clouds building in the southwest. The temperature had dropped, and he thought it was too cold for snow. Rain probably, he thought, sleet. Shows all the weatherman knows.

Sergeant Spencer parked his maroon Lincoln in one of the spaces at the rear of the pound offices and returned Clark's wave. He stepped out of his car into the wind, tugging the collar of his coat up under his chin and jamming his gray Stetson down hard on his head.

"Wild Bill," Spencer yelled into the wind.

"Thanks for coming, Spence."

Clark showed him into the PES bay where the yellow Lincoln stood sprawling, its hood and doors standing open like a prisoner being frisked. They had closed the trunk.

"You got it to yourself, today?" Spencer asked.

"Hernandez is around here somewhere. Boots and Smoky are in the office making some calls, backtracking the car."

"This the one you found the dead girl in?"

"Yeah."

"Did you rap it out yet?"

"We finally got our secondary numbers, but we may have to wait for NATB to build the VIN off of them. We're running it

82

on the new VIN/SLEUTH, but that just gives you possibles. But here's what I called you about, over here.''

Clark pulled back a tarp on the floor to show Spencer the gas tank from the yellow Lincoln. The top of it had been cut, a rounded square that they had pulled off.

"How'd you get it open?"

"Filled the tank with water and used a cutting torch. The bad guys had helia-arced it."

"Nice." Spencer nodded.

"Check this out." Clark pulled the tarp back to uncover the fifteen bundles they found inside the gas tank, in their loosened wrappings of plastic and oilcloth. "We were thinking dope at first."

"I still am," Spencer said.

"Look," Clark said, unfolding one of the packets to reveal an Uzi machine pistol.

"Somebody's smuggling guns in? Do you know how much coke you could stash in these bundles?" Spencer pushed his hat back. "How many you got there?"

"Ten Uzis. The five smaller packages are full of ammo. A thousand rounds of nine millimeter."

"How do you figure it?" Spencer asked.

"I think they're smuggling guns out."

"Mexico?"

"I know there's a market down there for hot cars. Add in the guns, it's a bonus."

"Makes sense, I guess."

"Spence, I need a favor," Clark admitted.

"Okay."

"Do you know any feds who could help with this—somebody at Alcohol, Tobacco and Firearms, maybe?"

"Yeah, I got a pal at ATF. Ex-deputy sheriff. You got the serial numbers off these guns?"

"Here." Clark handed him a slip of paper. "I'm not sure why, but there's a chill on with us and the feds lately."

"It happens. Did y'all get any prints off any of this?"

"Partials."

"Have you given it to any of your people in CID yet?"

"I called Marino in Persons, but he wasn't in."

"The slob. Probably watchin' the league play-off game at home with his family."

"I forgot about that. Who's playing today?"

"Who cares? It ain't the Cowboys."

"I appreciate you coming out," Clark said.

"I'm glad you called. This could be something serious."

"And, listen, if you see any of your state auto theft people, run this down for 'em, will you?"

"If I see 'em. Last I heard, they were off in Tyler or someplace working on a ring."

"I can't find out who we sold the burn-job to until Purchasing comes in for the auction Monday. If it's one of the yards outside the city, I may be calling on them to go with us. That's the best lead we've got right now."

"I'll leave word for them."

Clark had just stepped back inside the shop when the phone rang. It was Marino. He had not been home watching football on TV. He had been working, and he sounded as if he had been putting in some long days. Clark told him what they had found.

"Why don't you come by the office?" Marino asked when Clark had finished.

"You want me to schlep all this crap down there?"

"Nah, have your people book it into evidence. I've seen guns before."

"Then why—"

"We got a name. A guy who ties in with Charlotte Mayfield, your murder victim, and I'm going out to chat with him in about half an hour. I thought you might want to take a look at him. Meet me at the Denny's at Preston and LBJ. I'll buy you a cup of coffee afterwards."

"Sounds good. I'm on my way."

Sergeant Marino showed up with a partner, a youngish detective Clark did not know. Clark stepped out of his truck and leaned against a fender until Marino spotted him and pulled over. The right rear door of the brown Dodge Diplomat swung open and Clark slid in.

"Hi," Marino greeted him, from the passenger side of the front seat. "Haven't seen you around in a while, Billy boy."

"Trying to keep a low profile, man. How's it going with you?"

"Too damned busy. You know Al Lewis, don't you, Bill?"

"Don't think so. Good to meet you, Al."

"Hi," was all Al said.

"What's the deal?" Clark asked, not happy that the Persons guys were not volunteering anything.

"Snitch put this guy with the girl your people found in the trunk of the Lincoln," Marino said without turning in his seat to look at Clark directly.

"How?"

"Pussy deal. Snitch says our boy was helping her with expenses. Says he likes the life, thinks he's some kind of weekend character."

"Who was she?"

Marino looked down at the contents of a folder on the seat between him and his driver Al and read off what they knew about Charlotte Mayfield. She was twenty-two, with a stage name, a divorced mother in Mt. Vernon who had not heard from her in months, and a physical description that included a couple of tattoos.

"Yeah," Clark said, closing his eyes for a second to remember his copy of the notebook that he and his troops had put together. "I know her, or know of her."

"Yeah?" Marino asked, sounding almost interested and turning halfway around in his seat to look at Clark. "How's that?"

"She ran with a bunch of speed freaks we got into a while back, car thieves."

"Speed freaks, huh?" Marino raised his eyebrows. "Car thieves. Have you made the Lincoln yet?"

"It's stolen. We don't know where yet. Pro job, like I told you. I'm waiting for Purchasing to open Monday."

"She turns up dead in a stolen Lincoln." Marino nodded. "What's that about Purchasing?"

"The Lincoln was in our pound at one point, we gotta check with Purchasing to track down whoever bought it at auction."

"Hell of a deal. Somebody switched numbers?"

"Yeah," Clark said.

"She got mixed up with some serious car thieves. Does this M.O. match with what she was into the other time?" Marino asked.

"Nah. That was street thieves cranking Z-cars with screwdrivers. They'd either drive them until they got caught or swap 'em for dope. Some of them wound up out of state. We heard a couple of guys in Tennessee were buying hot Z's for five hundred apiece."

"*H-m-m-m.*" Marino made like he was deep in thought.

"Who's this we're going to see?" Clark asked.

Al was busy driving, and Marino did not answer at first. Clark nudged the big sergeant's shoulder.

"Huh?"

"What've you got on this guy we're going to see?"

"Not much."

That was that. Clark had dealt with Persons before, and he knew how they operated when it came to information. You tell them all you know and they nod and look wise, like an owl on a tree limb, like some FBI types he had known.

"Not so fast, Marino. I'm trying to write it down," Clark said with a sarcastic edge to his voice.

Marino grinned and snorted a little laugh. "Right," he said.

"So?" Clark insisted.

"So, what?"

"So am I supposed to know a password or a secret handshake, or what, motherfucker?"

"Hey, watch that shit, Clark . . ." Marino began.

"You bite my ass. Read your badge, Marino. You and I're on the same team, and we ain't supposed to keep secrets from each other."

This outburst was all out of nowhere for Marino, and he could not imagine any reason for it. He had been putting in a lot of hours and catching hell regularly over the lack of progress on a couple of major cases. He was in no mood on this Saturday afternoon, when he had better things to do anyway, to take this off Clark, a guy he had known a long time, but not been particularly close to, and whom he thought of more like a second-cousin than a brother officer. Car thefts and murder cases were not the same thing, after all. He wondered what the new guy, Lewis, was thinking, but he did not care enough about that to let it color his judgment. Marino was thinking a little action might not feel bad, and fighting always had been a tonic for him, inside and outside the ring. Maybe Clark did not know about his Golden Gloves career. It might be fun to go a round or two with this guy from Auto Theft at that, but Marino had learned on his way from the little house in West Dallas to his five-acre miniranch in Allen where his old mother had a room over the garage how easily you could win a battle and lose the war. He would pass up the insult and see what was behind it if he could.

"Pull over, partner," Marino instructed his driver, and Lewis found a handy spot in a strip shopping center on the right-hand side of Preston Road just south of Royal Lane. Marino turned all the way around to his left then, to look squarely at Clark. "You got no cause to talk to me like that."

"Probably not," Clark admitted. "And you got no call to hold back on your information. Or are you going to tell me that all you know about this guy we're going to see is that a snitch told you he helped the girl make expenses?"

"If I wanted to hold out on you, Clark, I wouldn't have invited you along with us in the first place. Would I?"

"Not unless you thought I might come across your boy on my own and you didn't want me going to see him by myself."

"Hell, it ain't worth the mental anguish." Marino shook his head. "Or you getting your goddamned feelings hurt. He's a local heavy-hitter—or his old man is, a developer. Daddy sits on half a dozen boards. Momma gets her picture on the society page every week or two doing something for charity. Name's Carlton Welborn . . ."

"The father or the son?" Clark interrupted to ask.

"Both. Daddy's the second, boy's the third."

"Figures."

"Yeah. Third's married for a couple of years, some blonde from Houston, same kind of family."

"So what's Third doing playing house with a speed whore?" Clark asked.

"*Quien sabe?*" Marino shrugged. "You can ask him when

we get there. Unless you've got something else you want to get
off your chest.''

"No, that's about it,'' Clark said, but he did not smile when
he said it. Marino might be holding out on him yet, and he was
tired of wasting time and energy playing games inside the
department instead of running down bad guys. "You got something?"

"Now's not a good time.'' Marino eyed him levelly, and he
was not smiling either. "But there'll come settle-up day, and I
won't forget that 'motherfucker' business.''

Clark nodded, and wished he had not called the big man that.
He wished he had gotten his point across without the insult, for
a couple of reasons. First, Marino was not a bad sort as those
things went, and the one-way business had been going on long
before Marino, or anybody with a Hispanic last name, for that
matter, had ever set foot in Crimes Against Persons, even back
when it had been Homicide and Robbery. Second, Clark, who
was a pretty good judge of these things, figured from the way
Marino looked at him over the car seat and the way the big man
carried himself that there very well might be a serious ass-
kicking in his future now. And he could have done without that.

CHAPTER 7

Saturday, 4:00 p.m.

Marino was about to knock on the front door of the house the second time when it opened and a black woman in her late fifties or early sixties looked out at the cops and asked if she could help them. She was wearing an unstained white apron over a black dress, and reminded Marino of the old woman who had been gunned down in the West Dallas hit.

If the cops had been friends of the master of the house, of course, they would simply have gone in past the maid and found the party in the den in front of a big-screen television. But they were not friends, and did not pretend to belong inside with the others, and so the maid was not impressed with them. When Marino told her who they were and he and Al Lewis showed her their badges, she was so unimpressed that she asked them if they would mind coming around to the back door. Marino thought she took rather too much satisfaction in that, and he told her that, yes, they would mind that very much and please just go get the man of the house and they would wait right where they were, thank you. She did that, with a look back at Clark, who had not shown her his badge and who did not look like the other two, which was about the way she would have expected plainclothes cops to look. She wondered if Clark was under arrest, maybe a suspect of some kind the cops wanted Mister Welborn to identify. The cops, Marino and Lewis, were clean shaven and dressed in sports coats and slacks, with ties, and

Marino was wearing plain-toed cowboy boots of black cowhide. Clark's beard had an uncommitted look, an in-between lack of development, and he wore an army field jacket over dirty Wranglers and a battered pair of Adidas, with a gimme cap jammed low over his face that featured the name of a local wrecker service stitched in fancy script.

"Wait right here," said the maid, closing the front door and leaving the three of them standing in the cold on the porch while she went for her boss.

The door was opened again, this time by a white man Marino guessed to be six foot five at least, with hair prematurely gray and thinning in front, worn long on the sides and in back to make up for it. Marino noticed the man's hands, how big they were, and guessed his game had been basketball. He did not look fast, Marino thought, but that was a hell of a pair of mitts.

The televised crowd went wild about something in the den, and the man in the doorway spat a soft curse and shook his head. Then: "Yes, may I help you?"

Marino showed his badge again, Lewis did not bother this time, and Marino explained to Mr. Welborn the Third that they needed a word with him, preferably a private one. Marino made it clear with a canting of his head that when he said "we" he meant himself and Lewis. As for Clark, that was for Mr. Welborn to work out for himself or to make an issue of if he cared to.

Welborn made some noise about always being glad to cooperate with the police but for heaven's sake couldn't they find a better time for this. Didn't they know the play-off game was on, and like that? He waved his hand at the half dozen or so cars parked around the circular drive in front of his house to let the cops know he had quite a lot of company for the game. While he did not go so far as to point out that the least expensive and impressive car in the bunch was a three-year-old Eldorado with a City Hall VIP sticker on the windshield, he did give them every opportunity to figure it out for themselves.

"Excuse me"—Welborn interrupted his own line of bullshit to address Clark in particular—"are you a police officer, too?"

Clark, who stood to one side with his back to the wind, his head tucked down on his shoulder and his hands jammed into

the pockets of his jacket, opened his jacket with his right hand
to show the badge on his belt.

"Oh," said Welborn Third. "Narcotics?"

"No thanks," Clark said. "I don't use 'em."

"I beg your pardon?" Third's eyebrow cocked.

"Uh, Mr. Welborn," Marino cut in, "if we can have a word
with you, we'll be out of your way before halftime, okay?"

"Well, I suppose so," Welborn offered, still looking at Clark
oddly. "What's it about?"

"You wanna let us in, Welborn, or hop your ass out here in
the fucking wind?" Clark asked in an even tone, smiling.

"I beg your . . . Oh, of course. Step inside, please."

"Thank you, Mr. Welborn," Marino said with a nod as he
and Lewis stepped into the warmth of the Welborn entry hall.

Clark thought that the entry hall, while it invited them to stay
longer than the windswept porch had, still was meant to impress
on them that they were intruders and not welcome long. Marino
brought up the Lincoln and the dead girl and hedged a bit about
the connection between her and Welborn Third, kind of swal-
lowing his words when it came to that. Clark, standing to one
side, thought the way Marino said it welcomed denial, and that
seemed to be the way Third read it, too. And he threw in a little
indignation for good measure, until Marino asked him again,
giving him a chance to reconsider, and this time Marino said it
more like he meant it, like he knew something.

"Come to think of it . . ." said Welborn Third, and then he
went into it about the dead girl. Not the truth, of course, not at
first, but this and that of it, keeping it general enough that he
could weasel in or out if there was a trap in it anywhere. Seems
he might know her, have known her, after all, not personally of
course. How, then, Clark wondered. Professionally?

Third talked and Marino listened, watching the man closely,
while Lewis took a couple of notes. Clark heard a door opening
in the direction of the den, and saw a tall blonde with high
cheekbones and blue eyes of a shade you don't see often,
peeking out at them. He smiled at her, but she was looking past
him toward Third and the other two cops. When Clark turned
back to Third and Marino, Marino was wrapping things up.

". . . appreciate your time," he was saying, and some more,

the usual thing. He held back a bit, the way he put it and the tone
of his voice, because he was pretty sure Third was holding out
on them and he did not mind if Third knew he felt that way.

"What kind of car do you drive?" Clark asked Third.

"A nine forty-four," the tall man said with a smile.

"That would be a Porsche?" asked Al Lewis, wanting to
keep his notes straight.

"Of course," said Third, managing not to sound too conde-
scending.

"And your wife?" asked Clark.

"What does that have to do with anything?" Third practically demanded.

"If you can't remember, I can ask her," Clark said, turning
in the direction of the den.

"She drives a BMW, light blue," Third said. "Why?"

"I was just wondering," Clark answered, smiling.

"Thanks," Marino said, wrapping it up.

Welborn asked if they had business cards, and Marino and
Lewis gave him theirs. Clark said he was all out, and Marino
wrote his name and telephone extension on the back of his own
card, and then the cops left.

Carlton O. Welborn III watched the cops walk to their car
through the fish-eye lens of the security peephole in his front
door. When they were gone, he went back into his den, ignoring
his wife and the look she gave him, and settled on one of the
sofas. Welborn told his friend about the cops, and especially
about the smart-assed one with the beard. His friend, Phillip,
was known to be in touch with City Hall, and promised he
would have a word with the assistant city manager for public
safety about it.

"Tell me again, Phillip," said Welborn. "What's his name,
the assistant city manager?"

"Bobby Klevinger," Phillip whispered, to keep from disturbing the other football fans in the room. "Robert, if you want
to humor him."

"Right. Right."

CHAPTER 8

Saturday, 5:00 p.m.

Pinky Lafayette smiled and waved back over his shoulder at his "constituents" inside the diner as he pushed through the double doors from the stifling cozy warmth and kitchen smells into the blustery biting edge of the wind kicking down Martin Luther King Boulevard out of the northeast, whistling in over the fairgrounds on Cullum Boulevard and down the broad street that used to be Forest Avenue. Pinky snugged the collar of his overcoat under his chin and tugged his hat down hard so it would not fly off. He leaned into the wind to make his way up the sidewalk of the long block to his office, cursing under his breath. He had not held office for a couple of terms, had not run for anything in that long, and his office these days was just that, his office. It was unofficial and unfunded except for contributions and a couple of small grants that had not been squeezed off entirely by the Republican spigot-tenders, but probably would not be renewed. He had been a fixture in South Dallas since the late 1950s—the first black man they had elected to any office that mattered, and the reason most of them had registered to vote, because he had convinced them that their votes would count. Any who were much under thirty paid him no mind because they did not know who he was.

Lafayette cursed more than the weather as he marched head down and leaning forward against the wind. He cursed time and the way things had of overtaking you, and the injustice of it. He had stuffed both local papers inside his overcoat, the front-page section of them, to reread alone in his office. But it had not taken him long to see what they were saying. They were saying it was over for Pinky, or soon would be.

The news was all about the killing of the two officers. Most of it was the black-and-white angle on the cops, and he had shaken his head and had a chuckle to see that Orville Knecht, the police chief Pinky had known since his days as a watch commander at the Southeast Division, the outpost on Bexar Street across from the ''Bon-ton'' projects, had taken the obvious angle and plagiarized or at least paraphrased something a New York cop had been quoted in a book as saying about the murder there of a black-and-white pair of patrolmen. ''Their color was neither black nor white . . . It was blue,'' the *Times Herald* had quoted the bereaved chief as saying.

That was all right. Pinky genuinely regretted the deaths of the young officers, and did not blame Knecht for speechifying. That was about all a chief of police was good for, after all. And he knew that Knecht would catch hell over it, as if anything he did mattered out here on the street. What bothered Pinky about the cop killing first and most personally was the press coverage, particularly the fact that he was nowhere quoted or even referred to in either paper. When had that ceased to be automatic? he wondered. When had they stopped calling him for a reaction to anything that went down in South Dallas? He knew some of the bylines on the stories, about half of them. Stuyvesant was still writing for one of the papers, and Pinky knew him personally, remembered him. Some of the others, he knew their names but not much else. And some he had never heard of before, like this guy who wrote about how one of the cops had tried to save the other one. Who the hell was Bobby Thurmon?

After what seemed a hike of miles, Pinky drew abreast of the two-story brown brick ex-clinic where he officed and shouldered open the door, glad to be free of the roar of the wind and the biting cold. He nodded and smiled a hello to the volunteer at the desk in the reception area, who looked up from a newspaper and raised her eyebrows as if to say she had not expected him to come in in this weather.

''Any calls?'' he asked.

"Not a one." She smiled back, then returned to her paper. "Were you expecting a call?"

"Not particularly, thank you."

She has no idea, Pinky thought, why I would be expecting a call. Sitting there reading the story, and makes no connection to me whatsoever . . .

Inside his office, with the door pressed quietly closed behind him, Pinky shed his overcoat and the gray hat and hung them on a coat tree in a corner. There was a full-length mirror on the inside of the door, and Pinky, ever meticulous, checked his reflection.

His hair, what there was of it, showed where his hat had been, and he combed out the crease it had left. That was better. He drew himself up and, since there was only he in the mirror and nothing to show scale, he pretended as he often did that he was taller than five foot four. He did not have to suck in his stomach anymore. The cancer had taken care of that, and he could not pretend that it did not show in his face, either.

John Henry Jones, aka "Zulu" Jones, former Panther, former pimp and doper, late of the Texas Department of Corrections, currently head of whatever he was calling his anti-drug youth center this week, that was the man the reporters went to now. He was the one they called the "community spokesman." Jones.

"Ain't that a bitch," Pinky whispered, shaking his head, as he looked from the file photo of Jones in the *Times Herald,* to his own image in the mirror. "A stone-cold bitch."

Dunk took no notice of the gilt hand-lettering on the big window of the ground-floor office in the two-story building on the corner as the gusting wind shoved him across the cross street and down the sidewalk. The lettering spelled out "Lafayette Community Action Center," but Dunk had things on his mind, and paid the lettering no more attention than the figure of the old man inside who stood looking out through angled venetian blinds onto the street.

Dunk was starving. He had partied late the night before, more to celebrate not getting killed by the Mexicans than for the money he had made. Smokin' rope and drinkin' dago red, and dance, dance, dance. He had not long ago rolled off of Irene and left her curled up in bed with her thumb in her mouth and her two babies taking turns crying in the playpen in the kitchen to go out and find something to eat. He had forgotten about eating the night before.

Dunk was navigating down the sidewalk with a tail wind and paying no particular attention to anything except that he still had his money on him, his pocket roll with a twenty and a pair of tens and the rest in his socks, and that he was not real clear about what time it was, exactly, and he did not hear the car coming up behind him until it was too late.

Sparky Filmore was riding shotgun in the Olds, a two-door brown-over-yellow model with a ragged vinyl roof and no hubcaps. Wheels Winager was driving. Winager eased alongside the curb and watched Filmore swing open the passenger door and pivot out of the car behind the hustling little guy. Dunk snapped on the deal too late, because he was hung over and hungry, and all wrapped up in an overcoat that was too big for him. He had found it in Irene's closet that morning, and meant to ask her about it if he ever made it back to her.

Dunk cut his eyes quick from the two white faces to their car, then downwind along the street to see if there were any witnesses. He did not like the looks of the car that stood angled into the curb beside him, its near door standing open.

"What's up?" he asked, trying to get something out of the two. With his shoulders set against the wind, he bobbed his neck up out of his collar to show his face to them, on the hopeful chance that they had mistaken him for someone else.

"Get in the car, Dunk," said the one nearest him. He was a head taller than Dunk, with a dark, stubbled face. In the couple of seconds it took for the touch of his hand between Dunk's shoulder blades to register through his heavy borrowed coat, Dunk was in the car, shoved in through the open door and tumbled over the folded-down passenger seat into the warmth of the backseat. He heard both car doors slam, and the car lurched forward with a squeal of tires.

"Who are you guys?" Dunk asked. They had not frisked him.

"We're friends of yours," the driver said over his shoulder.

"Only you don't know it yet," added the other one, who showed him a leather wallet that opened like a book. There was a green laminated card with a black-and-white photo. If it was of the big man, it was an old picture, Dunk thought.

"Y'all po-lice?" he asked, relieved.

"Who else?"

"You never know," Dunk offered, smiling wryly.

"Just keep your hands on your lap there. All right?" the passenger said.

"Huh? Oh, yeah."

He had started to slip his hands into his coat pockets, but the cop was not going to allow that, because Dunk had not been searched. Dunk could not see the passenger's other hand and figured he was holding a gun down in front of the seat. He was right.

"Where we going?" Dunk asked.

"Not far."

"Am I under arrest?" Dunk asked. His lawyer had told him always to ask that.

"You wanna be?"

His lawyer had not told him what to answer to that, so Dunk did not say anything. Neither of the cops did any talking for a while either, and left Dunk to wonder what this was all about.

After a few minutes' driving, they pulled into what had been some kind of warehouse or garage. There was no door on the front anymore, and there was nothing to the place except sheet-iron walls and a ceiling.

They got him out and did more than frisk him. By the time they let him put his shoes and shirt back on and then the coat, Dunk knew that for all that the garage's walls muffled the sound of the wind, it nevertheless found its way through chinks and seams and made the hard floor as cold as ice. Dunk hated being cold, the ache that settled into his bones and stiffened his joints, because it made him feel old. It made him think of his dead mother and all that had befallen her when everything he could do, all his high-school dropout hustling and thievery, had not been enough to keep her alive or even to make things easier for her in any way that mattered. She had died in wintertime, and he hated to be cold.

"Here's the deal," said the cop who had been the driver. "We need information."

"I ain't no snitch," Dunk said, careful not to sound smart-assed.

"Not yet," said the driver, with a tight smile.

Dunk said nothing. Why did it have to get complicated? he asked himself. He was just a thief. He took cars because he could. He didn't hurt anybody. Now he was mixed up with these Mexicans, cold-eyed Willy and Crazy Frank. How long can a man expect to live at all if he ran with mad dogs like Crazy Frank? And now this. Dunk had been rousted by cops before. He had two felony convictions, and he was doing probation for the second one. But these cops were not going by the book, and that worried him.

"Dunk, you got two options." It was the big man talking now, the one with the watch cap and the pea coat. "You can give us what we need, and we'll make sure nobody knows about it. We won't burn you, we won't put you on the spot. That's one option."

"Yeah." Dunk nodded.

"Yeah," the cop went on. "The second option is this: You can play the tough guy and tell us to get lost. In which case, we'll burn you right to the ground. We'll put a snitch jacket on you that you won't ever get off."

"Hey, man . . ."

"Hey, you," the driver cut in. "What part of the deal do you not understand? Either you live like a snitch for real or you die like one for drill. It's as simple as that."

"But I don't know nothing or nobody, man," Dunk insisted. "I don't know who you think I am, but . . ."

"You're a car thief," the big one said. "And you've been playing around with some pretty bad actors." He was being pretty matter-of-fact about all this, while the driver was acting nasty. Dunk had had the "good cop–bad cop" treatment worked on him before, but not quite like this. This was all happening in a place where there were no witnesses, and Dunk knew that this was all off the record. They weren't downtown, and there would be no written reports. He didn't know their names, and the car looked like one there might not be any record of at City Hall. He could be bluffing, Dunk knew. Probably was. But that didn't mean he wasn't dangerous. That business about the snitch jacket was serious, deadly serious, whether the cops were guessing or not.

"Lawd, lawd," Dunk muttered under his breath.

CHAPTER 9

Saturday, 7:30 p.m.

Dave White caught the image of Bob Marx, his partner, in the rearview mirror he had turned so that he could see into the blind spot to his right.

It was relief time, and Marx was coming on. Their target, Stefanie Nugent, lived in a "single city" apartment complex and Marx in his sweats looked as if he belonged, another up-and-comer out for a jog.

"Anything?" he asked as he let himself into the backseat.

"Nada."

"She's been in all day?"

"Since we put her to bed an hour after sunrise."

"So you've spent the day sitting on your butt here, just taking it easy?"

White was slumped down in the front seat against the passenger door, because that is the way you do it on a one-man stakeout. The theory is that a man sitting on the passenger side might look like he's waiting for the driver to come back, while a man sitting behind the wheel looks like a cop on stakeout.

"Something like that. What is it, only a quarter to eight? I wouldn't have thought it was a minute later than midnight." White spat with a grimace.

"Time really flies, doesn't it?" Marx grinned, leaning across the backseat on his elbow. If Stef Nugent or any of her friends showed, Marx would not be obvious. He and White both had room to duck out of sight.

"Screwed up a perfectly good weekend. That's all we've done here," White observed.

"Like you had something better to do." He was married, with two preschoolers. White, on the other hand, was single.

Lobo called for Maguire, whom he insisted on calling "Maggie," and the desk man in Vice agreed to try to reach him at home, after trying without any luck to explain to Lobo that Maguire did not work Vice anymore, that he had made sergeant and gone to Community Services, where he was in charge of the Police Athletic League or something. Lobo insisted, and the desk man made the call. You never know, he reminded himself. He had snitches of his own.

"Yo, Dogs," Hernandez answered the phone in the PES bay at the auto pound.

"Nacho, Clark here."

"Yeah, boss."

"Anything else on the car?"

"Nothing worth talkin' about. You get anything out there in North Dallas?"

"Yeah, I got a positive reaction off my bullshit detector."

"Did?"

"I'm telling you. See what you can find on a Preston Hollow type by the name of Clayton Welborn the Third."

"What do you want, Sarge, criminal history and stuff?"

"Nah, I could run CH on the radio, Nacho. Make a couple of calls. I'm interested in the scuttlebutt."

"Oh."

"Nacho, call somebody who works at the courthouse—see if they know any dirt about this guy. Okay?"

"It's Saturday, Sarge. Courthouse's closed."

Clark counted to ten. He did not want to hurt Nacho's feelings.

"Call them at home. Or try one of your friends in Intelligence."

"Got it," Nacho answered, full of confidence now.

"Fine. I'll check back with you."

"You coming back out here to the pound, Sarge?"

"No, Nacho." If I were, I wouldn't have asked you to do this for me, he thought. "I'm going to see if I can come up with anything myself."

"Yes?" Bobby Klevinger always answered the phone that way, because he liked simplicity. He confused it with efficiency.

"Phil here. Got a minute?"

"Sure," Klevinger answered, raising his lips in a smile because he knew that registered in his voice, made it sound as if he were happy to get the call. "What's up?"

It was nine twenty-eight, and Randi congratulated herself on making half a shift. Six and a half hours in a miniskirt, atop the spiked heels Charlie had insisted on instead of the sensible shoes she had brought from home. But the vest was the worst of it. It was open down the front, and there was a trick to serving the tables without exposing herself.

When the bearded man with the worried look came in, Randi noticed him, but table three was full of demanding car salesmen from a lot up the street, and she did not pay much attention to him. She did not suspect the bearded man was a cop, too.

"Hello?" Orville Knecht was at home when Klevinger called. He was lying on one side of a king-sized bed, his wife Eloise snuggled on the other, and the television was on. His son and daughter were in their respective rooms, doing whatever they did in there with phones of their own and TVs and stereos with headsets and whatever else Eloise had given in to their nagging about. The children were of an age to be troublesome, and Orville Knecht had enough to say grace over at the police department.

"This is Bobby. I hope I'm not interrupting anything, Chief?"

Klevinger was careful of titles in dealing with these people, but only because he knew they took them so seriously.

"What's up, Bobby?"

"I got a call," Klevinger said. A lot of his conversations with Orville began that way. "One of your guys got out of line with a community leader."

"Oh?"

"Yeah. A sergeant in Auto Theft, name of Clark."

Stefanie Nugent was coming alive in her apartment, not surprised to find it full of strangers. They were friends of Mack's, more or less, and that was cool.

She'd awakened nauseated and empty, sure she could feel her gut, strung like guitar string against her spine. She took a hit of speed for breakfast and started feeling better.

"Frank, come here," Willy called down the ladder hole from the attic of the big old house.

"Yeah, yeah," Frank answered, choking and snorting between his words.

"Leave that shit alone, will you?" Willy called down to him. "Half our profits are going up your goddamned nose."

Frank laughed at that, loudly enough for Willy to hear him, because Willy had said it jokingly. Frank knew that even Willy, the smart one, was afraid of him. When Frank thought at all, beyond registering his appetites, it was of what made one man more dangerous than the next. It was quickness more than strength, he knew. But above all, something in the heart. He thought hearts were of different colors. His was black, he figured, and that made him unafraid. That was the real secret of being dangerous, he had decided, and the significance of the black tattooed heart he had added to the collection on his chest. He liked that one, and had been considering some schemes to embellish it.

Willy stepped off the dimensions of the attic again while he waited for Frank. When the bad man's shaggy head appeared in the square of the ladder hole, Willy saw how the yellowish light from the naked bulb cast the shadows of his brows over his high cheekbones and the heavy stubbled lines of his jaw. From the dark hooded sockets of Frank's eyes, Willy saw the twinkling light of his pupils like the eyes of a wolf.

CHAPTER 10

Saturday, Midnight

Randi Stoner had a problem. With two hours to go before closing time, the place was getting rowdier. More of the customers were drunk, and they were making enough noise at a couple of tables to be heard even over the roar of the club's speakers.

There were drunks at plenty of tables and along the edge of the stage, where a couple of them were in danger of falling off their tall stools. But Randi's problem was one customer in particular, who was with two others who were playing pool.

"Hey! Hey, b-bitch!" Randi heard him over the rest of the noise, his voice high-pitched and rasping. " 'Nuther round, goddamnit!"

She carried a tray of empties back to the bar and was glad to see Charlie.

"How's it goin'?" Charlie grinned, leaning close to her to make sure she heard him.

"Fine," she answered.

"Glad to hear it. The costume fits good, huh?"

"Terrific. One size fits all, I guess." She could still hear the drunk at the small table whining for another beer.

"Hey, you got a thirsty customer over there," Charlie told her with a nudge against her arm. "Shake a leg."

"He's had too much already," she said.

"Not unless he's run out of money to pay for it." Charlie grinned again.

"Really, Charlie, he's on his butt. I don't want to lose your license for you on my first night."

"You let me worry about the friggin' license, kiddo. You just hustle your ass over there and keep the customer happy. You get me?"

"I get you."

"Hey, what is this here?" Charlie asked suddenly, and Randi felt his hand at her waist.

"What?"

"This right here. What is this?"

"It's a beeper, Charlie. What do you think?"

"What the . . . ? There's only two kinds of people wear pagers, sweetheart, doctors and dope dealers. And you ain't no doctor."

"And I ain't no dealer, either," Randi shot back, relieved he had not included cops in the list. "It's for my baby-sitter, in case the kid gets sick."

"You can afford one of these?"

"It was my husband's. The only thing he left behind when he ran off on us."

"Oh yeah? What kind of work did he do?"

"He wasn't no doctor, Charlie."

"I get you. So, okay, only keep it out of sight under there, will you?"

"Right." She had the thing clipped to the waistband of her skirt. Her costume was not designed to hide anything. The gizmo was not really a pager, although it looked like one. It was a transmitter, and if she pressed the right button it would send a duress code that Chapman and Potter would hear in their van across the street.

Charlie turned to leave, and then had a thought and turned back. "Maybe you better give me the number of that thing, in case I need to get in touch with you, okay?"

"I'm here three to two, five days a week. You can get in touch with me here."

"What, five days? Who said you get two days off?"

"Whatever."

Charlie shot his cuffs and moved on.

She told the bartender she needed three longnecks and balanced them on her tray with her right hand, careful to keep her money, separated by denomination, tucked around the fingers of her left the way Charlie had told her to do it.

"You know anybody named Charlotte?"

Betty, one of the two other waitresses, had slid into place next to Randi to place her order, and asked her the question in what passed for a whisper in the noisy club.

"What?"

"Charlotte," Betty repeated. "Maybe she was a dancer?"

"Who wants to know?" Randi asked.

"Guy over against the wall." Betty pointed across the big smoky room at the man with the beard, the one who had come in a couple of hours before looking worried. "Says he's looking for some girl named Charlotte, maybe she danced here."

"Hey, it's my first night," Randi reminded her.

"Oh, yeah. I forgot."

"Who is he?" Randi asked.

"Boyfriend, gangster . . . her daddy, for all I know. He said it was worth a couple of bucks."

Randi shrugged and hefted her tray. On her way to serve the drunk, she took another look at the bearded man. She did not recognize him. He must have felt that she was looking at him, because he turned his head and returned her gaze evenly. Maybe he had seen Betty talking to her, maybe he thought she might know something about Charlotte, and Randi thought he might be her daddy. He had sad eyes.

"T-t-took you long enough," the drunk snorted when she got to his table. He was a tall man, cadaverously thin with dirty-blond hair and bad teeth, wearing a black T-shirt with a denim vest.

"Here you go," she said, smiling without looking at the drunk as she put the beers on the table. She did not bend at the waist the way Charlie had showed her, with her butt in the air, but bent her knees instead, ready to move if he got out of line.

"Come here," the drunk insisted. "You g-gotta clean this up here." His friends called him Blondie and made fun of him because he stuttered. He looked at the waitress, and his left eye twitched.

"I beg your pardon?" Randi kept smiling.

"We got a b-bad spill here, b-baby. Clean this up. See?" Blondie thought she was smirking at him, and he did not like to repeat himself.

The drunk had spilled beer on the table in front of him. Randi stepped around the table and sidled between the drunk and an empty chair. With the bar rag she kept on her tray, she leaned down to wipe up the spill.

"That's b-better." Blondie giggled. "And while you're at it, let me ch-check your oil." His hand ran quickly up the inside of her thigh and she clenched her legs together too late to stop him from fondling her lewdly. She squeaked in spite of herself, like a rubber mouse. He laughed, showing his bad teeth in an obscene openmouthed grin that sprayed his spittle on her arm, and his hand worked up hard, trying to finger her tights aside. Blondie looked at his two pals at the pool table, Peter and Dick. Each of them had penises tattooed on their arms. Blondie wanted to be sure they were watching him have his fun with this bitch.

She twisted away from him and reached for his arm with her left hand, trying to push him away, but he was stronger than he looked. He pulled her toward him, and she slapped him with her free hand, balancing her tray in the other. Her open palm smacked his cheek, and he only grinned wider.

"That d-didn't hurt," he snickered.

Randi flashed on scenes from the police academy, hours on the mats in defensive tactics, but what she did had not been taught.

"Hey," Blondie called to Peter and Dick, "she's about a qu-quart low." They laughed with him and Blondie felt good. He'd show them.

With her right hand, Randi spun her drink tray hard at the drunk as his head swiveled back toward her, and she loved the dull crunch when it bit into the bridge of the bastard's nose.

"Jesus fuckin' Christ!" he cried, letting go of her to grab his broken nose.

Randi jerked free of him, delighted at the sight of blood on his face. She turned and stalked away, but he was not through with her yet. She heard the clattering of his chair on the floor and he was on her from behind. His fist in her hair yanked her back toward the table, her neck twisted over her shoulder, and he threw her off her feet, slammed her onto the tabletop so hard that she lost her breath. She was stunned for an instant, and with his free hand he yanked her vest aside. His ugly, bloody face leaned over her. His breath was hot and rancid on her eyes.

"I'm g-gonna fix you!"

His right hand left her and went to the flapped scabbard on his belt, and his right leg fell across her legs to keep her from kicking him. With his left hand still in her hair, he had her pinned. She reached for his eyes with one hand, but he ducked his face away and gave her hair a yank.

Randi knew he was going to hurt her bad, and she reached for the transmitter. It was gone.

The knife opened in his hand with a blur and a click that she heard, even over the thunder of the rock-and-roll music and the rowdy roar of the crowd. If anybody saw what was happening, no one cared enough to do anything about it. Except Charlie.

"Hey, man, put down that knife." It was Charlie's voice.

"Fuck you," the drunk answered, his eyes big as saucers on either side of his busted, bleeding nose. "You want some of this, too?"

"Think about it, buddy. You don't want to do this." Charlie was pleading with the drunk, and Randi knew from his voice that Charlie was not prepared to fight him.

And then suddenly the drunk's face was gone and his grip on her hair loosened. Randi squirmed free and looked up to see the bearded man standing behind the man with the knife.

Clark had his left hand in the drunk's hair, in a death grip, and yanked the man's head back so far that it would not be much of a trick to break his scrawny neck. But it was the cool, hard muzzle of the revolver that put a stop to everything. Clark pressed the snout of the gun hard against the drunk's head about a quarter of an inch in front of his ear.

"Lose the knife," he said, in a quiet voice that the man had no trouble hearing.

"Who the fuck are you?" the drunk demanded.

Clark thumbed back the hammer on his snubby magnum, knowing that to the drunk it would sound like the tumblers in the door of a bank vault.

"The knife."

And that was that. The drunk dropped his knife, and Clark dragged him back a few steps to give Randi enough room to roll off the table. The drunk's two pool-shooting friends made a move his way, but they could see that Clark, whoever he was, meant business, and they did not come very far.

"Get out of here," Clark told the skinny blond man as he let go of him and stepped back.

"This ain't over, motherfucker."

"You're probably right," Clark admitted, holding his gun level at his waist, aimed at the drunk's chest. "But it could be."

The two friends left their pool cues on the table and came to get the drunk away before he wound up dead over nothing. They grabbed him and slapped his back and one of them said something about getting his nose tended to, and neither Clark nor Charlie tried to stop them from leaving. None of them asked for the man's knife back, and it stayed on the floor where he had dropped it.

As the three of them made their way toward the door, Clark saw two linebacker types hustle in from the parking lot. They gave the guy's broken nose a quick look and headed toward the back of the place where Charlie stood facing Clark as if he was not sure what came next. They would be the bouncers, Clark thought. Never one around when you need one.

Clark slipped his gun back into the shoulder holster he wore under his field jacket before the bouncers got close enough to see it and get excited. He took a business card out of his shirt pocket and handed it to Charlie.

" 'Sergeant Bill Clark, Auto Theft,' " Charlie read aloud. "You're a cop, right?"

"You got any problem with that?"

"Nope. Absolutely."

"You see a need for any paperwork here?" Clark asked.

"Nope. Not at all."

"How about you, miss?" Clark turned to Randi, who was on her hands and knees on the floor, looking for something.

"What?" She got to her feet, looking shaken, and Clark saw that she had a pager in her hand. She must have lost it in the fight, he thought.

"They haven't gone far. You want to file a complaint?"

"I don't . . ." Randi stuttered, thinking fast.

"He's a cop, sweetheart. Do you wanna make a report?" Charlie explained.

"No."

"Good girl. There you go, Officer. Everybody's happy."

"What's up, Charlie?" One of the bouncers wanted to know.

"Nuthin'. Everything's okay. Those three that just left, go make sure they leave the property. That's all. Go on." The two big guys looked like they would have liked trying Clark out much better, but they did as they were told.

Looking around the place, Clark did not think many of the customers had even noticed the trouble. And if any of the employees had seen anything, they did not seem interested. "Are you all right, miss?" he asked Randi.

"Yeah. Thanks." She felt her heart pounding louder than the music, and her legs were shaky. "Thank you very much."

"What did I tell you about serving drunks, huh?" Charlie was waving a finger at her. "You could cost me my license serving a stiff like that, not to mention getting your throat cut."

Randi cocked an eyebrow at him and nodded her head with a tight little smile. "You're right, boss. I don't know what I was thinking."

"Well, just don't let it get to be a habit, okay?"

"Right."

"So, uh, get back to work there, already. You got thirsty customers all over the place." When Randi had left, Charlie turned to Clark with a look on his face like a conspirator. "You know how it is, Officer. You can't get good help. I tell you, she's new . . . It's her first night on the job, even. Can I buy you a drink?"

"Another time."

"Auto Theft, huh? What're you looking for in here, a stolen car?"

"Nothing like that. It's a personal matter. Girl named Char-

lotte. Charlotte Mayfield. Used to be a dancer. I thought somebody might know her.''

"Nah, no Charlottes, not since I been runnin' the joint. What
kind of a stage name did she use?''

"I don't know.''

"I could ask around. I got your card, right? I'll call if I come
up with anything.''

"Right. See you around.''

"You're leaving?'' Charlie made his face look disappointed,
but Clark thought he sounded relieved.

"Yeah, your place is too dull for me. Think I'll go see if I
can get into something.''

"Uh . . . Yeah, right. Exactly.'' Charlie grinned and patted
him on the back as he walked Clark to the door.

CHAPTER 11

Sunday, 1:00 a.m.

Clark left the bar and walked to his pickup, unaware that Larry Potter and J. D. Chapman saw him from their dilapidated van across the street. It was almost one o'clock in the morning by the time he got home to his apartment. He pushed the "play" button on his answering machine and listened to his calls while he made himself a Jack Daniel's and 7-Up in a tall glass, plenty of ice. The first message was the clackety metallic voice of somebody's computer, touting a dating service. One of the guys at work must have sent them his name. Very funny. Next, his ex-wife's voice, his most recent ex-wife. Her message had to do with the IRS and their taxes for the previous year, but Clark did not concern himself with that, only the sound of her voice. She sounded sad and lonely, and he was glad. There were a couple of hang-ups after that, and Clark wondered what time his ex had called. But he forgot about that when he heard the third message. It was his new lieutenant.

"Sergeant Clark, this is Lieutenant Bonny. Call me at home ASAP." Then a click.

Clark slipped out of his jacket and the shoulder-holster rig and tossed them on the couch beside his chair. Must be about that little run-in at the club, he thought. Didn't take long for Lieutenant Bonny to get wind of it. The department didn't mind you rescuing the odd damsel in distress, but it was a stickler for paperwork. There were supposed to be reports made when things like that happened, and he really should have put the asshole in jail, for all the good that would have done.

When the doorbell rang, he looked at his watch and hefted the comfortably heavy revolver on his way to the door. The fish-eye glass of his peephole made the face on the other side of the door look as if it were mostly a nose with eyes wrapped around either side. He didn't make the face at first, but the visitor must have heard him behind the door, because he called out.

"Bobby Thurmon, Sergeant Clark." Clark stood behind his door with a drink in one hand and a gun in the other and tried to place the name. "The reporter. I spent the night here last night, remember?" Clark set down his drink and opened the door.

"Yeah, sure I remember. What're you doing out this time of night?"

"I was by earlier, but you were out."

"Oh."

"I wanted to thank you for the tip."

"Tip?"

"The angle on the police shooting, the officer who tried to save his partner. You know, the black-and-white thing."

"You used that, huh?"

"Yeah. I guess you haven't seen the papers."

"I don't read papers."

"Oh."

"Well, you're welcome. Good night."

"Uh, Sergeant Clark . . ." Clark had started to close his door, and Thurmon edged forward.

"Yeah?"

"I've been thinking about what you said this morning, and, I thought maybe there's a story in it."

"What?"

"About how the courts turn the car thieves loose, how you catch them, but it doesn't do any good because the jails are overcrowded and they plea-bargain, and . . ."

"That's not news."

"It depends on how you write it."

"Okay. So what?"

"So, can I come in?"

"Well, I was just getting ready to turn in . . ."

"I won't stay long."

"Okay, come on in."

"Thanks."

Clark let the reporter in and noticed the look the kid tried to hide when he saw the gun in Clark's hand. What does he expect? Clark wondered.

"I gotta make a call. Make yourself at home. You know where everything is, I guess."

"Yeah, thanks."

The new lieutenant's wife or whoever sounded pretty groggy when she answered after the third ring. Clark told her who he was and why he had called, and then he listened as she woke up the lieutenant. She did not sound pleased.

"Lieutenant Bonny."

"Sergeant Clark. You called?"

"What time is it?"

"One something. What's up?"

"I left you a message at a quarter to ten. Where have you been?"

"Working. What's the deal?" Clark did not remind the lieutenant that he carried a pager twenty-four hours a day.

"I got a call . . ." the lieutenant began, breaking off for a yawn.

It did not sound promising, but at least it was not the deal at the topless bar. Not if the lieutenant had called before ten o'clock.

". . . from the captain. He got a call from the CID chief, who got one from . . . You know the drill."

"Indeed I do. What's the beef this time?"

"You got out of line with a heavy hitter this afternoon. A real . . ."

"Says who?"

". . . pillar of the community. Or maybe it's his daddy that's the pillar. One of those guys with numbers after their names."

"Out of line how?"

"This is not a trial board by telephone, Sergeant Clark. Just pull up on this guy. Leave him alone for the time being. No big deal.''

''It might be.'' Clark was focusing on not losing his temper. ''It might be a big deal.''

''Don't cop an attitude, Clark. Just get in line like a good troop. Cool it till Monday, and you and I'll sit down over it. Got it?''

''Yes, sir,'' Clark answered smartly, reverently, throwing the young lieutenant an unseen hand salute. ''Got it.''

''Good. What was it about, anyway?''

''What's that?''

''You called on this guy. What was it about?''

''No big deal.''

''Right. Monday, then.''

''Monday.''

''Good night, Sergeant.''

'' 'Night, sir.'' Clark hung up, and he had forgotten about the reporter making himself at home in his kitchen. ''No big deal, you pencil-neck cocksucker. Just a killing, a little gunrunning, an auto-theft ring, maybe some dope smuggling. You little . . .''

''What's that?'' Thurmon asked, joining Clark in the living room.

''Nothing,'' Clark answered, noting suspiciously that the reporter had a soft drink in his hand. ''You're not drinking?''

''After last night, I thought I'd give it a rest.''

''What happened last night?''

''I got drunk at the DPA Club, remember?''

''So?''

''So, I'm just going to take it easy on the booze for a bit. Who was that on the phone?''

''Nobody. Don't be an eavesdropper.''

''Right. I hear talk of killings, drugs, and gunrunning. Naturally, I wouldn't be curious.''

''It ain't for publication.''

''I won't quote you, Bill. We have a deal on that. I'm not here to capture any of your colorful quotes. I just want background . . .''

''You're looking for a snitch. Which I ain't.''

''Cops have snitches. Reporters have sources.''

''Same thing.''

''The hell it is. And if it was? You screw over your snitches, do you?''

Clark did not answer. He wished the kid would have a real drink. He would trust him more then.

''And I don't abuse sources. It'd be pretty hard to do either one of our jobs without 'em, wouldn't it?''

''And who gives a shit if your job gets done?'' Clark demanded.

''The people who voted you guys a pay raise in the referendum a couple of years ago.''

''Have a drink, you little prick. You're too quick when you're sober.''

CHAPTER 12

Sunday, 2:00 a.m.

"Did you get my little message, *bandejo?*"

"Who is this?" Carlton Welborn III cupped his hand over the mouthpiece of the phone and whispered his question with a look over his shoulder at his sleeping wife.

"You know who this is." Willy laughed softly into the phone. "How come you whispering, man? You afraid you gonna wake up that skinny blond wife of yours?" Willy was using his heaviest Hollywood *bandito* accent. "Too bad about your little 'tee-ty' dancer, ain't it? You want to see some pictures of her, man? It's a terrible thing to see, I'm telling you."

"What do you want?"

"How about if I drop you off a set of glossy eight-by-tens?"

"Listen, just tell me what . . ."

"I want the same thing I wanted before your whore girlfriend got sliced and diced, Carlton. Why you want to be so stubborn, man? It's a natural. You got the protection, I got the connection."

"I can't talk now."

"Meaning you can talk later?"

"Yes. Where can I reach you?"

"I'll get back to you, Carlton. You and the wife sleep tight, okay?"

The telephone was dead, humming dully in his hand for a long time before he put it back on its cradle.

"So they're calling you at home now," his wife said in a soft but biting voice.

"What? Who?"

"Your other women. You don't play innocence very convincingly, Carlton. Not even in the dark."

Carlton was offended by her lack of imagination, and said nothing. Where would we be now without poor Charlotte? he mused. Not living in this big house anymore, certainly. Carlton commended himself for having taken Charlotte out of the topless bar where he had found her, for giving her a taste of the good life at least. He wondered how it had been for her at the end, and a chill ran over him.

Willy killed the lights on his Monte Carlo as it rumbled up the long, deep-rutted drive into the trees beside the old house. The wind made the naked branches of the big oaks rattle like deer antlers scraping. There was a stand of cedar trees along the road itself, and a few more evergreens straggled across the front yard. There was a blink of light in a window at the corner of the house, and Willy bumped his headlights on and off twice to answer the signal. That would be Johnny, he knew, always standing watch as he was supposed to. Frank got bored if you put him on watch, but that was not what Frank was for.

It was colder than he could ever remember it when Willy stepped out of his car and jogged toward the warmth inside.

"Hey, man! How did it go, or what?" Frank bellowed from one of the rooms. "Did you make his shitter pucker up for him?"

"What are you doing in there, Frank?" Willy asked as he shoved the door closed behind him against the moaning wind and kicked the towels back under the door to close the crack.

"I'm reading all about your bombs and shit and jerking off, man. Where do you get all this shit?"

Willy poured himself a cup of coffee from the pot simmering on the stove. Then he walked up the long hallway and leaned on the door of the room where he had stashed all his reading material. There sat Frank, bundled up like an eskimo because he could not stand the cold even in the comparative warmth of the house, thumbing through one of his manuals.

"You weren't never in the army, Willy. Where'd you get all these books?"

"You can buy them at surplus stores, Frank. Or send off for them. What are you reading there?"

"I don't know, man. Somethin' about . . . 'impoverished devices.' "

" 'Improvised devices,' " Willy corrected him. "How to take everyday stuff and make bombs out of it."

"What do we need with bombs?" Frank asked.

Willy knew Frank did not think much of bombs. Too complicated, too remote. Frank liked to kill people up close. "You never know," Willy said. "Maybe you'll like the one about phone taps better, or infantry tactics."

"Ain't you got no books with women?"

"With you it's always *pinoche,* eh, Frank?" Willy laughed and walked toward the front of the house to find Johnny. "Hey, Johnny, how's it looking out there?" Willy softened his voice to talk to Johnny, because Johnny spoke softly, when he spoke at all.

"Cold," Johnny answered.

"No Jamaicans, huh?"

"Bad weather for them."

"Yeah."

Willy stood in the front room in the dark, nursing his coffee while Johnny kept watch. Without turning his head from the window, Johnny spoke again. "Are we hiding from them?"

"The Jamaicans? Nah, we ain't afraid of them."

"Maybe you ain't," Johnny answered.

"Maybe Frank ain't," Willy admitted.

They exchanged looks, and both laughed quietly.

"How much coke has he been doing?" Willy asked.

"He's been hitting it pretty good."

"What do you think about this place for a warehouse?"

"Looks okay. When?"

"Not long. I spoke to our friend tonight."

"What did he say this time?"

"He mostly listened. I'm gonna talk to him again tomorrow." Willy was thinking, making plans, figuring out all the ways the thing could go wrong, all the angles the gringo could try to play on him. He thought this place would be all right. It was a relic from the old days when this part of Oak Cliff had been practically out in the country. It was called "Cigarette Heights," because what streets there were had been named after cigarette brands, back around World War II. It was hilly and wooded, with privacy because the houses were scattered apart in the old way. The weather would help, if the guy with the bow tie on Channel 8 knew what he was talking about. There would be a little warming the first of the week, then rain and another hard freeze. That would keep the few neighbors they had holed up indoors. The attic was big enough for one of their regular loads, but it was the old barn out in back that Willy had his eye on.

Willy worried about the Jamaicans. They were crazy, like some of the Colombians he had heard about. It came from their Third World upbringing, where they didn't have nothing and life was so damned cheap. Somebody gives them a car, clothes to wear, and a couple of bucks, and they'd rather kill somebody than go back. Or get killed themselves.

Willy thought he had fixed the Jamaicans. He had paid a man to sic the cops on Curtis and the boys. That was his mistake; he should have made the call himself. He had been thinking he did not want his voice on the cops' tape, but you can't trust nobody to do shit like that right. He would have told the cops it was some serious Jamaican posse action and all about the machine guns and everything. They would have gone in there like the Marines and that would have been the end of it. But this shithead he gave the job to, there was no telling how he ran it down. The town was crawling with the funny-talking motherfuckers, but it was this dude Curtis he wanted taken care of. He was the one that would be trouble.

Chapman and Potter stirred in the cold darkness of their van as the door of the topless club opened and a knot of people spilled out into the parking lot. They watched the dancers and the waitresses, the two bouncers and the manager all scurry around the lot, their breath making clouds in the stinging clear night air. It was after three o'clock in the morning, and the place had been closed just over an hour.

"It's about time," J.D. groaned. "What the hell took so long?"

"They have to count the money," Larry answered, stretching and wiggling his feet to make sure his toes were not frostbitten. "Split the tips, settle up, all that shit."

"Which one is Randi?"

"There. The overcoat and sock cap."

There was a marked security service car sitting on the parking lot, backed up against the side of the building where the driver could keep an eye on things without getting out in the weather. They watched the manager climb into the security guard's car with a bag in his hand, and the two of them sat there until all the employees had gotten their cars started and were on their way.

"That's nice of him," J.D. noted. "He makes sure they all get off before he leaves to make the bank deposit."

"It's a people business, J.D."

They watched all the cars sputter to life and crunch across the hard, cold gravel of the lot into the street, and when there were none left, J.D. gratefully cranked the old van and turned the heater on full blast.

"No tail," Larry said.

"I don't see any. Looks like she made it through her first night, huh?"

"Guess so."

It was not obvious that they were following Randi's car. Most of the time they did not even have her in sight, but they knew the route she would take, the one they had laid out for her, and they were looking for anyone who might be following her. There was not much traffic and the street was slick, the wind spitting ice at them as they drove. When they passed the 7-Eleven where she was to make the call, they saw her there, just coming out of the store. She walked with a cup of coffee to the pay phones as they pulled into the big parking lot across the street. The cellular phone rang, and Potter answered it with a grin.

"Cold enough for you?" He laughed.

"Screw you, Potter," Randi shot back. "It had to be an outdoor pay phone?"

"Thought the fresh air would do you good—you been cooped up in that smoky fleshpot half the night while your loyal backups been seriously freezing their asses off in this shitcan van."

"You're breaking my heart, Potter."

"So how did it go?" She took long enough answering that Potter looked up across the lot to the 7-Eleven half a block away to make sure nothing had happened to her. She looked okay, just standing there kind of bunched against the cold. "Randi?"

"No problem," she said, finally.

"Are you okay, kid?"

"No . . . I'm freezing. So is this it, or what? Am I off the clock?"

"Yeah, that's it. We'll tail you on home just to be safe."

"Thanks. See you in the morning. I'm working the day shift tomorrow."

"Why?" Potter asked.

"Charlie didn't say. Just to come in early. Ten o'clock in the morning."

"Whatever."

"Okay. Good night."

" 'Night."

"She sound okay?" J.D. asked.

"Yeah . . . just tired, I guess."

Back in her car, a battered but gutsy little Honda that had been seized from a low end dealer months before, Randi locked her door and made sure the heater was all the way up. You should have told him, she scolded herself as she caught the light at Northwest Highway. She saw the van in her mirror, and did not mind that Potter and Chapman would be there behind her somewhere on the drive home. "I should have told him about Blondie and the guy from Auto Theft," she said aloud. "But if I did, they would have pulled me off the job."

Stef finally got tired of waiting for Mack to come back to the party, and the dope he had given her wasn't any good. She was coming down already, and she was tired of the way some of the shitheels in the house were carrying on. A couple of them in particular were going apeshit with a Polaroid, taking each other's picture with all the women in the place and making them show their tits. They made a pass or two at her, and finally she had enough of it and grabbed one of them by the goddamned lip and damned near twisted his face off his skull. She was pissed with Mack for dumping her here with them.

"I told you already, pecker breath, you ain't carrying no weight, you don't take my fucking picture."

He fell down and got back up and made a show like he wanted to fight, but she wasn't scared of him. She'd kill him bare-handed if he made a move, and he was just drunk, not high enough to try her. The other one said something about her being Mack the Knife's bitch, and they moved on.

So Stef split. Fuck you all, she thought as she stomped out. She had to show up for work in a few hours anyway, and she wondered as she tugged her leather coat tight around her what the hell time it was anyway. She stalked down the sloping drive to her Mustang.

Across the street and up the block, Investigator Marx snapped the last of the day's photographs and checked his watch: 4:18 A.M.

CHAPTER 13

Sunday, 10:00 a.m.

Bill Clark awoke on his couch to the sound of his telephone ringing. He took a moment to orient himself because he had only been living in the apartment for a couple of months, and heard a woman's voice on the answering machine.

"I don't give a shit about the IRS!" he barked at the phone. "That's the lawyer's job. Call him." Clark untangled himself from the quilt he could not remember getting out of the closet and staggered to his feet.

It occurred to Clark that something was missing, or someone. He'd had company the night before. That kid, the reporter. He started toward the kitchen to see if he was in there and stumbled over an empty Jack Daniel's bottle. It was when he put his hand on the coffee table to steady himself that he found the note.

"Bill, sorry to skip out on you, but if I spent two nights in a row at your place, people might start to talk. I'll call you. Bobby T."

Clark stumbled barefoot into the kitchen and put on a pot of coffee, trying to remember all he had said to Bobby T. It worried him that he might have gotten drunk and said too much, and he knew it probably should worry him that he couldn't remember. The hell with it. If anything he said made the morning paper, somebody would tell him. He wasn't going back on his principles and buy an issue just to find out.

It was not until he had his first cup of coffee in his hand that he made his way back to his chair and switched the phone machine to play.

"Sergeant Clark, this is . . ." It was not his ex-wife, and Clark could not place the voice. ". . . I'm the waitress at the club, the one last night. I, uh, just wanted to say I appreciate what you did. Thanks, 'bye."

Well, that's nice, Clark thought. Nice of her to call, I guess. Then, after a couple of sips of his coffee, he finally woke up enough to wonder how she had gotten his home phone number.

He checked his watch. Ten o'clock. Good timing. His ex-wife always went to ten o'clock mass. The kid liked to sleep in and go later. He called and woke her up.

"How's it going?" he asked.

"Fine." She sounded sleepy.

"I just thought I'd check up on you, kid. I've been pretty busy, and . . ."

"Mom's at church."

"I know. That's why I called. I wanted to talk to you. Are you awake?"

"Yeah, kinda. Are you okay?"

"Fine. How's school?"

"About the same."

"And Larry?"

"Gary."

"Whatever. You two still an item?"

"An item? Dad, how quaint."

"Give me a break, I'm old. You're still dating?"

"Yeah. He'll be here in . . . What time is it?"

"A little after ten."

"He'll be here in a couple of minutes."

"You're still in bed."

"Dad, he's coming to take me to mass."

"That's at twelve."

"We'll have breakfast first."

"Where?"

"Lighten up." She laughed. "We'll go out somewhere."

"Maybe I should let you go so you can get dressed."

"You're a stitch. What are you worried about? You think we're going to . . ."

"Never mind that. I just . . ."

"God, Dad. On Sunday morning?"

"Don't knock Sunday morning, kid. You'll . . . Never mind. I just wanted to . . ."

"I know."

". . . hear your voice, you know. See how you were doing."

"I'm fine. Really. How's it going in your bachelor pad?"

"Some pad. It's . . . I'm getting the hang of it. Kind of."

"You and Mom have your hearts set on this divorce thing, huh?"

"Looks like it."

"Yeah, it looks that way on this end, too."

"I guess you hear plenty over there, kid. But, I'd like you to remember, there's two sides to everything."

"I know."

"Well, I . . ."

"Just a sec, Dad. There's somebody at the door."

"Larry, I imagine."

"Gary."

"Whatever."

The Mexican on the phone had suggested a grill in Old Town, and Carlton had no idea what to expect. All he had to go on was the voice, the thick accent like the *bandito* in *The Treasure of the Sierra Madre*. The voice had told him to take a table near the window, that he would be contacted. He had not been there long when up walked a young man in a tasteful and expensive gray glen-plaid sport coat, navy slacks, and a powder blue shirt, a London Fog overcoat folded neatly on his arm.

"Good morning," said the young man.

"Good morning," Carlton answered, looking up into a strikingly handsome face with strong, lean features and just a bit of a sign of weariness around the eyes. The eyes themselves were clear and so black they glistened as they locked on his. Carlton looked away first, because looking into the young man's eyes made him nervous, and he did not put much stock in that business of outstaring people anyway.

Willy took a seat opposite Carlton that put his back to the room, and gave no sign that this concerned him. Carlton had expected it would, and had made a point of taking the chair with its back to the wall because he thought that was important. He did not realize that Willy was not worried about that because Johnny had preceded him and was watching his back.

They spent a not unpleasant hour together, and when they were through, Carlton finally knew exactly what Willy wanted from him. He already knew the downside, what was in store for him if he did not go along. If I could be sure he would only do to my wife what he had done to Charlotte, Carlton mused, I might call his bluff. She's become quite the nag lately. But he did not demand specifics of the young Hispanic; he did not even ask the question he wanted to ask. He wanted to ask if Willy had been the one on the phone, and he was toying with the idea that Willy was just the front man for the real bandits. Willy seemed too civilized for the work. That was how little Carlton Welborn III knew of the business he was in. When their conversation was ended, Willy rose and they shook hands on their deal. It was all very civil, and might have been about real estate for all anyone else in the place would have known. Carlton had given his word, and Willy had given him the details. It was a done deal. Pleasure doing business with you.

Clark put the question of how the waitress got his phone number on hold and around noon he made the rounds of his troops, calling them at home. They all were enjoying a day off, and the weather was too bad to be out and about. Nacho had not come up with anything solid, just a couple of people who had heard that Carlton Welborn III moved with a pretty fast crowd and did not mind cutting corners to make a buck. There were a few people who claimed he owed them money, a couple of lawsuits over business deals, nothing firm. Winager said he and Filmore had run down a half a dozen hooks and made them offers. He thought they might hear something in a day or two. That was about it. They'd know more on the Lincoln they'd found Charlotte Mayfield's body in tomorrow when the world went back to work. Clark called Spencer and learned that the DPS didn't know much more than he did. And his friend at Alcohol, Tobacco, and Firearms hadn't gotten back to him with anything on the Uzis. So that was it, nothing happening and nothing much likely to happen before tomorrow. Clark resigned himself to having a day off, watching a little football on the tube. The remaining two play-off games were on, and it beat staring at the walls. It was almost time for the first kickoff when he got a call from Sergeant Marino.

"Clark, you're not working today?"

"Can't find any work to do. You?"

"Nah, I'm at home. For a while, anyway. I'll probably go in this afternoon, try to whip some paperwork into shape. Got a call you might be interested in."

"Yeah?"

"Sergeant Maguire in Community Services."

"Yeah, I've been meaning to call and give him a hard time about the promotion. What did he have?"

"I guess you know he's fresh out of Vice. One of his snitches has a case to work off. Says he can do us some good on the van shooting in West Dallas."

"Really."

"Says it was a Mexican they call Crazy Frank."

Clark walked into the Crimes Against Persons office a little after one o'clock in the afternoon and found a lone clerk-typist at work in the big room in front. She was hammering out a stack of reports that made a slanted pile in her "in" basket. She knew Clark from before, and the beard and rough clothes did not throw her.

"How's it going?" Clark asked when he saw her.

"It's going. What did you think of the Broncos yesterday?"

"Didn't catch 'em. How'd they do?"

"Fumbled it away in the last two minutes."

"That's a shame. You lose any money on it?"

"Don't be silly, Sergeant Clark. It's illegal to bet on football. You know that."

"Yeah. Lost my head there for a second." Clark laughed a little as he made his way toward the offices. They called the Broncos "Cowboys West" these days, because of all their ex-Dallas players and coaches. The Cowboys had fallen on hard times, and local fans had to root for somebody.

He heard voices as he stepped around a corner into the

doorway of Sergeant Marino's office, and found the big sergeant leaned back in his swivel chair with his feet on his desk,
in conversation with a young-looking man he had seen around
but whose name he did not know.

"Sergeant Clark." Marino looked up. "Nothing better to
do?"

"Yeah, it comes from not having a personal life. I thought I'd
drop by and see what you'd come up with. You mind?"

"No, I don't mind. We're all on the same side, right?"
Marino said it in a pleasant tone, but with a bit of an edge to let
Clark know he had not forgotten about the name-calling the day
before.

"Right," Clark answered. "Am I interrupting anything?"

"Nah." Marino waved him in. "Come on in. You know Jim
Grimes, sergeant in Narcotics?"

Grimes leaned forward in his chair to offer his hand and
Clark took it, thinking he looked awfully young for a sergeant.
He was thinking that more and more these days, how young
sergeants looked, even lieutenants.

"Yeah, I've seen you around, don't think we've ever been
introduced."

"Grimes has some pretty good files on some of our dope
gangs," Marino explained. "I thought he might be able to make
Crazy Frank for us."

"Can you?" Clark asked.

"I'm not sure." Grimes nodded. He had a couple of spiral
binders on the floor beside him. "The gang thing has really
taken off in the last couple of years."

"They're into drugs?" Clark asked.

"Yeah. Crack, mostly. It's raised stakes all the way around."

"Kids?" Clark offered.

"A lot of it. Anywhere from nine years old into their early
twenties."

"So how many Crazy Franks you got in those books?"

"A few, probably. Nothing really rings a bell, though. We've
had your occasional drive-by shooting, but nothing on this
scale. Four bodies, automatic weapons, none of the dope taken
from the van. It's not the profile for our boys and girls."

"Don't we have some kind of nickname file on computer, Marino?" Clark asked.

"Yeah. I ran a query already. Nothing that matches."

"We've got our own file, of course," Grimes put in. "Same deal. We have a couple of Franks, but I checked and one of them was in the county jail when the killing went down, the other one is out of town, supposed to have moved to Houston with his family back in September."

"In Auto Theft, we keep books on our pro car thieves, but I can't say I remember any Crazy Franks," Clark said. "Besides, most of ours are speed freaks, biker trash, that kind. This was a crack deal, so . . ."

"Yeah, and I'd expect bikers to take the dope and the van if they made the hit," Grimes offered.

"Exactly," Clark agreed.

"Anybody home?" boomed a voice down the hall.

"Nobody but us chickens," Marino answered.

Two men appeared in the doorway, and Clark knew them both.

"Bill, you know these old hooks," Marino said, playing host. "Sergeant Grimes, this is Barney Oliver from Intelligence, and that is Captain Angstrom of TAC. Come in, gentlemen."

"You ain't got enough room in here, Marino. Don't CAPers have a conference room somewhere?" Oliver bitched amiably.

"Nah, we're working cops, we don't have time to have conferences. How about the outer office? Plenty of room out there."

"You do have a coffeepot, don't you?" Oliver asked.

"I think we can find you some coffee."

"Can I help you?"

Bobby Thurmon looked past a pair of empty desks toward the sound of the voice.

"Mr. Jones?"

"What is it?"

"I'm Bobby Thurmon, *Times Herald*. We spoke on the phone yesterday."

Zulu Jones stepped through his office door.

"Thought I'd stop by for a follow-up."

Bobby was surprised. Jones looked like a tight end in his file photo, but he was well under six feet tall. Jones waved the reporter into his office at the rear of the Black Pride Community Center and they settled into chairs on either side of a scrupulously neat desk.

"Follow-up on what?" Jones asked.

"The shooting."

"Been a lot of shootings."

"The one with the two dead cops."

"A black man died, too," Jones intoned, an eyebrow arched.

"One of the cops was black, Mr. Jones."

"Man in your paper said they were both blue."

"What are you doing?" Bobby asked, closing his notebook.

"Let's say I'm making a point."

"Let's say 'fuck it,' Mr. Jones. See you around."

"An attitude, Mr. Thurmon?"

"Long hours, mostly. You want to do this or not?"

"I can live without the press."

"Yeah. They tell me that's what Pinky Lafayette used to say, too."

Carlton Welborn III had a second meeting that Sunday, and he reflected upon the differences between the two as he pulled his Porsche off the pitted, curbless street and stopped in front of the gate. The gate, like the fence, was eight feet high chain link, with metal posts and four strands of rusty barbed wire on top. He honked his horn three short blasts, followed by a longer one, and sat looking over the fence at the sheet-iron roof beyond. He could not see through the fence because there were wide bands of some kind of plastic material woven among the spaces in the chain link to keep things on the inside private.

Willy had made a nice impression. Brunch in a familiar place, a quiet conversation he had no reason to mind being seen at by friends of his. If someone he knew had come over to their table, Carlton could have introduced Willy as a business associate. Everyone knew Carlton did business in Mexico. The oilfield equipment thing, even some speculation in resort development. It had all been very convenient, very deniable, an enormous relief after all he had imagined from the voice on the telephone, and what he knew had been done to the girl Charlotte.

The gate swung inward, and he drove into the lot. It was still cold and the sky was clearing, but the two men who closed the gate behind him wore only T-shirts and denim vests, and their breath vaporized and drifted away over their heads. Carlton parked the Porsche and stepped out gingerly, holding his pants legs up to keep his cuffs out of the mud.

Inside the sheet-iron building he wiped his feet on the concrete slab floor and noticed one of Mack's men, the blond one, had a bandage across his nose and a purple half-moon under one eye. There were the usual cars in various stages of cannibalization. On a rough iron rack to one side there was what he recognized as a gas tank from a luxury sedan; they had begun to cut it with a torch, and he saw that a hose ran from a spigot beside the wall and rested inside the neck of the tank so there would be no fire from gas residue in the tank. That much he had picked up from his infrequent visits to this place, that you had to fill a gas tank with water before you cut it with a torch. It was more than he had ever wanted to know, and he did not like coming here at all. He was out of his element here, and in danger of being compromised, exposed. Not at all like having brunch.

"He's in his office," one of the dirty henchmen said, grinning. "He'll see you now."

Carlton wiped his shoes again and rapped a knuckle on the closed door perfunctorily before entering.

"Ten-Four, roger and out, good buddy," said the man behind the battered wooden desk. He tossed the walkie-talkie down and met Carlton with a crooked smile. "You wasn't followed."

Carlton knew him as Mack, and beyond that knew hardly more than his pager number and this place where he seemed to do most of his work. The man had a face that put the lie to his smile.

CHAPTER 14

Sunday, 2:30 p.m.

"It's not any of your kid gangs," Barney Oliver explained to Sergeant Grimes. The five of them had arranged themselves in chairs around a couple of desks in the CAPers outer office, which was empty because everybody working the Jackson-Terry murders was out on the street. "None of this high-school shit."

"Really?" Grimes was sensitive about being by far the youngest man in the room, and it was narcotics they were talking about, after all.

"Really. Crazy Frank never saw the inside of a high school unless he burglarized one."

"You know him?" Marino asked.

"Yeah. He runs with two of his cousins, Willy and Johnny. They have Mexican names, but they like to Americanize for some reason."

"West Dallas?" Clark wondered aloud, thinking Barney enjoyed knowing secrets a little too much, wishing he would just let them all in on it without the joy-popping.

"Yeah, originally. That's their main turf, and that would be why they'd hit your Jamaicans if they were trying to expand into that neighborhood," Barney replied.

"It makes sense, then," Marino said, shaking his head. "Sounds like Maguire's C.I. could be for real."

"Did he give you his name, Sarge?"

"No. Maguire's at home—I told him I'd call if we came up with anything."

"I'd like to know who his boy is." Barney smiled softly.

"We'll see how it shakes out," Marino said. The mass murder was his case, and he made it clear without saying so that he would call the shots. He appreciated all the help he could get, but it was still his case, and he knew you had to be careful with snitches, for more reasons than one. Like calling them confidential informants, or C.I.'s, for instance. "What do you have on these guys? Got a hangout, headquarters, like that?"

"They're cagey. They move around, don't stay in one place more than a few days at a time." Barney Oliver was not checking any notes. Clark noticed he had not brought any binders with him, as young Sergeant Grimes had done. This was all coming off the top of his head. "I ran it by Organized Crime before I left the office . . . All they've got is rumors."

"O.C. works Sundays?" Clark asked.

"Nah, I called a guy at home."

"Restores my faith." Clark chuckled.

"So what do we do next?" Grimes wanted to know.

"I'll call Maguire. Maybe he can get a little more out of his man," Marino said.

"Do we have pictures of these Mexicans?" Clark asked.

"We don't," Barney admitted. "As far as I can find, they've never been handled. Not in Dallas, anyway."

"I'll check the county," Marino said, making a note for himself on the pad he carried in his pocket. "You got their real names, Barney?" Oliver pulled a scrap of paper out of his shirt pocket and read them off, and Marino wrote them down. "Anything else?"

"Yeah, I've got something," Captain Angstrom spoke up. "I was in the office going over some tactical intelligence reports . . . FYI stuff we share with other jurisdictions on special ops. I bumped into Barney and thought I'd sit in with y'all. I'm seeing things I don't like."

"What's that?" Marino asked, in his assumed role as moderator of the little group.

"Around the country, the gangs and dopers are going military. Automatic weapons, demolitions, small unit tactics. Whoever pulled that van ambush . . . we don't want to underestimate them. I've seen reports of claymore mines . . .''

"Where do they get claymores?" Grimes asked.

"Steal 'em, buy 'em black market from GI's," Barney put in. "We ran on a house in East Dallas last year, remember? Guy had enough army crap in there to blow up a couple of city blocks. LAW's, ammo, you wouldn't believe it. We couldn't even make a case stick, because the friggin' army wouldn't say it was their shit."

"You're kidding."

"Nah."

"Why?" Grimes was amazed.

"Go figure the goddamned army," Barney spat back. "Politics, who the hell knows?"

"You been talking to ATF about this?" Clark asked Angstrom.

"We try to stay in touch. You know anybody over there?"

"A friend of a friend."

"Ask him. I'll take anything I can get."

"Okay." Clark nodded. "How about the FBI, DEA? They got anything?"

"If they do, they're not telling us about it." Angstrom shook his head.

"Why not?" Grimes asked, thinking he knew the answer.

"They don't say," Angstrom replied. "Word is they think we have internal problems."

"Like what?" Grimes insisted.

"A leak maybe."

"Bullshit," Marino spat.

"Probably, but the lines are down, bullshit or not." Angstrom did not want to say any more than that, did not want to put too fine a point on it by saying the leak was thought to be in Narcotics.

"I know. We're feeling it, too," Grimes admitted.

The door opened and Bob Marx walked in with a manila envelope under his arm.

"Raise up, goddamnit!" Barney Oliver yelled in mock alarm. "Internal Affairs. It's a raid!"

• • •

"That's it?" the big man asked idly, gnawing on a dirty fingernail. "That's what he wanted?"

Carlton had not taken a seat in either of the mismatched chairs opposite Mack's desk. He had not taken off his hat, his gloves, or his coat. He had expected an ugly snarl of rage at the news, but there was just this troubling pensiveness. Carlton liked to imagine he understood Mack the Knife. In his private thoughts, lying awake in bed beside his skeptical wife, he even flattered himself that he handled the big man. He did not like being surprised by him now.

"Isn't that enough? He wants to muscle in on my . . . our operation. He wants to up the ante beyond all reason. A hundred kilos of cocaine, for God's sake! An increase of that magnitude simply redefines the whole thing. We're not . . ."

Mack waved a paw to silence him and replaced the finger in his mouth with another one.

"So much the better," he said. "Let the little greaser have his big deal. Make the call."

"You're not serious."

"The hell I'm not. We let him use our connections . . . excuse me, your connections, on the Mexican side to load up. His people get it across the border. Once it's here, we muck the little cocksucker and we're sitting pretty with a hundred keys of coke, no overhead."

"Muck him?"

"Rip him off, whack him and take the goddamned dope. I like it."

"Jesus . . ." Carlton felt suddenly too warm in the shabby room. This thing was expanding beyond his limitations, which he knew well enough, if he admitted them only to himself. "Kill them, you mean?"

"Or else they probably wouldn't let us have the dope, stupid."

"We couldn't just . . . steal it?"

"You're a goddamned riot, you are." Mack laughed aloud, genuinely amused. "You want them little fuckers looking for you the rest of your life, which would probably be less than a week? You haven't forgot what they did to little what's her name, have you?"

"Charlotte. No, I haven't."

"And they weren't even mad at her, man. That was just to let you know they are serious people. You ever heard of a 'Colombian necktie'?"

"I . . . I don't think so."

"It's a cute little trick the greasers do. You take a guy, see, and you cut his throat, longways." Mack raised his chin and drew a line from above his adam's apple down to his collarbone with a thumb to illustrate. "Then they reach inside his neck and grab his tongue, see. And they pull his goddamned tongue out through the slit and they lay his tongue down over his chest like a friggin' necktie, see?"

"I see."

"And they leave him like that for his friends to find. That's the kind of people we are dealing with here. You arc dealing with, I mean. You're the one who had fuckin' brunch with the guy."

"They aren't Colombian. Are they? I mean, they're Americans, Mexican-Americans . . ."

"Same thing. Fucking greasers. You want to take any chances?"

"No. Of course not."

"Me neither. So we'll do it my way. Find a pay phone. Make the calls and set the thing up. You told this asshole Willy you had a deal, didn't you?"

"Of course, but I didn't . . ."

"Crossing your fingers behind your back don't count in this business."

"Uh, my people . . . down there . . . they might balk at something this big. What do I tell them?"

"Nothing. It's one load, like the rest. All they're gonna see is payday. Don't worry about it."

"Okay. That's it, then?"

"Not quite. What's his offer?"

"Offer?"

"He wants your Mexican connections, what the hell's your cut?"

"Oh. Twenty percent on delivery here. Twenty percent cash, or a third of the dope. My choice."

"You'll take the dope, not the cash. He'll jump at that, because he's got expenses. Did he say anything about your dealers up here?"

"No, nothing."

"Figures. He wants you should take the dope, not the money, so he ain't gonna fuck with your peddlers . . . not yet. That comes later."

"You think he's going to try to take me over?"

"I think he's gonna take your ass over and kill you and fuck your wife and then kill her, and live in your house and drive your goddamned Porsche and wear your nice cashmere overcoat there. That's what I think."

"I see."

"Because he's a fucking greaser and that's the way they are. Not like me. You can trust me."

"Of course."

"Say it like you mean it, Carlton."

"I do mean it, Mack. I trust you, or I wouldn't be here," Carlton said with all the conviction he could muster, wishing he had the last year to live over again. "Obviously."

"You bet your ass, 'obviously.' I've been straight with you, ain't I?"

"Absolutely."

"Yeah. So don't you forget that. Don't you get to thinking this smooth little bastard is your kind of people. Don't start thinking maybe you'd rather do business with him than with me, will you, Carlton?"

"Don't be . . . Of course not. Farthest thing from my mind."

"You supposed to talk to him again today?" Mack asked.

"Only to let him know when I have things set down there," Carlton said. "He doesn't know . . . I didn't let on to him that I had . . ."

"That you had an associate you'd have to confer with? Good, keep it like that. The simpler the better, and the less he knows about my part of the thing, the better. I've got my heart set on surprising the guy, get me?"

"Naturally."

"You supposed to call him or does he call you?"

"He'll call me. I don't have any way of getting in touch with him."

"The boy's not dumb. Okay, set it up as soon as you leave here. And when he calls next time, act like it's all set and everything, but act like you're still kind of reluctant, like you did today when you met. These guys are like wolves, they can smell you when you play around with them. And get a number where you can call him, let him convince you he'll come through with his side of the thing when the dope comes in. I ain't worried about that, he'll be in touch all right, because he ain't through with you yet by a long shot, but you act like you're worried about that part of it, because that's how he'll expect you to be. Get me?"

"I get . . . I understand."

"Good. Now get outta here."

"Yes, I'd better see to things. You'll want to hear from me after I've spoken with him?"

"Yeah, call and run it down for me. On my pager. I won't be far from a phone. I've got plans tonight, but you won't be interrupting anything."

"Plans?"

"A little R and R for the boys. We got a bitch needs her attitude adjusted."

"Yes, women need a firm hand, don't they?"

"I'd say so. See ya around."

"We're clean, honest," Marino cracked as Marx joined the group. "You don't have pictures, do you?"

"I wanna see my lawyer," Barney Oliver chimed in. "I ain't talkin' without my mouthpiece."

"Knock it off, will you, guys?" Marx shrugged with a good-natured grin.

"It comes with the territory," Clark admonished him.

"Yeah, it's what you get for working with the Kefauver Committee," Barney put in.

Clark thought the Kefauver thing was a little too close to the mark to be very funny. Kefauver had investigated the rackets with his Senate committee, and a Dallas lieutenant had testified about the time mobsters came to town with plans to buy their way in. The whole mob thing was a touchy point as far as he was concerned. He had known that lieutenant, who wound up working in the jail until he retired, and they had chiefs who'd insisted there was no organized crime in Dallas, which he and almost everybody else knew was bullshit. For that matter, he thought it curious at least that with all the gambling in Dallas there did not seem to be many cases made on bookies from year to year. Intelligence handled those cases, and for that and other reasons Clark thought it irksome that Barney was the one to bring up the Kefauver thing.

"You guys having some kind of a summit conference in here?" Marx asked. "Am I interrupting?"

"Nah, we're just cutting up a little business. What'cha got?" Marino, still the emcee, spoke for them.

"Well . . ." Marx hesitated for only a second, but long enough that the others took note of it. "I've got a couple of shots here . . . some people I'd like to get ID'ed."

Marx opened the manila envelope and tugged out a wad of black-and-white glossies. He handed the top half to Marino, the rest to Barney Oliver.

"Where'd these come from?" Barney wanted to know.

"Casa Linda. Off of Ferguson Road," Marx replied, as if he did not understand that Oliver had meant what kind of operation. "Know any of these people?"

Barney scanned a few and passed them to Clark, who wished he had brought his notebooks, the stuff his guys had put together on their active car thieves. He spotted a familiar face in the second photograph. There were two men and a woman walking down a steeply sloping driveway, with the rear ends of three cars at angles to one side. It was a nighttime shot and the light was not very good, but the definition was decent. A surveillance photo, and a pretty good job.

"This guy here," Clark said, holding up the photo.

"Yeah?" Marx looked hopeful, a little surprised.

"Yeah. He's a speed freak. We handled him a while back, when they were stealing 280-Z's like there was no tomorrow. Righteous name escapes me, but he goes by 'Turbo John.' We ran on a fleabag motel off of Thornton, out toward Buckner Boulevard. Got him and two speed whores out of one room."

"Great. Turbo John you said?" Marx was writing it down.

"Yeah. Hang on a second." Clark turned around to face a computer terminal and entered the nickname. "Shit," he said.

"What's the matter?"

"System's down," Clark answered. "The library must be logging overdue books."

"You're kidding," Marx said.

"What do you think, we've got a dedicated system?" Clark slapped the keys to cancel his query. "Anyway, that's him. You can run it later. Or I'll check our files manually in the morning."

"That's fine," Marx assured him.

"Or I could run down the hall to Auto Theft and see if I can pull the case report."

"Don't go to the trouble, Sergeant Clark. I'll run it down later. This is great, thanks."

"We handled this one," Grimes spoke up. "I think I may have him in one of my books."

Grimes thumbed through one of his binders and came up with a name and mug shot of another of the guests leaving the party where Stef Nugent had been the night before. Clark borrowed Grimes's other notebook and was not surprised to find familiar faces in it.

"See, this is what I've been trying to tell the bosses for I don't know how long," Clark announced to the group. "You guys in Narcotics, Intelligence, us in Auto Theft, we're all chasing around after the same bunch of scumbags. You've got files over there, we've got 'em over here, and you never know what's what unless we get together like this and compare notes. I don't know what the hell Organized Crime has on any of them, because I don't have a high enough security clearance to even park in their lot. I'm telling you, we gotta get our shit together here."

"Nice speech, Clark." Barney pretended to applaud.

"Yeah, you got my vote," Marino joined, standing up to mean the meeting was over. "Okay, I got work to do. You guys make anybody else for IAD here?"

"A couple look familiar," Grimes said, balancing a notebook on his lap and holding a couple of the photos between his fingers. "Why don't you come down to the office with me, Marx, and we'll look 'em all over, see what we come up with."

"Fine," Marx agreed, thinking there was a lot to what Clark had said, and thinking he had been dumb lucky to walk in on this crowd sitting around on a Sunday afternoon.

"Oh, speaking of bikers," Grimes began as an afterthought, "Vice is working on something . . ."

"What?" Clark asked.

Grimes hesitated. He had been briefed on the Vice-Persons undercover operation targeted at a biker, but part of the briefing had been the importance of playing it close to the vest. "Operational security" somebody had called it. And this guy from IAD, what was the deal with him and where did the photos come from? IAD didn't work crimes, they worked cops.

"I'm not sure," he said. "Something with CAPers. You know what it is, Marino?"

"I heard something," Marino admitted. He didn't seem eager to cut it up with them either, and Grimes felt he had made the right call. "But my plate's full with this multiple. You know how it is. My crew has all they can say grace over . . ."

"How about you, Marx?" Barney Oliver cut in. "What kind of a deal are you working on? What's the story on these pictures of yours?"

"Hey, I . . ."

"Too big to talk about, huh?" Barney laughed harshly. "Same old shit. You guys are worse than the FBI."

"Knock it off, Barney. He's got orders and that's that," Marino said. "Green is handling it for us. He's after a biker they call Mack the Knife. I don't know how it ties in with anything or if it does, but it's not a secret from you guys as far as I know. Green's working it with Grouton in Vice. They've got a couple of people working undercover, keeping tabs on his hangouts. He's some double badass likes to cut up women. Runs whores, steals cars. That's all."

"The hell you say!" Clark put in.

"What?" Marino demanded, hearing some kind of accusation in Clark's voice or his attitude.

"The blonde in the Lincoln, Marino. The case I'm trying to get somewhere on. How did she compare with your boy's work? Is that the way he cuts 'em? Does he have some kind of signature?''

"I don't know, to tell you the truth," Marino admitted, not liking that he had been too busy to put the two together, and even more that Clark had a point. "Green has the file. I didn't make the connection . . . You think there's a link?''

"I don't know," Clark answered. He had meant to follow that with something pointed about being cut out of the loop, but he saw that Marino did not want to fight about it and decided to soften it a little. "I'd like to see the file on this guy, see what your people think.''

"We can do that. I'll call Green at home. Anything else?''

"Yeah, I'd like to know who this guy is you and Vice are laying traps for. We might have something on him," Barney put in. "We keep files, too, you know.''

"All right, all right, you guys." Marino put his hands up to say he didn't want to fight about it.

"Maybe we ought to start over, play like we all work for the same department," Angstrom offered. He said it softly, with a little smile. He was the ranking officer present. He liked what had been going on here, the sharing of information, and hoped they might have stumbled onto something that could become regular. "Sounds like we have a couple of closely held operations that may overlap. What advice can IAD give us? Are there risks in cutting this up among everybody represented here?''

"That's not my call, Captain," Marx said, with an apologetic shrug. He saw the potential, too, but he was not going to be the one to let it out that they were tailing Stef Nugent.

"Okay, let's do this," Angstrom said. "Let's say we reconvene this meeting in the morning, when all the bosses are in the house. Everybody get everything cleared or closed, one way or the other. Then let's sit down again and put our cards on the table. Anybody think that's not a good idea?''

Nobody objected. Marino and Clark nodded vigorously, and Angstrom had decided they might be the two most critical anyway.

"Okay, let's say ten o'clock. That's time enough to run it by the bosses, not enough time for any of them to have second thoughts.''

"Where?" Barney Oliver asked.

"How about our place?" Angstrom offered. "We've got the room, and it's out of the way."

Nobody had any objections to that, either. TAC's offices were on the second floor of the Central Patrol Division on the east end of downtown, what had been the Murray Gin property. It was not City Hall, which was in its favor. Angstrom thought there might be objections, the political kind, if somebody thought he was trying to put a show together. He could justify his involvement on the grounds that, whatever happened, when the bad guys were located, it would likely be TAC who went in after them. But he knew that would be a poor defense if a boss felt his turf threatened.

CHAPTER 15

Sunday, 5:00 p.m.

Clark went back to his apartment after the meeting that turned into a summit conference at CAPers and sat down and deciphered his notes. Before he even made a drink, he got on the horn to all his junkyard dogs and gave each of them his chores for the next morning, including one to catch any new business that might come up, like impounded cars that did not check out for ID numbers. His Salvage Unit had one advantage over most teams of investigators, in that they did not work an assigned caseload. The routine auto theft beefs that came in every day went to the regular auto theft investigators. The dogs pulled salvage yard inspections and followed up anything that turned up. When they saw a pattern, they worked it out, and that was how they made cases on auto theft rings. Theirs was a particularly arcane area of technical expertise, and they had been called out around the state to help other cops. They exercised initiative, and that was one reason it was important for Clark to be on good terms with his boss. That had not been a problem with Lieutenant Felty, but he did not think it would be easy breaking in the new kid, Bonny. First he would have to get past this thing with Carlton Welborn, the calls from the chief and all that business. It was a bad time to be breaking in new talent, but Clark could not do anything about that.

He called Spencer again and took it on himself to invite him to the meeting Monday morning at TAC. What the hell, Clark thought. Nobody said not to invite outsiders. And he had been a cop long enough to know that if you asked permission first you just gave somebody a chance to say no. When he had done everything he could think of to set things up for Monday morning, he got up from the phone and made himself a drink. Mostly Jack Daniel's this time, with just a touch of 7-UP.

Then he decided to do something that would really help him relax. He climbed the stairs and opened the door of what he liked to think of as his "studio." It was the unused second bedroom, but he had rigged it up to suit him.

There was a table against the window where the light was best. There was not much light now, because the winter days were so short, but he peeled the moist cheesecloth off the clay figure and took a seat to plan his next move. He was pleased with the way the rider had begun to take shape, and fiddled with a couple of his sculpting tools, a looped wire and a scraping blade, as he pictured how he wanted the horse's neck to bend. It would be a piece of frozen action, the cowboy's right hand thrown back over his head, his left on the reins, low over the pommel of the old-fashioned saddle with the high cantle. Clark rested the blade on the damp clay where his cowboy's left arm disappeared into the lumpish unworked stuff. He looked up at the pictures he had tacked to a bulletin board on the wall for reference. There were photos from books on equine anatomy, a couple of photocopies of Remington prints. The telephone rang. He cursed softly and listened for the sound of a voice on his machine.

"Sergeant Clark, this is . . . the lady you rescued last night. I . . ."

Clark broke in. "Yeah, I'm here. How's it going?"

"Okay. You got a couple of minutes?"

"I guess so. What can I do for you?"

"Well . . . I've got a little time on my hands myself. How about if I buy you a cup of coffee or something?"

"Uh, yeah, that'd be all right. You mind telling me how you got this number?"

"No, I don't mind. What would be a good place for you? For coffee, I mean."

"You name it," he said. Okay, so she does not want to tell

me on the phone. Interesting. "What part of town are you in?"

"Let's make it Denny's on Central."

"Okay, when?"

"Say in about an hour?"

"I'll see you there."

He hung up thinking about it. He wanted to know how she had gotten his unlisted home number, and there was always a chance she knew something. Maybe she had a line on Charlotte Mayfield. He had seen the waitress he had asked about Charlotte talking to this girl right before the scuffle, and maybe that was what this was about. His broncobuster would wait.

Mack called back a few minutes after Carlton paged him.

"What's up, partner?"

"I spoke with . . . the guy, you know."

"Yeah, yeah. So?"

"So it's set. This week."

"He's got his end set up?"

"He says no problem. Friday at the latest. What do you think?"

"I think he sounds like a mover. He'll call you when the shipment arrives?"

"Yeah, that's the deal."

"Okay. Keep in touch."

"Right."

Carlton Welborn looked up from the phone to find his wife watching him over a martini.

"Who was that?" she asked.

"Business."

"Do you have to go out?"

"Why?"

"You've been doing a lot of your business at odd hours lately."

"Things are tight, you know that. I have to hustle to make it these days."

"Are they? Are things really bad?"

When everything had collapsed underneath him, oil and real estate, the savings and loans, and finally the stock market crash, Charlotte's friends had shown him a way out. They taught him that people will always find the money for what they want, especially when they can't afford what they need. Yuppies who could not keep up the payments on their BMWs would still pay cash for drugs. Carlton knew people in Mexico from his business dealings there, and Charlotte's friend Mack had shown him the value of Mexican friends. Mack sent stolen cars south to the border for Carlton's friends, who did not mind bringing cocaine across to pay for them. Later, they added stolen guns, and were paid with even more cocaine.

Carlton thought of it as commodities trading. He did not worry about the law because he never touched the cars, guns, or drugs. It was a profitable joint venture, practically risk-free. But now there was trouble.

"Nothing I can't deal with."

She sipped her drink and tipped her chin to strike a thoughtful pose. He was slouched in his overstuffed leather chair in their tastefully appointed den. The room was dark except for a lamp on over his shoulder. She stood leaning against the doorway. He turned to look at her and she seemed to be smiling at him, but he could not be sure because she was silhouetted by the light behind her.

Willy was wrong about her, Carlton thought. She was not skinny. She still had the lean, tight body that had caught his eye when she was a sorority girl at SMU, when he had been a frat stud. They were made for each other, he had thought then, and he did not like to admit mistakes.

"Would you like a drink?" she asked.

"Please."

He had been right not to tell her he had no plans to go out. She reappeared with a pitcher of martinis and an extra glass, and he watched her coil her legs underneath her on the couch at the end nearest him. When she handed him the cool long-stemmed glass, she made a point of brushing her hand over his and fixed a warm gaze on him that he returned blankly, as if he did not suspect her intention.

"You've been stoic about your business troubles," she said.

"Stoic?" He chuckled. "Hardly so noble, babe. I'm holding my own."

"It's difficult, I know." She smiled. "You'd tell me if I should cut back, wouldn't you?"

"Cut back?"

"I know I'm not . . . I don't particularly make a point of managing money, Carlton. If you need, I could . . ."

"Don't be silly."

"I want to be supportive," she purred. "You can tell me anything, you know. I'm not . . ."

"You needn't worry," he assured her, laughing inside at the thought of how she might react if he told her everything. "We're in good shape. It just takes a bit more . . . effort these days, that's all. It won't last forever. Really, don't worry."

"All right, I won't. Did you say you have plans to go out?"

"I didn't say. Why, do you have plans?"

"As a matter of fact, I do."

"Oh?"

"Yes." With that she dropped her empty glass soundlessly to the carpet and rose, uncoiling toward him. He smiled as she loomed over him and tilted his head, still slouching in the chair, to meet her lips with his. Unmoving, he felt the weight of her as she crossed the space between them and settled over him, her hands on his chest.

"But if I did . . . have to . . . go out . . . " he teased her, murmuring his words between her kisses.

"But you don't, do you? You don't have to go . . . not if I could think of something you could do here . . . something that would be . . . better . . . ?"

It reminded him of a time when they were dating and she was jealous of another girl. Determined to keep him, she had made love to him with such conviction that he would never need anyone else. She had always reacted this way. First the biting remarks and sarcasm, then this.

"But if it were business, babe . . . Something important . . ."

"You tell me, Carlton. You tell me what's important." Her hands were on him then, opening his pants, and she was kissing his throat, his chest, his ribs, playfully, as she worked her way down and took his sex in her hands. "You tell me."

And then she did not talk any more for a while. He put one hand on her head and held his drink in the other. He put a stop

to her teasing and made her do it the way he liked it. She would
have resisted, but he insisted with the hand and sipped his drink
at the same time, and she relented and made the noises he liked.
He told himself that he might be losing control of the under-
world thing, that Mack the Knife and this hard, smooth kid
Willy might be muscling in on him there, but there was still this.
He still had this. He laughed silently, his mouth opening to
show his teeth as he came in her mouth.

The Denny's on Central was almost as busy as usual, with the
break in the weather. Clark did not see the girl, but it had been
smoky and dark in the club and he knew he might not recognize
her in the brightly lit restaurant. He let the waitress, a lady who
looked about his mom's age and who was too far into her shift
to waste any energy on a big smile, lead him to a booth by the
window where he took a seat facing the door.

She came in before he finished his coffee, and he noticed that
she looked the room over and seemed to register the two young
uniformed cops in a booth toward the back. He could tell she
saw him but she only showed it with a bit of a smile, nothing
that would attract attention. She waved off the waitress and
made her way down the aisle between two rows of booths
toward him. When she was close, Clark slid out of the booth
and stood up.

"Clark?" she asked.

"Yes, ma'am."

"Are you going somewhere?"

"No, ma'am."

"Oh, I see. Guess I'm not used to manners."

Randi Stoner slid into the booth in the seat across from him,
and Clark took his seat again. She was dressed for the weather,
in jeans and a sweater under a down jacket she took off and laid
on the seat beside her with her purse. With her hair pulled back
into a ponytail, she looked awfully young, and he did not see
any signs of the hardness he expected. She was attractive, in a
natural and unpremeditated way, the way a young woman can
be. She looked . . . healthier than he had thought she would,
somehow. A waitress stopped by to refill Clark's coffee, and
Randi said she would have coffee, too. When the waitress had

left, Randi looked down at her hands and Clark waited for her to speak.

"I appreciate you meeting me like this," she said.

Clark nodded, still waiting for her to get down to it.

"I, uh . . . I'm not sure how to go about this," she said.

The two cops passed by on their way out, both of them young guys Clark did not recognize, and Clark noticed that the girl looked up as they passed and thought he caught something in her face. Neither of them spoke to them, but one of them looked from her to Clark as he went by. Clark watched her for some reaction, but she looked down at her hands again and the waitress brought her coffee.

Clark watched the cops settling up at the cash register. The same one who had paused to look him over on the way out shot a look in their direction again. Then they shared a laugh with the cashier and went out.

"Did he know you?" Clark asked.

"Who?"

"That officer."

"Yeah."

"Okay."

She put sweetener and a little cream in her coffee and stirred it, then looked up at him. "Look . . . I don't know your first name."

"Bill."

"Okay, Bill, the thing is . . ."

"He busted you for something, right? It happens."

"We were in the academy together."

"Excuse me?"

"I'm a police officer, Bill."

"The hell you say." So, the officer made her, of course, but he did not know Clark, so he did not speak to her because he figured she might be working some kind of undercover deal. Good for him. Clark was glad to see somebody was still teaching them that.

"Randi Stoner, Vice."

"Okay." He drank a little coffee. "Guess that explains how you got my home phone number."

"Yeah, I thought we'd better check signals."

"You have your ID with you?"

"I'll show you mine if you'll show me yours," she answered. "All I saw last night was a business card."

"Yeah, I try not to flash the badge around if I can help it. But then, you did get my number from the Report Section."

"Humor me. It's my first time out."

Bill laughed and reached into a pocket of his field jacket. He showed her the badge case with the badge and ID card without being obvious to anyone else in the place. She put her purse on the table and did the same.

"Okay, we're both official." Bill smiled.

"I don't know."

"What?"

"The picture on your ID. When was that thing taken? That's a baby picture you've got there, and with the beard, I'm not sure . . ."

"Yeah, it's a Matthew Brady tintype. Might be worth something someday. Show a little respect, will you?"

"So, that's the main thing I had to tell you. No big mystery."

"You could have done that over the phone."

"There is one other thing."

"Oh?"

"I didn't report that little incident in the club last night."

"I guess you have a good reason."

"Nice response. I appreciate that."

"You can explain it to me. Start with what kind of a deal you're working on."

A little over an hour later, they had eaten, the waitress had cleared their table and freshened their coffee several times, and Randi Stoner had told Bill Clark everything she wanted him to know. As it turned out, it was more than she had thought she would tell him, and it went beyond her first undercover assignment. Bill found he did not mind listening. He told her about his daughter and his pending divorce, but not about his trying to sculpt. Funny the secrets you save, he thought. She said she had heard stories about him, and asked why they called him Wild Bill.

"Ancient history." He smiled ruefully.

"Like the time you called in drunk from Nuevo Laredo half an hour before your shift?"

"It was Matamoros. But yeah, that kind of stuff."

"No wonder you're getting divorced." She wished she had not said that.

"Yeah, I had it coming the first time. But I really worked at this one."

"Sorry, it's none of my business, one way or the other."

"Don't worry about it."

"Level with me," she said, changing the subject. "Did I screw up by not reporting the incident?"

"Did I, by not arresting the guy?"

"You didn't have a complainant."

"It happened in my presence. I could have charged him with disorderly conduct if nothing else."

"Why didn't you?"

"Truthfully? I didn't want to screw with the paperwork or the court time for a pissant misdemeanor, which I figured was all it would be because this little waitress wouldn't stand up, probably wouldn't even be around anymore by the time the case came up."

"If you'd known I was an officer?"

"I'd have killed him."

She looked at him hard and knew he meant it.

"You were trying to get a line on a dancer?" she asked, as if the matter-of-fact way he had mentioned killing the man made her want to change the subject.

"Name's Charlotte Mayfield. She turned up dead in the trunk of a Lincoln at the pound."

"I'll ask around."

"No you won't. You've got enough to worry about with your own deal. I'll handle mine."

"Okay."

"Give me the vitals on this mad dog you're looking for."

She rattled it off and he jotted it down on the back of the page off the legal pad he had brought from home. She had it all memorized, and he did not think she left anything out.

"Another thing," he offered, when that was out of the way.

"I wouldn't be surprised if your friend with the broken nose showed up in the club again."

"You think?"

"Stranger things have happened. Tell your backup about him."

"What do I tell them?"

"That's up to you. Tell them what he did, only say he did it to one of the other girls. Say he gave you a hard time and leave out the details. Just don't think you're going to handle that stupid little fucker by yourself."

"Okay."

"And give some thought to your hardware. That pager deal didn't work so well last night."

"I think I've fixed that. I did some tailoring on my costume."

"I don't guess you've figured out a way to carry a gun in that outfit."

"Are you kidding? It's all I can do to hide my . . ."

"Tits?"

She nodded and laughed, looking away. "Oh yeah, that's right," she said. "You got a pretty good look last night, didn't you?"

"I was busy. Honest, I was keeping an eye on your friend with the deviated septum."

"Guess I'll have to take your word for that."

"Have I ever lied to you?"

CHAPTER 16

Monday, 1:00 a.m.

Peter and Dick went in the club to look the place over and Mack the Knife waited outside in the van. Blondie, with his broken nose held in place by a dirty bandage, waited with Mack. He would not go inside at all until Mack and the boys had things set up, because they did not want the manager to spook and call the cops, which he might do if he saw Blondie walk in.

"I'm t-telling you, man. I'm t-t-telling you . . ."

Mack was tired of hearing it. The skinny little son of a bitch had been at it all day, talking about what he was going to do to the bitch.

"You ain't telling me nothing," Mack muttered. "I do the telling, and if you could handle your business I wouldn't have to waste my time on this shit, so just shut the hell up."

Blondie was in the passenger seat of the van, Mack in back where he would not be seen if anybody got nosy. He had business, and he did not want any extra trouble. It was the principle of the thing with Mack. People at the club knew Blondie was one of his people, and he couldn't have some beer slinger breaking his nose without some payback. And if the dude with the gun dealt himself in, so much the better.

Mainly, what Mack had on his mind was this thing with Carlton Welborn and the Mexicans. That could make a score worth shouting about if it worked out right. But before he could enjoy it, he would have to cover his tracks on the girl he and

Blondie had killed out in Pleasant Grove. He had a couple of things working. This cop bitch, Stef Nugent, was supposed to do something about that. She said she could find out what the homicide cops had on the case. Maybe she could lose their evidence, or screw it up.

Mack had turned her out with good dope. He had her tied up every way you could think of, videotapes, Polaroids, the works. Stef was not going to make any trouble for him, but lately she had been acting like just another speed whore, and he had all of those he needed. She had been aces at first, put him onto some competitors ripe for rip-offs. Mack and the boys went in like they were the cops. They had raid jackets and ball caps, the whole nine yards. Half of the guys he burned probably thought it really was the cops that ripped them off. He liked that.

Another thing he might do about the murder case was let Blondie take the rap. He was next to useless. Maybe if Blondie did this waitress the same way they had done the thing in the Grove, Mack could make a call and Blondie would take the fall. He mulled it over. It needed work, he thought. And the thing with the Mexicans came first.

Dick and Peter came back cussing and shaking their heads. They climbed into the van like they thought he might take it out on them.

''What?'' Mack demanded.

''She ain't in there, Mack.''

''Why not?''

''She worked the early shift today. Got off at six.''

''Give me a break. Who told you that?''

''One of the other waitresses.''

''Her name's Betty,'' Peter volunteered, like Mack gave a shit about her name.

''And the manager, what's his name?'' Dick added.

''Charlie somethin'.'' Peter was the one for names.

''You asked the manager about her, about the waitress from last night?''

''Yeah,'' says Dick, looking at Peter out of the corner of his eye. ''It was his idea.''

''Yeah, yeah. So did he recognize you from last night, from when you was in there with Blondie last night?''

"I . . . I don't know. Prob'ly. I guess."

"And you told him you was looking for this waitress for . . . ?"

"Huh?"

"For what reason? Why did you tell him you was looking for her?"

"I didn't say. I didn't give him no reason, man."

"Okay. Okay, screw it. Let's get out of here. She'll be back tomorrow night?"

"Yeah, she works till closing."

"Okay, so it's tomorrow night instead. Come on, let's get the hell on the road. I got things to do."

Blondie crawled out of his seat and into the back, and the other two settled into the seats. As they pulled out of the parking lot into the street, Peter remembered the waitress's name. He was trying to be thorough.

"Her name is Randi, Mack. With an *i.*"

"Thank you," Mack said from the dark rear of the van, and Peter, oblivious of sarcasm, smiled. He had done good, he thought.

Doing sixty-five in the big rented Olds was like sitting still, but Willy left the cruise control on and put up with it because he did not want to get stopped by the Highway Patrol. The credit card he had used for the rental matched his bogus driver's license, and it had gone through without a hitch. He did not mind paying top dollar for ID he could use without making trouble for himself. It was his cover identity, like it said in his mail-order books. Frank could make fun of his reading material, but he was serious about his business, and there was good information out there if you knew where to look.

Willy was wearing his gray slacks and tassle loafers with his blue blazer. He did not look like a gang boss, and he thought he could con his way out of a stop if he had to, but there was no point in taking chances.

Frank snored on the the seat beside him, like a kid on a trip with his daddy. It was not so much that Willy thought he might need Frank on this run; it was that he did not want to leave Frank behind with just Johnny to watch him. Johnny was too

cool, too low-key, to handle Frank if he got the itch to do
something stupid, so Willy had him along. He would have to
find something to do with him when it came time for the meet,
because you couldn't take Frank anywhere he didn't piss somebody off, and these were people Willy definitely did not want
upset. They were sitting on the key to his future. A hundred
keys to his future, Willy thought, and laughed softly behind the
wheel of the Olds, shaking his head and laughing quietly at his
own joke, as the big car breezed through the night headed south
on I-35. It was just over four hundred miles from Dallas to
Laredo; at sixty-five miles an hour, with a couple of stops for
gas, they would get there about breakfast time.

Everything had turned to shit, as far as Ned could see. Reggie
was dead, and Curtis spent all his time making sure Ned and
Stone knew he was still calling the shots. Ned could not see
where anything was being done to get them out of Dallas. Split
the hell up and get on the damned road; that was what Ned
knew they ought to do, ought to have already done. But Curtis
was having none of that, and Ned was through trying to talk
sense to him after one half-assed try that nearly ended up in a
shooting. These goddamned Jamaicans did not even want him
going out for something to eat or to use the phone, or a damned
thing. It was plain to see that they did not trust him and he
thought that was pretty funny, in a no-laughing way, that here
he was the outsider again. Still, he told himself. Still the odd
man out. Just like in the army, in the white man's world, you
name it. I just had to throw in with these ignorant-assed Jamaicans, he thought, careful that nothing he thought showed on his
face. Serves me right.

They were holed up in what Curtis assured him was a "safe
house," a place picked out ahead of time for just such a situation. It did have some food stashed in a closet, but these Jamaicans were so ignorant that they had not put up stuff in cans, and
a lot of it was spoiled. It was a little shotgun frame house which
Ned knew from growing up in Dallas that white people used to
live in, but he had trouble believing it. They had made it to the
car after the shooting in the apartment building and went fast
but legal out Hawn Freeway before the cops got everything in

South Dallas shut down. He knew this neighborhood used to be called "Hungry Heights," and he could remember when the old Kaufman Pike drive-in theater used to be a big deal. Here they sat in one of these shacks the white Grovites had left behind when blacks moved out of South Dallas and Oak Cliff into Pleasant Grove. All the streets in the little neighborhood had girls' names, and out the back window Ned could see the lights of Hawn Freeway not far off across vacant fields, and in the daytime he could see the used-car lots and whatever else on the other side of the freeway. Safe house my ass, he thought, at his post watching out a back window. Ain't nothing in this son of a bitch gonna stop no bullets except me.

It was ten minutes after nine Monday morning, and Lieutenant Bonny was explaining the importance of community relations to Sergeant Clark in the lieutenant's office in Auto Theft, downtown. Clark was listening patiently, or pretending to, having made a point of being at his own office at the auto pound early to get the junkyard dogs started on their respective chores and to pick up all his files. He was waiting for an opening so he could make some kind of apology that he would try to make sound sincere and then he could get the hell out and get ready for the meeting in TAC at ten o'clock. After the session in CAPers the day before, he had allowed himself to entertain high hopes, and he wanted to be ready to contribute. He had been waiting in Bonny's office, which Clark still thought of as Felty's, since eight o'clock, hoping to get this out of the way. But Bonny had ambled in at a quarter to nine and screwed around after that getting coffee and looking over the weekend paperwork.

". . . which brings me to the crux of the matter."

"Crux." Would it kill them, Clark asked himself, to put people in charge of line outfits who had done a little bit of the work themselves? Felty had been about the last of the CID bosses with any time as an investigator. The problem was the department had streamlined the promotional system to the point where nothing counted except your score on the written test, with no points for seniority or job performance. So these book-smart types were making rank before they got any experience.

Three years was the minimum for an officer to take the sergeant's test, one year in each rank after that. In three years in Patrol, you're just starting to show a return on the department's investment. Clark was glad he was not just getting started, the way things were going.

". . . the crux of the matter is this: What were you doing at Welborn's house in the first place?"

"I was working a case."

"Crimes Against Persons is working the case."

"It's a stolen car. It's related."

"You've confirmed it stolen?"

"It's hot, Lieutenant. We should have something back from NATB today."

"I beg your pardon?"

"The National Auto Theft Bureau."

"Oh."

"It's your first day."

"In other words, you have not confirmed that the car is stolen. Isn't that right?"

"Yes, sir. That's right."

"And even if you had, CAPers is working the homicide. It stands to reason, if they clear the murder, they clear the auto theft. Why duplicate effort?"

"It doesn't actually work that way, Lieutenant."

"I don't . . ."

"It might actually work the other way."

"Nevertheless . . ."

"Lieutenant, I really didn't go out there on my day off with the intention of pissing the man off. And to tell you the truth, I'm not sure what I did, unless it was maybe I didn't dress for the occasion."

"That's beside the . . ."

"Or maybe I hit a nerve."

"Meaning what?"

"Meaning the guilty dog barks loudest. Mr. Welborn struck me as . . ."

"Your clairvoyance aside, Sergeant Clark, you are to focus your energies on stolen cars, cars we know are stolen. Auto thefts are up like rockets in Dallas, the rate's been climbing out of sight for months. What are you doing about it?''

''Putting car thieves in jail.''

''It doesn't seem to be having much effect, does it?''

''They don't stay long enough.''

''Well, that's not our department, is it?''

''Obviously not.''

''Okay, okay.'' The lieutenant looked at his watch and checked the datebook he had laid on his desk, centered in the clean white blotter with the green corners. ''I think we understand each other.''

''Yes, sir.''

''Sorry to have to call you down like this on my first day, but we might as well have an understanding right up front. Do you have any questions?''

''No, sir.''

''Good. Well, I guess that's it, then.''

Clark nodded and stood up. He was not sure he shared any understanding with his new lieutenant, and if that had been intended as an ass-chewing, he'd had better in grade school. But at least it was over.

''You should have used it,'' Lenny Stuyvesant said, leaning his chair against the pressroom wall.

''He's a prick,'' Bobby Thurmon answered, defending his decision to walk out on Zulu Jones.

''Pricks are news.''

''You would have quoted him?''

''No, I wouldn't have gone to him in the first place. But that's because I've been at this too long. I'm too close to the cops.''

It was the first time Bobby had ever heard the old man say what everyone else said about him.

''What about Pinky?'' Bobby asked, not wanting to follow up on Lenny's *mea culpa*. He needed advice, not a confession. ''Is Old Man Lafayette still news?''

''You're shopping for a minority spokesman here. That's not good business.''

''We make 'em, we can break 'em.''

''You're too new at this racket to be cynical. That's my job.''

''I'm serious. Who elected Zulu Jones spokesman of anything?''

''It's too early in the morning for philosophy. How's your series coming?''

''Not bad. What did you think of the piece yesterday?''

''Decent.''

Bobby was doing a series, ''Dallas's Bloodiest Week.'' The first installment had run in the Sunday editions, along with follow-ups on the deaths of Jackson and Terry. The second was due by noon, and he had not written it yet. He had planned to center it on the aborted Zulu Jones interview.

''High praise, considering the source.''

''What's your angle on the next installment?''

''Good question.''

''Call him up. Give him another shot at it.''

''Zulu?''

''He's the one who matters.''

''I was thinking about using Lafayette instead.''

''The historical perspective?''

''More or less.''

''Do 'em both. Use the contrast.''

''I could do that.''

''I would. If I gave a shit what the minority community thinks in the first place.''

''Don't you?''

''The readers do. That's what counts.''

''What about your readers, Lenny? What are you doing on this?''

''I'll just stick to the facts. Call me old-fashioned.''

By twenty minutes to ten, Captain Angstrom had the second-floor Special Operations Bureau meeting room set up with coffee urns and legal pads. Smoking was not allowed except in private offices throughout the building, but he had taken down the NO SMOKING signs and made sure there were plenty of ashtrays. He wanted this meeting to go well, and thought it might lead to something. And he was a methodical person who liked details. He had come to the TAC job more or less by chance in the normal rotation, but he had fallen in love with the job.

Angstrom had spoken with his deputy chief, the SOB commander, about the meeting the first thing that morning, and had not gotten much of a stir out of him. Tell them we'll be glad to help any way we can, the chief had said.

By a quarter past ten, the meeting room seats were all taken and Angstrom had sent out for some extra chairs to be shuffled in wherever there was room. Everybody who had been there when they broke up the impromptu Sunday session showed up, and most of them brought friends. McCluskey, a forty-eight-year-old black man twenty pounds over his playing weight as a fullback at East Texas State, was in charge of the Shooting Team, investigating the killing of Jackson and Terry. Angstrom made sure McCluskey took the chair at the head of the table.

Angstrom tried not to act surprised when Sergeant Spencer from State Narcotics showed up. Sergeant Clark made it clear that he had invited Spencer. Angstrom had no problem with that, and hoped no one else did, either.

The murders of the officers and the West Dallas multiple homicide were the major cases. Everything else branched off of those, so it was logically a CAPers show.

"We're not making much headway on the two officers," McCluskey admitted. "The shooters left us plenty of empty brass, which isn't worth a shit until we find a gun for comparison. Nothing on prints yet. We did bring a copy of the dispatch tape of the call. Marino?"

Sergeant Marino put a tape recorder on the table and turned it on. It was a small one, and the volume was too low for the size of the room, but all the officers attending sat still and strained to hear. It only lasted a few seconds.

"I don't know if all of y'all could make that out, but I have a transcript here of what he said, which was not much. Let's see . . . He says there's some kids smoking crack in these empty apartments, which is not unusual at all, according to the beat officers . . ."

"This wasn't their beat, Jackson and Terry?" Marx asked, not because it had anything to do with his job at IAD, but simply because he sensed the irony of it.

"No," Marino answered. "One Fifty-three was out on a call already. Jackson and Terry were one beat over, so they covered. Routine."

"I know," Marx said with a raised palm to show that he hadn't meant anything by his question. He had worked Patrol more than the three-year minimum, and he knew that the calls you got were the luck of the draw. "I just . . . I don't know, I wondered."

"Yeah, it's a crapshoot sometimes," Marino said, nodding. "Anyway, there was nothing about guns or Jamaicans, or anything to suggest more than the usual threat at the location. Just some kids smoking crack."

"So it looks like a setup," Sergeant Byner, Angstrom's A-2 squad leader, interjected. Angstrom had asked him to sit in and take notes.

"Maybe," Marino said, looking up from the typed transcript. "But *why* is the question."

"How so?" Angstrom asked. To him dealing drugs and shooting cops went hand in hand. Did there have to be a reason?

"Because"—Barney Oliver spoke up from his seat on the far side of the table—"Jamaicans sell dope. That's their thing. The guns are for security, or going to war over turf. Why ambush cops? Who needs that kind of heat?"

"Exactly," Marino agreed. "And heat them sonsabitches got, believe me. Grimes there and his people been running on them ever since the shooting. Ain't that right?"

"Yeah, we've closed 'em down pretty good, as far as we know. If they're dealing from places we don't know, I don't know who they're selling to, because we've put the word out that Jamaicans are poison until this thing is cleared. They got to be hurting."

"Exactly," Barney said. "Which is why it doesn't make sense that they ambushed the cops. Don't you think, Marino?"

"Yeah, we been kicking that around." He exchanged looks with McCluskey, who nodded. "Personally, I think there may be a connection with the van killing."

"Turf war." Oliver grinned, pointing his finger at Marino. "Exactly."

"That's what I'm thinking. We got this Jamaican van making relief on a crack house they put in over in West Dallas, and somebody screams up in a Monte Carlo and two guys bail out and they whack them like the fucking Marines.''

"You said they were in a Monte Carlo?'' Clark spoke up for the first time.

"Yeah, dark blue, maybe black, could be gray. We don't know what year model, no license numbers or identifying damage or anything.''

"And two men got out. The shooters?'' Clark was jotting this down.

"That's right. The driver stayed in the car.''

"Sounds like you found some witnesses.''

"It wasn't easy.'' Marino shook his head. "They won't stand up in court, and they ain't that sure what they saw as far as the car goes, but we're pretty solid on the Monte Carlo, dark color, and there were three guys.''

"Okay,'' Clark went on, seeing the pattern develop. "How does that match with Maguire's informant? His tip on Crazy Frank? Barney, you said you had a Crazy Frank that runs with a couple of his cousins, didn't you?''

"I checked back at the office, ran it around the room. All we have is speculation: it's supposed to be Frank and these other two. One of them goes by Willy, we're pretty sure, and he's supposed to do the thinking. Frank is the badass. The third one, nobody knows much about him.''

"They're into gangs?'' Marino asked, to clear it all up in his own mind after all that had been said the day before. "You said they were or were not ganged up, Barney?''

"They run gangs, is what we hear. They got the little high schoolers and street bandits peddling their dope. They're a gang of three is how I get it, bossing and wholesaling.''

"So we're saying it's a gang war, if I understand you correctly,'' Angstrom asked. He wanted to keep it clear. "These three wholesalers own West Dallas, the Jamaicans try to expand, that's the van killings. Now, before the Jamaicans can get off a counterpunch, the Mexicans sic the cops on them and . . . What? The heat for the cop killing puts them out of business?'' Barney and Marino nodded. "Why wouldn't they make the trap work the other way? They could have set it up where we shoot the Jamaicans.''

"They know how professional you guys are up here in TAC, Captain," Barney volunteered. "They figured you'd take 'em alive and they'd just bond out."

"Are you serious?" Angstrom asked.

"I don't know. Who the hell knows how they think for sure?" Barney threw up his hands. "Marino, was that a Hispanic who made the call?"

"We played the tape for a linguistics professor at SMU, and he said what we all thought in the first place," Marino answered with a shrug that said he did not think that much of professors. "It's a black male, twenties or early thirties, local."

"So Frank and Willy and the boys have some pretty good intelligence going on," Barney said with a hint of admiration. "They've got somebody who tipped them where the Jamaicans were, and somebody to make the call. They're pretty sharp, these boys."

"So, anyway, that's it," Lieutenant McCluskey summed up. "It sounds like Crazy Frank and his pals may be good for the van killing, and the murder of the officers could be part of a gang war. For shooters, we're looking at two, maybe three Jamaicans. I'd guess they're long gone. And the chances of getting our hands on those guns, I'm not optimistic. Anybody see it otherwise?" Nobody did. "Okay, what else?"

CHAPTER 17

Monday, 11:00 a.m.

Willy stood in the uncharacteristically brisk wind at the Laredo pay phone waiting for Johnny to answer. He checked the number he had dialed. It was one of a dozen pay phones they used. Even though he was as sure as he could be that the cops had no records on him, Frank, or Johnny, Willy insisted on good telephone security. He had books on electronic surveillance, and he knew how easy it was to get tripped up that way. So they only talked business on pay telephones, and not on any one phone very often. It was like having cut-outs, something else he had learned from his books. You don't have anybody who can trace stuff back to you. You use different guys, so that no one person can tie you up with more than one little thing. You keep yourself in the clear that way. Finally, Johnny came on the line.

"Where the hell you been, man?" Willy barked. "I told you I would call at eleven sharp. What's the matter up there?"

"Nothing, Wi . . ." He caught himself before he mentioned Willy's name. "Nothing's the matter. I had a flat tire, man. It happens."

"Yeah. If you say so." Willy let his tone of voice make it clear that he did not like it.

"So, how's it going?"

"We're here. That's about all so far. We got stuff planned for later. Everything is all right up there?"

"Fine."

''The deliveries went out all right, and the pickups? Sales are going all right? No trouble from the foreign competition?''

''Everything's fine. Normal. The competition ain't been seen in the sales territory. You know what I mean?''

''Okay. Keep an eye on everything for me, and don't let on to anybody that I'm out of town, remember that. Act like I'm just busy with something, but everything's business as usual. You got it?''

''I got it. We been over this.''

''I know, and we go over it again so there's no problems. You don't mind, do you?''

''Of course not. You're the boss.''

''Good answer. And, hey, get that nigger. What's his name?''

''You mean Dunk?''

''Don't say his name, stupid. You know the one I mean, just get ahold of him and tell him I want another car, a Monte Carlo, and make it black this time.''

''Okay.''

''And tell him I'll pay him the same price and even trade in the Firebird I got from him last time so he can do something with it and make a little extra change. He ought to like that.''

''How come we're so nice to him?''

''We've got plans for him, that's why. And tell him I'll be around to see what he's decided about my business proposal. You got all that?''

''I got it.''

''Okay, I'll talk to you later. You straight on the time and the phone?''

''Yeah, no problem.''

''Okay then. *Adiós* for now.''

It was this one thing he had, he admitted to himself as he walked back across the street to the motel where he had left Frank asleep again on one of the beds. The Monte Carlo. He did not want to drive nothing else, because that was like his trademark. But he liked to be seen driving different ones because he thought that had some kind of effect on people. And why buy them off a lot when he could buy them cheap from Dunk? Let him take the chances. As far as when he was driving them around, he always made sure he had good enough papers to get him by the uniformed cops. It was a thing, like a quirk, but he knew it and he handled it.

Frank's thing was the women—believe it or not from looking at him. If he was not smelling blood, he was smelling pussy, and he was awake and on the scent when Willy got back to the motel room.

"Women!" he grunted, sitting up in the bed. "We got to get us some goddamned women!"

"Why not?" Willy laughed. "With any luck there's no killing today, and you already ate."

In the Special Ops meeting room Angstrom shifted in his chair as the cooperative spirit of the meeting unraveled around him.

"Let me get this straight," Bill Clark was saying, his voice rising. "You IAD guys come in yesterday showing pictures around and I tell you I make some of the people in those pictures as speed dealers . . ."

"And I knew a couple of them, too," Barney Oliver put in.

"Right, and Intelligence has files on a couple of them," Clark went on. "And, you being Internal Affairs, it stands to reason there's a cop tied up in it somewhere or else you think there is, and you can't tell us what the hell's going on here? Have I got that right?"

"Bill, take it easy, for Christ's sake." Marx had brought Dave White with him this time. "We understand how you feel, and we'd like nothing better than to open up the books and let you read over our shoulders. The point is, that decision has been made. It wasn't made by me or Bob, and it's not going to change. There's no point in jumping on us about it."

"I don't believe it," Clark muttered, pushing back in his seat.

"Hey, we didn't have to come to this meeting," White pointed out. "We're trying to work with you guys the best we can."

"And I'm sure we all appreciate it," Angstrom put in, trying to smooth things over. "We all take orders here."

"Well, let me ask you this," Clark said. "Does Jefferson Lee 'Mack the Knife' MacAnnaly have anything to do with it?"

"Who?" White asked.

"I've heard that name," McCluskey said, turning to Marino.

"Biker type, isn't he?" Marino offered, looking from McCluskey to Clark. "Isn't he that biker badass Green is working on?"

"Yeah, that's right," McCluskey confirmed it. "What's he got to do with Internal Affairs, Bill?"

"Ask them," Clark said, pointing at Marx and White with his thumb. "Who's here from Vice, anybody?"

"Uh, Vice wasn't in on this," Grimes pointed out. "I'm Narcotics."

"Are y'all working on this MacAnnaly thing over there?" Clark asked. He was worried about Randi Stoner, but did not want to say anything that would put her on the spot with her bosses, get them asking why she was cutting up her business with some guy in Auto Theft.

"Yeah," Grimes said. "Our undercover people are keeping their eyes out, checking some of his hangouts."

"How about Vice? They got anybody on it?" Clark insisted.

"I'll check." Grimes made a note.

"What's the connection?" Marx asked. "And who's Mac-Annaly?"

"The connection is he's a killer. We could screw around and get somebody hurt with too much secrecy. See what I mean?" Clark explained.

"We don't have any evidence of a connection," White said, as if that were an answer.

"Well, I just . . . Okay. I'm not mad at you guys," Clark said, reminding himself about his temper. He still had Marino to contend with when all this was over from shooting off his mouth, and he didn't need anybody else mad at him. He noticed the bemused look on Spencer's face. "I'm just saying we may be playing this one a little close to the vest. If we've got a bent cop, yank the bastard. Make him go to court or the Civil Service Board to get back in. Unless he's in deeper'n a mine shaft, it's not worth getting somebody hurt over it."

"You, uh, got something in particular in mind, Bill?" Grimes asked.

"What do you mean?"

"I don't know. You sound like you know something . . . Anything you want to tell us?"

"Nah, nothing in particular. It's just the principle." Touché, Bill thought. Got me there, youngster. He wasn't ready to put all his cards on the table either. It was a judgment call, and he was by no means sure he wasn't screwing up his own priorities. He could get Randi hurt trying to keep her out of trouble, and he knew it, but he let it go. He would call Randi and tip her to the IAD deal before she went to work that afternoon.

After that it was the rehashing that all meetings deteriorate into after an hour or so, and the noise of chairs being scraped away from the table as the men prepared to leave. Dave White was joking with a couple of the others to smooth over any feathers that might have been ruffled.

Angstrom rose and spoke in a loud enough voice to make himself heard, trying not to sound like he was making a move. "What do you think about another meeting to follow up on what we've covered here today? Anybody feel like it would be helpful to get together again?"

There was the general murmur of a couple of dozen cops saying that they did not think it could hurt, and it was left to Angstrom to set a date. He offered the following Thursday, same time and place, because he knew if he set it too far ahead the impetus that had brought them together would dissipate. Nobody objected, and he did not bother to mention that he would have notes of the meeting typed up. He had not decided yet if that would be a good idea.

CHAPTER 18

Monday, 2:00 p.m.

"Ah, he wants a woman, that's all that's the matter with him, Jefe." Willy smiled and shook his head, full of deference to the older man, trying to make it clear that his friend was a simple man, a fool almost, but with redeeming qualities that made him worth having around. He could not afford to look foolish himself in the eyes of the man he had come all this way to see, and yet he knew that one must not demean his associates or risk demeaning himself.

Willy was still wearing his navy blazer. Frank was taking turns growling like a dog and laughing his crazy laugh. Frank was impossible, Willy told himself. You are afraid to leave the son of a bitch, but you can't take him anywhere. This was not one of their West Dallas dives where he could fix anything Frank fucked up. This was the audience he had dreamed of since he was old enough to know that there were men in the world with such power.

They had the cantina to themselves, Willy and Frank and the old man and his *pistoleros*. The old man was a legend. Mexicans on both sides of the border made up songs about him. They did that for their heroes down here, the ones who stick it to the gringos and are generous with the poor.

"Such men have appetites," the old man said. "And they have their uses."

It was meant to put Willy at ease and to bring him around to

172

the business at hand as well, and neither purpose was lost on the young gangster.

"Of course," he said. "My proposition . . ."

"Yes, I know it," the old man said. "A hundred kilos, on credit."

"Well . . ."

"It's not completely unreasonable," the old man said. "I have known your family back to your grandfather and his brothers. I know both your uncles, and their word is good. You come highly recommended."

"I appreciate that."

"Still, it is a big debt to undertake."

"I understand, and I would die before I'd default," Willy promised, meaning every word.

"Naturally." The old man smiled. "But dead, you are of no use to me. In the business sense, I mean."

"Of course."

"Do you always dress this way? Like a gringo, I mean."

"No. Of course not, Jefe. It was for the drive down, in case I was stopped. I like to be prepared . . ." He wanted to tell the old man about the books he read, how he tried to anticipate everything that might go wrong.

"Julio!" the old man roared suddenly.

"*Sí*, Jefe." A man to Willy's left uncoiled from his chair.

"Give our friend there the white woman."

Julio motioned for Frank to follow him and marched across the room and up the stairs, leering. Frank looked at Willy, who nodded, and then sprang up from his chair and followed.

"And you, my young friend?" offered the old man.

"It is not necessary, Jefe. Thank you, but I impose on your time only for business."

The old man grunted appreciatively, and Willy congratulated himself for his answer.

"It is to be envied, I sometimes think," said the old man. "To be so easily amused as your friend. We smart ones, we demand much more, don't you think?"

"Yes, but we achieve much more, Jefe."

"Indeed. Indeed we do. Tell me, do you follow the religion?"

"I beg your pardon?"

"Santeria, Palo Mayombe. What do you believe?"

"I . . . I was brought up in the Church, Jefe."

"Not what I asked, if you don't mind my saying so. We all were brought up in the Mother Church. But do you worship Saint Barbara, or is she Shango, whose lust is for the blood of the heart? Do you know Saint Barbara?"

"I remember her."

"With the sword in one hand, in the other the flaming heart. Are you of the priests, my young friend? Or are you of the people?"

"I . . . I'm sorry, Jefe, to disappoint you in this. But I don't believe in anything," Willy admitted, adding, "Except in myself."

"I see."

It was the last thing he had expected, and for Willy, who prided himself on his anticipation, it was daunting. For the first time, he considered how he would deal with the old man's dismissal, and this unanticipated reversal weighed on him even more.

"It is no matter," the old man pronounced, smiling, and Willy felt the warmth of the great man's smile like a warm sun. "You live among the *yanquis,* and you cannot be expected to know. We will teach you."

Willy nodded, not knowing what to say. Teach him? How long would that take? He was a businessman after all, and time was as real a value for him as money, in its way.

"You will come with us?" the old man asked as if he thought he might be imposing.

"Anywhere, Jefe."

The old man smiled again. He reveled in a young man who knew the value of respect. At a nod from the old man, all of the men in the cantina were on their feet and he and the youngster from Dallas led a procession out the front door to the fleet of Blazers and Jeeps that awaited them. Willy's rented Olds would stay behind, along with Frank and the man Jefe had assigned to keep an eye on him.

Upstairs, in a room off a hallway where the white woman

spent her days sleeping and her nights doing what was demanded of her, Frank was at play.

She was skinny, as white women often were to Frank's way of thinking, but she had heavy breasts with pink nipples, and freckles across her collarbone, a feature that fascinated him. Her hair was blond, on her head at least, and it did not matter to Frank that she wore no makeup. She had blue eyes, and a generous mouth with pouty lips.

Frank announced his presence by storming through the door Julio opened and kicking the bitch, still asleep, off the bed onto the floor beyond. She screamed, savagely awakened from her recurring dream that she had found her way home again. But by the time Willy and his new friends drove away, she had regained her refuge of hopeless resignation, and offered no resistance to Frank's abuses. She took him up her ass as he insisted, as she had done others before him, and deafened herself to his animal noises, deadened herself to the rending of his cock inside her and to the blows he rained down on the length of her body, and tried to crawl back into her dream of home.

Back in Dallas, in "Hungry Heights," the Jamaican Curtis returned from a walk to a pay phone at the combination self-serve gas station and convenience store by Hawn Freeway. He rapped on the door frame in the prearranged cadence and sidled into the little house through the door opened for him by Stone, who was standing watch in the front. Curtis's face was slit from side to side in a smile that showed his teeth like a knife wound exposing a rib, and there was a look in his eyes that Stone had not seen since before the Mexicans hit their people in the van.

"They're coming," Curtis said. "They're coming."

At his shop in Grand Prairie, Mack the Knife sat on a toolbox making calls on a cellular phone he was sure would not be intercepted or traced. As he talked, Blondie, who had not volunteered for the job because he was afraid of nothing as much as upsetting Mack with a poor job of barbering, cut the big man's hair. Mack paused between calls to inspect his progress in a rearview mirror he had yanked off the door of a wrecked car.

"Shorter," he told Blondie. "I want it shorter. Then do the beard."

Blondie started over, using a pair of barber's shears he had bought that morning for the job, as Mack punched in a number, reading it from a dime-store spiral notebook.

"Who the fuck is this?" Mack demanded of whoever had answered. "I'm calling for the Dago. Tell him to call Mack. Pronto. Just give him the message, bitch. He'll kick your ass more than you like it kicked if he misses out on this. Tell him I said that." He disconnected from the call and studied Blondie's progress in the rearview mirror.

"What do you think, M-m-mack?"

Mack looked at Blondie's reflection, at his twitching left eye. "Not bad, Blinky."

"Aw, M-m-mack. I asked you n-not to c-call me that."

"You're too goddamned touchy. Ain't your fault your old lady raised you with a pint of hooch in one hand and a Louisville Slugger in the other."

"D-d-d-don't talk about my m-m-m-mother . . ."

"Or what?" Mack pivoted to face him. He liked teasing the little fucker, and doing it when he had scissors in his hand made it more fun. He knew how Blondie was about blades.

"N-n-nothing. N-nothing, just I d-don't know why you want to d-d-do me that way . . ."

Mack watched Blondie's eye going crazy.

"I'm just teasing. It means we're pals."

"Yeah, w-w-well . . ."

"Go back over my hair. I want it shorter. Then get rid of this beard." He did not know if the cops were looking for him on the murder rap or not, but he needed mobility, and did not want to take any chances. "Did you get the dye, too?"

"Yeah, M-mack. Just like you t-told me."

CHAPTER 19

Monday, 4:30 p.m.

Bill Clark sat at his desk in the Salvage Unit at the auto pound cursing into a telephone. For the fifth time that day he was listening to Randi Stoner's recorded voice inviting him to leave a message at the tone. He did not bother this time to leave a message, unless you counted his whispered curses. He slapped the cradle of the phone to disconnect and dialed the number of the Vice Control Division.

"Is Sergeant Grouton in?" he asked the clerk who answered.

"He's out of the office. May I take a message?"

"How about Randi Stoner, is she around there anyplace?"

"No, she's out, too."

"This is Sergeant Clark. I left a message earlier, around noon. I wanted him to call me as soon as he came in. Did he get that one?"

"I don't know. I don't think he's been in yet."

"Do you know where he is?"

"Only that he's out working on something. Shall I page him for you, Sergeant?"

"I'd appreciate it. Ask him to call me at the Auto Salvage Unit, please. It's important. If he misses me here, let me give you my pager number."

She repeated the number as he read it off to her. "I'll get word to him as soon as I can," she promised.

"Thanks." Clark wanted to think that Grimes had touched

177

base with the Vice people. Narcotics and Vice shared an office, for God's sake. He wanted to think that Randi's undercover gig had been canceled, or put on hold, or at least, that she had been tipped to the possibility of a leak.

His junkyard dogs were holding over after their three o'clock quitting time because Clark wanted to see what they had come up with, and he only wanted to go through it once. The boys were in their usual adolescent mode. Back and forth across the big room they traded off-color jibes and launched the occasional tightly wadded memo, all with the air of a junior-high math class left unattended. Clark braved the cross fire of a rubber-band fight to freshen his coffee, and turned from the coffee maker backed up to the post in the middle of the room at the sound of Sparky and Wheels coming in.

"Anything to it?" he asked.

"Nah, but it was a good call by the uniforms. Guy had a pickup somebody'd redone, and the replacement dash covered the VIN plate. Looked hinky enough, but we found it okay and it checked."

"How pissed off was the driver for having to wait?"

"Waiting's better than bonding out. We explained it to him," Wheels said.

Sparky and Wheels pulled the batteries out of their PDT's, the "portable data terminals" they carried on shoulder straps. With the little computers, they could run registration and wanted checks, even send messages and distress calls if they needed to. They dropped the batteries into the rechargers on their desks, and signed the terminals in in the squad book, a brown cardboard binder.

Clark waved his men into a ragged circle toward the open middle of the room, and he liked the way they put aside the bullshitting now that it was time for business. You had to know how to play and blow off steam when there was time for it, and his guys did. They also knew when it was time to bear down.

"First, any new business since Saturday that we need to take care of?" Clark asked. Nobody had anything. "Anything come up at the weekly auction?"

"Routine, boss," Nacho Hernandez spoke up.

"Yeah, and I just want to make sure we've got all the routine stuff covered, nothing new coming up we have to concern ourselves with, because we are about to get busy on this business with the Lincoln. No problems with the impounds over the weekend?"

"Routine," Crash mimicked Hernandez.

"Okay, Boots, you and Smoky bring us up to speed on the Lincoln so far." Clark leaned back against the post and yielded the floor to Boots, his second in command.

"Well, we helped Purchasing open up this morning, and ran down the sale of that burned car Nacho came up with off the VIN on the Lincoln. It was bought by a salvage operator over off of South Central, name of A to Z Wrecking. Y'all probably never heard of them," he added with a smirk.

"Not much we ain't," somebody moaned. They all knew A to Z, one of the seven or eight outfits they still had trouble with. That was down from the three dozen shady operators of a few years ago. The dogs had seen to it that the rest of them had squared up or gone out of business.

"So we went out to A to Z and we found the wreck, the burned car sold at auction. And lo and behold, the VIN plate was gone off of it. A to Z still had the papers from the city, where they bought the car."

"Meaning the thieves didn't plan to file for a salvage title," Clark said. "Which fits if they're gonna take the car to Mexico and sell it."

"Right." Boots nodded.

"Okay, did you hear back from NATB?"

"Not yet. Janie was supposed to call me back, but I haven't heard from her. I told her to page me, but they don't, sometimes."

"Give her a call. We need the complete VIN off that secondary we raised on the Lincoln. We're going to have to know where it came from before we can get anywhere."

Boots went to his desk to make the call, and Clark addressed his troops.

"Okay, until further notice, I want all of you to keep your pagers with you around the clock. Double-check your gear bags and keep them handy." Since they had lost their lockers in a remodeling, the dogs kept what they thought they might need in workout bags in the trunks of their personal cars. "We are going to work this Lincoln back and forth until we tie it in with the murder victim, the thieves, the killers, or somebody, and break this deal loose. I was at a little meeting this morning, and we may be looking at a gang war that could get even uglier. Here's what I know about it so far."

Clark pulled his notes from the meeting out of his shirt pocket and went through them. There was no grab-assing now, and the dogs took notes, exchanging looks among themselves with eyebrows cocked to show that they thought this had the earmarks of a real shitstorm. When he was through, Clark asked for questions.

"I don't like the IAD angle worth a shit," Boots offered.

"Neither do I," Clark agreed.

"You're saying we've got a bad cop in with the bikers?"

"I'm speculating."

"When the smoke clears, that's all the hell we're going to see in the papers, is the part about that son of a bitch."

"You're probably right," Clark admitted. "But press relations ain't our concern."

There were more questions and plans were made, and Clark set things up for the next day. But in the back of his mind a couple of things were kicking around. For one thing, there might be something he could do on the press relations, and he wondered if he could trust the new kid, Bobby Thurmon. The other thing was about trust, too, but it was a hell of a lot more unsettling. If there was a cop mixed up with the bikers, how did he know it wasn't Randi Stoner? That might account for her not reporting the deal with the blond guy, might even be behind his jumping her in the first place. And if she was dirty, she had sure roped him into some trouble with that story of hers. He wondered about that and about why she had not returned his calls.

CHAPTER 20

Monday, 7:30 p.m.

Randi Stoner flattered herself that she was getting the hang of the job. Like the hand-to-hand drills at the academy, waiting tables in a skimpy outfit was largely a matter of balance and position. Footwork was the key to it. With the improvement in the weather, the early crowd was heavy, and she had noticed customers coming in for the past half hour had been damp but not soaked, so the rain had started. It would be dicey at closing time, she knew, if the hard freeze came as predicted and the wet streets iced over.

You can adapt to almost anything, she told herself, and even the noise level inside the club was less annoying than it had been at first. She had begun to learn to look at her customers' lips when they ordered, so she could make out their words without having to get so close to hear them that they could put their hands on her. Not all of them tried. Maybe because it was Monday and a workday, she saw a difference in the clientele. The early crowd particularly had been fairly well behaved, men in suits stealing time from their jobs for drinks and a show, contenting themselves with language that was lewd but not threatening. Words did not hurt. She was comfortable enough in her role that she found she could operate on a kind of cruise control, freeing herself to think of other things. She thought of her mother.

A widow for several years now, her mother had recovered

from her loss and devoted herself to the business that had been
a hobby before her husband, Randi's stepfather, had died. Now
she was a businessperson in earnest, with a shop that ran itself
and the freedom of time as well as a comfortable living. She
was at a loss over Randi's wanting to be a cop, of all things, but
had resigned herself to it. They both looked forward to an
occasional long chatty lunch and a little shopping. Mondays
were good days for it, Randi having worked weekends most of
the time since the academy, usually on evenings or late nights.
Her mother was thinking of remarrying, and debating how
much to tell Randi about the man she was seeing. Randi knew
more than her mother seemed to imagine already, just by the
changes in her over the past weeks, the signs in her eyes and her
stride and the extra touches here and there that belied her sexual
reawakening. Randi was happy for her.

"So how's it going, kid?" Betty slid her tray onto the bar
beside Randi's and smiled at her.

"I think I'm getting the hang of it."

"Sure, it's all in your head." Betty nodded knowingly.
"And your feet. Charlie and his frigging high heels."

"I haven't worn heels in a while, and I don't think I've ever
been on my feet this much. Listen," Randi said, leaning a little
closer to Betty as if she thought someone else might overhear.
"This girl the guy was asking about Saturday, what was her
name?"

"I don't remember, kid. I've slept since then."

"Charlotte, wasn't it? Charlotte Mayfield, something like
that?"

"Uh, yeah, could have been. Why?"

"Said she might be a dancer, so did you know her? Did she
dance in here, maybe?"

"I couldn't tell you the names of the girls we got dancing
in here right now, much less somebody used to work here.
What's your interest?"

"You know what happened."

"Sure I saw it. That skinny shit roughed you up and the guy
with the beard stuck a gun in his ear. Only I didn't see nothing,
okay?"

"Yeah, so I told him I'd ask around. I owe him a favor, don't I?"

"Maybe you do, kid. I don't owe no man nothing. They do what they do for their own reasons."

"You're probably right. So who would know? Charlie? Maybe the cashier?"

"Ladies, ladies." Charlie appeared behind them, shaking his head and smiling. "What are you doing here, organizing a union or something? We got thirsty guys all over the place."

Betty smiled sweetly and called Charlie a shit and Randi did a little curtsey and off the two women went to serve their drinks.

Rain drummed dully on the windshield of Stef Nugent's car as she studied her face in the mirror and touched up her makeup in hopes of finding Mack inside the club. He liked her to look as if she retained her pretensions. The things he did to her meant more to him that way.

From the cold rainy night, Stef hustled through the vestibule where the cretin sold admissions through a hole in a window to men but buzzed women through free of charge. She was glad she was here, where it was too loud and musky with odors of sweat and spilt beer to think.

Betty the waitress recognized her and tipped up her head to say hello, both her hands full with a tray carrying two pitchers of beer for a table of fraternity boys from SMU. Stef found a place at the bar near the space where the waitresses picked up their orders.

Mack had not returned her calls. She knew he was cross with her for walking out of the party Saturday night. And he knew she would be needing his drugs by now. He could be sure of her on that count, of the control her appetite gave him over her. She detested him for that and harbored the hope that she would destroy him for it. There was no sign of Mack or any of his boys. It was early for them, but she was restless with her awakening need, and had to find him.

Betty made her way back with an empty tray and with a look over her shoulder at the tables in her area decided that there was time for a quick smoke. "What's up, kid? Haven't seen you around for a while." Betty greeted Stef with a smile.

"Nothing to it. You seen him or any of his friends in tonight?"

"Not tonight. Blondie and a couple of 'em were in Saturday. Did you hear about that?"

Stef shook her head no, thinking about where she would look next.

"Blondie got a little out of hand with the new girl, and she broke his nose." Betty rolled her eyes and laughed.

"You're kidding." Stef laughed with her. "What did he do to her?"

"Not a damned thing. Some guy cut in on 'em and run Blondie off."

"What guy?" Stef knew Blondie was dumb enough to fight anybody, and would either cut or be cut before it was over.

"The one that put a pistol in his damned ear. Charlie said he was some kind of a po-lice."

"No shit?"

"You know I don't ever see nothing, but that's what Charlie said."

"What kind of po-lice? What was he doing in here?"

"The kind with a beard and some kind of army coat. Not young, not real old. All I know is he was asking me about some girl he thought used to work here. That was before the fight broke out."

"What girl?"

"Charlotte somebody. You know her? I can't remember the last name. Mayberry or something like that."

"Doesn't ring a bell," Stef said. It did, though. She knew who Charlotte Mayfield was. "What did you tell him?"

"What's to tell? Same thing I told Randi this evening." Betty ground out her smoke in the ashtray on the bar and reached for her tray.

"Who's Randi?"

"The new girl. The one Blondie tangled with. Over there." Betty pointed in the direction of the tables Randi was working and Stef followed the gesture and saw Randi Stoner coming toward the bar with a tray balanced above her head as she slipped between two crowded tables. The raised arm opened her vest and the smooth swing of her hips as she came clear of the men who watched her pass made Stef think she might be mistaken, because these things were a part of someone who had done this before, was comfortable with the place and all it implied. But she was not mistaken. It was Randi Stoner, all right, the new kid in Vice.

"See ya," Betty smiled with a wave as she turned away from the bar to get back to her customers.

"I was never here," Stef said as she turned her shoulder to the approaching Randi.

"You know me, kid," Betty assured her. "I never see nothing."

Randi saw Betty on her way from the bar and the woman in the leather coat moving toward the door, her collar turned up against the weather outside. She told herself it was really going pretty well, and that she hoped she wasn't wasting her time. She hoped Mack the Knife would show up.

In the foyer, Stef paused. If Randi was undercover, she had backup. Inside the club would be too obvious, hard to have a couple of guys nursing beers from open to close, and Vice did not have enough people to work it in relays. She felt sure about all that, but then who was the guy with the beard Saturday night? He did not figure to be backup. A coincidence, maybe.

Most likely, she has somebody outside, regardless of this business with the mystery man, Stef thought. She made herself think it through, vibrant with perverse delight, knowing that she was doomed and that beyond the door they might be waiting to end it for her. Stef knew she was as addicted to the adrenaline rush as to Mack's drugs.

"You got an umbrella?" she asked the old woman behind the ticket window.

"Sure do. Why?"

"How much do you want for it?"

"Ain't for sale."

Stef took cash from her coat pocket and shoved a twenty through the window slot at the old woman.

"Oh, uh, okay, then."

The old woman pushed the cheap plastic umbrella out

through the round hole she talked through and Stef took it. Thinking it was supposed to be bad luck to open an umbrella indoors, she punched it open as if taunting the fates and stepped through the door.

No one was waiting for her, only the parking attendant huddled under the awning. It was raining harder now, and it was colder. Stef held the umbrella low over her head and walked to her car, trying to step around the puddles, glad she had worn her high-topped boots with the high heels. She knew now that she would see Mack before the night was out, and that added to her excitement.

She started the engine and locked her door, then reached under her seat and pulled the pistol out of its zippered case and laid it in her lap. It would be somewhere close, first of all, so they could get in quick if Randi needed them, but not close enough to be obvious. Preferably line of sight to the front door of the place. Two men. A car would not be any good. Nothing in the buildings around, no place she could think of they could rent or borrow that would work. A van. It would be a van. She scanned the block or so of the street that she could see and the lot across the street where . . . There it was. It was over half a block away, in a good spot, really. That had to be it. Even in the rain and darkness, she thought she recognized it. She laughed. It was a van they had seized off a buy she had made. If they suspected me, they would not use that van, she told herself.

When she pulled off the club parking lot, she turned right, away from the parked van, and held her breath until the next intersection, where she turned left, drove a block, and then turned right. She slowed to a stop against the curb, ready to make a U-turn if she had to, and counted slowly to one hundred. No one was following her. She laughed again and drove on until she found a phone and dialed Mack's cellular phone. Blondie answered and gave her the same song and dance as before.

"Fuck you, Blondie. Tell the son of a bitch I know he's there, wherever the hell you are. It's a portable phone, goddamnit! It's important."

"To you or to him?" Blondie asked, laughing.

"Tell him that snatch you grabbed Saturday night was a cop, shithead! I'll wait thirty seconds."

He did not come on the line in thirty seconds, but it was not long, and she waited.

The meal was excellent and the brandy afterwards even better. The Mexican cop was extravagant in his praise of the old man's cigars, and Willy was impressed with Welborn's connection. The man was fiftyish, with hair gray at the temples like a soap opera doctor. His suit was banker's gray and his smoothly knotted tie a subdued rose. He spoke with a polite air of assurance. This is a cop? Willy thought. Not like any he'd ever run into. He was a colonel. Maybe that made a difference. It came time at last for the colonel to excuse himself, reluctantly. When he was gone, the old man turned to Willy, smiling.

"You have done well, young man. This man is a good friend to have. You know him?"

"A friend of a friend," Willy answered modestly.

"You have good friends indeed, then," said the old man, who looked much different this evening than he had in the afternoon, wearing a soft white linen suit and robin's-egg blue shirt. But no tie. He had not gone that far. "Politicians are the hardest crop to grow, you know. You fertilize them with bullshit, you water them with money, but who knows what the hell you will reap? You see what I mean?"

"Yes, I think so."

"Just now we are in a period of reform. We have your government to thank for this, in large measure."

"My government?"

"A figure of speech. Mexico is a big, fine country. If only we weren't so close to fucking America! It overshadows us. But, where else would we find fools to buy the shit that we sell? Fools with money, that is the great gift of America to the world. But now there is reform in Mexico. That business with the DEA agent in Guadalajara. They killed him down there, and now we have reform. Do you know what reform means in Mexico?"

"I'm not sure."

"It means that new people, the reform people, take over the business. Nothing changes except the pockets into which the money goes. I have seen it many times. Did you know that they have my name in Washington?"

"Really?"

"I have been assured of it. I am a symbol of something. It is not clear exactly what, but that is not important. What matters is that my arrangements have all expired." The old man laid his cigar aside. "For all the years we have been in business on the border, mine and the other families, the fickle winds of politics have not been kind lately. It is for this reason that I am so pleased you have come to me with this distinguished connection."

Willy chose not to divulge unless asked directly that he had no real idea who the man was, only that Carlton Welborn had arranged for them to meet for the first time this evening, less than an hour before the two of them met the old man. Welborn's insistence on keeping his operation small and manageable had misled Willy as to the quality of his contacts in Mexico. The old man's reaction made it clear that there was enormous potential here, and Willy was working hard to keep his face deferential and calm, while his mind whirled at the possibilities.

"I had no desire to take my proposal to anyone but you, Jefe," Willy assured the old man, and it was true. He knew of no other major trafficker except by rumor, and only of this old man through his uncles.

"Your proposal. One hundred kilos on your word is an enormous debt for a young man. Failure is betrayal in this business, you understand."

"I do, Jefe."

"And I believe you appreciate the consequences of betrayal."

Indeed he did. Willy knew one thing above everything else. He would happily die before he would fail the old man with the kindly face who sat across the table from him.

"I have a counterproposal," El Jefe said, pausing while a waiter in a short white jacket hovered over them long enough to pour more coffee in their cups. "Not one hundred kilos, but one thousand."

"Jefe, that's . . . that's . . ."

"It's over a ton of cocaine."

"It's more than I ever . . . It's impossible . . ."

"You'd think so, wouldn't you? What do you suppose the

gringos do with so much of it? They must give it to their
children, to their dogs and cats!''

''I'm speechless,'' Willy admitted.

''It's just as well. I'm not finished. Three things. First, dealing cocaine is not dealing marijuana.''

''With all due respect, Jefe, I . . .''

''I know about you in Dallas, Willy. You can organize, you
can manage. But now we are talking about cocaine in volume.
We are talking about the Colombians. You know of them?''

''Of course.''

''Of course. You watch *Miami Vice,* I suppose. Why do you
think we have taken up the old religion, for protection against
the police? Money does for them. It's from the Colombians we
would like a little protection. If you fail in this, you will find
them much harsher than I am. Is that clear? Second, you must
understand that Dallas is not the end, only the beginning. From
there, the cocaine goes north, and east, and west.''

''I see.'' Willy saw himself stepping up to a level of play that
he had only imagined. It couldn't be happening this fast, this
easy.

''A lot of people would be depending on you. You sense the
responsibility, I hope.''

''I do.''

''Good. I'm almost through.'' He sweetened his coffee and
tasted it. ''Third, there are families on the Texas side who have
handled deliveries for years, but they have the reform, too. In
time, it will all be arranged satisfactorily again. It is always so.
But for now, there is a link missing from the chain. I used the
chain analogy before, didn't I?''

''Yes, Jefe.''

''Good. The missing link is your opportunity. Here's my
proposal. You take charge of the thousand kilos and see that it
gets to Dallas. You provide safekeeping for it there. My associates will come to you for their portions. Understand?''

''Yes, but what . . .'' Willy could not think of a respectful
way to phrase it.

''What's in it for you? Ten percent.''

''I beg your pardon?''

"You move a thousand kilos, you keep one hundred. It is fair, isn't it?"

"Of course." Willy had already done the math. The old man was talking pure profit, no cost to him except his time and the incredible risk of failing. It was the chance of a lifetime.

"Understand me, Willy. This is the last thing. I am a broker, not God. I am in no position to forgive you, because, like you, I am responsible. Do you understand?"

"I do."

"And you will not betray my trust in you, either through carelessness or greed?"

"I will not."

"You must not. This is not a business for a man who can't be relied upon."

"I won't fail."

"I hope not. For both our sakes." He said this last with a wry laugh.

"I will make you proud of me," Willy swore.

"Then let's drink to it."

CHAPTER 21

Monday, 11:00 p.m.

"Get in the back."

Stef sat in the passenger seat of Mack's van and watched Blondie and the other two disappear into the raining night in her car. They were going for beer, with orders to stay out of trouble and be back in an hour.

"Nice for a price," she said.

"I got your price," he smiled, patting the pocket of his shirt.

The physiological unfairness of it, its inevitability and *déjà vu* sameness, drained from her arms and legs the energy she had deluded herself that she was saving against this moment. When she needed him the most and wanted him the least, she was at her weakest. After a hit of his speed, she would be a match for him, or almost. And then there would be nothing to fight him for, because he would have had her then, he would have put her through her paces. She dared not kill him, although a hundred times she had imagined it, suspected he had made himself vulnerable to it, daring her to do it. Because without him where would she get the speed she had learned to need? What would she do, buy it from dealers on the street? Rip them off for it? Skim it off the shit they seized? All those were dead ends for a junky cop, and she knew it. Only because she was scrupulous in her professional life except where Mack was concerned had she survived this long.

"Mack, don't be a shit," she said, making her words sound

tough in her mind, but they came out of her lips pleading. She hated herself when she begged. He was the only one who had ever made her beg. "It's not the time. We've got business."

"I mean business, baby."

"Come on, man. Let me get straight and we'll do it right."

"You do it my way, bitch."

"Let me have some, Mack."

It was coming down on her, and the weather was perfect for it. The cold, dirty rain and the glowering watching woods in front of the van across the bike trail clearing that led down to White Rock Lake out of sight in the darkness, it was all her. The night was her turned out to show the world how she felt inside. Fatigue. Bone-numbing, profound fatigue, and the gaping maw of depression that threatened to swallow her without a trace like a cold, black sea. It had come to this, again. She told herself it would be all right in a little while. No matter how bad it got, soon it would be all right again, and getting herself right was the first step to winning, somehow.

She crawled over the seat into the back of the van. He had turned off the engine and it was cold. She hoped he would let her keep the boots on.

"Get it off," he said. He did not say it mean, because they both knew he did not have to, and he was not a fool. It was all she could do to hold herself erect and look him in the eye as she unbuttoned her leather coat and let it slide down her back. She felt much worse than she had moments before, as if knowing he was there and the time was near she had no more reason to hold herself together, and whatever reserve she had been drawing from was draining out of her. He motioned for her to change position, from sitting on the nasty mattress they kept in the back of the van to kneeling on it, and she did as he wanted.

As she took off her sweater to reveal her breasts, her eyes fixed on his hand as it came clear of his shirt pocket and she saw the stuff in his hand. He held it out toward her but she knew better than to reach for it. Instead, she raised herself on her knees and with her thumbs tugged the waist of her blue jean skirt down over her hips. It felt like slow motion to her, as if she were watching it happen to someone else again, and when she lifted herself on one knee and then the other to slip the skirt all the way off, she caught a glimpse of herself in the windshield, her reflection staring back at her as if it were surprised.

When she was naked except for her boots, she knelt on the mattress and looked at him across the darkness inside the van, trying to look at his eyes and not the dope in his hand. The dope this time looked strange, different, but she tried not to look at it.

"What do you want?" he asked.

"I want you, Jeff."

"What do you want, baby? Really."

"I want you."

"You want the dope, don't you?"

"Yes."

"And my dick."

"Yes. I want 'em both. You know what I want."

"Which first?"

"You first, Jeff."

"You're lying."

"Yes."

"Why do you call me Jeff at times like this?"

"It's your name."

"I'm Mack."

"Not now. Now you're Jeff."

It was a litany that he varied only enough from one time to the next to make her listen, to make her think about her answers, so she would really be with him and not absent in some secret place in her mind. He moved close to her and pressed her down on the mattress on her back. She heard a zipper work and felt him pressing himself between her legs. At his touch, she opened herself to him and closed her eyes for what she knew came next.

"Do you want me?" he asked.

"Yes."

"Who are you?"

"Investigator Stefanie Anne Nugent, badge number 2349, Vice Control Division, Dallas Police Department."

He entered her gently, holding himself back.

"Why are you here?"

"To fuck you."

"Why?"

"I love you, I want you. You make me come."

"It's for the dope, isn't it?"

"Yes."

"It was a lie that you love me, wasn't it?"

"Yes."

"But you want me?"

"Yes. Do it, Jeff. Please, just do it."

"Tell me a story, Stef. Would you do that?"

She did. The story was about a policewoman who thought she was tough. She went after a bad guy, a dope dealer and a real badass. Nothing would do but that she would bring him down. She was drawn to him because he was the only man who made her genuinely afraid. It was her pride that was her undoing. The only way she could get close to him was to do drugs, because he did not trust anyone who didn't use. He was smart. She thought she could fuck around with speed and not get hooked. She thought she could handle it. She was wrong. He hooked her and he ran her and he turned her out. He made her whore for him with his friends. She got all fucked up on drugs one time and let him make videotapes of her and take pictures. Now he owned her.

As she told him the story, he moved deeper inside her. Bit by bit, he moved into her. It was her only resistance to him that she did not move against him, because he would not start in earnest until she moved, to prove something to her.

The rest of the story, his favorite part. This bad man owned the policewoman now, but even more than that she had fallen for him. Not in love with him, she did not love him, but she needed him. She hated him. She needed to hate him. If anything happened to him she would miss him even more than his drugs, because she could find dope, but there was no one else like him.

He won again. She moved against him because she could not hold herself together any longer against her need for the drugs and the feel of him inside her and the time that was passing and knowing the others would be back soon. If she resisted, Mack would make it last until they came back and he would let Blondie and the penises watch. So she gave up and fucked him, and in her need and fatigue she felt it all happening inside of her the way it almost always did and she knew she would come and she tried not to give him the satisfaction of crying out.

When it was over he held her tenderly for a moment, and whispered things to her, and she cried a little. She thought she heard her car coming back, and she wanted to cover herself, but he would not let her. Now was the time for the thing she wanted and needed most of all, and he always made her do the drugs naked, no matter where they were or what was happening. It was a rule he had made, and he allowed no exceptions.

"What's this?" she asked.

"New shit."

"I don't want new. You know what I want."

"You gonna shoot up between your toes again? You ain't going to be able to wear shoes if you keep that up."

"What is it?"

"Call yourself a narc. It's ice, the latest thing. The dawn of the Ice Age."

"You don't shoot it?"

"Nah, you smoke it. Don't you cops keep up with the market?"

She drew herself up to lean on one hand as he got the shit ready for her to smoke.

"Here you go, take a hit of that."

The first two or three draws, nothing. She was not a smoker except for a joint once in a while. Another. And, in a flittering heartbeat, she was up. She sucked in the smoke, held it deep inside her, and she loved it. She was up. Goddamn! A glow came alive in the pit of her stomach and warmed her, naked in the damp, chilled van on the nasty mattress. She felt the heat of it curling with the beat of her heart, throbbing out through her veins, down to her fingertips, her toes. Goddamn!

"Yeah, I thought you'd like that."

"You got any more?" she asked.

"You don't need any more. You're up for hours, whether you know it or not."

"I want some more."

"Well, you ain't getting any more. Trust me, you're up."

"What is this shit?"

"Ice, crystal meth. New stuff, new way of making it. It's

gonna sweep the country. Gets you up like crack, only it keeps you there longer.''

"How long?''

"Hours.''

"How do you know it won't kill me?''

"If you die, you die. You know the best thing this stuff is gonna do?''

"I know I'm up. I don't give a shit if I do die.''

"It'll put them greasers in Colombia out of business. We don't need their coke if we got this shit. American dope for American dopers, that's my position on the goddamned trade deficit. Fuck 'em.''

"It was good tonight,'' she said.

"Quit lying, bitch. You got your dope.''

"I mean it. With your hair cut off, and your beard . . . black hair. It was like fucking somebody else.''

"That does a lot for my ego.''

"Let's do it again.''

"Put your clothes on, nympho. They'll be back any minute.''

"Who?''

"Blondie and the boys. Jesus, you get your dose, the whole world goes away, don't it?''

"Could we make this brief, Bobby?'' Chief Knecht said, swirling his glass impatiently. What was left of the ice in his drink tinkled. He had been nursing the one whiskey sour since dinner. "I had a long day. Two funerals.''

"I know, Chief. You did a good job, your remarks. Everybody said so.''

"You didn't come.''

"The mayor was there. Somebody had to mind the store.''

Klevinger settled into a comfortable chair and put his drink on the upholstered arm, wrapped in a linen bar napkin so he would not ring the fabric. They had finished a dinner at an exclusive country club in far North Dallas, planned long before the murders of the two cops, and impossible to cancel. Important people had turned out, all the men in tuxedos. The women had engaged in what the bachelor Klevinger understood they called "competitive dressing." He had not been nursing his drinks, but he could handle his liquor. He knew Knecht was not a drinking man, or else he was careful who he drank with.

"Have a seat, Chief."

"I'm fine, thanks." Knecht preferred to stand, to pace. The sounds of after-dinner voices mumbled in the big room outside the double door Klevinger had pulled closed so they could have a word alone.

"Damned shame," Klevinger mumbled into his drink.

"What's that?"

"I said, 'damned shame.' About your two officers."

"You sound like you mean that."

"Of course I do. What in . . ."

"I've seen it both ways with these shootings, don't forget. When we win, there's hell to pay. When we lose, all's sweetness and light."

"What are you trying to say?"

"When cops die, nobody sues the city. We all dress up and make speeches. We hand the widows flags, everybody has a good cry."

"Come on, now."

"The mayor takes a brave stand against crime, even Pinky Lafayette chimes in, or used to. I guess that's Zulu Jones's department now."

"You're upset."

Knecht looked at him with a wry smile but said nothing more.

"You've seen the papers?" Klevinger asked, rhetorically. They all read the papers religiously.

"Yeah. No surprises."

"What are you going to do about going to the wonder-nines?"

"The what?"

"High-capacity nine-millimeter semiauto pistols your officers are screaming for, and their spouses. Where do we stand on that issue?"

Knecht had been a policeman a long time. High school, a hitch in the army, and then the police department. He was in the lucky majority of officers who had never heard a shot fired in anger, at least not close or personal. Like most cops, he had been in dozens of situations when he thought he might have to shoot, when he was ready to, but it had not come to that. It was a curious thing, the way that went. He knew five-year officers who had been in two, even three shoot-outs. Luck had something to do with it.

"I didn't know you were so knowledgeable about guns," Knecht said, smiling.

"I don't know shit about them, I know about running a city. And it doesn't matter anymore who's right about the damned guns. We have to give them the new ones. Period."

"Money's not a problem?"

"It's always a problem, but not as much as a mutiny. Or a protest by the spouses on the City Hall steps. I shouldn't have to tell you this. You should be telling me."

"We're talking about two million dollars. Maybe two-five."

"Jesus! How much do these goddamned guns cost?"

"It varies, but you don't just hand them out like neckties. You have to buy the leather gear, a thousand rounds of practice ammo per officer, magazines, training. It adds up. We'll have to survey the research, see what other departments have done . . ."

"Make the announcement tomorrow; that won't cost anything. I'll start looking for the money, but I'm telling you right now, two million is too much."

"You know what I'd like to do with two million."

"Yeah, AFIS."

Automated Fingerprint Identification System was Knecht's crusade item. It compared fingerprints by computer and could do in seconds what it took months to do by hand. But two million for pistols would bump AFIS down the line, off the short list for sure. You could not go to the city council for four million in projects, not the way the Dallas economy was waffling. Not and stand up for pay raises and staffing, and all the pacekeeping you needed with a department like his.

"That's right. We need it. Dallas has been at the front on this kind of thing for years. We're talking slippage without it, Bobby."

"We tried, Chief. The negotiations unraveled on us."

"I know. We should do it ourselves. If we're careful with the specs, we could be talking about plugging into a national system. You don't know what it could do for our clearances." The city and county had tried to lash together a treaty, cosponsor the thing, charge suburbs for time, but it had caved in, hard feelings all around.

"And make the bulletproof vests part of it, too," Klevinger added. He had not been thinking about AFIS.

"We have a vest for every officer. Anybody who wants one can have one."

"It's gotta be mandatory. Terry and Jackson weren't wearing them. We could have liability here."

"Vests wouldn't have saved them, any more than automatics."

"It's not the reality," Klevinger insisted. "It's the perception."

"Jackson died a hero, you know. That's real."

"They both did, Chief."

"Yeah, I said that in my speeches today. They're all heroes, all the KIA's. None of them have to do the job. But, Jackson . . . he might have got out of it if he hadn't tried to save his partner. I don't know what makes a man . . . do that. I honestly don't."

"Let's say in the morning at eleven for the press conference, Chief. I'll get with you on it beforehand."

"Right."

"Tell all your people they did a good job on the funerals today."

"Yeah, we know how to do funerals. We've had the practice. Do you think . . ." Knecht looked up from his drink at Klevinger, who gave the impression he was waiting for the chief to get it off his chest. "How would it be tomorrow if I told them what would really make a difference?"

"Chief, courts and corrections are not our . . ."

"Not our bailiwick? No, but they're sure as hell our problem."

"We'll talk in the morning, Chief."

"Between the two of us, Bobby, you think buying 'em new pistols will keep them from going union?"

"That's not fair of you. We're talking about officer safety here."

"Right."

Knecht found a place to put down his glass and walked out of the room to find his wife and take her home. Klevinger watched him go and shook his head.

"Charlotte Mayfield is the dead blonde they found in the Lincoln at the auto pound, the car you did the VIN work on for Welborn."

"I don't care, I didn't do the bitch," Mack insisted, not angry, just firm.

"She was cut up like the one in Pleasant Grove, the dancer they found with the beer bottle in her."

"Why would I lie to you about it, Stef?" Mack eyed her calmly. "The one in the Grove, I did that one. It was business. But for the record, the beer bottle, that was not me. Must have been Blondie."

"He was there? He can put that on you?"

"He knows better."

"You're supposed to be smarter than that." Stef shook her head.

"And you're supposed to be of some use to me. You were supposed to find out what the deal is on that case, anyway."

"I will."

"You said you'd do it yesterday."

"No way. There was a crowd in Persons yesterday. Some kind of summit conference."

"What about? About me?"

"Read a paper, will you? Two cops went down Saturday night."

"So did they make me on the bitch in the Grove, or not?"

"I don't know. I don't think so, I'd have heard something."

"I hope you're right. Anyway, this Mayfield bitch was supposed to drive the Lincoln to Mexico, but somebody did her and put her in the trunk."

"Who?"

"Some Mexicans. They're trying to muscle in on Welborn, but that's all right. I got plans for them."

"So the cop waiting tables at the club is not a problem."

"Nah."

"Not even if they think you're good for Mayfield?"

"I ain't worried. I didn't kill her, and they ain't going to connect me to the Lincoln. Cars are what the hell I do. That I ain't worried about at all."

"So there's no problem."

"That's what I been trying to tell you, goddamnit. Get it through your head."

"Okay." Stef, having dressed now, was sitting on the dirty mattress, her elbow resting on a spare battery that was among the junk in the back of Mack's van. "You don't have any plans for her, then?"

"What kind of plans?"

"Don't play dumb with me," Stef flared. She knew she had had no choice but to tip Mack about the cop in the club, this girl Randi. So she could get her dope, if for nothing else. Also, because Randi could pose a hell of a threat to Mack, and by extension to Stef as well. If anything happened to Mack . . . But this part had been worrying her all along. She did not want anything to happen to this kid Randi, not because of her. If she could believe Mack about this, the whole thing could actually work out all right. All Mack had to do was stay out of the club until Stef got word to him that they had pulled Randi off. They wouldn't run the undercover thing very long if it didn't get results—a week at the most. They had too much to do to tie down three people, Randi and her backup, for maybes. "You know perfectly well what plans."

Stef was up, and she could hear her teeth biting off the ends of her words, knew she was talking too fast, saying everything twice, and she felt like she could see through walls, like she could see through the closed door of the van into the wet cold night, through the trees across the bike trail to the streets of the city, inside the cars on the wet, sloshing streets, into the lives of the people in the cars. She was not cold anymore, the heat inside of her kept her toasty warm, and she could see the past and the future, watched herself lying on her back on the mattress with her legs sprawled and limp at first as she told Mack/Jeff her story and then her legs wrapping around him, her heels digging into him as she surrendered and moved under him. She could see it all, and it would be all right. She would destroy him, bring him down. And this kid Randi would never know how close she had come.

"Nothing whatsoever. I'll tell you the truth . . ."

"Because she broke Blondie's nose. Don't forget that."

". . . we went over there to the club last night, as a matter of fact, and we had it in mind to . . ."

". . . teach her a lesson, right? I knew you'd have that in your mind, because you can't let people get away with that kind of shit," Stef said, nodding her head too fast.

"Because people there at the club, they know . . ."

". . . that Blondie works for you, he hangs with you, and you gotta protect the image." Stef was thinking faster than he now, finishing his sentences for him. She knew everything he was going to say before he said it, she was way ahead of him.

"Exactly. Only she was off last night. And, actually, I have business to take care of, and I was thinking we'd just blow it off, forget the whole thing. I mean . . ."

". . . business comes first, always."

"Exactly."

"What kind of business?" Stef asked, leaning toward him, her eyes wide, almost luminous in the darkness.

"That's for me to know and you to find out, Officer."

"Cars? Guns? No, it's dope, right? Big business?"

"I'll tell you when the time comes. Now, get out of here."

"What?"

"The boys are back. Get out."

"Nothing happens to whatshername, the kid working the club, right?"

"Not from me it don't."

"Okay. I have your word on that. You'll call me?"

"I promise."

"Don't make me come chasing after you."

"Is that an order, Officer Nugent?"

"How about a little something for the road?"

"You don't need it. I told you, this shit you smoked, you're gonna be up for hours. I'll be with you again before you need. I mean it."

"Right. So, you're just gonna take care of a little business now, right?"

"No, some big business." Mack closed the side door of the van, leaving her standing there in the rain looking at the closed door, probably still talking a mile a minute, she was so high. He crawled back into the driver's seat of the van and motioned to the boys through the passenger window.

Blondie came up grinning, showing his bad teeth, and elbowed Stef aside so he could climb in. Peter and Dick piled into the back. Mack was glad to be driving again, now that Blondie had cut and dyed his hair and shaved off his beard. He cranked the van and put it in gear, leaving Stef Nugent talking in the rain, gesturing to emphasize whatever the hell she was saying.

CHAPTER 22

Tuesday, 1:45 a.m.

''It's almost t-t-two o'clock, man. They're g-gonna be closed.'' Blondie was nervous, shifting around in the passenger seat and bobbing his head up and down.

''You look like a fighter waiting for the bell,'' Mack told him.

''Yeah?'' Blondie grinned. Nobody ever called him a fighter before. ''And in this c-corner, wearing n-no trunks!'' he said, trying to sound like an announcer. He laughed at his own joke, and looked into the back to see if the other two were laughing with him. They grinned to let him know that they got his joke, that he was a funny guy all right.

''No, I take that back,'' Mack said, one eye on the traffic and the treacherous street, slicker now that the temperature was really dropping again. ''You don't look like a fighter. You know what you look like?''

''What?''

''You look like this guy I heard about. He was at this thing, where they were doing research on sex, see? These guys in white lab coats were asking everybody how many times a week did they get any, how often they got laid, and this one guy, he's like you, Blondie, he can hardly fucking sit still. He's bouncing around, he's hopping, and he's got this big shit-eating grin on his face. So they ask him, 'And you, sir, how often do you get any?' and this little guy, he says, 'Once a year.' 'Once a year?'

says the guy in the lab coat. 'But if you're only gettin' it once a year, how come you're so excited?' And the little guy, this is you, he says, 'Tonight's the night!' ''

Mack roared with laughter at the joke and at the stupid look on Blondie's face. He checked the mirror and the two in the back were laughing too, poking each other in the ribs and pointing at Blondie and laughing their asses off. ''Get it? 'Tonight's the night!' ''

"Okay, okay. I g-get it," Blondie said, looking out the window on his side and making a face. He liked the one about the fighter better. ''Only it's g-going to be closing t-time before we get there and that b-b-bitch'll be gone.''

"They close at two. They don't leave at two," Mack explained patiently. ''We got plenty of time.''

Mack was thinking about putting some muscle together to take on the Mexicans for their dope. He knew who he could trust and who he couldn't. Stef kept him posted on who got busted and needed to work off a case, so Mack knew who was set up to be snitching, and kept clear of them. Stef was an investment, in addition to which he was heavy into this game the two of them were playing. She had not won a round yet, but that didn't mean she wouldn't win the game.

Mack drove carefully, watching for cops and thinking about sex with Stef. When she needed the dope and he made her do things, she hated him and then she wanted it and she hated him even more. Stef was the only woman in a long time who felt anything for him, and hate was better than love, for all he knew. He knew hate was real, and the way Stef hated him and even herself when he was in her, it was the hottest thing he had had going for a long time. That was the part he would miss the most when it was over.

Mack parked across from the club's parking lot. From there he could not see the backup van, the one Stef had told him about. But that was okay. If he couldn't see them, they couldn't see him. It was when everybody left the lot after the place closed and Charlie had settled up, that was when he would worry about the cops in their van. There was plenty of time.

• • •

Dunk got off the bus on Gaston Avenue at East Grand. He was practically invisible in his disguise, a gray cotton ball cap and a gray khaki jacket. He had all he needed in a tool pouch, and if he had to he could get rid of it quickly. The location was good for him: lots of cars parked around the clubs and if he did not find what he wanted there, there were plenty of cars in the apartments across the street. Weather was good, too, because cops minded their own business in weather like this. It was too cold for them to be getting out of their cars and messing with people, and the streets were too slick, so they would be laying up in places where wouldn't nobody run over them.

He was in no hurry. The Mexican had said that Willy wanted this particular make and model, black and it did not have to be right away. He had a couple of days to find it, so if this was not the night, no problem. He knew that when he delivered the car Willy was going to be on him about the dope business. Dunk had not decided what he would say about that. The two cops that rousted him on Saturday were on his mind, too. Snitch for real or die for snitchin'. Ain't that some shit.

For the thousandth time that night Randi pressed her right elbow against her hip to feel the reassuring bulk of her ''pager'' there. She was proud of her needlework, and wondered how she would ever tell her mother about it. She had taken up the waist of the miniskirt to hold the clip of the transmitter more tightly, and stitched a piece of elastic into the waistband for extra measure.

As she got better at her job, she realized that Saturday night had been a waste. She had been so self-conscious that she probably would not have known it if Mack the Knife had sat at one of her tables, unless he had given her a hard time for screwing up his drink order. Tonight, she was making progress.

She wasn't even worried about the creep with the broken nose. He wasn't worth blowing her cover. She'd asked J.D. and Larry to keep an eye out for him, as Clark had suggested. If he showed up they would move inside. At the first sign of trouble, they'd run him in for disorderly conduct or public intoxication, anything to get him out of the picture. That wouldn't burn her, Vice cops hung out in clubs like this all the time. She might have to get a new backup team, but that would not be a problem, either.

Randi was getting comfortable in her role, even finding time to joke with some of her customers, and wonder about what she was supposed to do with the tips she was making.

At ten to two the club began to empty. Charlie ran his wall clocks fast like all the clubs, Mack knew, because they wanted the serving and drinking shut down with minutes to spare. The Alcoholic Beverage Commission was shorthanded, but they still checked up on late service now and then, and nobody wanted trouble with their liquor license over such chickenshit stuff as that.

"Here they c-come!" Blondie barkcd, all excited.

"Them's the customers, stupid," Mack told him. "They run off the customers, then they divvy up tips, they balance the register, and like that. It'll be a while before the employees come out. You better take it easy. You're gonna shoot off in your pants if you don't watch out. That'd be hell, wouldn't it, Blondie? If we got this chip for you and there she was and you shot off before you even got it in? That'd be a damned shame."

"It's going to be a war," Ned said, after Curtis had finished explaining it all to him and Stone.

"Did you think we would take this kind of treatment from them Mexicans, Neddy boy?" Curtis asked him, with that funny singsong way they had. "Did you think we would run away?"

"I was wondering why we didn't get out of town while we had the chance."

"And was you wondering why we didn't get rid of these guns?"

Curtis pointed to the weapons from the shooting with the cops. The AK-47 and the Uzis lay wrapped in a blanket on the floor of an open closet. Each of them had different guns now, little Uzis like pistols, with long magazines that stuck out of the bottoms of the handles. Ned didn't like them at all, did not think they were worth a shit at any distance. He wasn't a Jamaican, and he didn't like to fight the way they did, spraying bullets around like water out of a fire hose. He had been a real soldier, he was a trained professional in the use of small arms. He liked to work at some distance where you did not run so much risk of the accidental hit coming back at you, where you could aim your weapon and pick out your targets and knock them down.

"I was wondering about that, as a matter of fact."

Ned did not care for the nine-millimeter round either, because to him it was a pistol bullet, no matter what you shot it out of, and he liked the real bullets his AK used. You could put one of his AK bullets next to one of their nine millimeters, and they looked like a father and son. He wanted a gun that shot real bullets, one you could hit with from a decent distance, but he did not say any of this to Curtis. He had not got past their suspicions yet, he knew, because they all knew somebody had sold them out to the Mexicans.

"These are cop-killer guns," Curtis crowed. "We left them enough brass to make a statue. They ever get their hands on these guns, they gonna know what they got."

"Exactly," Ned agreed glumly.

"So we gonna make sure they find them. Ask me where."

"Where are the cops going to find the guns, Curtis?"

"In them Mexicans' hands. In their dead hands, that's where. And then we're off the hook and back in business. In South Dallas and in West Dallas, goddamnit. You see where I'm going here, Ned?"

"Hell of a plan."

"You damned right it's a hell of a plan."

"Only how are we going to arrange for all these Mexicans to be dead?"

"Ned, you insist on underestimating us. It's our killers we going to go to war with, killers from out of town. I done told you they're coming."

"Fine, only . . ."

"Only what?"

"Only I done been in one war, Curtis. I had not meant to get into another one."

"Don' worry. This time, you going to win."

• • •

Mack realized too late that he could not tell which of the bundled-up women who came out of the club was Randi Stoner, and he did not know her car. Charlie, the manager, solved the problem for them, without knowing it. The rent-a-cop was there, keeping warm in his fake squad car, and Charlie had walked over to get in when he turned around and yelled out across the lot.

"Hey, Randi!" he yelled. "Come here a second."

When Mack saw one of the scurrying figures stop and turn toward Charlie, he knew that his problem had resolved itself, the way things do when something is meant to happen.

"What?" Randi called across the frosty lot.

"Amateur night. I want to see you up there."

"We'll see."

"You'll make some money, kid, I'm tellin' you. They love it when a waitress dances. Think of your kid."

"I'm freezing, Charlie."

"Do it!" Charlie laughed, his breath like smoke in front of his face, his teeth chattering. He was not wearing a hat.

"We'll see. Good night."

Randi walked away, waving her hand as if to say either good-bye or get outta here. Charlie could not tell which. When the guard put his car in gear and started to move, Charlie told him to hold it a second. He wanted to be sure Randi's car would start, that she would get off all right.

Randi's little Honda fired right up, and she revved the engine a couple of times and turned on her lights. As she pulled across the driveway to the street, she beeped her horn lightly at Charlie to let him know she appreciated his waiting. And then she turned right and was gone in the swirling rain, taillights going away.

"Okay, let's go," Charlie said to the guard, and they went the other way to make the night deposit in the bank.

"There she g-g-goes," Blondie jabbered.

"I know, shithead. Hold your horses."

The taillights of the Honda were still in view to his right when Mack saw the headlights of the van across the street and half a block down come to life. He watched the backup van roll down onto the street and turn to its left, rumble past where he was sitting, and continue in the direction Randi had gone. When they were well past, he followed.

Most of the way, Mack could see only the van, but that was all right. He wondered if they would tag along all the way home with her. That would mean a break-in. The cops in the van had their eyes on Randi, and they were worried about the cars between them and her, was anybody tailing her. It never occurred to them that somebody might be following them. Tailers are the worst at spotting tails, Mack knew, and thinking that made him check his mirrors to make sure his own butt was clear.

The cop van rolled up and stopped in the Medallion parking lot to watch Randi make her call from the 7-Eleven, and Mack laid off a safe distance to see what happened next.

"So how did it go tonight?" J.D. asked.

"Nothing to it."

"We didn't see any sign of that blond guy you told us about. Did you?"

"Nah, no problems."

"Okay, mount up and we'll tag along home."

"No need, you guys go on to the house."

"No dice. Let's go."

"I'm gonna gas up the Honda and maybe get a hot chocolate. You got time for that?"

"I didn't know you had to put gas in a Honda. I thought they did that when you bought 'em and they ran forever."

"Really, I'm fine. I'm heeled and there's no tail. What's to worry?"

"Okay, you're a big girl."

"See you in the morning."

Mack could not believe his eyes when he saw the cop van turn a sharp U and head out of the parking lot. The girl hung up the phone and walked to her car by the self-serve pump. Mack watched the backup drive away down the side street and the girl fumbling with the gas pump, and he could not believe how it was all falling into place. This thing is supposed to happen, he told himself. That was all there was to it.

"Get ready, boys," he said. "Here we go."

CHAPTER 23

Tuesday, 3:15 a.m.

Randi stood at the pump with the nozzle in her hand and jiggled the switch from Off to On and back again. Nothing was happening. She looked into the store to see if the clerk knew she was out there. Maybe she was supposed to pay first. She saw the clerk look up from the register, in her direction. She waved her hand at him and pointed at the pump. He nodded and waved back.

She heard the van roll in behind her and thought at first it was J.D. and Larry, but a quick look told her it wasn't, and she looked away because she had been about to smile and say something cute, and she didn't want to get into anything with strangers. She assumed the van would swing to its left and park head-in. With her back to the van, her eyes on the rolling numbers on the pump, she did not realize at first that the van had pulled straight into the lot, parallel to her car, between her and the store. What was in her mind in the last few seconds was should she get a receipt for the gas. Technically, she was entitled to reimbursement. It had just occurred to her that she had forgotten to ask J.D. what to do with her tips when it happened.

An arm snaked around her throat from behind and the force of a body drove her into the pump so hard she heard herself grunt with the impact before the arm squeezed shut on her windpipe. Hands on her arms, pinning them. She felt the ground fall away beneath her as her feet came up, the arm choking and

211

lifting her, and the dark sky above her, rain hitting her face and then even the night sky was falling away and she knew she was blacking out. She soiled herself and then everything closed down on her.

She came to in the lurching van, atop a smelly mattress. Her arms were free and she twisted her body to get her hand inside her coat. There were voices above her and the sound of the engine, the tires on the wet slick street, and the closeness of men huddled around her, dirty men she could smell. It was dark and one of them pressed himself down on her. He was giggling and chanting something. She worked her hand inside her coat, beneath the long sweater she had slipped on over her costume and fumbled for the transmitter in the waistband of her miniskirt. Once she thought she thumbed the switch to On, but she couldn't be sure so she let her body bounce up more on the mattress as the van careened down the road and tried it again. She was sure she had it that time, but she did not know how far away J.D. and Larry would be by now, or how far the little transmitter's signal would reach.

The van turned left, then right onto what sounded like gravel, sloping down. It occurred to Randi that this might have nothing to do with who she was, that it might be a random thing. Her revolver was in the Honda, along with her ID, in a zippered bag to keep it clean. How far would the transmitter reach, she wondered.

"What the hell?" J.D. and Larry exchanged puzzled glances. Between them the square black box sounded a tone and the bulb on its top blinked red, off and on, insistent.

"She's sitting on the goddamned thing," Larry offered. "Setting it off and doesn't even know it."

"You're clear," J.D. advised, checking Larry's blind spot in the mirror.

Larry pumped the brakes to get his speed down without skidding then stayed on them as he swung the steering wheel around, making a top-heavy U-turn, the old van rocking up on its right wheels as he came around.

"Hundred dollars she's set the damned thing off accidentally," Larry said, his voice full of conviction.

"No bet, that's what she did, all right. Clear."

J.D. looked as far up the cross street to their right as he could see while Larry watched to the left, and they bounced through the intersection against the red light. Well under a minute after they got the signal, he heaved the rattling van hard left and skidded precariously around the corner onto Abrams and both of them saw her Honda sitting at the pump in front of the 7-Eleven. They grinned and shook their heads at each other, but Larry did not slow down, caroming off Abrams up the turn-in and screeching to a stop in front of the store. They were on the ground before the van quit rocking from the sudden stop, and J.D. went into the store with his gun drawn. Larry took a quick look at the Honda and did not see any sign of Randi, so he moved toward the store, too, to his partner's left and behind him. They were both thinking that Randi had stumbled into a robbery at the 7-Eleven, but they could see the clerk at the register. Somebody's got a gun on him, or he's the hijacker faking it. No sign of Randi.

The clerk fell back as the two men came in, both of them crouched and wide-eyed, the black snubby revolvers in their hands.

"Please! Please!" the clerk cried, backing away, his hands in the air.

"Be still," J.D. told the clerk, showing him a badge. "We're police. Where is she?"

"I beg your pardon?"

"The woman in that Honda, where is she?"

"She vanished."

"Do what?"

"No sign of her," Larry reported. He had looked down all the aisles, kicked open the door into the back room, stuck his head and his gun around all the corners.

"What do you mean, vanished?" J.D. demanded.

"Well, it was very curious, now that you mention it . . ." the clerk began.

"Slow talker," J.D. said. "Put it out, let's get some uniforms rolling. Get the chopper if you can."

Larry raced out of the store and went to Randi's Honda first, just in case. It was locked and he could see nothing amiss inside. The nozzle of the gas pump hose had fallen or been pulled out of the tank of the car and lay abandoned on the driveway. The pump had shut off, showing six point eight gallons sold.

"Tell me what happened," J.D. told the clerk, not yelling because if the little man got any more upset he might forget whatever it was or faint.

"She was pumping the gas. The van came. There." The clerk pointed. "It stopped, only for a moment, and then it went. And she was gone."

"A van. What kind of van?"

"I'm sorry, I don't . . ."

"What color?"

"Gray, I think."

"Gray?"

"Yes, with . . . spots."

"Spots?"

"Yes, on this side." The clerk showed with his hands and a turn of his body that he meant the left side of the van.

"The driver's side, then. You saw the driver. What did he look like?" J.D. asked, talking fast.

"I don't know."

"What do you mean?"

"Hey, J.D.," Larry came back into the store, his portable radio in his hand. "They say no go on the chopper on account of the weather. Low visibility."

"Tell 'em to turn the headlights on on that motherfucker and get it in the air!"

Larry ducked back out through the door and talked earnestly into the radio, his head bobbing up and down. A siren growled from the direction of Northwest Highway.

"He was wearing a mask, the driver," the clerk put in.

"What kind?"

"Like a cap, a woolen cap that you pull down. With holes for the eyes."

"Shit! Which way did they go? The van?" The clerk pointed north, in the direction of Northwest Highway. "Did they turn or go straight?"

"Maybe straight, maybe to the right. I didn't see. But if they turned left, I think I see them. I was watching because I did not know . . . The lady just vanished.''

"Okay, thanks.''

J.D. rushed outside and took the radio to put out what they had. An unknown make and model van, gray in color, with primer spots on the driver's side, left the fifty-eight-hundred block of Abrams within the last two or three minutes. Direction of travel either north on Abrams or east on Northwest Highway. No license number. Driver wearing a ski mask. Believed to have abducted a Vice officer, female.

The first Patrol officer roared up, siren drifting, more sirens on the night air. The dispatcher relayed from the Helicopter Division that one bird was en route, another would be airborne ASAP, estimated arrivals twelve minutes on the first, thirty on the second.

"Relay to all channels. Get some units into the lake area, into White Rock Lake,'' J.D. said.

"Eight-ten to all TAC units on Channel Two, Signal Forty-five, Flagpole Hill, Code Three. Do not acknowledge, radio discipline.''

A Park Police unit checked in on Lawther Drive, heading into White Rock Lake Park, then another. The Northeast Patrol Division watch commander proclaimed a command post at fifty-eight-hundred block of Abrams and ticked off the numbers of the four units nearest to the lake to report there. The dispatcher advised him that two of those units were out of service, but the officers working the units broke in to say they were clear and en route. It was crackling on the air by now from one end of the city to the other. An officer was in trouble, and God help the ones behind it.

The van stopped, and the man who had ridden all the way on top of her, bouncing on her, rolled off now and reached under her to grab the front of her coat.

"Roll over, B-B-Beethoven!''

Randi looked up at a yellow ski mask with red around the mouth hole like smeared lipstick.

"Gotcha now, b-bitch!''

He straddled her and pawed at her coat, yanking it apart,

popping off buttons. She pushed his hands away. He giggled and punched her with his fist on the side of the head. One of the others grabbed her arms and held them. She tried to raise a knee to push Yellow Mask away, but hands out of the darkness pinned her legs to the floor. She could not get any leverage with her arms or legs, and all she was doing was flopping around, her hips bouncing, trying to work something loose so she could hurt one of them. Jesus, how many are there?

She screamed as loudly as she could and hoped the sound of her voice made it out of the van, thought she could hear it echoing out into the night, bouncing off the low clouds like radio waves. She screamed a second time and Yellow Mask hit her again, full on the mouth this time. She tasted blood.

"Stick something in her mouth," came a voice from up front somewhere.

"I got something right here to put in her mouth." Another voice.

"You do and she'll bite the son of a bitch off."

Her third scream died in her throat as a fistful of fabric shoved into her mouth and she gagged and tossed her head but could not spit it out. It tasted of gasoline and grease, and the taste and smell of it choked her as much as its bulk and the pressure of the hand that fed it to her.

"That's better."

"Okay, let's see what we got here."

"Close your eyes, bitch. I said close your eyes."

The one who said that jabbed his fingers at her eyes but stopped them short, making her blink. She left her eyes closed.

"I w-w-want to see what we g-g-got."

They rolled her from side to side, pulled and pushed her legs and arms, and one of them kneed her hard in the ribs to make her turn the way he wanted her to. All of that was to get her clothes off, and when the coat had been peeled away and her long sweater pushed up, one of them laughed.

"She likes this costume so much she wears the son of a bitch home. Look."

A hand pushed inside her vest and squeezed her breast, hard, until she cried out into the rags in her mouth. A hand ran up the inside of her thigh and grabbed her roughly, and she gasped with the shock of it and the pain.

"Let's get down to business."

"Go for it, man."

They shoved her legs together to make it easier and then tugged at her tights, pulled them down over her hips and rolled them and pulled them down over her feet, the hands hopping quickly up her legs as the pants went by so that when she felt them release her it was too quick for her to break away. Next the miniskirt, the same way, and she was naked except for the stupid vest, and they swapped her wrists around among themselves so that she was never free of them as they pulled her coat and sweater off over her hands and then they laughed like boys being naughty and talked about her as if she could be made to care what they said.

I will not die, she told herself. Whatever happens, I will not die.

"What do you think of this, huh?"

She felt something touch her between her legs and squirmed to get it off of her.

"She's hot, m-m-man. She wants it!"

"Spread out, goddamnit! Give me a little room to work here."

She felt them scurrying around her, felt the van move with their shifting weight, and opened her eyes enough to see the figures of the men who were doing this. All in masks, dark shapes with big shoulders. She saw a tattoo of a penis on a thick forearm.

"Turn loose of her hands there. You don't have to hold her now. Just tell her what you want. She'll mind. Won't you?"

When her hands came free, she covered her breasts and between her legs, but one of them slapped her with an open hand down across her eyes, on the bridge of her nose.

"Don't do that, idiot. Why do you think we took your clothes off?"

That one hit her again, in the same place, and tears came to her eyes. She moved her hands.

"See? All you have to do is explain it. She ain't stupid. Are you? Here, sit up here."

A hand in her hair lifted her head and shoved her back against the side of the van opposite the side door. The metal was cold, and she arched her back to get off the cold metal.

"Proud of them little titties, ain't she?"

"I said lean back."

She did as she was told.

"You've got your eyes open. That's cheating."

She closed her eyes, having seen that it was the yellow one who squatted between her legs. He put his hands on her knees.

"Spread 'em, b-bitch."

She opened her legs.

"Now open your eyes. You see what this is, don't you?"

This one had a black mask and his eyes looked black, too, in the darkness, with the white of his skin around them in the mask holes. In his mouth hole she saw only white teeth in a crooked row, like tombstones. She had read that somewhere, a description of a man with teeth like tombstones. He had something in his hands.

"This is a jumper cable, just like you use to start your car when you fuck up and leave your lights on all day. You with me so far?"

The yellow one with the red like lipstick around his mouth hole moved his hands up her legs and touched her. She started at his rough touch, but made herself hold still. She heard the stuttering wingbeat of a helicopter invisible in the rain outside the windows of the van. In the distance she thought she could hear sirens.

Z-z-z-z-z-t!

A ball of fire popped on the sole of her left foot and she jerked up, banging her head and back on the side of the van, making a helpless noise in her throat behind the gag. Her hands shot up at the touch of the fireball, reached out toward the source of the noise and the searing smell, the burning tender flesh of her instep.

"No hands."

She obeyed, lowering her hands to her sides.

"You with me so far?" the black mask repeated.

She nodded, making more noises because the pain in her foot was excruciating. She was ashamed of crying from the pain.

The yellow one probed her with one of his fingers, and she looked down at his hand on her and saw his thumb lying on top of her there and the thumbnail was black with grease. She jumped when he put his finger inside her, his nails scraping her. It hurt, and she jumped again. Instinctively her hands moved toward the pain, but she had learned about her hands and she kept them at her sides, balling them tightly into fists.

The one in the black mask reached out toward her with one of the clamps from the jumper cable and fastened it like a mouth onto her right breast. She cried because it hurt so badly and her foot hurt and she could smell the burned flesh on the sole of her foot. Push, push by the yellow man. She cried.

"Get the picture?"

The one in the black mask held the second clamp of the jumper cable, its jaws open, menacing her left breast.

"Get the picture?"

She nodded, crying.

"Gimme a beer, willya? Nah, stupid. That one, the hot one." Black Mask held the bottle of beer toward her and then turned it over in his hand, pouring the warm beer over her chest. He moved his hand to the left and the right, soaking her breasts in the sudsy warm beer. It felt like urine and she remembered she had pissed herself when they choked her and they must have seen that and she cried. Her foot hurt. "No point wasting a cold one."

Black Mask opened the jagged-toothed clamp and tugged it free of her breast, holding the two clamps up in front of her, close to her eyes. He touched them together. *Z-z-z-z-z-t!* It made blue sparks and she flinched away, throwing her hands up over her eyes.

"No hands, please."

She put her hands down.

"Now, listen to me."

The clamp from the jumper cable bit into her right breast again. The yellow one hurt her, poked into her, giggling. She heard herself whimpering behind the oily rags in her mouth and she was ashamed. I will not die, she told herself. No matter what . . .

"Listen to me."

She had closed her eyes and at the insistent tone of his voice she opened them to see that he had the second clamp of the jumper cable open again. It surrounded her left breast and she looked down at her breasts, shiny with the warm beer like piss, the alligator mouth of one clamp chewing her, eating her alive, working deeper into her flesh as her breasts rose and fell. She was crying, sobbing, and her breath was ragged. I will not die. I will not . . .

"Are you listening? Are you?"

She nodded.

"Tell me everything."

She made a noise through the gag, started to lift her hands to take the rags out of her mouth but did not.

"Don't worry about that. You are a cop, aren't you?"

She nodded her head.

"Your name is Randi Stoner, isn't it?"

She nodded. The yellow one, pushing, hurting.

"You're going to be a good girl, aren't you?"

She nodded. The helicopter again, closer now. No sirens anymore.

"Why were you working in that club? What were you doing? You'll tell me, won't you?"

She nodded.

"When I take out the rags, you won't scream, will you?"

She shook her head. No.

He pulled the wadded rags out of her mouth and she gulped the cold damp air, and closed her eyes. She breathed deeply and fought against crying aloud.

"Tell me."

She started to speak, but the black mask stopped her with the soft touch of a fingertip to her lips.

"I'll know if you lie, and I'll put my little friend here on your other tit. If it don't kill you, it'll fuck you up for life. Understand?"

She nodded. The yellow one hurt her, worse this time, and her nod froze as she flexed herself and gasped at the pain he did to her. When he stopped for a moment, and she could control her movements, she nodded again. The yellow man giggled.

"Good girl," said the black mask. "Why?"

"Looking for a murder suspect."

"Don't make me play twenty questions."

"Jefferson Lee MacAnnaly, aka Mack the Knife. He killed a girl, a dancer, in Pleasant Grove. He's supposed to hang out at the club. That's all."

They heard the helicopter, too, now, and she prayed that it was not lightning that she saw dart across the sky through the window behind the one in the black mask. She prayed it was the "Night Sun," the probing eye on the police helicopter that would see through the rainy dark and whatever cover these bastards had thought would hide them.

"What the hell is that?" one of them asked.

"A chopper, stupid. What else?"

"They're looking for us."

"Why would they be? Who reported her missing, that camel jockey at the 7-Eleven? Don't be stupid."

"Them other cops, in the van."

"They were long gone when we grabbed her. Get a grip, asshole. The chopper's up all the time around here."

These men knew who she was, they knew about the club, about J.D. and Larry. One of them was the man who killed women. Randi remembered the crime-scene photos of the girl. Sprawled on the ground with the beer bottle.

The yellow one hurt her bad. Sweet Jesus, she prayed. I will not die.

"Enough of the third d-degree. Let me at her!"

"Go for it, shithead. Who's stopping you?"

The yellow mask shoved himself at her, and she saw his fly was open, his sex was out. He drove her back against the cold wall with his clumsy shoving, and lurched his weight onto her, bearing her down along the wall, her head banging against the wall and the back of the seat as he crawled onto her, his dirty hands pawing at her. She put her hands on his chest to push him away.

Z-z-z-z-z-t! Blue sparks in the black stench of the air.

"Hands, please," said the black mask.

She let her hands drop, let them fall beside her shoulders on the mattress. He's the one, she knew. The black mask was Mack the Knife.

"Where's that damned chopper?" somebody yelled.

"Keep your voice down," said the black mask.

"Listen to it, will you? Where is it?"

"See the light, stupid? Over there. Way over there, the other side of Abrams, going that way, toward the friggin' lake."

"Goddamn!" grunted the yellow mask. "I n-n-need some room."

"Get it!" one of the others encouraged him.

"Ouch!" Another voice. "You kicked me, stupid. Watch where you're putting them feet."

"Pace yourself," cautioned the black mask. "Wouldn't it be hell if you shot off before you even got it in? That'd be hell, wouldn't it?"

"Aw, m-m-man."

"Watch your fucking feet!"

"Aw right, aw right, you guys. Yank that door, give the lovebirds a little room. That's it, let's step outside and make sure there ain't no blue meanies sneaking up in the bushes. Give 'em a little privacy."

The yellow mask giggled. Randi knew who he was, too.

Lieutenant Rampling was driving the second bird, closing fast, with Officer Chessman cross-checking landmarks from the first helicopter, talking him in. Rampling was glued to the infrared display, the FLIR, for "Forward Looking Infra-Red," which made the inky black jumble below a flickering green world where nothing with body heat could hide.

"Upstream, north of Park Lane, west of Abrams. There's a gravel road, a cleared right-of-way, then like a trail into the trees where the bridge crosses. Left, left. Okay, should be eleven o'clock," Chessman coaxed him along. To the first helicopter, the one rigged with the Night Sun high-intensity halogen lamp: "You say you had visual, Oh-Four?"

"Affirmative. Confirm a van, dark in color. No occupants visible. Nobody in the area. They've pulled it in tight on the west side of the trail clearing, into the trees, but coming in from the south you can see the right side of the van. We were afraid the Sun would spook them. We're orbiting southeast to cover your engine noise."

"Ten-Four. We're coming up on it, coming . . . We have them. Dispatch, we have visual on a dark gray van. What is TAC's location?"

Sergeant Byner and two of his men were close. They had been turning onto Park Lane off of Abrams to check White Rock Creek upstream of the lake when the first bird squawked. They were dismounted, deployed in a skirmish line at twenty-meter intervals.

"We are forty meters north of Park Lane on the west side of the creek. Can you confirm distance to target?"

"I make it sixty meters, due north."

"Ten-Four."

Byner had Castleberry with him, and Castleberry had his rifle. The third man filled the entry-one position and carried one of the little German MP-5 submachine guns. Byner had an M-16. There would not be time for help to get to them. He would get within sight and take it from there. He knew a couple of things the bastards could be doing to the officer, and he didn't aim to let either of them go on any longer than he could help.

Cold air and rain drove in through the open side door of the van, and the yellow mask cursed and grumbled, shifting his weight toward the door and dragging Randi down onto the mattress.

"You g-got this coming, b-bitch!"

He slapped her. Again. Again. She cried. He forced her legs apart and pawed at her with his dirty hands. Sweet Jesus.

With more cursing and a mindless urgency, he hunched against her and she felt his hot fluid spray over her belly and she lay perfectly still. He slapped her and slapped her, cursing.

"S-stupid f-f-fucking whore!"

"What's the matter there, soldier?"

"You psyched me, m-man. You head g-g-g-gamed me and look w-what you d-d-did to me!"

"That's awful, ain't it." This one leaned his head into the van and she could see it was the black mask. "Go to all this trouble and look at you, shot off all over the lady before you ever got it in. That's a shame."

"You d-did it to m-m-me, man."

"I'll hook my jumper cables to your balls and maybe we can get you going again."

"It ain't f-f-funny!"

"I think it is. Who's next?"

A man leaped into the dark square hole of the door.

"I'll do her."

"Get to it," said the black mask. He was in charge.

"I'm f-f-first, Mack," the yellow mask whined.

"You had your turn. Get your ass out of the van."

The yellow mask screamed. He threw himself off of her, with another slap for the hell of it, and clambered noisily out of the van.

"Take it easy," the black mask told him. "Have a beer. And watch where you leave the empty this time."

"I have them," Castleberry whispered. The three TAC officers were wearing infrared night-vision goggles and they had moved carefully, silently, among the trees within sight of the creek. "There." He pointed.

The van was dark, shiny in their goggles, square edged. They saw figures swarming around the near side of it.

"I count one, two, three men."

"Three."

"Check."

"No guns showing."

They moved closer and found firing positions. Castleberry worked his goggles off his face, down onto his chest, and brought up the rifle. He switched on the infrared scope and swept left to right, right to left. Three men wearing masks. Two looked like they were arguing. No sign of the girl. Wait. Inside the van.

This one said nothing, only crawled across her sprawled legs which she had not closed because she was afraid of the blue sparks the black mask would make on her, the teeth of his clamps on her. She lay still as this one crawled onto her.

• • •

The TAC cops heard a car door slam in the distance somewhere, impossible to tell how far because of the way sound carried at night, even on this kind of rain-soaked night in the cold air. Voices from the van, a man's voice. What was he saying?

"Get it done, man. We've been fucking around here long enough," growled the black mask from outside the van.

"Yeah, yeah," groaned the one on top of her, hurting her where the yellow one had ripped at her with his black fingernails. He reached under her and pinched her ass. "Do something for me, bitch. Shake it. Shake your ass."

He pinched her hard. She choked back a scream, and moved under him, praying. *I will not die. No matter what.*

"That's it. That's it! Goddamn!" He threw himself at her twice, three times, and fell on her, cursing.

"Okay, okay. You got yours, now get her out here."

"Yeah, yeah." He crawled off of her and stepped outside. He reached back for her and pulled and she tumbled out of the van naked and fell heavily on the ground and was surprised that it was littered with small, smooth stones. Where were they?

The rain tumbled down on her and she was cold. Her foot hurt and her breast throbbed. She was sick at her stomach and there was pain and a seeping of fluids from her insides, and the rain was cold but it washed off the yellow one's jism from her belly and the stale beer. *I will not die. No matter what happens, I will not . . .*

"We have to kill her now," said the one in the black mask.

"What?"

"I said we have to shoot the bitch."

"I ain't had my turn," one spoke up.

"I thought you said . . ." one of the others protested.

"Blondie called me by name," the black mask hissed. "I promised somebody I wouldn't do it. Pete, you fucked her, you shoot her."

"Don't mind if I do," said that one.

"L-l-let me!" the yellow mask whined.

Randi looked up and saw guns in their hands. She scrambled to her feet and tried to run, but her burned foot would not bear her weight over the stones, and she fell. One of them caught her easily and dragged her back toward the van.

"Naw, Blondie," drawled the black mask. "I'm afraid you'd shoot too soon and miss the bitch again." Laughter all around, Blondie in the yellow mask muttering curses. Pete leveled a silver automatic at her head.

Randi heard a flutter of furtive whispers, three or four in a quick stutter. Gunshots? She curled into a tight ball, but felt nothing. When she looked up at Pete, she saw that he was all wrong. There were too many holes in his mask, and steam curled up out of it in the cold night air. He stiffened awkwardly and pitched over backwards, banging and clattering as he fell like a log against the van and lay still on the ground.

Randi pushed herself up with her hands and saw Pete's buddy, the quiet one, dance like a puppet for a long second and go down. She saw the one in the black mask dive prone on the ground and she heard bullets thumping around him. He yelped suddenly like a kicked dog and slammed back against the van. He was hit.

Yellow Mask threw himself to the ground beside her.

"G-get up," he whispered.

He held her tight and walked like a crab, keeping her between him and the darkness where the shots had come from. She looked back and saw the black mask scramble madly around the front of the van and disappear.

"No. No," she said, in a quiet voice.

"It's you and m-m-me now, b-bitch," Blondie muttered, the muzzle of his gun to her ear, and squeezed her to him with his free arm around her throat.

She did the thing they had showed her in the academy, hard and fast. It almost worked. She got the gun away from her head, and they both had their hands on it now, but he held on to her and did not let her drop to the ground so the cops in the trees could get a clear shot at him. He bear-hugged her and they both had the gun, both her hands against his right hand, because he was afraid to let go with his left. They struggled for the gun, pressing and twisting against each other and Blondie giggled. His fly was still open and she felt his erection against her leg. She tried to hook her foot behind his leg, but he kicked it away.

Their labored breathing sent billows of steam roiling around their heads, their feet scuffling, scattering stones over the soggy ground. She drove her knee up hard and he screamed and went down, holding on to her, dragging her down on top of him.

The muzzle flash erupted between them like an orgasm of heat and light. The boom of the report reverberated like thunder. Yellow Mask looked at her, and she was glad he did because the last thing he ever saw was the smile on her face.

"Stay down, Officer!" came the voice from the woods.

"He went that way!" she pointed, screaming. "Around the front of the van. He's wounded."

"Yes, ma'am. Stay down, please. We see you. You're all right."

She crawled to the van and climbed in, the dead man's gun tight in her fist. She was pulling her clothes on when Sergeant Byner came up, his face like a frog's in the night-vision goggles.

"Are you okay?" he asked.

"Jefferson Lee MacAnnaly, aka Mack the Knife," she answered him. She gave Byner Mack's physical description. He let her tell him all about it, even when she started describing Mack's van, forgetting that she was sitting in it, hugging her coat tightly around her, and Mack was in the woods somewhere with a bullet in him, running for his life.

CHAPTER 24

Tuesday, 4:30 a.m.

Dunk missed the place the first time and made a U-turn in the black Monte Carlo he had stolen an hour earlier. He had draped a hand rag over the steering column to cover the minor damage he had done getting the car started after he used the folding "slim jim" he carried in his tool bag to unlock the driver's door. He had not broken the window, which was the quickest and simplest way to do it, because he did not want any complaints from Willy.

On his way back he finally spotted the break in the thick row of cedar trees. He turned in, clicking his headlights on bright because it looked like the kind of place where he might run over a cow or a bear or Lord only knew what up in there. A light flashed on and off to his left, and he stopped. It flashed again. He popped off the high beams and waited for some long seconds. Another light flash. He cut off the headlights altogether, and looked in his rearview mirror at the dark crooked driveway behind him. He could not see the road anymore because the drive curved as you came in and now all he could make out was the black mass of the cedar trees. Lawd, lawd, he muttered. He rolled down his window to stick his head out, thinking he maybe ought to put the Monte Carlo in reverse and make a run for it. He did not need this shit.

"Hey, man." The voice was soft, but it popped up out of

nowhere right beside him through the open driver's window, and Dunk jumped so high he hit his head and cursed.

"Take it easy, Dunk." It was Johnny, the quiet one. "Park it over there."

Dunk felt his heart twisting like a kitten in a burlap bag. Won't have to worry about getting old, he told himself, if I keep messing around with these damned Mexicans.

"What is this, man, secret headquarters?" Dunk asked as he climbed out of the black Monte Carlo holding his tool belt, his cap tugged down over his forehead. A fine drizzle now shimmered in Johnny's flashlight beam, turning to ice. "I almost never found this son of a bitch."

"Nah, it's just a place we do this car shit," Johnny told him. It occurred to Johnny that letting Dunk know about this place was maybe not the smart thing to do. But he could only do so much, and he had to hang around the place because Willy had left word for him to round up some guys he could trust and have them waiting there when he got back. "We're West Dallas boys when it comes to the serious stuff. You know that."

"Whatever. You got my money?"

"Here. And there's the trade-in."

Dunk counted his money.

"Any problem with the money?" Johnny asked.

"Nope. As agreed. What's the deal with the other car? Willy didn't like it or something?"

"He likes to change cars a lot. It's a thing with him. There ain't nothing wrong with it. He said you can drive it or sell it or whatever. His gift to you, because this money covers the one you're delivering tonight. Right?"

"Yeah, right. How come he's so good to me?"

"He wants to bring you into the business. He's got plans for you. The South Dallas thing."

"What do the Jamaicans think about that?" Dunk dared to ask.

"Don't worry about the Jamaicans. We handle them foreigners."

"Of course you do," Dunk smiled, wondering where the hell this Mexican got off calling anybody a foreigner. "And I'd love to stay and chat, but it's too goddamned cold out here for me."

"Willy wants an answer pretty soon."

"I'll get back to him," Dunk promised, hustling over to the Firebird he had stolen only a few days before and sold to the Mexicans. Crazy people.

Johnny stood in the cold rain as if he did not feel it and watched Dunk get into the car. He waved as Dunk made a circle and passed on his way out toward the road.

As he circled the car to leave, Dunk saw the barn in his headlights. It was old and leaning, but he saw the doors were closed and there was a chain running between them. A new chain, shiny in his headlights.

"I'll bet y'all do some car stuff out here," he muttered. Then as he saw the driveway curving ahead back toward the road, he returned Johnny's wave and thanked the Lord that he was leaving. No more with these guys, he promised himself. They can get somebody else to run South Dallas.

He hated this weather. The streets were getting slicker with the rain making ice and slush that sprayed up on the windshield and the headlights and he could not see where he was going, and he knew people in Dallas did not know how to drive in this stuff. As he neared the Trinity River bridge going back into South Dallas on Old Central, he thought he saw a police car behind him in the lane to his left. Dunk slowed so it would pass him. He was worrying about that and forgot that his lane merged left at the foot of the bridge. When he looked up and saw the painted stripes that meant he was not supposed to be there and the car coming up the entry ramp on his right, he instinctively braked and swerved and felt the impact. He looked out his window at the face of the cop in his car only a couple of feet away and saw that he had his mouth open, he was saying something, and the grinding metal of the two cars sounded like a machine eating metal. In what looked like slow motion, he saw his car and the cop car like they were welded together, yawing and spinning, skittering on the slick pavement toward the guardrail in the middle of the freeway, and he hoped he would die in the crash.

Mack pounded through the trees, as the deep burn of his wound punished him for the labor of breathing. They were coming after him, and he wondered how the cops found them so fast. He did not try to hide or move quietly because he knew he was hurt badly.

The two TAC men spread out on either side of the line of movement where they had last seen the man in the black mask and moved into the woods after him. They swept the woods with their eyes as they went, their goggles showing them a pale green world as they hunted him.

Twice Mack changed directions, the last time at a sharp angle that brought him out of the woods at the base of a concrete ramp, a bridge. He scrambled up as far as he could make his legs take him, then fell on his hands and knees to stop himself from sliding all the way back down again. Spitting blood on the concrete, he made it the last few feet and tumbled over the retaining barrier onto Abrams Road.

Castleberry raised his rifle but the picture he saw in his scope was a "Don't Shoot," the hunching figure of a man disappearing over the railing. Castleberry put it out on the radio and started up the ramp after him.

Mack dodged cars and angled across the lanes of the divided road toward the lights across the street at the south end of the bridge. He did not look back because he knew they were close, but he did not think they would shoot across the road with the traffic. It had to be after four in the morning, but still there was traffic. Where are they all going at this hour?

Castleberry reached the bridge railing and yanked off his goggles because of the streetlights. Mack the Knife was no-where to be seen.

Carlton Welborn awoke, trying to remember the sound he had heard. He checked to make sure his wife was asleep, then rose lightly from the bed and slipped on his robe. He slid his feet into his slippers and went downstairs to investigate.

He checked the front and back doors, and when he went into the kitchen he saw glass on the floor. Glass from the door to the driveway.

"Morning, partner."

The voice startled him; and he spun around to find Mack seated at the kitchen table.

"What in God's name are you doing here?" Carlton demanded, whispering. He did not want to wake his wife.

"A little trouble. Hand me another rag, will you?"

The room was dark, and Mack's face was in shadows, his legs in the trapezoid of light from a window.

"A rag?"

"That one on the fridge'll do fine."

Carlton plucked the dishrag off the handle of the refrigerator and tossed it onto the table in front of the big man. He watched Mack fold the rag and shove it inside his shirt. He saw that Mack pressed his left arm hard against his side.

"Trying to stop the bleeding," Mack explained. "Or slow it down, anyway."

"Bleeding?"

"I got shot."

"What's going on?"

"I was taking care of a little business, trying to make sure the cops weren't on to us. Things got out of hand."

"I don't understand."

"You don't have to. What you have to do is come through for me."

"What do you mean?"

"Money and transportation. If I can get out of here, I'll be okay. There's people in Oklahoma I can trust. I can get well there, stay low. Arrange it for me, Carlton."

"How?"

"Somebody's company plane out of Love Field, with a pilot who can keep a secret."

"You're crazy. I can't . . ."

"You'd better."

"You don't know what you're asking. I can't involve people like that."

"Oh. How about the money part?"

"I don't have any."

"You're not much help."

"Well, there's a little cash, but . . ."

"Get it."

Welborn did not turn his back on the big man in the shadows, kept his eyes on him as he moved across the kitchen, then hurried to his den and opened the wall safe behind the painting above his desk. He took all the money out of the quart-sized hole and left the safe door open in case Mack wanted to check for himself. He went back to the kitchen, with a nervous look up the stairs. Most of all, he did not want his wife to wake up and find him with this man.

"It's all I have."

"How much?"

"Less than a thousand."

"Christ, Welborn."

"Not much less."

"That's all?"

"Look for yourself if you don't believe me. The safe's open."

"Why wouldn't I believe you? Car keys?"

"What do you want with . . ."

"The Porsche."

"You're going to take my car?"

"Nine hundred bucks and no help on a plane. Least you could do is loan me your car."

"All right. The keys are there by the door, on the rack."

"Okay. Guess this is it, then."

"Just be quiet leaving. My wife is asleep upstairs."

"We wouldn't want to wake her," Mack said. Welborn could not see his smile because he was in the shadows. "I don't think these rags are going to do the job, partner. You got a pillow or something?"

"Sofa cushions."

"That'll do."

Carlton hurried to get a couple of cushions and brought them back. He wanted Mack out of his house.

"Here."

"You're a pal," Mack said softly, smiling his invisible smile. He pushed the barrel of his gun into the center of the two pillows and with his left hand cupped the stuffed fabric firmly around the barrel. "Thanks."

The pillows muffled the sound of the gun, and Mack waited to see if he had awakened Mrs. Welborn. He sat in the chair at the kitchen table and waited for over a minute, a wall clock somewhere in the room ticking it off for him. Nothing from upstairs. Good. He would not have gotten anything out of killing the wife. It was bad enough she would come downstairs in a few hours and find this mess.

Mack noticed, as he stood and the pain in his side made him catch his breath, that Carlton Welborn III looked surprised. Welborn had a splotch of blood on his pajamas, high on his chest, just where the lapels of his bathrobe veed, and there was blood running across the white tiles on the kitchen floor. As Mack stepped over the corpse, the blood that had puddled in his chair dribbled onto the floor, mingling his blood with Welborn's. He took the key from the neatly labeled hook on the wall. Above the key rack there was a cork bulletin board with a couple of cartoons thumbtacked in place. Mack tried to make them out as he opened the door with the broken glass, but there was not enough light in the room.

They drove Randi out of the place in a squad car because she insisted she did not want an ambulance, and when they showed her which car it would be, she opened the door herself and sat in the front. The backseat was for prisoners and victims. On their way out of the place, up out of the bottoms along a gravel road that made the squad car bounce the way the van had, she saw a village of white buildings with rows of small windows. From the windows, heads of all colors looked out at her, long heads with big ears that wigwagged at the noise the squad car made. Horses. It was a riding stable. They had taken her out onto a bridle path.

"What's her condition? I see. Yes, have a car come right over." Chief Knecht sat on the edge of his bed next to his wife.

"She's alive, though?" she asked.

"Yes."

"What's it coming to?"

"They kill my officers. Now they're raping them."

"Get dressed, I'm on my way." It was Dave White.

Bob Marx blinked and cleared his throat. "What's up?" he asked.

"I'll tell you when I get there. Twenty minutes."

Marx hung up the phone and pushed himself out of bed. He looked at the pale light outside his window. A streetlight. The sun was not up yet.

Bill Clark came up off his couch as if he'd been jumped by a burglar and stood wide legged and groggy in the middle of the room. A knock on his door. Another. Gun in hand, he went to the door and looked out the fish-eye peephole. A uniformed officer.

"What's up?" he asked.

"Message. Open up, Sergeant Clark."

"What is it?" he asked, opening the door the length of the chain.

"Randi Stoner's at Parkland, hurt. I don't know how bad."

"Jesus. What happened?"

"All they told me was she asked for you."

Stef Nugent was awake, staring at her reflection in a mirror. She heard footsteps outside her door and before Mack could knock she opened it and he stumbled inside.

"What happened?" she asked.

"Got shot." He leaned on her and she walked him to her couch.

"Who did it?" she asked.

"Long story."

"And you came here. Only place you could think of. Terrific."

"I brought you some more 'ice.' You don't . . . even have to be nice . . . nice for a price, nice for the 'ice' . . . get it?"

She sneered at him, but she did reach into the pocket he was fumbling with and took the "ice." She dropped it into the deep pocket of her robe. When she closed and locked the door, she saw blood on the threshold.

"Who did it?" she demanded.

"Long story," he repeated.

"What about Blondie and the penises?"

"Dead."

"All of them?"

"Dead. Cops . . ."

"Cops killed them? Cops? What the fuck did you do, Mack?"

"Long . . ."

She jabbed two fingers against his throat and felt his pulse tapping light and fast. "Let me see where you're hit."

"Nah, it'll only . . . start bleeding again . . ."

"Jesus, you're in bad shape."

He nodded, his head sagging onto his chest, and she checked him again for a pulse. He was alive. He might even make it. She turned on the television and the radio. The TV was some canned late-night bullshit, and she turned down the sound. She tuned her radio to KRLD and heard some of the details.

"You rotten bastard. You said . . ." Stef was not sure he could still hear her. "She was no threat . . ."

She looked at him, then she looked at herself in the mirror again.

Clark was ushered into the Rape Trauma Unit where doctors were treating Randi Stoner. In the unit's waiting room, he found J. D. Chapman and Larry Potter standing, smoking cigarettes, in front of a door. He had known them both a long time.

"She asked for you," J.D. told him.

"We did all we could," Larry said. "We did good . . . after."

Clark nodded and thought they looked like they wanted to ask him why she wanted him there, but neither of them did. He tapped on the door, and it was opened by a nurse. He told her who he was and she motioned him to come in.

"You think Stef is involved?" Marx asked, as he and Dave White climbed out of their car in the parking lot of Stef Nugent's apartment.

"I think we better find out."

"You want a little backup?"

"No, I want us to handle this."

That was bad thinking, Marx told himself as they hustled up the long walk toward her door.

They found the door ajar, and Dave White drew his gun as he pushed it open all the way. He palmed the little Smith &

Wesson Chief on his hip as he moved into the room. Marx stayed close behind, gun in hand.

"Police! Don't move!" White shouted at the figure on the couch. He approached slowly.

Marx dropped to one knee and saw it was Mack on the couch.

"Don't move!" White repeated.

"He ain't moving, Dave. Now what?"

"I'll cover him. You check the bathroom and the kitchen."

More dumb thinking, Marx muttered under his breath. They needed backup, some uniforms. He edged his way down a wall and around a corner into the kitchen.

"Come here, Dave," he said.

"I'm covering this guy," his partner shot back. "What is it?"

"Stef Nugent. She ain't moving either."

"I hope you don't mind I asked for you," Randi said.

"I don't mind. You look good. I didn't know what to expect."

"Right, I look terrific."

She was on an examining table with her feet in stirrups, which had made her laugh, having just come from a bridle path, and that had made the doctor and the nurse look at her a little strangely. She was covered with a sheet, and she saw that Sergeant Clark made a point of looking at her face.

Her lip was badly bruised, and her cheeks were purple from the punches. Her foot felt better now; they had done something about that, one of the injections they gave her. Her right breast hurt terribly. She had demanded a douche and when the doctor objected, she remained calm and explained that he needn't worry about collecting sperm to identify her rapist because he was lying on a bridle path in North Dallas with the top of his head popped up like a trash can lid, the kind where you stomp the pedal and the lid flies up. So they did as she asked.

"You did good," Clark said.

"You don't know what I did."

"You're alive."

"Yeah."

"That's the point, isn't it?"

"Yeah."

"So you did good."

"I killed one of them," she said, wincing at something the doctor was doing to her under the sheet.

"I'm glad."

"It was Blondie, from the other night in the club. You were right, he came back."

"I should have killed him when I had the chance."

"Yeah. I wanted you here."

"Here I am."

"You're the one I tell my secrets to."

Chief Knecht faced the TV cameras, the news crews looking sleepy and cold in their quilted jackets and turtlenecks, their stocking caps. This was all happening in the driveway in front of Parkland Emergency, because the chief did not want this herd of newsies inside getting in the staff's way. He had told them what he knew about the abduction of Officer Stoner. He had given them her name because his people had located her next of kin, her mother, and she was being brought to the hospital by squad car. He kept it simple, did not say anything that would cause them any problems later, and waited for questions.

"Have you ever seen such a week?" Bobby Thurmon asked, holding a tape recorder in front of Knecht. "All the killings in the last four days—what does it mean?"

"Read your own newspapers, ladies and gentlemen," Knecht said, although he did not see any women in the group. "Watch the news you put out on television every evening. Last year in this country one of every five police officers was assaulted, eighty killed. If cops were soldiers, we'd have handed out over twenty thousand purple hearts in this country, last year alone. We've had more than our share of it, and frankly I don't see any reason to think it's going to get any better."

"Is it gangs or drugs, Chief?"

"Same thing. American cops seized over forty tons of cocaine last year. Problem is, Americans used two hundred tons. Yeah, I'd say our problems are drug related."

More questions, a buzz of voices canceling out each other.

"And I'll tell you another thing," Knecht went on. "I'm tired of political hacks making brave speeches and then throwing dimes at this problem like they were manhole covers. If we can afford Stealth bombers at five billion dollars a shot, why not jails to keep convicted felons off the street? I'll make y'all a deal. When we get the men involved in this thing tonight ID'ed, I'll bet you two of 'em were on probation or parole. And you'll have to trust me, we don't have that yet, but I bet you I'm right about this."

"Who are you calling hack politicians, Chief?" Bobby asked.

"Most of them. I'd say all, but I don't know all of them."

"Does that include the mayor?"

"Did the son of a bitch run for office? That's all for now, ladies and gentlemen. I think you've got enough there."

Knecht worked his way through the reporters to the hospital doors, ignoring the rest of their questions. They shouted questions at him until the doors closed behind him.

"Well?" Knecht shot a nearby captain a look.

"You pissed on some pretty big pants legs out there."

"I didn't say anything about Bobby Klevinger."

"I admire your restraint, Chief."

CHAPTER 25

Tuesday, 6:00 a.m.

"Early morning is best," El Jefe explained to Willy. "When a man yawns and looks down and he has a hard-on. His mind is not on his work then, is it?"

The two of them leaned against the fender of Willy's rented Oldsmobile beside a narrow road, looking across from their low hill to the snaky brown break that was the river, the border. Frank stood not far away, talking with El Jefe's driver and a couple of his men.

"There it is," the old man said, pointing.

Willy saw the tanker truck easing forward in the short line of cars and trucks on the Mexican side.

"Every Tuesday and Thursday morning for a year, this truck has crossed here, coming north. Every Monday and Wednesday evening, it crosses going south. At first the gringos searched it every time. But not so much lately."

"Excellent," Willy whispered, shaking his head. "The planning, the resources . . . Will they search it today?"

"Probably not. But we don't take the chance. Observe."

As the tanker reached the border station, an ancient pickup with sideboards straining against a load of chairs and boxes pulled alongside. Willy saw steam billowing suddenly from the hood of the pickup and then, just as a guard stepped forward, it burst into flames. Willy could hear the shouts of the guards across the distance and he saw them waving their arms and the tanker truck groaned into gear and lumbered across the border.

"There, you see!" the old man exclaimed.

"Excellent," Willy congratulated him.

The tanker truck picked up speed as it headed north on the road toward the interstate.

"So, then you're off, young man." The old man shook his hand and looked him in the eye. "I don't need to remind you of all we have talked about."

"No, Jefe. I won't disappoint you."

"Good. *Vaya con dios,* then."

And that was that. Willy and Frank were on the road, on their way back to Dallas, tailing a ton of cocaine. And ten percent is mine, Willy told himself, like a schoolboy in a dream. Free and clear.

Knecht was in his office with his bureau commanders. Many of them were standing, because his office was hardly roomy enough for a command conference. They ordinarily used the media conference room, but this morning it was full of press, and Knecht's already-announced press conference had been moved up. There would be live local television coverage, he had been told.

"Stef Nugent is at Parkland, too," the head of his Internal Affairs Division was explaining.

"Who?" the chief asked.

"Stef Nugent, Chief. Narcotics, undercover."

"We've got two women in Parkland?"

"Yes, sir," the IAD commander said. He would have preferred to brief Knecht on this in private, but things were happening too fast. "Separate deal, sir."

"Okay."

"We've been keeping an eye on her for several days, got information she might be the leak we've been worried about . . ."

"What kind of information?" Knecht demanded. He had not heard any of this.

"Her picture showed up in some notebooks we took off of dealers."

"Pictures?"

"Yes, sir. So when they got word of this deal last night, the abduction of an undercover officer, my people went to her apartment . . ."

"Nugent's."

"Yes, sir. That's where they found MacAnnaly, this guy Mack the Knife."

"Yeah, I got word we had him. DOA, right?"

"Yes, sir, dead on arrival at Parkland. One gunshot wound to the torso, probably nine millimeter. Doctors said he bled to death, basically."

The Criminal Investigations and Special Operations deputy chiefs spoke up, out of sorts that IAD was getting into this part of it.

"Sounds like our people got him, Chief," the Special Ops commander put in. "My man fired on him with an MP-5 beside the van, nine millimeter. He said he thought he hit him at least once. They did some good shooting under tough conditions out there, sir."

"I'm sure they did . . ."

"Chief, we have investigators with Nugent to get a statement . . ."

"She didn't tell my people anything when they found her in her apartment. She was already out. Overdose, we're not sure what it was yet."

"All of which brings up a damned important point," said the Vice Commander. "IAD was looking at Nugent, and I didn't hear a goddamned thing about it. This came out in a meeting the other day. IAD flat refused to come with the information."

"Wait just a minute there . . . " the IAD commander sputtered.

"What meeting was this?" Knecht asked. "I don't remember . . ."

"A working group," the Special Ops deputy chief explained. "Over at my shop . . ."

"The hell you say!" said the CAPers commander. "First I've heard about it."

"Your Lieutenant McCluskey was present, and a sergeant . . . Marino."

"What kind of a deal are you guys trying to pull over there . . .?"

"Where do you get off . . . ?"

"Getting back to the question of operational security . . ."

"Knock it off!" Knecht boomed, standing up from behind his desk. "Now . . ."

The door opened and Bobby Klevinger strode in, just as the chief's intercom buzzed, his administrative assistant trying to warn him that the assistant city manager was on his way in.

"Good morning, Chief."

"Morning, Bobby. What can I do for you?"

"I'd like a word with you." Klevinger's jaws were tight, and he looked less carefully groomed than usual. "Privately."

"All right, people. We'll adjourn for the moment. Stand by outside if you please." The commanders filed out, and Klevinger closed the door behind them.

"What the hell got into you, Knecht? Were you drunk?"

"In reference to what, exactly?"

"In reference to that show you put on for the reporters at the hospital. Have you seen the papers?"

"No, I haven't. You mean we made the morning editions?"

"Front page."

"I wouldn't have thought they could get it in that quick."

"Well?"

"Well what, Bobby? You want some coffee?"

"No, I don't want any goddamned coffee. Orville, I demand an explanation!"

"Fair enough. Bobby, this city is swirling clockwise like a turd in a toilet, because the people in charge don't have the balls or the brains to do what needs to be done, and I'm goddamned tired of it. That's all."

"What is this, your resignation speech?"

"No. You're going to have to fire me."

"Don't think I won't."

"You've been working up your nerve for a couple of months now."

"Where do you get your information? Whoever said . . ."

"Maybe you didn't interview a candidate for my job that last trip you made."

"That's neither here nor there, Orville. You cannot make remarks like you made this morning to the press. You . . ."

The chief's door opened again, and in walked Gene Madigan, president of the Dallas Police Association.

"What are you doing here, Madigan?" Klevinger demanded.

"I got business here."

"After me," Klevinger snapped. "Get out."

"Why don't you throw me out, Bobby?" Madigan glided across the room toward Klevinger with a tight little smile on his face. "If you've got the balls."

"Now, now, gentlemen," the chief put in. "I won't have any of that."

"He just barged in," Klevinger complained.

"So did you," Knecht observed. "What can I do for you, Madigan?"

"I'm delivering a message."

"Great!" Klevinger threw up his hands. "Union bullshit, at a time like this."

"The DPA's not a union, Bobby," Knecht pointed out. "What's the message?"

"I've never been a fan of yours, Chief. You know that."

"I do."

"To us you've always looked like a patsy for the shot callers over at the leaning tower of bullshit. You don't demand a damned thing, and you don't ask for enough . . ."

"Thank you for stopping by to share that."

"But I liked what you said on TV this morning. I've been getting calls, and the association officers got together, and here's the thing. We're behind you on this . . ."

"On what?"

"We figure Klevinger's gonna try to shut you up or else outright fire your ass. Am I wrong?"

"Probably not," Knecht admitted.

"So we're behind you on this, like I said. If he fires you, the association walks."

"A strike's illegal," Klevinger pointed out patiently.

"So put us in jail," Madigan retorted. "Twenty-two hundred of us." The two exchanged looks that both meant from their hearts. But only Madigan wanted to back his up, so nothing came of it. "That's the message, Chief. See you around."

"Thank you for stopping by." They shook hands, and Knecht walked Madigan to the door. When he was gone, Knecht turned to Klevinger. "I need to brief with my staff, Bobby. There's a press conference in less than an hour."

"You're hanging yourself," Klevinger said. "Committing professional suicide."

"We could make it a joint press conference. Would you like to share the podium?"

"No, thank you," Klevinger said as he stomped out.

Knecht rubbed his eyes and called his people back in.

The word was out that Mack the Knife was dead, and Sergeant Spencer got a call from a Grand Prairie auto theft detective who had a line on a shop where Mack had done his car work. Spencer agreed to meet the Grand Prairie people over there.

Ned and his two Jamaican friends heard the news on the radio but it meant nothing to them, except that they joked about kidnapping a lady cop someday. When the noon news came on television, they watched it, and had some things to say about Randi Stoner when they saw her file photograph on the screen.

Curtis was too edgy to watch much television. He spent most of the morning away from the house, and once he took the car and was gone for over an hour. When he came back, just before the noon news came on, he was singing, and Ned looked out through a window shade and saw him cutting some dance steps on the front porch.

"It's happening!" he sang as he came through the door. "It's a beautiful sight, man. They're coming in from all over. Beautiful black warriors with blood in their eyes. You just wait, Neddie boy. We going to show them Mexicans a thing or two."

Clark stopped by his apartment to clean up and get dressed for the day, and his phone rang.

"Sergeant Clark, this is Bobby Thurmon."

"Yeah, kid. What's up?"

"Did you hear the chief's press conference?"

"What press conference?"

"At the hospital, early this morning. You know about the policewoman, right?"

"Yeah, I know about that. What did the chief say?"

Thurmon read him part of his story.

"Didn't know Orville had it in him. Good for him."

"You have anything to add?" Thurmon asked.

"Quote me, you mean?"

"Why not?"

"Get outta here," Clark growled and hung up the phone.

The next call, as he was toweling off after a shower, was Boots. "Any instructions?"

"Just stand by. I'm on my way. Everybody's there?"

"Except Filmore and Winager. They spotted a familiar name on the county jail roll this morning, and they're on their way down there to lean on a car thief."

"Anybody I know?"

"Small-timer, they call him Dunk, I don't have his right name. Get this, last night he's driving a stolen car and he sideswipes a squad car on South Central. Totals both cars."

"Officers hurt?"

"Nah, bumps and scratches. Can you believe that?"

"A real master criminal. Okay, I'll be there in a minute."

Dunk was not surprised when a guard ushered him into an interrogation room and he found himself looking across a table at the same two cops that had rousted him the Saturday before.

"Morning, Officers," he said, smiling.

"Give me something," the big one said.

"I don't know what . . ."

"No time for games, Dunk," the other one said. "There ain't but three of us in this room, and we all know who we are and what we are. Now you get right or get screwed to the fucking wall."

"First, we're gonna yank your probation," the big one promised. "Then we got you cold as ice on this auto theft. We might file on you for assault to murder for attacking them po-lice with your goddamned stolen car, if we can find the time . . ."

"And," the other one said, talking in a quiet voice that Dunk knew really meant business, "we're gonna put the high bitch on you."

"That ain't right!" Dunk flew up out of his chair. "Now, you know that can't be right. I ain't in no way up for no bitch, man."

"Add 'em up, Dunk. This Firebird here that you ran into the squad car with, that's going to be conviction number three. Habitual criminal. And that means life."

"I got probation last time, man."

"It's still a conviction, Dunk, because you didn't serve your probation right. Like I said, we're going to get you violated on that, today."

"Aw, man . . . Am I all you two have to mess with? In this whole goddamned city, am I the only criminal you two officers can lay your hands on?"

"Can you do life living down a snitch rap? Dunk, that's the question you have to ask yourself."

"What do you want?"

"What have you got?"

Filmore and Winager called their office to let them know that they were taking Dunk on a "down and out" to show them something. Some Mexicans, he said. They'd be in the office in a couple of hours.

Long before noon, Willy started getting the Dallas stations on the radio in the Olds. He caught the news about Randi Stoner and this guy Mack the Knife.

"Did you hear that, Frank?"

"What about it?"

"That Mack guy, he was Welborn's muscle, don't you get it? That ugly biker dude. He's dead, man."

"How far to Dallas?" Frank asked.

"We'll be there by . . . Wait a minute. Listen. Listen."

More news. Dallas developer and investor Carlton Welborn III was found murdered in his Preston Hollow home this morning. His Porsche was missing.

"Goddamn, Frank, I can't believe it."

"What?"

"Ain't you listening, man? It's like angels came down out of heaven during the night and gave me my fucking wishes, Frank. That biker dude is dead, Welborn is dead, and here we sit watching a ton of cocaine roll down the highway. Man, life just keeps getting better and better, doesn't it?"

"Semiautomatic handguns will be issued and body armor is mandatory, effective immediately. That is a review of the cases to this moment, and my announcements in summary. Thank you, ladies and gentlemen." Chief Knecht stalked out of the media conference room without taking any questions. Press releases were handed out covering everything, and the chief went directly to his office, where his full staff was waiting. He left word he wanted no calls and addressed the group.

"Ladies and gentlemen," he began, noting with pride that there were ladies in his command staff, three captains and a deputy chief. Blacks and Hispanics, too. They had come a long way. His office was even more crowded than it had been earlier, with people standing, but that could not be helped. He wanted to talk to his people now, and he did not want to wait until the media room cleared out.

"I have several things to go over with you." He brought them all up to speed on the events of the previous twenty-four hours, including the most distasteful part, the business about Officer Nugent and her involvement with MacAnnaly. He read them a copy of the note Stef left behind. It explained everything. Her condition did not look good. Quoting a doctor at Parkland, Knecht told his staff that she was still alive, but only "technically."

He commended Officer Stoner for the way she had handled herself in a situation he said that he could not presume to appreciate fully. He had high praise for officers involved in her rescue and singled out the helicopter crews for the job they did in bad weather. He also mentioned the three TAC officers by name who rescued Stoner and said he was proud of them.

Next, what he thought was an important lesson of the last few days.

"I heard disturbing reports in my office this morning about a plot brewing in our department. It involves some investigators, a lieutenant, and even a captain. Do you know what they're up to?'' He paused for effect.

''Cooperation! Some of our line people have figured out a way to share information, to merge their files, in spite of us. In spite of the compartmentalization we insist on, they have found a way to do their jobs. They have overcome us! Now, I want you people to make what our troops have started a part of the way we do business. Put it in writing and get it to me by noon Thursday. Bob, you're project manager.''

The Criminal Investigations chief nodded.

The chief turned to his executive assistant chief. ''Today, fix our problem with the FBI and the DEA. If it was Nugent, that's old business now.''

''Right.''

''One last thing,'' Knecht said, his tone softening. ''We're going to issue semiautos to the troops who want them, and body armor is mandatory, effective immediately. Now, let's be clear on this. Automatics and vests are all right, and I should have made the armor mandatory in the first place. But they wouldn't have saved Jackson and Terry. Sharp minds and strong hearts keep cops alive. And a little luck.'' He looked over the room. ''Questions?''

A staff captain stood. ''Chief, you mean armor is mandatory for field officers, don't you?''

''If you carry a gun and a badge, you wear a vest.''

''But, sir, it seems silly for me to wear a vest in my office over in . . .''

''No problem, son. Turn in your badge and your gun and you won't have to wear the goddamned thing.''

BOOK THREE

THE KILL

CHAPTER 26

Tuesday, 2:30 p.m.

Clark was in his office talking on the telephone to Sergeant Spencer. The DPS investigator was filling him in on what they were finding at Mack's shop in Grand Prairie.

"Okay," Clark said, as he looked up and saw Filmore and Winager come in. "So that ties him in with Welborn, too, then? Great. I knew that bastard was wrong. Okay, thanks for calling. Yeah, you'll be the first to hear."

Most of the dogs were there, and Boots was ready to announce his results on the Lincoln.

"Listen up," Clark called the crew to order. "Boots, you're on."

"Okay, I heard from NATB and ran down the complainant on the original theft of the Lincoln. I talked to Lunas up at the office, he had the case. Reported stolen a couple of weeks ago by a North Dallas credit-card millionaire type. Lunas said he smelled an insurance rip right off the bat, but he couldn't nail it down. Lunas and I called on the complainant, and with all the killing going on, he upped the deal. Welborn arranged for his car to disappear for no cut in the settlement, as long as our boy didn't report it stolen for twenty-four hours."

"Okay, good work," Clark said. "I just got off the phone with Spencer, and they popped a shop out in Grand Prairie where somebody's been changing up car numbers and rigging gas tanks like the one we found on the Lincoln. He says our boy

MacAnnaly is all over the place, including a pound or two of hair where he got a haircut and a shave. It all ties in with Welborn. They were stealing cars, faking the numbers, loading the tanks with guns, and sending them south.''

"And deadheading back?'' Hernandez asked. "I would have figured a way to make the return trip pay, too, if I was him.''

"Yeah, we're looking at that. It stands to reason he was bringing dope back, but we don't have anything yet. Anyway, they're all dead, so who cares?''

"So how come the dead girl in the trunk, Sarge?'' Smoky asked. "Who did that?''

"Marino was thinking our boy Mack at first, but now he's leaning to somebody else. He doesn't know who yet, somebody who wanted in on Welborn's action. Doing the girl was to get his attention.''

"Jesus,'' muttered Hernandez. "What a waste.''

"Really,'' Clark agreed. "Anybody got anything else?''

"We got something,'' Winager announced.

"Is this off y'all's 'down and out' this morning? What was that guy's name?''

"He goes by Dunk,'' Filmore answered. "Real name's . . . let's see, Nathaniel Lee Black. He's the one wrecked out with a squad last night.''

"While driving a stolen car,'' Clark added, for the dogs' information. General catcalls and derision.

"Y'all lay off our snitch, now.'' Winager held up his hands in mock solemnity, pretending to demand respect for old Dunk. "Excuse me, 'our confidential informant.' He has stole a whole lot of cars in his career, and only been caught five or six times. Besides, he put us on to something. Tell 'em, Sparky.''

"What was that Mexican's name you had on the West Dallas shooting, Sarge?''

"The one Maguire's snitch gave us? Crazy Frank.''

"Well, our little C.I. showed us a place where he says some people keep stolen cars. Matter of fact, says he had just dropped one off there and picked up another one when he had that run-in with the law on South Central.''

"He dropped one off and picked one up?'' Clark asked.

"Yeah, it was a trade-in. I mean it, that's what he said."
More clowning. A trade-in.

"I don't know about your man Dunk," Clark put in.

"Neither do I, but he says these are Mexicans. Three of them,
Willy, Frank, and a quiet one he thinks is named Johnny."

"Are you sure about the names?" Clark asked.

"That's what he said."

"Okay, write up your warrant application. I need to make a
couple of calls."

By six it was dark, and the return of the hard freeze settled
in with the night as promised. Inside the old house in Cigarette
Heights, all was warmness and light, and everybody was happy.

"Johnny, I told you to get me some fighters. I told you we
might be going to war. And what did you get me? A bunch of
West Dallas punks, man. How many did you end up with,
anyway?"

"Twenty-four."

"And none of them worth a shit. Look at them."

"Hey, some of them are okay, Willy. I picked some of them
myself."

"I wanted you to pick all of them, man. I wanted to have
gunmen I could count on, not these wetbacks who don't know
no fucking English and these here little gangsters."

Johnny had not seen Willy smoke dope often, and he knew
this must be a special occasion, but he had been waiting ever
since he and Frank came in to hear what it was all about. What
was the deal with the gasoline truck they had stashed in the
barn? Nobody told him nothing.

"Ain't you going to ask me how come there ain't going to
be no fighting after all?" Willy insisted.

"How come, Willy?"

"Because the other side"—Willy looked at Frank to make
sure he was listening—"is all dead! Is that weird, or what? Can
you believe it?"

"Who died?" Johnny asked.

"Welborn and his biker got killed."

"Oh," said Johnny. He had not known it was Welborn and

bikers they meant to have a war with in the first place. "What about the Jamaicans?"

"Fuck the Jamaicans." Willy dismissed them with a wave of his hand and then did his impression of a Jamaican, mincing around the room and talking in a singsong falsetto. Everybody who could see and hear him in the house laughed at him. They knew he was the boss, and when he made a joke they laughed. When he was done with that, he came back to Johnny. "We already took care of them. They are all either in jail or out of town. The ones that missed the bus, they're hiding out over there in South Dallas somewhere. We win, man! We're the fucking champs!"

There were more sides to the drug wars in Dallas than bikers, Jamaicans, and Willy's gang, and that was on the mind of the young man who had been assigned to stand watch at the bottom of the driveway.

His name was Tomas, but he made all his friends call him Tommy. Willy and Frank and them used American names, and he wanted to be like them. Tommy wanted to be exactly like them right now, by which he meant he wanted to be inside the warm house instead of sitting on a tree stump freezing his ass off. All the man had told Tommy was Willy needed some guys to help him with something. All this shit about guns and signals and standing watch, that all came later. He didn't know who he was watching for, but he counted on his numb fingers who all it might be. There was the Colombians, there was some of them in town, he had heard. Cubans, too. Plus the Jamaicans, but they stayed in South Dallas, Tommy had been assured. Two or three different Mexican gangs out of the prisons—he couldn't keep them straight. He stopped counting. That was enough enemies for him. There was a moon, and he had enough light to see the gun lying across his knees. He checked it again to make sure the safety was on. They hadn't said anything about staying all night, either. His mother would be pissed.

It was the first time Ned had been out of the hideout in days. He had given up on getting away from the Jamaicans, just as he had given up on getting to his money and flying out of Dallas.

So here he was in the backseat of a station wagon with Curtis driving and three dudes he had never seen before. They went in circles for a while, and Ned decided Curtis was lost. Why don't they let me drive the goddamned car? I was born and raised in Dallas, and I've been driving all my life. These bastards ain't seen a car till they came to this country.

Finally Curtis got it straightened out. He motioned with his hand for all of them to get down, and he put on this hat that was supposed to be some kind of a disguise. He slowed down, and they cruised by the place. There it is, Curtis says. All Ned saw was a bank of cedar trees at the side of the road. As they went on by, he thought he saw the flickering light of a fire back in the trees. Somebody camped out, maybe. Damned cold night for that, he thought.

Captain Angstrom was sitting at his desk in the Tactical Section, mulling over the numbers. Of his four on-duty squads, two were deployed on robbery stakeouts, hoping to surprise a nasty pair of hijackers who had been shooting up convenience stores. It was an indication of the kind of week it had been that these characters had not made the front page. Angstrom's analyst had a tight pattern on the pair, and they were due to hit again that evening. Narcotics had another squad tied up backstopping a bust they were trying to put together. Now Clark had a search warrant to run, and he wanted TAC to run interference in case Maguire's snitch was right and the Mexicans were good for the van hit.

He punched the intercom to his desk man and gave instructions to start making the calls. He was putting A-Unit on standby, which meant a forty-minute maximum response time anywhere in the city. And he thought of Bette Davis in *All About Eve:* "Fasten your seat belts. It's going to be a bumpy night."

"I don't understand," Lieutenant Bonny said.

Clark looked at the phone in his hand. "Which part?"

"If the Mexicans are suspects on the van killings . . ."

"It's a search warrant, Lieutenant. We're going in looking for a stolen Monte Carlo. We put auto parts in also so we'll be legal going in the house. But the Mexicans may be there, and we've got word from a snitch . . ."

"So you're taking Persons with you? And TAC?"

"Yes, sir."

"I don't like it."

"I thought you just didn't understand it, sir."

"Are you trying to be funny, Sergeant?"

"No, I'm trying to get a warrant run. You said you wanted to be notified."

"A little earlier in the process was what I had in mind."

"Why, you want to pass on my warrants?"

"Why not?"

"That's the judge's job."

"It's obvious you and I don't see eye to eye on the concept of supervision."

"Supervision's my job. I'm the sergeant."

"Then what the hell's my job?"

"Beats me, Lieutenant. I was hoping you'd know."

"Look here, Sergeant . . ."

Clark could almost hear Bonny counting to ten. "Yes, sir?"

"I think I'd better come with you on this one."

"Good idea, Lieutenant. We'll probably be at it all night. It'll give you a chance to get some grease on your hands, see what it is we do."

"Yeah . . . that's right. Let's see, it's a quarter past six. With traffic, I should be out there in, what? About thirty, forty minutes?"

"Terrific. I'll tell the men."

"Uh, what's the weather supposed to do tonight, Sergeant?"

"It's colder than a well-digger's ass right now, sir, but it's supposed to drop another twenty degrees or so. High winds, freezing rain. Perfect night for a raid."

"Yeah. Okay, I'll see you at your office."

When Clark's pager went off, he was sure that it was Lieutenant Bonny again. But when he found a telephone, he took another look at the number on the digital display and realized that it was not his lieutenant's. He did not recognize the phone number or the lady's voice that answered.

"This is Bill Clark," he said. "I was paged to this number."

"One moment, please," said the voice.

Then Randi Stoner came on the line. "Bill?"

"Randi—how are you? Where are you?"

"At my mother's. She's nursing me back to health." She said it in a way that Clark knew meant her mother could hear. "Am I interrupting something?"

"As a matter of fact . . ."

"Oh."

"But I'm glad you called. What can I do for you?"

"I was wondering if you had plans this evening. Sounds like you do."

"Just business. How about a rain check?"

"Call me. I don't think Mom and I are going out."

It was almost seven by the time Clark and his people showed up at the Southeast Patrol Division for the preraid briefing. The TAC troops were already there, and Sergeant Marino arrived minutes after Clark. Lieutenant Bonny had called to say he would not be able to make it. Clark was to keep him posted; he would have his pager with him.

Southeast had been Clark's old station; he had worked most of the 1960s and some of the 1970s out of it, but it had changed. A new locker room had been built onto the back and most of the old one was offices now.

Since it was the Salvage Unit's search warrant, Clark opened the little meeting. While he went over the background, Winager and Filmore pinned some stuff on a bulletin board.

"First, I guess I could do introductions," he began. It was more than good manners in a mixed-force operation like this to make sure all the good guys knew each other.

Clark and his Salvage Unit investigators would handle the actual execution of the search warrant. Sergeant Marino was along in case they found anything that tied in with the van killings.

Captain Angstrom was there to command the TAC troops. He explained that the lieutenant who was the E-Unit commander was laid up in the hospital with a ruptured vertebra. Angstrom would call the shots until his troops secured the house and grounds. Sergeant Byner and his squad would handle the operation. Angstrom made it clear that if they ran into a shitstorm they would rely on the investigators to support them until TAC reinforcements could respond. They were stretched pretty thin, he said, but that could not be helped. He had coordinated with the Southeast Division commander, and the TAC office downtown was running a log and monitoring the TAC ops channel.

Angstrom sent one of his men to his car to get a raid jacket for Marino. Clark's men all had their own, windbreakers with POLICE in four-inch white letters, and ball caps with the logo Clark had designed.

Everybody gathered around the bulletin board where Winager and Filmore had pinned blowups of street maps and sketches that they had made from their drive-by with Dunk. The helicopters were down due to weather, and were not likely to chance it even in an emergency. They had taken some big chances in the search for Randi Stoner, and did not want to push their luck.

They ran through it a couple of times—what everybody was to do, the men they expected to find, everything. Their information from Dunk was that the one called Johnny was there alone, but there could be as many as three. The search warrant was for stolen cars and auto parts, but the three amigos also might be good for the van hit in West Dallas, and that meant maybe automatic weapons.

They were ready to go by seven-thirty, when Filmore called from the courthouse to say he had found a judge to sign the warrant. He and Winager were on their way.

Angstrom called a vest check, and he and Sergeant Lupton went around the room tapping cops on their chests. Marino and two of the "dogs" flunked, with alibis. Byner's troops went into the trunks of their cars and came up with three vests for them.

Clark drove his unmarked car and Winager drove their van with all the equipment. Boots and Smoky rode with Clark, the rest of the dogs in the van. Marino drove his own car in case his part of it did not pan out. The TAC squad buddied up into two marked cars and a van. Winager and Filmore would join up with them on the way.

Five cars and two vans. As they pulled out of the Southeast parking lot and headed for Oak Cliff, Clark thought they looked like an army convoy.

Tommy rocked back and forth on his tree stump and cursed in the frigid air, blowing steam that he would have realized gave away his position if he had not been so cold or if he had been more interested. Since he did not have a watch, he did not know how long he had been sitting there, but he could hear the laughing and talking inside the house, and see the warm lights in the windows through the drawn shades. They forgot all about me out here, he muttered. Ain't nobody going to come relieve me, man. He was hungry, too.

He turned around the other way and looked around the corner of the house and he could see the light of a fire of some kind. It was far enough back there that you probably could not see it from the road, but he could see the light off it dancing on the ground and making shadows. I wouldn't mind going back there for a minute, he told himself. That fire looked cheery, inviting. Maybe they got food back there. Everybody's having a party except me.

Here we go again, Ned thought. They had dropped the first three men off in front of a motel on Hawn Freeway and then picked up three more at another place. Now they were going again, back down Ledbetter with Curtis at the wheel, steady talking.

What Ned knew about this he did not particularly like. These guys, these three and the first three, were part of Curtis's gang, their "posse" they called it. All of them had come in from out of town, and they had brought all these stone killers in with them, to hear Curtis tell it. Ned had not seen any killers, or any cars that brought them to town, either, and did not care to. What this was about, he gathered, was that Curtis had got a line on the Mexicans' hideout and now he was driving his out-of-town guests by to look the place over. What they could tell about it in the damn dark, he did not know. It was not what he had been taught as to recon, but they had not asked him, either. He was just along for the ride, in more ways than one.

• • •

Lights out, Clark let his car roll to a stop at the side of the road with just the emergency brake, so he wouldn't show any brake lights. If Winager and Filmore were right, the Mexicans' place was almost straight ahead, through a scraggly stand of scrub oak that looked in the moonlight like men with their hands in the air. The road curved here, and dipped to cross a shallow swale before it reached the house itself. They would watch from here until TAC signaled them to come in.

Clark stepped out of the car, taking his sawed-off 12-gauge, the one they called "Puff," with him out of the seat. They had removed the bulbs from the dome lights of all their cars, so no lights came on to give them away. He stepped into the road to check behind his car and accounted for everyone, all his people and Marino. TAC had preceded them, and was out there in the dark somewhere getting ready to start their part of the operation.

"So we just stand around here and wait for the SWAT team to round up the bad guys, eh?" Marino drew alongside Clark, shaking his head and stamping his feet because he was so cold.

"That's the plan," Clark answered cheerfully. Investigators had mixed feelings about TAC and these deals. The General Orders called this a "High-Risk Apprehension," and dictated that TAC would be called to precede the investigators and deal with any resistance. There were good reasons for doing it that way, but like most of the rest of them, Clark did not like working a case up to a point and then letting somebody else kick the door and bag the bad guys. It was up to the investigator on the case to declare a raid an HRA, and Clark considered fudging on this one, but it would have been a shaky call. Marino had been emphatic about not wanting to bring TAC in, but Clark had seen it the other way. It wouldn't be easy to explain any automatic weapons the next day. And he didn't aim to have to explain anything to any widows.

Though it was too cold and the rain was coming in fits and starts, Clark wanted his people out of their cars where they could see and hear. He did not want anybody sneaking up on them. Clark thought he saw some movement in the trees at the edge of the road down by the house, but he could not be sure.

TAC had left their cars somewhere on the other side of the house, and Clark was hoping that if any of the suspects got away from Angstrom's boys they would come his way.

He had a radio that transmitted and received one of the two channels the TAC portables used. Angstrom had explained that his people would be using the other channel, and that he would switch to the channel Clark was monitoring if he needed to communicate with him. So Clark was holding his silent portable in one hand and his sawed-off shotgun in the other, waiting for something to happen and trying not to freeze to death. He also found himself trying not to think about Randi Stoner. Probably sees you as a father figure, he told himself. And that made him think of his daughter.

Tommy sat fidgeting on his stump, holding the rifle between his knees. He would give them about ten more minutes, and if they didn't come relieve him, he was going to relieve himself. He would walk around the house to the back and see if they had any food or anything. At last he would get warm.

He stopped watching his breath make clouds when he heard something. A city boy, he had been amazed how many noises there were at night in the woods. This was not really the woods, but it looked like a forest to Tommy, especially in the spooky moonlight. It was worse when the moon went behind clouds and the whole world turned black. In the city, he realized, it is almost never really dark. That sound again.

Thunk. *Z-z-z-t!*

Tommy lay spasming, voiceless, on the ground beside his tree stump, his gun on the ground beside him. He looked up, bewildered, as a giant frog with a smooth round head and enormous green eyes hovered over him. The frog must have zapped him with his tongue, Tommy figured.

The TAC officer, E-3's scout, checked the kid's pulse and recovered his TASER darts. He rolled the kid over and slipped flex-cuffs on his wrists. The small electrical darts fired by the unit delivered a pretty healthy wallop. The officer knew how the kid felt, because part of his training had been to take a couple of hits himself. It beat shooting the kid. The officer looked side to side with his night-vision goggles to make sure no one else was moving across the front of the house in his area of responsibility, then gave the signal on his hands-free throat mike for the men he was leading to move up. Before moving himself, he stripped the kid's rifle and removed the bolt. He couldn't afford to leave it armed or lug it with him.

Forty-five seconds later everybody had checked in with the ready signal, a team of two at each of two predesignated diagonal corners of the house for containment, a four-man primary entry team and a two-man rescue team which included the captain.

"Voice and lights in three, two, one," Angstrom counted it down and then remotely armed the high-intensity halogen field lamps they had sneaked into position. One man in each of the three primary positions was designated to maintain visual on the target, without goggles, while all the others shielded their eyes to preserve night vision. The lights were aimed to concentrate their effect on the interior of the house, and would not shine directly at any officer, but even looking into the brightly lit target area would ruin night vision for thirty or forty seconds. To anyone inside, the light would blind them immediately, and leave them impaired for several minutes after the lights were turned off.

When the lights hit the house, it looked like the place had come alive with a swarm of ants. There were people everywhere in there, impossible to count. The electronically amplified voice of Captain Angstrom gave them a warning in English and in Spanish, quickly and clearly, and then the shooting started.

One long burst of automatic-weapons fire kicked glass out of the windows along the front of the house. Then the TAC officers in front, the entry and rescue teams, heard another long burst screaming over their heads.

From the rear of the house, where one cover team had reported four or five male subjects gathered around a fire, and where the bulk of the house spared the men from the full effect of the field lamps, shooting started almost immediately. The men scattered away from the fire toward the shadows, unslinging and firing their weapons at random, to either side of the house, yelling as they ran.

Cover One, the two TAC officers nearest the fire barrel, were not immediately threatened by the shooting of the men in the yard. They had chosen positions with cover and concealment, and they were low to the ground. The men were shooting high and wild.

Angstrom's booming voice ordered the suspects to stop firing and surrender, just as a burst fired from the house knocked out one of the field lamps. A door banged in the rear of the house, and Cover Two confirmed subjects exiting the house. Several men were running from the house, in what looked like an effort either to escape or outflank the officers' position at the front.

"Commence firing!" came the order, as Angstrom killed the remaining two lights, and the TAC officers went to work. From their low cover positions, with their night vision goggles, they had clear targets on the men running and screaming around the house. Their positions precluded endangering each other with cross fire, and all the TAC officers would maintain static positions until the command to enter or advance. This meant that anything moving was a bandit, and they pressed all their advantages.

Angstrom listened to the shooting and monitored the ops channel. There were a hell of a lot of people in the house and on the grounds, and he wished he had begun the operation with two squads instead of one. But he picked up his own men's short, three-round bursts among the long rattling bursts and yelling of the enemy, and no one had called in any casualties. It could be worse, he told himself. They could have lain low and let us enter before they started shooting.

Cover One knocked down three of the screaming shooters in the backyard with quick aimed bursts and watched the fourth dive under the house. When the yard looked clear, they turned their attention to the house, slapping fresh clips into their M-16s. Movement at the windows, two more short bursts from Cover One. Good group. No more shooting there.

Cover Two shifted position slightly, low-crawling right and left to improve their angles, then opened fire on the group charging out of the house. Count 'em, count 'em, one officer told himself. They were firing full auto, and it took a bit of concentration to shoot as they had trained, three rounds at a time. Don't spray 'em, he reminded himself. It's a gun, not a garden hose. Don't shoot yourself dry. Cover Two knocked down each of the men who had rushed out of the house, the last of them falling between the two officers. He had run the last ten meters with solid body hits, and fell to the cold ground breathing pink froth from a wounded lung.

Screaming inside the house, orders at the top of the lungs. Somebody was taking charge in there. The shooting stopped.

Angstrom tried the loudspeaker again. English and Spanish. Throw down your weapons. Come out with your hands up. Silence followed his instructions.

Angstrom was on his radio to the TAC office. "Advise we are under fire. Notify the standby unit. Call up A-Unit, roll full response to the staging area, we will advise deployment on their arrival. Advise Southeast Patrol and Channel Two dispatch. Advise ambulances standing by and request additional. Hold them at the staging point. It ain't over out here yet." It was standard practice for TAC to have a Dallas Fire Department ambulance standing by at a safe distance from any operation like this, to cut response time to a minimum, just in case. Angstrom knew they would need more than one ambulance this time. He switched to the channel Sergeant Clark was monitoring.

"Yeah, Cap'n. You need us over there?"

"Negative now. There's not a safe route to bring you in. Heads up, though. This looks major."

"Ten-Four. How do we help you?"

"Stand by there. If we can't hold them, they may come your way. Be advised, if it's moving, it ain't us. You got that?"

"Right." Clark put his people into the brush alongside the road, in positions facing the house where the shooting had subsided. He told them to be alert to suspects trying to sneak out of the area. "Let them get close," he said. "Be sure they're in range before you start shooting." He then found himself a place near the road where he could see the area his people were covering and the house itself.

"They're coming out!" He heard Angstrom's voice on the

radio, then firing from the direction of the house. Heavier this time.

At the house, Angstrom heard the doors slam open against the walls of the house in the rear an instant before chairs and tables crashed through the windows in front, followed by a heavy fire to the front. He heard shooting in the back, heavier still.

"Coming out!" a voice on the operations channel, probably Cover One.

The officers in front of the house burrowed down in their positions and waited for targets. The shooting across the front of the house stopped suddenly, and picked up dramatically in the rear.

Cover Two was on the flank of the mob that boiled out of the house. The bandits were shooting better now, down at the ground and generally into the locations from where they had drawn fire the first time. Somebody had pulled them together during the break, and they were deadlier now that the startle effect had passed. The officers were glad that they had relocated, taken new firing positions ten meters to the left of their original spots, because they could hear rounds impacting over there, screaming along the ground, thumping into trees, and whining ricochets sailing out through the air. Cover Two opened up, slapping bursts into the side of the mob, and they saw people going down, but even more still running. The gang of men from the house swerved to their right, driven like cattle, angling away from the fire from Cover Two.

The two officers in Cover One saw what looked like a battalion pour out of the back of the house, firing at the place the officers had just left.

"A fucking banzai," one of the officers muttered, raising his weapon, trying to remember to point shoot, pick targets. The mass of men coming straight at him made it almost impossible to miss. How many were there, he wondered, but he did not waste time counting. He touched off a three round burst, then another. He heard his partner firing beside him and saw two, three, four of the gunmen in the front of the charge stagger and fall. The rest of them, like a human wave, broke around the fallen ones and came on. The officers fired to the front, then to their left and right, as the screaming gang split and passed on either side of them. Muzzle flash from ten feet away, the hammering of a submachine gun driving slugs into their position. One officer felt the rounds hitting him, pounding down on him like claw hammers, and he registered the fact that his weapon was dry. He tried to tell his partner that he was reloading, but his mouth did not work for some reason, and he noticed that his right hand did not work, either. The last thing he noticed was that his partner had stopped firing, too.

"Cover Two to Boss, they are out. Repeat, they are out. Looks like they overran Cover One and beat it into the boonies."

"Roger. Hold position, Cover Two. Entry stand by." Angstrom advised Clark of the situation and asked TAC center for an ETA on the E-Unit squad en route to the location. He was told they would be at the staging area in eight minutes. He advised TAC center to send them directly to the location. Suspects had broken out, and he would search and secure.

Clark passed the word for his men to look sharp.

Sirens, first one then another, then a whole pack of them, like wolves on a hunt. The night was alive with the screaming of sirens, the banshee wail that said there was killing tonight.

Willy had no idea how many of them he had lost at the house or in the breakout. Most of the rest of them were scattering, panicked and just running to get away, in twos and threes because all of them were afraid to be alone out here after all that noise and fire at the house. Willy brought the band with him up short as soon as they were deep enough into the trees behind the house to be invisible. He grabbed them and waved his gun at them and cursed them, and managed to make four or five stop their crazy dash and stand still for a minute. They knelt on the ground or leaned on their knees, sucking in the cold air. One of them puked, and another one discovered he was wounded.

"Frank! Frank, Johnny!" Willy called out, looking at the faces around him, trying to see into the woods. "Frank!"

"I'm right here, man. Stop that hollering before they call in a fuckin' air strike on the woods."

Willy turned to see Frank kicking himself free of brambles

grown up beside a bois d'arc tree. He had three or four men with him, too, and Willy saw that Frank had the two men who had brought the tanker truck up from Mexico. They had faces like death masks, and Willy knew why. They were El Jefe's men, and they knew what would happen to them if they lost the cocaine. They preferred cops, who, after all, would only shoot them. And he knew he could count on Frank.

"Frank, where's Johnny? You see him?"

"What's left of him. He's in the yard."

"In the yard?"

"When we come barreling out of the house, he got in the front, like a dumbass. They knocked his head off, them mother-fuckers. I had to step over him, and that was when I got that cop, man. He was laying there in the bush, you know? He had this weird-ass hard hat on and these big green goggles. I never seen nothing like it. I stick out my gun like this, and man, I gave it to him. Nailed his ass."

"Okay, okay. That's one of them. How many did we lose, a dozen?"

"Who cares? They wasn't no good anyway, you said that your—"

"Okay, I said that. Now how many we got left?"

"You can count as good as me. This is it, whatever we got right here."

Willy counted three, excluding the wounded man, who had lain down on the ground and was trying to die or something, plus himself and Frank and the two from the truck. That meant seven. "The Magnificent Seven," he laughed bitterly.

"Seven what?" Frank asked.

"Seven of us. To go back and get the truck."

"What are you, crazy? You get shot in the brain or some-thing? You know how many cops is down there?"

"Approximately. Four covering the sides. I think we killed two of them. Another three or four in the front."

"And what about all them sirens? What you think that is, fire trucks?"

"The place will be swarming with 'em in a few minutes, but right now, they got to be patching theirselves up and wondering what the fuck they ran in to. Where's the last place they're going to look for us, Frank? Right back there at the house. You scared or something?"

"Fuck you, man. I'm up for it."

"And I know you two men will go back with me," he said to the two from the truck. "How about the rest of you?"

The other three were kids, street gangsters who had been dragged into this thing with no idea what was involved. They looked at each other and at Willy and wished they were already wounded like the one lying on the ground, so they could be out of it. Then they heard shooting from the hill up the road from the house.

"There you are," Willy said. "You hear that? The cops have this place surrounded. Our only way out is to go back to the house, where they don't expect us. We grab the truck and haul ass. We run over them. They ain't gonna shoot at no gasoline tanker, man."

"Yeah." Frank grinned sarcastically. "We'll outrun them."

CHAPTER 27

Tuesday, 8:45 p.m.

After the big shooting spree at the house and the word from Angstrom that the suspects were breaking out, it was quiet for a couple of minutes, and Clark knelt in the spot he had chosen for himself near the road and strained to hear sounds of movement. He looked back toward the cars he and his men had parked and saw that they were far enough beyond the crest of the little hill that men running through the woods would not see them.

Voices in the woods. He heard the men from the fight at the house, some of them yelling back and forth to each other. It was hard to tell exactly where the sounds were coming from, one overlapping the other, echoing through the woods. He thought at least one of the yelling men was moving his way, coming toward the road.

Someone was running through the woods and weeds to his front. Clark heard the sounds clearly, the feet pounding on the hard cold ground, labored breathing. He worked the action of his short-barreled shotgun as quietly as he could to chamber his first round, then drew a shell from his pocket and thumbed it into the magazine. That gave him five.

"Police! Halt!"

Clark recognized Marino's voice, and cursed. He heard shooting in the direction of Marino's voice, and a loud surprised curse. Then gunfire erupted all along the crest of the low hill as the dogs opened up and took return fire from two or three automatic weapons. Clark moved his eyes from side to side, keeping his head still, and heard footsteps coming his way. The shooting down the line had made somebody decide to swerve toward the road, in his direction, and he waited. A voice cursed in Spanish almost on top of him, and Clark heard a bolt drawn back on a weapon. Two shapes, coming right at him. He took the farthest one first and shot both of them, working the pump action of his shotgun quickly. In the fireballs of the shotgun's muzzle flash, he saw both their faces and their guns. They looked surprised, and their guns tumbled out of their hands. All this was in slow motion to Clark, and the sound of it all was muffled. They both went down. He duck-walked a few yards toward the road, watching to his front as he fed two more shotgun shells into his magazine. The shooting had stopped.

When there had been no more sound in front of them for almost a minute, Clark moved forward to check the two men he had killed, then worked his way down the line to see about his men. None of his dogs was hurt, but Marino was lying on his back, cursing in Spanish. He had taken two hits, both in the chest, and he was mad as hell. Clark knelt beside him.

"Good thing Angstrom loaned you a vest, huh?" he said.

"Don't rub it in." Marino glowered at him.

They put in gas first, to stir up anybody waiting inside, then Angstrom sent Sergeant Byner in with his entry team. They moved quickly but carefully and pronounced the house clear three minutes later. There was not much to the place, and they had found only casualties and the one man who had dived underneath the house early in the firefight. He was uninjured, but offered no resistance. He seemed happy to be arrested, in fact.

The totals ran to four suspects dead, eight wounded, two captured unharmed, the one from under the house and Tommy, the kid the scout bagged before the shooting started. Two of the TAC officers were wounded, both of them on Cover One, one of them seriously. They both had taken multiple hits, but their body armor and the new ballistic helmets had kept them alive.

Angstrom surveyed ammo and found they were running low.

He took some from a few of the men and gave it to the four he posted in a skirmish line that ran behind the ramshackle barn. He sent one man back to their panel truck to bring more ammunition and notified TAC Center to send the ambulances in quickly, no lights. He still had hostiles in the area, and he was concerned about snipers. He did not want his people spotlighted by the light bars atop the ambulances, and he did not want much light at all until he was satisfied the place was secured and the fighting was over. Night-vision gear gave his people an edge, and he did not want to lose it, just in case.

As the first ambulance bounced into the driveway, directed by a TAC officer standing at the edge of the road, Angstrom called Clark for a status report. Clark reported no police casualties, four suspects dead, no more action on the hill. Brown told him to bring his people to the house in their vehicles, lights out.

Angstrom checked his watch. His reinforcements were less than four minutes away, and he knew that Patrol elements were roaring into the staging area now. Their supervisors would have them formed up and ready to move in a matter of minutes. He asked to have a request relayed that Patrol close down the road that ran in front of the house as far away as they could manage. There was no telling what they were onto here, and he could not rule out chemicals or explosive devices. That was one reason he did not conduct a sweep of the area with the people on hand. He just wanted to hold what he had for the moment, get his wounded taken care of, and wait for the second squad. Then they would look the place over carefully. They could use some of A-Unit, now assembling at TAC Center, if they needed them. You always have somebody in reserve.

Clark and his people climbed aboard the dogs' unit car, riding on the hood and trunk, for the ride down to the house. Two of his people drove their van, and Marino rode in the car with Clark. His chest ached like hell, and he felt like he'd been hit with a hammer, but his heart was still pumping and he knew he would be okay. He was mad. He had not shot anybody.

Clark was halfway to the house when the shooting started again. He thought it was from in back of the house somewhere, by the barn, maybe, and he hesitated. He didn't want to screw up the TAC guys with their layout, and he was not sure for a moment whether he should haul ass to the house or stand by, maybe even go back up the hill.

"What the . . ." Angstrom turned toward the sound of the firing, behind the barn. "Status, Three," he spat into his radio, wanting a report from the skirmish line point directly behind the barn. Nothing.

Number Three, rifleman Castleberry, died almost instantly, as he knelt in his skirmish line position and scanned his area of responsibility through his night-vision goggles. The report of the first burst of the counterattack only just registered in his mind and then the rounds found him and he sagged to the ground. They would find him with multiple hits, some off his helmet, a couple to the vest, one in his left arm, and two in his face. His would be a closed-casket funeral.

Willy left the three kids he did not trust to shoot at the cops he had watched taking their posts along a line at the back of the place. If they would stay with it long enough just to make the cops duck, make them react, that would be good enough for him. He led Frank and the two truckers on a straight line up out of the woods, up the gentle slope, toward the back of the barn. There was a small door there with a chain and padlock on it, just like the big doors in the front. The four of them reached the barn without drawing fire, and Willy shot the wood away from the lock and yanked the door open.

"We're drawing fire . . ."

"Repeat!" Angstrom demanded, but got no answer. E-3's scout was hit and down on the skirmish line, shot in both legs as he tried to move to a location that offered cover from the source of fire. He tried to answer, but it didn't work, and he lay still, wondering how long it would take for all his blood to run out, worried that he could not make his arms work, either.

Sergeant Lupton and the entry team got low and formed up to face the threat. Angstrom ran toward them to tell them . . .

With a roar and the sudden blast of horn and lights, the tanker truck screamed to life inside the barn and the unexpectedness of it froze Angstrom in midstride. He looked at the barn and saw the ramshackle old building move. What the hell?

As the driver gunned the engine and the truck leaped forward against the door, the old tired barn gave way and fell on the truck. The truck roared and screamed, its horn blasting and its headlights on full, and finally it pitched forward, driving the barn doors down and underneath its big tires, splintering them. The tanker truck waddled and rumbled down the drive toward the road, tossing the debris that had been the barn off its back like a dog shaking off water.

The lights of the truck blinded Byner and his men in their goggles, and as they scrambled to move out of its way and claw off their goggles, the men on the running boards of the truck opened fire.

The two paramedics with the first ambulance were working on the two wounded officers in the front yard when the shooting started. They threw themselves on top of the two wounded men and hoped like hell lightning would not strike them a second time.

"It's a tanker," Angstrom muttered. "Flammable."

As he turned to warn Byner's team, out of the corner of his eye, Angstrom saw the slugs making what looked like sparks on the ground, a racing line of sparks coming down the rutted driveway at him. They weren't really sparks. They were ice chips banged up off the frozen ground by the bullets.

He thought the bullets chasing down the driveway got him, but in fact the bullet that hit him came from Frank on the other running board, shooting across the hood of the truck, making sparks fly where some of his bullets caromed off the hood of the truck itself. Angstrom mistook Willy's short ineffectual burst for the one that got him and he went down in the driveway, his right leg mangled and turned under him. He saw the big tires coming and rolled over as far as his ruined leg would let him and then the big tires rolled over him, the front one, then the tandem ones on either end of the tank itself. Miraculously, he was still alive after that, but not for very long. He turned his head to watch the truck continue down the drive, but he did not see it. He did not see anything.

Byner and his men had too much to do in too short a time. They lost vision in the headlights, they had to dive for cover because they had not expected to draw fire from the direction of the garage, they had to raise their weapons and find targets, and then they had to process the information that Captain Angstrom had been yelling at them. Flammable. The truck was flammable, a gasoline tanker. All of this added up to enough hesitation that Byner and his men did not manage to shoot either of the men on the running boards of the truck, or get any bullets into the cab, either. They weren't hit, but that was largely because both Frank and Willy were concentrating on Angstrom in the driveway.

As the truck thundered past, Sergeant Byner rolled over and opened fire, holding low, trying to make his rounds skitter along the hard ground like stones on water, and he heard the sounds of tires blowing. He saw the truck lurch precariously as it took the turn from the driveway onto the road too fast, and he and one of his men let loose a barrage at the tires on the left as it turned to the left into the road. At first he thought that the tank had gone up, but it was only more of the tires exploding.

The driver wanted to turn right at the road, but when he got there he saw the second and third ambulances coming at him and he turned left instead, almost turning the truck over onto its right side because of his speed.

Clark saw the tanker turn toward him, and instinctively he whipped his car across the road in the truck's path. He jumped out of the car as his men clambered down off the hood and he saw Marino struggling out of the passenger door. The van was behind him and it turned sideways too, making a roadblock to stop the truck. All the officers in Clark's party went to their right, into the ditch and up the slope toward the overgrown fence.

Willy was on the running board on the left side of the truck working to reload when he saw the car and the van up ahead. He slammed a fresh magazine home and pivoted to rake the men in the ditch, firing his Uzi from the shoulder with one hand as he held on to the driver's door. The cops in the ditch returned fire, and it sounded to Willy like a hailstorm pounding the side of the truck, all the lead thumping around him. He did not realize he was hit until he found himself airborne making a crazy slow-motion somersault through the air among the heavy cold raindrops. He landed in a pile on the hard road and bounced like a stiff-legged mannequin. He felt no pain when he came to rest.

The truck was bouncing and slewing coming down the road. The wheel rims made sparks on the hard ground and a crazy noise as they banged and wobbled over the shreds of the blown tires. When it hit the car, the truck jolted hard, throwing Frank off his running board into the ditch on the other side of the road from the cops. Then the truck crunched into the car, wadding up the front end of it and shoving the whole thing backwards. It might have been able to keep going, but the van was right behind the car and finally there was too much sheet metal and mangled machinery wedged underneath the front of the truck, and it ground to a halt.

The driver was working frantically to shift into reverse, and he looked down once at the cops running toward the truck. He heard them screaming at him in English, and he did not care. He knew what he had to do, and if he couldn't do it, he wanted to die. When he saw there was no hope of getting the truck going again, the driver picked up the gun from the seat and stuck it out the window, thinking he might take a couple with him. But the cops were having none of that, and they poured so much fire through the window and his head that from the back he must have looked like a mask with a dozen eyeholes.

For the second man in the truck, getting shot by the cops beat going back to El Jefe, but he still had hopes of escaping. When the truck stopped, he jumped out and ran into the ditch and up the other side toward the fence. He had no idea where he was going, but jumped quickly over the fence and sprinted across the field beyond, hoping the darkness would swallow him. The sirens and lights of the TAC reinforcements came over the crest of the hill where Clark and his dogs had made their stand, and lights from the lead car fell on the running man. The oncoming TAC officers, who had been listening to Angstrom's radio transmissions as they drove, saw the truck and the two police vehicles in a pile in the road and Sergeant Byner was screaming into their radios for them to hurry up. The lead cars screeched to a stop and officers bailed out and called to the running man to halt. He dodged right and left to get out of their lights, but the cops were working their hand-held spotlights now, and he could not get away, so finally he dropped to his knees in the field and threw up his hands.

Clark's men were worried about the tanker exploding, and edged around it gingerly for a look inside the cab to make sure everybody was accounted for, and two of his men backtracked up the road to check on Willy, who lay motionless and broken-looking in the road.

Marino did not want to get close to the truck because of the gasoline, and he stood reloading his revolver with his last six rounds. He had been knocked down right off the bat at the fight on the hill, and had not gotten off a shot. He had put six into the truck along with everybody else, but he could not know if his bullets had done any good or not. Now here he stood with six rounds left, and . . .

First there was a movement in the grass in the ditch on the other side of the road, which made Marino turn that way, and then the crazy look on the face that rose from the ditch, a big-eyed crazy grin showing white teeth, with the round ugly muzzle of the submachine gun rising just below the teeth.

"Hey!" Marino shouted. Nothing else came to mind, and he knew he should let the others know.

Clark turned at the shout and saw Marino pivoting and bringing his gun up. It was a chrome magnum, and Clark saw moonlight sparkle on it as it came up. Marino ducked into a crouch as he turned toward the ditch, and then Clark looked where Marino was aiming and saw Frank coming up out of the weeds.

Frank fired his submachine gun, laughing out loud, and Marino squeezed off his magnum, two, three, four times. Clark watched the two of them blazing away at each other, Frank standing up straight in the ditch and firing from the hip, Marino squatting, his arm extended. Then Clark saw the welding-torch tip of Frank's gun rise to point almost straight up, and Frank toppled over into the ditch. Marino remained squatting, squeezing off the rounds. His revolver was empty, and Clark heard the hammer falling on dead primers as he ran to see if Marino was all right.

That was the last of the shooting. After that, it was assholes and elbows taking care of the wounded. Once all that could be done had been done, they started mopping up, processing the crime scene, and dealing with the media. Word was, Chief Knecht himself was en route to the scene.

With all the confusion at the roadblocks that Patrol had thrown up to keep traffic out of the area, no one paid any attention to a station wagon being driven by a man in a hat, with four passengers. Curtis drove his out-of-town friends back to the motel where they were staying, jabbering away at them. Ned sat slumped in the backseat chewing on the knuckle of his trigger finger, shaking his head.

CHAPTER 28

Wednesday, 11:00 a.m.

For the most part, it was old news by the time Knecht stepped in front of the cameras again for another news conference in the media conference room. There had been live Minicam reports from the scene of the shootout, each of the local television stations breaking into their regular programming with special reports.

Orville Knecht had gone on the airways live from the scene to say quite a lot about the general situation of crime in our cities, but all the TV people had used was a couple of terse sound bites over B-roll of the aftermath, bodies covered with ambulance sheets, bullet holes in the walls of the old house, discarded medical supplies, uniformed and plainclothes officers apparently wandering aimlessly around the crime scene, Patrol officers guarding the perimeter, and of course a lot of shots of the tanker truck and the two police vehicles. What they used of Knecht's comments included his insistence that Dallas was no worse than any place in America, that the problem was national in scope. The footage they aired might have been designed to contradict this. The other thing they used was a remark of his to the effect that America was becoming Colombia, with all that implies. That one seemed much more in line with the video, and attracted a lot of attention. That night on *Nightline,* Ted Koppel opened with a report on the shootout in Dallas, and the theme of his show was "Is America Becoming Another Colombia?"

The final casualty figures, killed and wounded, were twenty suspects and five officers. Zulu Jones was quoted in a story by Bobby Thurmon as saying that the disparity meant the cops might have executed some of the prisoners. The two men captured unharmed at the house, Tommy and the man from under the house, were made available to attest that they had received humane treatment. The man described as a "foreign national" who had been captured in the field as he ran from the truck was made available but refused to answer any questions. The widows and children of the two officers who died were contacted by the press for reactions. They were contacted repeatedly, to the point that the widow of Captain Angstrom responded to one reporter with such fervor that the unfortunate young woman was treated and released at an area hospital with what were described as "minor injuries."

All this and much more was known to the press and the public before Chief Knecht's press conference the following morning. Reporters and camerapersons in attendance tried to outguess each other as to what Knecht would have to add, if anything, and the speculation was that they were in for a rehashing, with the chief hoping to see himself on television from that point on in the more flattering lighting of the media conference room. The cynics among them were not disappointed at first, because Chief Knecht did review and summarize the events of the past several days for them. He saved the news for last.

"Additionally, our investigation at the scene has resulted in our seizing a sizable quantity of a substance believed to be an illicit drug." Having read that, Knecht looked up from his notes at the media assembled and waited for the inevitable questions.

"What kind of drug, Chief?"

"Field testing indicates that it may be cocaine."

"How much?"

"Approximately one ton."

The room fell silent, except for the noises the machines made.

"Could you repeat that, Chief?"

"One ton. Over a ton, actually. Preliminary investigations indicate that the seizure consists of approximately one thousand packages, each of them one kilogram. A kilogram is approximately two point two pounds, as you know.''

Big fuss now, everybody talking at once, voices buzzing like hornets, nothing coming clear but the volume of the chaos. Finally, after Knecht motioned for decorum, they came more or less to order and he could answer some of their questions.

''After processing the crime scene, a thorough search was made of the area and the cache of drugs was located at that time. My information is that a dog reacted to the stash and that led to the search.''

''Would that be a 'junkyard dog,' Chief?''

''What? No, ah, that would be a regular dog. An actual dog.''

''You mean one of your dope-sniffing dogs?''

''That's right.''

''What's the deal on these 'junkyard dogs' we heard about last night?''

''I'm not sure I follow you.''

''Last night at the scene, some of your officers . . . they were wearing caps with bulldog logos. We heard them called 'junkyard dogs.' Is that some elite unit you've formed, Chief?''

''Not exactly. That is a nickname that has been adopted by a group of officers who . . . The official name of the group is the Auto Salvage Unit.''

''What do they do?''

''They work out of Auto Theft.''

''And they were involved in the seizure last night?''

''They developed the information and got the warrant to search the property. That was related to an auto-theft case. And, yes, they were on hand for the incident that led to the seizure. And I would like to add that our Crimes Against Persons Section was also involved.''

''Why?''

''There was believed to be a connection between these individuals and the murders last week in West Dallas. The four murders at a van in West Dallas.''

''Have you cleared that case, too?''

''We are awaiting results of ballistics tests being run on the weapons taken from the suspects last night. I might add that we are optimistic.''

"How much is a ton of cocaine worth?"

"Now, that is a question that I think it is foolish to answer. It depends on the purity of the drug, and a great many other factors, and . . ." He was interrupted by the predictable question of how pure this particular cocaine was, and he said that would have to wait for the lab results. ". . . but I am advised that the average price of cocaine in this area is in the neighborhood of sixteen thousand dollars per kilo, so you can see that if you do the math you come up with something on the order of sixteen million dollars."

More hubbub, yielding finally to a demand to see the seized cocaine. They all wanted to see it, take pictures of it, shoot video of the packets for their newscasts.

"We will be looking at that possibility. I have no announcements to make on that at this time."

"And where was the dope found, Chief?"

"Inside the gasoline tank, on the tanker trunk. There was a second tank inside, filled with the drugs, and then gasoline was put in on top of it. Top-notch job, I am told."

"Where did the cocaine come from?"

"We are working now with the DEA on that, but our first indication is that it probably came from Mexico, that it probably crossed the border in that configuration."

Reporters will dream up questions as long as you let them, and Knecht was in no hurry to leave them this time. He had nothing else on the calendar except a meeting with Bobby Klevinger that he had every reason to believe would be acrimonious, and then calls to be made to the wounded officers and their families, and to the dead officers' survivors. He appreciated the value of these calls, and he did not mind so much the wounded ones, but he dreaded the survivors with a passion. He was never able to conceal from himself or them that he felt responsible for their loss, and he was not sure that he did not upset them more than he comforted them.

Ned had sat in the ratty little hideout shack in "Hungry Heights" with Curtis and the unspeaking Stone ever since they dropped off their visitors at the motel. They had not missed a word of radio news, and Curtis had rushed out of the house at one point and come running back in breathless with a little black-and-white television under his arm. They got the set working pretty well, although the video was poor, and then they watched the television and listened to the radio. Curtis sat watching *Nightline* as if he were hypnotized by it. When there was no more news to watch, he took the radio into the front room and did not reappear until nearly sunrise, when he grabbed a paper sack to write on and disappeared into the front room again.

About nine o'clock Wednesday morning, Curtis came in yelling for Stone to get up. He wanted Stone to take the car and go pick up the men from out of town and bring them over for a sit-down. Tell them I have a multimillion-dollar plan, he said. Tell them that.

Marino walked into the hospital room to talk to Willy with a disappointed look on his face. He had just been told Willy would live, and that pissed him off. Before he was there five minutes, though, he realized that Willy was more upset about it than he was, and Marino felt better about the way things had turned out.

Willy thought he was dead. When he got shot and fell off the truck and bounced on the road, things went black for him, and he thought he would never have to wake up again. He thought he was beyond the reach of the old Mexican and the Colombians, but then he woke up in Parkland, and the gringo doctors had worked their own evil magic and kept him alive. All he had on his mind was getting out of there, one way or the other.

Marino understood. He knew living was going to be harder than dying for Willy, and he decided that he was going to have a talk with the assistant district attorney on the case. Marino was going to convince the A.D.A. not to seek the death penalty this time. He wanted this bastard to do life.

Ned caught the drift of Curtis's plan and made up his mind what he would do about it. Curtis was too stupid to live, and Ned knew that nobody just quit the Jamaicans. He was wanted for the murder of the two cops, even though he had thought they were the Mexicans at the door. He would not have done any shooting if he had known they were cops. Now Curtis was not only too dumb to run, he was making plans to steal that goddamned ton of dope from the cops! That was this big plan he was so excited about. Before Stone got back with the heavyweights from out of town, Ned knew he had to make a move, so he told Curtis he was stepping out to the store. Did Curtis need anything? Ordinarily, Curtis would not stand for Ned to go off by himself, but this time he was so far off into his masterpiece plan that he just said go on. He didn't need anything. Ned had a phone call to make.

Clark finally got home about the time the noon TV news came on, and he watched the coverage of Orville Knecht's press conference as he slumped onto his couch and tugged off his shoes. He was dirty and tired, and enormously relieved that none of his people had been seriously hurt. They had turned up with the odd nicks and dings, and Nacho had a gash on his gun hand that he was at a loss to explain. He would do his drinking left-handed for a while, but they had been lucky. Clark knew now as never before how much luck had to do with it.

Angstrom's boss had dragged them over to the TAC office even after they had given statements to CAPers and IAD, and put them through a debriefing, complete with maps and timetables, sketches down to the square foot, before he let them go. Clark knew it was good to get it all down on paper and tape while it was still fresh. But he was exhausted now, and sat staring dully at the television, wishing he had a drink in his hand but too done in to make one. He looked down and saw for the first time, now that it was all officially over, that his hands were shaking.

The call was routed to Lieutenant McCluskey in CAPers. He reached across a cluttered desk to take it.

"Yeah?"

"I got something for you."

"What?"

"Cop killers. Jamaicans."

McCluskey signaled for one of his investigators to listen in and tape the call, for another to start a phone trace, and wrote a note which he handed to the clerk who had come over. She looked at the note, then at him. He nodded and flicked his hand at her to say she should hurry.

The note said CALL TAC. STAND BY. RAID.

Clark called his daughter to let her know he was all right, and let her con him into meeting her boyfriend, Gary, one day soon. They would have dinner.

After a hot shower and a cold Jack Daniel's and 7-Up, Clark felt better. He mixed himself another drink and considered his plans for the day. After what they had been through the night before—not only the fight and the paperwork and reports afterward but the recovery of the stolen Monte Carlo and the processing of the scene with the Physical Evidence Section and CAPers—Clark had given his people the day off. He tried to remember if he had mentioned this to his new lieutenant, but put off calling him to check. If he knew his guys, most of them would be at the DPA Club that evening, and Clark decided he should be there, too. Surviving a deal like what was quickly becoming known around the department as the "Cigarette Heights Shoot-out" demanded a certain ceremony of reflection, a thanksgiving and rekindling, and he knew that each of them had operated within his own isolation of the moment. They needed to get together and patch the whole thing, their collective memory of it, together. It would be therapeutic, a kind of personal debriefing that they all needed.

Part of what they all needed had to do with the officers who had not survived Cigarette Heights. Clark mourned Angstrom and Castleberry like family. There were three others in the hospital that he thought about, too. Two were supposed to be in pretty good shape, but the other was still in danger. It felt like war, and he knew that it all had not sunk in on him yet. He thought about Randi Stoner, and wondered if she felt that way, too.

He called her at her mother's house.

"You've been in the news," she said.

"That was TAC. We just watched."

"You're okay?"

"I'm fine," he said. "You?"

"Restless. Mom's been great, but . . ."

"I don't guess you'd like to have a drink with me tonight, would you?"

"I could use a drink," she said.

"We're all going to end up down at the DPA Club, I imagine. Okay with you?"

"I'd like to hear what happened, and you'll have to get drunk to tell me."

"My reputation precedes me."

She laughed, and so did he.

It was after dark by the time the Jamaicans got together in Curtis's little frame house. Two had gone back wherever they came from by then, leaving word they could get by without hearing whatever Curtis had to say. And two had sent word that the business had been down too long already, that they were going to be busy that evening getting some crack houses back into operation. So only two showed up, which Ned thought was a good sign. He did not know how many soldiers these two represented, but he knew there was no shortage of these bastards willing to kill for a ton of cocaine. Curtis's plan was still plenty damned dangerous.

Just as Curtis was getting ready to make his big presentation, with a Dallas street map and newspaper clippings taped to the wall behind him, a dog started barking out in the yard.

"What the hell is that?" Curtis demanded.

"That dog, belongs next door," Ned said. "Why don't you take him back over there, Curtis? Can't hear anything for that dog barking."

Ned could not imagine that they did not hear it in his voice. He had made his phone call and he had his deal. The part he had not planned on and the part he did not care for was this right here. This homicide lieutenant had cut him no slack on this. He had to go back to the house and stay there until he got the signal the cops were on the scene. That way, his Jamaican friends would not miss him and get hinky, maybe relocate. Easy for you to say, man. That was what Ned was thinking when he heard the dog bark. This was it. He did not want to jump up and volunteer to go out and take care of the dog, because that would give them something to remember when they thought back on this. That was why he suggested Curtis take care of the dog. He knew how he would react to that.

"You get the dog, motherfucker!" Curtis glowered at him. "Who the hell do you think you are?"

"Okay, okay. I'm going."

Ned went out the front door into the cold night without bothering to put on his jacket because he wanted the men he left inside to think he did not plan to be gone long. But when he stepped off the porch and felt hands drawing him into the darkness, he knew he was gone for good. Whatever else might happen, he was done with the Jamaicans.

"I'm Sergeant Marino," said the man they took Ned to. "Tell me about it. The layout, the people, everything."

Ned began, and he had been careful to prepare for this question. He leaned over the board in the back of the van and drew in the layout of the house.

"They're making plans, you know," he said.

"Plans for what?" Marino asked.

"They're going to raid police headquarters and steal that ton of cocaine."

"Jesus."

Ned heard someone whisper that word, but when he looked up, nobody was talking.

"The audacity of it!" Curtis exclaimed. "The boldness!"

"The goddamned foolishness."

"Who said that?" Curtis demanded, spinning around from his maps and articles.

"I did. What the hell do we want to declare war on the Police Department for? You saw how that come out last night for them Mexicans, didn't you? Why steal the cops' dope? It don't cost us nothing to buy dope, fool, because we sell it for more than we pay for it. What the hell you want to go to war for? We ain't about war, man. We about business!"

Curtis pointed his finger at the man, forgetting himself in the passion of the moment. "You," he said, "don't think big enough! Imagine the impact! We swoop in out of the night in the sleepy hours. Grenades, rocket launchers, machine guns, we have all these things. You have them. We disappear, leaving death and destruction behind, and we take a ton of cocaine. A ton! Can you imagine . . .''

With a sound like the switches on a row of electric chairs being thrown, the walls of the little house seemed suddenly to disappear, as the light of the sun itself shot through, blinding them all. The walls were almost invisible, the light was so pure and bright. And then came a voice like the voice of an archangel:

''This is the police! The house is surrounded!''

Epilogue

Joe Miller's bar had changed since Joe himself passed away. There was a piano now, a big classy job that sat unplayed between the bar and the overstuffed couches in the front half of the place. There was not much of the old crowd, the reporters and the courthouse people, that used to make it one of the more interesting watering holes in town. There were only a few of the diehard regulars leaning on the bar and a smug gaggle of lawyers at a table.

Bill Clark sat across from Sergeant Marino in the back half of the bar at a corner table, a small table that did not encourage people to invite themselves over. But Marino had happened into the place and he had brought a beer over from the bar and made himself at home. The first thing Clark had thought of when he saw the burly Mexican headed his way was that they still had business to settle over that name-calling thing. He had hoped Marino had forgotten about that.

Now they sat across the table with drinks and empty glasses in front of them in the comfortable gloom of the place. It was dark, and some decent jazz was playing over the speakers. That much had not changed.

Clark saw her come in, pushing through the inner door of the little vestibule at the front where the bar made an L and there was a poster that said "Make Love Quiet." It was about an antinoise campaign at Love Field, the old airport. But it was a picture of a nude blowing the propeller of a little model airplane, and Clark had always liked it. Randi Stoner paused for a moment to let her eyes acclimate to the darkness, and Clark looked at her and the poster. Out of the corner of his eye he saw Marino swivel in his seat to see what he was looking at.

When Marino saw Randi, he pushed himself up from the table.

"I'd better be running along," he said.

"It's early," Clark told him.

"Not for an old married man. See you around."

"Good night."

Marino stood to one side at the narrows between the piano and the bar to let Randi by, and they exchanged nods and smiles. She smiled differently at Clark as he rose from his seat and she joined him at the little corner table.

"Hi," she said, her hand touching his arm as he held her chair.

"Hi, yourself."

The waitress cleared the table and took Randi's order and then they were alone.

"How did it go?" Clark asked.

"Pretty well. They said I'm coming along."

"We knew that."

"I'm glad . . . that I decided to try it."

"Me, too."

Randi had been in counseling at the Dallas Rape Crisis Center since a couple of weeks after it happened. Thursday evening her group met, and drinks afterward had gotten to be a regular thing for her and Clark. She had not wanted to go at first; she had not thought she needed to.

"And I'm glad you didn't try to talk me into it. Or out of it, for that matter."

"You're a big girl."

"Good answer. Did you hear about Chief Knecht?"

"Yeah."

"Klevinger was on the radio. He said Knecht resigned 'to pursue opportunities in the private sector.' "

"I heard."

"What do you think?"

"Klevinger fired the poor slob for calling the mayor a son of a bitch on television that night at the hospital. He just had to wait for the heat to die down. I guess two months is long enough. That's longer than people remember anything these days."

"Two months." Randi looked at him and laughed softly. "It seems longer ago than that."

"Good. I also heard my hero, young Lieutenant Bonny, made captain today."

"I guess you're glad he's out of your hair."

The waitress brought them fresh drinks.

"I should be, the dumb little shit. Except that he got TAC. They put him in Angstrom's slot. Those poor bastards. 'What a falling off was there,' huh?"

They drank and did not talk for a while. Clark liked that about the way things were with them. It was comfortable, with quiet silences like friendship. And there was the other, too, the electric quickening at a touch or a look. It was remarkable, and neither of them worried where it would lead.

"What was Marino doing in here?" she asked finally.

"That worried me, at first. I thought he might have looked me up to kick my butt for calling him names."

"It didn't look that way."

"No, we talked it over and decided to buy each other a drink."

"That's what I like about older men." She laughed. "You're so reasonable."

"Yeah, or just tired."

"I'd prefer to think you were saving your energy."

"Oh? Am I going to need it?"

"If you play your cards right. I like Marino, myself."

"Why?"

"Because he knows an exit cue when he sees one."

"Yeah. He's a little nuts, though."

"Who isn't, Wild Bill?"

They shared a naughty leer. That had become a private joke with them.

"He's made a career of that Mexican kid, Willy. That's what I mean. He's obsessing over the little asshole."

"And?"

"Marino's been keeping tabs on him down at Huntsville. Said Willy's tried to kill himself a couple of times, but the screws keep saving him. That really pisses old Willy off, and Marino loves it. They've got the kid in a special cell now. Suicide watch. They're gonna keep the little bastard alive forever. Marino says Willy wants to die because he's afraid the people he got the cocaine from are going to find a way to get to him."

"And do what?" Randi asked.

"Beats me. Whatever it is, it must be worse than dying."

"Sounds like justice."

"Or a reasonable facsimile. You ready for another?"

"No, thanks. I'm driving."

"So am I, but I'm going to have another drink."

"No you're not."

"I'm not having another one?"

"You're not driving."

"The hell you say."

"Because I'm going to take you home."

"Your place or mine, hotshot?"

"I haven't decided."

"You're sexy when you take charge. Have I ever told you that?"

"Mmm, I believe you have."

He leaned toward her and she turned her face to his. They kissed, and he held her close, enjoying the slow spread of warmth from her.

"When is all this going to happen?" he asked.

"Now is good," she whispered, her hand on his cheek, playing with his beard. "I have bourbon at my place."

"You silver-tongued little devil."

Clark caught the waitress's eye and signaled for his tab.

"I told my group about you tonight," Randi said.

"I hope you had the common decency to exaggerate a little."

"They said you were probably good for me."

"Probably?"

"Maybe I didn't exaggerate enough."

"It wouldn't be easy."

"Oh, I meant to tell you. Mrs. Angstrom was on the radio, too. Did you hear?"

"No. What?"

"Captain Angstrom had a son in college. Did you know that?"

"No, I didn't think he was old enough. Hell, he was younger than me."

"I'll pass on that one. I don't want to hurt your feelings."

"Ha ha."

"She said he's going to be a cop."

"What?" Clark stopped counting his money into the waitress's tray to look askance at Randi. "Here? The DPD?"

"Yeah. He graduates in May and he'll start the academy this summer."

"Well, I'll be damned."

Clark was silent in contemplation and none too steady on his feet. Randi put his arm around her shoulder and they walked out of the bar leaning on each other. When they stepped outside, into the starred and balmy night edged with the lights and bustle of the city, he hugged her close.

"Life goes on," she said.

"Yes, ma'am. I guess it does."